WES

HOP

NORFOLK COUNTY L
WITHDRAWN FOR

C000051567

the last date stamp

NORFOLK COUNTY LIBRARY
WITHDRAWN FOR SALE

THE ULTIMATE APHRODISIAC

By the same author

A Bedtime Story

THE ULTIMATE APHRODISIAC

John Hole

Hodder & Stoughton

Copyright © 1996 by John Hole

First published in Great Britain in 1996
by Hodder and Stoughton
A division of Hodder Headline PLC

The right of John Hole to be identified as the Author of
the Work has been asserted by him in accordance with the
Copyright, Designs and Patents Act 1988.

10 9 8 7 6 5 4 3 2 1

All rights reserved. No part of this publication may be
reproduced, stored in a retrieval system, or transmitted
in any form or by any means without the prior written
permission of the publisher, nor be otherwise circulated
in any form of binding or cover other than that in which
it is published and without a similar condition being
imposed on the subsequent purchaser.

All characters in this publication are fictitious
and any resemblance to real persons, living or dead,
is purely coincidental.

British Library Cataloguing in Publication Data

A CIP catalogue record for this book is available
from the British library

ISBN 0 340 65398 1

Typeset by Palimpsest Book Production Limited,
Polmont, Stirlingshire
Printed and bound in Great Britain by
Mackays of Chatham PLC, Chatham, Kent

Hodder and Stoughton
A division of Hodder Headline PLC
338 Euston Road
London NW1 3BH

NORFOLK LIBRARY AND INFORMATION SERVICE	
SUPPLIER	FARR
INVOICE No.	C984195
ORDER DATE	29-11-96
COPY No.	

For Gertraud Johanna Anna
and in memory of George Vincer,
my wonderful parents,
with love

and with grateful thanks
to Ernest Peter, Morag, Fiona, Ginnie
and George (without whom, nothing)
for their time, consideration, criticism,
mixed food and
bountiful encouragement
in the writing of this novel

CHAPTER ONE

Better is a poor and wise child, than an old and foolish king.

ECCLESIASTES 4:13

WHIT SUNDAY 28 MAY

'You can look but you can't touch!' she laughed in her oddly deep voice. The girl he had met for the very first time less than an hour before shot him the briefest, most winning of smiles, stood unsteadily at the other end of the punt and proceeded, without any hesitation, to peel off every stitch of her clothing.

Then she slid, with a stifled shriek, into the shining waters of the river Cherwell.

Norman Ranburn, retired businessman, yet another swift month beyond his sixty-ninth birthday – a man previously resigned to a life pretty nigh done, bar the occasional jolly to Lords, Beaulieu or Glyndebourne – could hardly believe his eyes. While he had looked away like any decent fellow, he had seen enough to be both extremely diverted and delectably shocked. Young girls just didn't do that in front of older gentlemen. More was the pity.

One minute she was poling the ancient wooden punt along with surprising expertise, affording him the safe and covert pleasure of watching the muscles of her thighs flexing, her long bare toes pressing the bottom-boards, while he made much of pretending not to notice the falling waters of the river splashing her T-shirt. The next it was almost as if she had sensed his private fantasy and had undertaken to realise it – the electric shock of her smile, the momentary sidelong glance that sought, yet didn't seek, a reaction, and then the scoop of white cotton off and over her head. There was a momentary glimpse of dark-brown nipples, like upended olives on taut boyish breasts, the flash of fit brown limbs and the pitch-black bush at her crotch and it was over. The curved flank of her turned buttocks was but an etched memory. Had it really occurred? Did she actually do that? How astonishingly brazen of her.

Now she was no more than a dark head silhouetted on a surface glistening with ripples, worried in the sunlight by a solitary, busy dragonfly. 'Cold,' she yelped. 'Yucking muddy too.' She swam energetically away from him towards the jungle of young willows on the other bank, her shockingly naked shoulders cutting the surface. Norman almost extended his fingers to touch the denim of her sawn-off jeans tumbled in the bottom of the boat. They would still be warm. They would smell of her if he held them to his nose. He made himself examine the bullrushes instead. Very carefully.

She called herself Amy Shakespeare. She was a friend of his granddaughter Francesca. A New Zealander, from Wellington it was said. A shameless young New Zealander. She would be about twenty-four. She and Francesca had been schoolfellows together until six years ago at Sherston College in Somerset. For one of these modern brutish young women she was exceptionally fetching. And probably a bit wild.

He seemed to recall a rumour that even at school she had a crazy reputation. He half-remembered hearing some tale of her challenging the school groundsman to climb the school's famous Sherston Oak one midsummer night whereupon she handcuffed the poor lad to one of the topmost branches and didn't release him until dawn. And he without his trousers. She was clearly a bit of an oddball, not all her oars in the water. She certainly didn't know the form. But, then, which of these colonials did?

Norman could already hear Gilbert's voice booming on fifty yards downriver. Very shortly, his brother, who, being Gilbert, was proud of his cunning dexterity with the punt-pole, would join them with the second punt. Norman hesitated to think what the remainder of the party would make of it. After all, finally, the stupid girl would be obliged to emerge from the water when she had finished her dip. It would look mighty odd. Maybe it didn't matter. Maybe that was how youngsters were these days. Christ alone knew.

There she was now, in the shadows on the other side of the main stream, being dragged gently by the flow, one long white arm languidly attached above her head to a tangle of branches. He tried not to appear to be looking, but he had a shrewd notion that she was hanging there in order to be able to watch his reactions. She damned well knew it just wasn't on, behaving like that. She was presumably only too aware of his likely discomfiture and was probably enjoying it.

It was all right for her – they could get away with most things, nowadays, these kids. But it was damned embarrassing for him. After all, his daughter and granddaughter were in the other punt. He could almost sense the corners of the girl's wide, liquid mouth flickering with knowing merriment. She could obviously be a tricky devil, this one.

He heard a splash and the black prow of Gilbert's punt hove into view around the bend, propelled by Norman's blazered younger brother. Back-lit by a glare of golden reflected sunlight, the two women, his daughter Joan in her straw hat and his granddaughter Francesca trailing a limp hand in the water, looked like something in an Edwardian sepia photograph.

This burst of late-May high-summer weather lifted the heart. Everywhere the trees and bushes seemed to be loaded suddenly with vibrant lettuce-green leaves. Nature and life were well on their way again for another year. The sap was rising. Norman could never remember blossom such as he had seen during this spring. Burgeoning, wasn't that the word? Maybe when one has retired, these things are all the more clearly noticeable, he thought. When all's said and done, you suddenly have an infinite amount of time when your life's not really in the fast track any more.

'Gotcha! There you are, Norman,' Gilbert called noisily. 'Good golly, I thought little Ms Shakespeare had an outboard motor in her pocket or something.'

The women turned their heads. 'Where, actually, *is* Amy?' called Francesca. Their punt slid towards him. Norman was still not quite sure why *he* had been the one who'd finished up in the one craft with the picnic baskets and the bold young woman, while his offspring finished up in the other with Gilbert.

The girl was swimming back towards the two punts, working energetically against the stream, ducking her head into the water with each stroke.

'You poser, Amy,' shrilled Francesca. 'You don't know what's in there. You'll contract lockjaw.'

'Undiluted effluent, I shouldn't wonder,' mused Gilbert, who was beginning the business of parking his punt along-side that of Norman and Amy. Joan already looked disap-proving, but, then, that was often all too customary with her. Norman guessed his daughter would look rather more than merely disapproving when Amy Shakespeare deigned to haul herself out of the water in the total thoroughgoing nuddy.

Joan had looked depressed from the moment they had arrived from Manchester. She was unfortunate enough to take her looks from himself and her rather serious nature from her mother, Grace. For Norman it had always seemed a most unfortunate genealogical baton-pass. At the age of forty-four she was settling into a middle-aged thickness that she had fought hard to stave off. And light-hearted wit, he thought sadly, would be an element in her character sadly absent without leave.

Joan's daughter, on the other hand, had taken her delicate

blonde looks from her own father, the effortlessly charming Sven Nielsen. The two women, mother and daughter, were, in truth, so different in appearance that it was sometimes impossible to believe that they were related at all. Particularly as Francesca had in recent times adopted the brazen image of punkish slash-attack lipstick and sticky-looking blonde dreadlocks or hair-extensions or whatever they called those absurd sausage things she had on the top of her head.

It was the recent separation of Francesca's ill-assorted parents, Joan and Sven, that had triggered off this rare visit down from Manchester of Norman's sole issue. It was very sad – quite clearly yet another Ranburn marriage had hit the rocks. Thank God for Gilbert and his wife Mary. At least their partnership seemed destined to last. But, then, Gilbert always fell butter-side up.

Amy's slender fingers gripped the side of his punt. The brown waters swirled lasciviously about her, lapping over her ears and her sharp chin. For a split second she made fleeting visual contact with him with huge dancing grey eyes. Beneath one perfectly arched eyebrow, her eyelid dropped swiftly in a surreptitious wink. Then it was as if nothing had occurred between them. Norman looked away. Oh Lord, this was so embarrassing.

Amy stood up in the water.

She was perfectly properly clad in a neat, shining, gorgeously shaped, black, one-piece swimming costume. She must have taken it over the side with her and put it on under the water while swimming up there away from them, by the little island. Norman realised he had been sweating lightly. But it was such a warm day. Especially for May.

He busied himself taking off his glasses and polishing them with a handkerchief. The girl hardly gave him another look. Muddied and licked with fronds of lily, she waded across and joined Francesca, who was now sitting on the bank laughing at her, with her skirt up round her bottom and her shirt all unbuttoned to hell.

Joan and Gilbert began to pass out the spread to the bank. Cold white wine was spilled into neatly stemmed plastic wine glasses. There were Tupperware boxes of salad and smart blue plastic plates and much was made of the various dressings that arrived in a range of carefully washed peanut-butter jars.

These had been Grace's picnic baskets, of course. Years ago. Norman's ex-wife Grace had always done these things with elan. Joan took after her mother in that. Although doubtless that patron saint of first-class picnicking, St Michael, had probably been quietly drawn into assisting with the provisioning.

Norman lay back in his cushioned reclining seat and raised the Château Cissac to his lips. He must concentrate on helping Joan through this distressing time. She was going to need his support. Only he, her father, knew how much. At one and the same time Norman felt a tired impotent anger and a profound sadness for his daughter that rekindled the grief of the death of his own marriage all those years ago. However solid Joan had been, it was inexcusable for Sven to have waltzed off with the Dutch arts sorority or whatever, just as his wife was beginning to have to face the grim reality of her mid-forties. But, then, in Norman's own case, Grace had been a damned diligent wife to him for twenty-one years, before she had suddenly upped and evaporated and finished up in conjugal bliss in bloody West Lulworth.

Were the Ranburns just no good at long-term personal relationships? He rather thought as much. Perhaps they were just no good at sex. Good at thinking about it – not much cop at doing it. His father Magnus's marriage had failed spectacularly as well. To lose one marriage, Norman thought, might be regarded as a misfortune; to lose three looked like bloody incompetence.

When one came to think about it, apart from the ill-fated business with that Caroline Oakley, seven years before, he himself had had no proper personal relationship for two decades now. Two whole decades, for goodness' sake. Not since the seventies. His only proper relationship, of course, had been with work – with Chandos House. And now that was denied him too.

But it had been all right. He had never been overly bothered. He had always been able to appear outwardly adjusted, good-naturedly calm, never lonely and hardly ever bored. People always thought of him as nice, kind, friendly and even quite good-looking. He had all his own hair, for God's sake, and not a few of his own teeth. He was always thought of as everyone's favourite uncle. Gilbert's and Mary's boys adored him. And, at work, he had been the sort of boss secretaries were prepared to die for – thoughtful, listening, never one to raise his voice. But a total butterfingers where women were concerned. Pathetic really.

Because whatever had been his advertised, public persona, what went on underneath that urbane, shy surface hardly bore thinking about. And, of course, he *did* think about it.

All the time.

Well, some of the time.

Too often anyway.

But no one would ever know. Even Norman himself from day to day tried very hard to blank out that morass of hideous lusts, twisted fantasy and idiotic yearnings. Bumping into a lass like Francesca's ex-school friend, Amy, on this hot spring Sunday tended to bring such dreadfulnesses bubbling closer to the surface. Bumping into his little prick-teaser of a granddaughter as well, to be brutally honest. It all troubled him to the quick.

Of course, it was completely appalling to think of his granddaughter, Francesca, in such terms, but she didn't allow a fellow much choice. He did all in his power to excise such ideas from his consciousness. However, Fran ensured, willy-nilly, that the gentlemen of the party had absolutely no alternative but to register the lacy intricacy of her black brassiere, displaying as it did her youthful cleavage. Francesca made sure she was on display and that was all there was to it. The result was immoderately blatant but presumably no more than part of the job-description of her adopted world of what Sir Malcolm Sargent used to call roll-and-rock.

Amy, on the other hand, just had so much bloody class.

There was no comparison. One seemed no more than a schoolgirl in full advertisement mode. The other had the magnificent, magnetic, sexual confidence and the teasing decorous restraint of a Greta Garbo, a Marlene Dietrich or a Jacqueline Kennedy.

But Norman fervently promised himself not to look at Amy's body any more. She was just a child, for God's sake. Yet he could not strip from his mind the graven image of the taut, sculpted, black material that covered her breast as she had raised herself out of the river half a hand's-breadth away from his fingers. That vision seemed almost to sing in his head – the sharp momentary shape of her nipple crying out to be pinched, her body running with water, the hard muscles of her upper arms and those taut shoulders. And her long neck. And the fleeting wickedness of that cool appraising eye. Oh to be able to be there.

But he never would be. That was all well over now.

Not that he ever had been there, in truth, even when young. And now, whether he liked it or not, the world saw him as an old gentleman. With a life over, and opportunities not grasped.

He must stop thinking these things. He would go mad. He *was* mad. But, quite against his will, his eyes were constantly drawn back to her.

Why in heaven's name was she so damned compelling? Was it just her looks? Or was there something else that gave her a kind of added electric magnetism? A sort of innate energy? Hunched there in the long grass of the riverbank, chatting intimately to his brash granddaughter, her lean arms wrapped around her legs, her chin on her knees, she looked like some kind of prehensile stick insect. Yet, though she was long-limbed and absurdly slim, she was in no way bony. Aquiline really – her bum and her breasts were all there, present and correct and pleasantly collected. He had been wrong when she'd wickedly given him that original naked flash of her bosom – under the scooped neck of her black swimsuit there certainly lurked a shadow of cleavage. A shadow of brown cleavage, brown shoulders, brown arms, skin like flawless silk licking over her collarbones. How could she be brown like that and it not yet be June? And, of course, full of lithe, pent-up, almost arrogantly mocking youth. Youth that for an old chap like himself felt like toothache, it hurt so.

But it was the eyes that did it for him. Those astonishing, washed-out, pale-grey eyes, which seemed as if they might be able to see through concrete. Oh yes, and the fairy dust of freckles gracing her cheekbones, decorating that straight, no-nonsense nose. And her mouth, her wicked letter box of a mouth – so wide it seemed to be making a determined effort to reach both of her ears. Its curling, knowing, expressive lips, which gave vent to this uniquely energetic, hooked-on, life-affirming way of talking – those long, double-barrelled New Zealand vowel sounds. Why did every 'o' and 'a' and 'u' seem to possess two or even more syllables down under?

So, yes, she was a stunning looker all right. She could unman anybody. Over his turkey sandwich on walnut bread, Norman kept an amused eye on Gilbert, who was deep in conversation with Joan about the merits and demerits of the wretched Ford Mondeo. But Gilbert, too, time and time again, flicked his eyes over to the two young girls and allowed them briefly to cruise Amy Shakespeare's young limbs and to stroke their way over the dark shiny cap of her hair, the ends of which had the good fortune gently to stroke her square shoulders. That afternoon, absurdly framed by a cliché of Maytime cherry blossom, it was as if the girl could conjure magic. So much so that she made Norman feel positively tired, so touching was she in her strength and in her youthful vulnerability.

Norman found his thoughts constantly turning to whom she might be bedding. Because they usually were, weren't they, these kids? And, what was a good deal worse, he fell to thinking how much he would give to see them at it.

Oh God, she was no more than a sharp nineties kid, though, wasn't she? It was just her youthfulness that was magnetic, and that was all. Nothing more. Spend half an hour with her, one to one, and he would surely finish up gagging with boredom. He was allowing himself to be a stupid, drooling old dunderhead.

But her overall engineering was simply superb. She had the magnificent fortune to be put together like the pistons of a Silver Ghost. And, in turn, *he* had had the magnificent fortune of spending a long warm afternoon in her presence, watching her unaffectedly move and play and eat and smile and strip and, for one secret intimate moment, wink.

It would have to do.

Later, when they had completed a lengthy – and welcome – boozy luncheon and returned their hired punts to the pectoral-flexing Jack-the-lads at Magdalen Bridge, Norman found himself driving Joan back to his home in the Daimler. Gilbert had snaffled the two girls and folded them into his new Porsche for the return to Coombe, the village outside Oxford where Norman lived.

Norman half-thought that being alone together in the car might provide a secure moment or two for his daughter to unburden herself of some of her unhappiness about what had happened between Sven and herself. He still knew little about the whole sorry mess. Loevborgs, the Dutch sports equipment people, had taken Sven, their UK manager, back from Manchester for a two-month sojourn in Rotterdam and there he had fallen lock, stock and penis, for some fierce younger woman. It appeared that she owned a high-profile, and no doubt obscurely newfangled, art gallery and was, by all accounts, a deft catch.

Driving in the car, passing through Thame, both of them stolidly looking out through the windscreen at the abundant countryside, should have been providing an excellent opportunity for a moment of fatherly succour and advice. But Joan didn't seem to want to know anything about that. Probably their father–daughter relationship would not now allow for any such thing. In the last ten years or so they had been together in the same room only a couple of dozen times. The Ranburns were a typically dysfunctional 1990s family.

'He's given me the house.' That was all she would vouch-safe as far as her marital disaster was concerned. Keeping Joan's household going was about to cost Norman even more in the future. That was all he allowed himself to conclude.

There was silence in the car as they pulled off the main road and began to travel a little too fast through the country lanes. Norman filled the time by allowing himself to be entertained by elaborate notions of handling parts of Amy Shakespeare that he would never actually see again.

'It's good they've kept in touch,' he said.

'Who?' she asked shortly.

'Francesca and, um, whosit – Amy.'

'I don't think they have. She suddenly rang Frannie out of the blue just like that. Some story about having lost her phone number. Don't think they've seen one another for three or four years. I don't know what that's all about. When we said we were coming to Oxford to see you she apparently jumped at the chance – said she'd drive up and join us. Bit of a trollop if you ask me.' What a very nice idea, thought Norman: 'a bit of a trollop'. Lovely. He liked the word 'trollop'.

'Funny word, "trollop"' he said.

'Well,' Joan snorted dismissively. She was doubtless right – particularly when one had, as he did, the private information about the state in which the trollop had entered the River Cherwell. Joan was a dear girl, but grumpy – practical, kind, able, a good mum, but basically giving off an air of disappointment. However angry he might be with Sven, Norman could easily envisage some tidy-looking arbiter of Dutch artistic taste bringing more than a little life back to someone who might have imagined a final spoke had been put into his mid-life cycle. He had a brief vision of Sven, in some spotlessly clean, minimalist Dutch hotel double-bed lustily giving it to . . . well, to Amy Shakespeare actually.

'What does she do?'

'Amy? Oh I think she's working in films. Mostly. It's a bit on and off.'

'Actress?'

'Good God, no. She's a deputy deputy deputy location

11

manager or something for a company called, would you believe, Reach For My Gun Films. They make telly films. Things like that *Juliet Spring* series. Bodice-rippers for video rental.' Joan savaged the whole industry in one quick sneer.

'I'd've thought she could have been an actress,' Norman said, thinking aloud.

'Everyone fancies her, Daddy. They always have done. You should have seen you and Gilbert at lunch. Tongues hanging out. It was disgusting. Neither of you could take your eyes out of her itty-bitty bathing costume. And you're both well past it now, Daddy. Actually, in fact, I do believe she does some cabaret act or something. Illusions. Yes, adult illusions, whatever that means. Sounds dirty to me. She works with some young man she's thick with. I shouldn't be at all surprised if it wasn't public bonking or something,' she said crudely. 'Dodgy anyway.'

Joan turned to watch two elderly lambs skipping as they arrived at the outlying parts of Coombe.

'That's a hell of a big motorbike she's got. Frightfully expensive,' she mused. 'I wonder where she gets the money. From what I know of her, I rather fear the worst.'

'Fear' was the wrong word, thought Norman – Joan probably meant 'anticipate'. What in heaven's name was this girl, Amy, doing fiddling about on the fringes of the film industry – trying to be a 'best boy' or a 'gaffer' or whatever the devil they were called – when by rights she could be swanning around the world in Concorde being one of these sought-after super-models?

Joan very firmly changed the subject and began to talk about Francesca's plans to set up a recording studio in Cheadle-Hulme close to where what was left of the Nielsen family resided.

It was only when they were back in his living room at the Aviary that Norman got the first suspicion that within this mother-and-daughter-trip-from-the-north might lurk a subtly secret scenario. It seemed as if this recording studio thing might be one such hidden agenda. Ten minutes after Mrs Clarke had brought through the Earl Grey and her very worst rock-like rock-cakes, the penny slowly descended and Norman began to understand, also, why it was that brother Gilbert had been drafted into this family get-together. He was there to add persuasive weight. This was not about the collapse of his offspring's marital relationship: this was about a neat forty-seven grand required to capitalise a small recording studio facility in an old glue factory in Cheadle-Hulme. The plan being that his darling, flaunty little granddaughter would then endeavour to record uncouth youth at play with their Sludge, or their Nurofen or their Lavatory music, or whatever they called it these days.

Even before the tea was ready to be poured, Joan had produced files and papers and business plans for this proposed extravagance. Large full-colour letterheads and a specially designed logo that looked like some Gruyère cheese with a dashboard cigarette lighter pushed into its centre, announcing 'Synchromesh Sound' of Cheadle-Hulme. To Norman, with the best will in the world, it didn't exactly sound like a goer. Joan made some joke about the name that Francesca had come up with – that he would like it because it came from the world of motoring. The said Francesca sat there, beseechingly, her shirt slit to her navel, looking all of thirteen and a half – very pretty and adorable with her pile of beaded blonde cigar-butts on her head, but not very much like someone who could keep a load of drug-smoking, combat-booted and grossly tattooed guitar-thrashers in very much order.

Joan did all the selling. As he knew, she said, Francesca had done a two-year course in sound engineering at her local tech. And had spent a number of long nights in one of the most famous Manchester recording studios – no doubt learning about how to look hard, smoke marijuana and put herself about, thought her grandfather, probably unfairly.

Norman already supported Joan and Francesca, each with a modest monthly allowance. He could probably find forty-seven grand if it was really required of him, but it seemed like such an unlikely idea. Surely, he ventured, Frannie would be wiser to get some more work experience under her skimpy little belt, before launching off into this madcap expensive scheme. A scheme, moreover, that in the current economic climate could so very easily come to no good.

He could see the top of his daughter's cheeks colouring. Norman was renowned for being careful. Gilbert, in fact, often called him 'stick-in-the-mud' to his face. Sometimes in front of the staff. That was one of the reasons why he had been obliged, three years before, to resign as chief executive of Chandos House and put the whole thing into the dubious care of his younger brother. This reputation had Joan expecting him to bathe Francesca's rickety edifice in the baleful and unforgiving light of reality. For this reason she was now launching herself on a full-scale charm offensive. It was not her strongest suit.

Yards away from the house, out on the lawn, in the early-evening sunlight, sat Amy, now in her leather motorcycle trousers and the hulking great medicine boots that all these goofy kids wore nowadays – boots with silvery metal plates and hundreds of straps and buckles. She had taken herself out through the french windows once it was clear that this was going to be a Ranburn family Maastricht. She was wearing a fairly feminine long cardigan over that tight white T-shirt and was sitting by the pond that had the little dolphin fountain, throwing bits of rock-cake at the ducks. She hit quite a few of the ducks, but they seemed happy enough with this as it meant plenty of rock-cake, along with the humiliation.

She seemed to be entertaining herself and her duck disciples with a programme of harry, hurry and high tea. Norman found it difficult to concentrate on the discussion in hand and not to allow his eye to return to the tight black leather encasing the girl's sharp knees and her long straight thighs. She was just too beautiful, that was the problem with Amy Shakespeare. She ought not to be allowed out. She gave old gentlemen palpitations.

With a slight turn of her head, Joan summoned up her biggest gun to the fray. It was almost as if it had been rehearsed. Leaning against the marble mantelpiece, his head framed by Norman's favourite Dale Riddlesden painting, Gilbert launched into about two dozen reasons why his

elder brother shouldn't turn down this opportunity for pro-
moting the world of the arts and his granddaughter's career
advancement. Gilbert talking about art was a pretty good
joke. Gilbert always reckoned taking his various progeny
off to Disneyland, Paris, had been an 'art' experience. And
probably about the only one he had ever encountered.

Gilbert's main thrust was that Norman had a lot of money,
could easily afford it and, at this stage in his life, what else
was he going to do with it? Joan nodded in much vehement
agreement.

Amy had disappeared from the lawn. The grass was deserted again, clad now only in long evening shadows. The
ducks looked mortified. Where had she gone?

Norman embarked on a light defence of his position, suggesting that while Synchromesh Sound was clearly a praise-
worthy and attractively thought-through scheme, he was
obliged to have his doubts. Was it right for someone as
young as his granddaughter to be in charge of such a large
capital investment?

Then something happened that almost caused Norman to
stop speaking in mid-sentence. There was a small octagonal
summerhouse perched on the edge of his lawn in front of
some towering laurel hedges. Over the top of the sloping
edge of its roof, looking at him with rudely baleful eyes, was
an enormous face: big rolling eyes, long boxer's ears and a
crude bright red haircut. And this astonishing creature was
lurching about, apparently sticking its tongue out at him.
Norman was the only person facing out towards the garden,
so only he was in position to take in this grotesquerie.

In spite of this extraordinary turn of events, Norman
managed to soldier on with various anodyne philosophical
remarks about how it was necessary for the young to have to
struggle. The distorted face or mask, or whatever it seemed
to be, was, he now realised, constructed of a huge piece of
newspaper, torn, folded and painted in a fairly abandoned
fashion. The tongue licking its way around its fantastical
mouth was actually a slim pink female hand. Now whose
hand could that be?

15

Meanwhile, at the family Ranburn plenary session, Joan was now quite unable to stop herself from interrupting Gilbert. She could see they were losing Norman. She was having to control her anger. She wasn't doing it with enormous aplomb.

On the summerhouse roof, a second, equally gross, head appeared. The building was taking on the role of a full-scale puppet booth. This newcomer had a rude long nose and crinkly brown hair very like Gilbert's. In fact the face and its accompanying pipe could possibly have been a puppet version of his brother. Norman stopped himself from snorting out loud with amusement. Amy, for it must surely be she, was no mean draughtswoman. And damned swift.

Norman had begun to formulate the idea that he might stand at least as guarantor on a bank loan for Francesca to raise the capital for the project. It would mean that the enterprise would have to pay for the costs of such a loan – but that would be all to the good. Nothing like the cold wind of commercial truth to beef up your attitudes, sort out the wheat from the chaff.

Then, suddenly, a third figure began to cavort about the summerhouse roof. This, to all intents and purposes, appeared be a female puppet of gross elongated appearance. It had a bustline that would have made even Jane Mansfield feel glum. The two puppet men's faces that remained in attendance either side of this storming new character seemed to ooze prurience by their ogling. Did either of them represent Norman himself? He couldn't easily see a likeness. But then, he thought, one could never recognise oneself when one's voice was played back on a tape recorder.

The spectacle on the other side of the lawn was more than riveting. It was very hard indeed for him to keep his mind on the subject in hand.

Finally Joan said it: 'Daddy, I know you're going to live for years and years yet, but when you do go, the beastly old tax man will come along and take so much of what you have and give it, no doubt, to some high-spending extravagant Labour government. How much better to pass some of it on now to your own granddaughter. What better investment could you make? It's not as if you travel the world or anything. Or enjoy an extravagant social life. This is the time when young people need their family's help. There aren't any jobs out there. Well, not interesting ones. Fran's made something like a hundred applications since she left Uni. She needs your help. Please, Daddy.'

Norman stood silent as if he was thinking all this through. But he was hardly listening. Anyway, he knew perfectly well the general sort of tack that Joan would take. He had been her father for forty-four years, after all, so he did have a modicum of experience in these matters. She always went at things like a fan in a feather factory, did Joan. Norman, meanwhile, was overoccupied watching theatrical developments on and about the garden-shed roof.

It was difficult to apprehend the precise narrative thrust of this instant piece of al fresco theatre. He suspected the basic underlying motif had something obscurely immodest about it, but the materials that the girl was using were necessarily devoid of much subtlety. There was a lot of cavorting about in the tradition of Mr Punch. Indeed there was cavorting, capering, bouncing about, tripping the light fantastic and a fair amount of falling down flat. There was a deal of indistinct but nonetheless merry and lustful abandon. Norman's mind was more and more drawn to the amazing fact that it was apparently possible for a man to get the giggles from the sight of various bits of paint-splattered newspaper being thrown about on a summerhouse roof thirty yards away. Theatre had, it seemed, a powerful magic.

Norman took himself out of the line of sight of Amy's bizarre show and sat with his back to the light. The teatime discussion was over. Gilbert thought he was a poor, unadventurous sap. But that had always been Gilbert's secret view of his rather careful elder brother. Joan thought he was just a bloody dog-in-the-manger and was pink with disappointment in spite of Norman's perfectly reasonable proposal to act as a guarantor. Francesca probably thought that her grandfather's offer at least might keep her scheme flickeringly alive. She tugged her skirt down and buttoned herself away. It was cooler now and the show was over. But she smiled at him quite amicably. God, thought Norman, almost reaching for his cheque-book, he had always been such a sucker for a pretty face, even if he had never actually done anything very positive about it.

Norman actually felt pretty gloomy about his reluctant intransigence. It was the right thing to do. But it was sometimes exceedingly painful to do the right thing. Particularly when it hurt your potentially very pretty and one and only grandchild. It was difficult to deny someone one loved as much as he did Francesca.

The party broke up very quickly after that. Joan had come down from Manchester with Fran to get some money. She had failed. Now she felt she needed to get off. They were both going to stay with Gilbert and Mary at Abercrombie Hall at Witney before going back to Cheadle-Hulme in the morning. Joan seemed to think it was preferable for them to stay in her uncle's swarming family residence rather than in one of her father's myriad spare bedrooms. Even given Mrs Clarke's catering. And Nola Clarke dished no mean breakfast.

Joan had stopped even trying to look him in the eye. Francesca gave him a hug. And enveloped him in perfume.

And there was Amy, by the big barn, where the cars were parked, her disturbingly perfect features entirely suffused with unengaged, butter-wouldn't-melt innocence. She, too, seemed to be making much of not catching Norman's eye. She was now entirely cling-filmed in black leather all the way from her long white throat to her big-booted feet. Delectable.

Parked by Gilbert's car was Amy's dynamic steed. Amy's ultra-macho power symbol. The motorbike shone with red and black and seemed to have a Lloyd's-Building-like lattice-work scaffolding framework, the like of which Norman had never seen. Actually it was ages since he had even been close to such a blatantly vulgar display of modern technology. True, it was small, but extremely fast-looking. Italian. Something called a Ducati Monster 900. Big bucks, he imagined.

'It's the business. I've only had it a while,' she said, when he asked. 'Brilliant in traffic. In my view. Totally torrid.' She lapsed into cod-Italian: '*La bella bika con attituda*. You can coast to a standstill and keep your feet up, for aeons longer than the girlie alongside expects. And then, yabadabadoo, you're motoring again. It totally blisses me out.' She grinned cheerfully. 'I salivate over it. Wet, wet, wet, as they say.' How could she afford such a beast? he asked himself. She must have some sort of private income. He wondered who her parents were. Sherston hadn't been a cheap school. As he knew to his cost.

'Powerful then?'

'Finger-licking,' she said obscurely. But it seemed to mean that it was. It had been a stupid question to ask – 900 cc was obscenely potent. Sexy even. Amy slid her big black helmet slowly down over her head. Look at me, look at me, just once, he wanted to say. But she didn't. She swung an elegant leg over the machine and switched it on. She stroked the shiny red petrol tank with both gloved hands as it nestled there, rumbling between her thighs. 'Yeah, a girl needs something like this to ride. Talk about ego-tickle.'

It was time for the young people to take their leave of one another. Francesca embraced Amy, throbbing motorbike, helmet, leathers and all. 'Get the vibe?' enquired his granddaughter.

'You know it,' Amy replied, an obscure mantra that presumably meant something to them both. Norman wondered if they might shortly be moved to roll up a trouser leg and indulge in complicated handshakes.

'Anyhow, Amy, mega to see you,' said his granddaughter. 'Yonks it's been. Don't lose touch again.'

Then, in a burst of noise and slammed car doors, they had all gone. And Norman felt empty. And saddened at his earlier lack of generosity of spirit. He also felt it was salutary to be on his own again. One got used to it. And got to enjoy it. Visitors always needed to be dealt with, and left an awful lot of washing-up. They were nice to have but it was also good when they had gone. He was a happy hermit really.

He walked round the barn to the summerhouse. Behind

it, strewn on the ground, was an array of small pieces of puppeteer's jettisoned newspapers. Then he toured the dustbins grouped where the pigsties presumably once used to be. In two of them lay all kinds of torn and battered wooden sticks and newspapers and smearings of bright red and black paint. The paint was still wet and had marked the insides of the bins. So it *had* happened. But it was difficult to equate the crude devices that he found pressed into the dustbins with the truly illusory magical devices that had presented themselves to him in performance only an hour or so before, floating above his father's summerhouse.

By that time in the day, it being Sunday, Mrs Clarke had gone home, so he would have to go in to clear up the tea things for himself.

But he left it for a little while. Desultorily, he watched the early-evening news. As usual he was more absorbed by the newsreader's motionless upper lip as she spoke, than by the various news stories that she wished to impart. He was suddenly weary.

His daughter Joan was right, he thought – what need had he of all that accumulation of funds? How was it that he had been unable to give Francesca even a little pump-priming cash? It might at least have made him feel useful again, even involved. It often crossed his mind that he had felt properly alive only when he had been running Chandos House, emulating his bullying old father. Now, as a purely figurehead chairman, more or less forced into retirement by Gilbert and, to some degree, the distressing scandal of the Austin Peacock embezzlement horror, he hardly had so much as a toe-hold in the company.

But Chandos House itself was changing. The recession had forced Gilbert to turn more and more of their facilities into retirement homes for the elderly. It wasn't the same. It might be profitable and secure and plugged into the ever-expanding grey-haired pound, but it didn't have the adventure and vision that Chandos House used to represent.

So here he was now, marginally bored, frustrated, unproductive, less fit than he used to be, but clean and tall and perfectly healthy. But with no great sense of purpose. And eternally beset, the while, by screaming, feverish, fantastic, obscene, sick-making, masturbatory dreams, none of which had he the courage to do anything about.

And today, of course, these slimy fantasies had been further inflamed by the sight of a bright, wild young woman taking herself off for a swim. And his mind had gone apeshit with libidinousness. But she would never know. No one would ever know. And he would die having done nothing about it. The world of women was safe from him.

And it always had been. Grace had gone after twenty-one years. He always told himself, and other people, that it had been because of his dreadful dedication to Chandos House and to work. And that was partially true, but it was also true that he had stopped feeling sexually attracted to his wife early in the marriage, sometime in the fifties for God's sake. It wasn't her fault. Nor his for that matter. He had just ceased to – what did they call it? – fancy her. Had it been because she had not cared for it all that much? She had certainly never complained when their conjugalities drifted to a halt.

After years and years, about the time his twenty-one-year-old daughter Joan had married Sven Nielsen, Grace, who had never glanced at any other man in her life as far as he knew, fell in love with a short, round-the-world yachtsman with the ridiculous name of Fraser and left. In six quick months first Joan had gone, and then, astonishingly, Grace had evaporated as well.

In truth, Norman hadn't felt all that discomfited by his sudden solitariness. Being a single man for the first time in his life appeared to give him the opportunity of seeking out some of his dirtier destinations. But he never did. Well of *course* he didn't. The only change was that his isolation allowed his fantasies to run ahead of themselves and get all the more dirty.

It gave him space, too, at times, to wonder what it was that Grace had left him for. She and the stunted yachtsperson Fraser Ward settled on the south coast and, on the rare occasions he saw her again, she looked vaguely younger, certainly more tanned. She took to wearing white double-breasted trouser-suits with elastic under the instep and chiffon around the throat. She seemed thinner than he remembered. He once bleakly asked Joan what she thought her mother saw in Ward. 'Sex, I suppose,' said his daughter, sneeringly, by way of comfort. But it couldn't have been that, could it?

Sex had been a part of the heaven and earth never apparently dreamt of, in Grace's philosophy. So unlike the teeming ruminations of her first husband. And so Norman, abandoned and purposeless in Coombe, continued to lust after young, writhing, ecstatic, gasping female bodies but did absolutely nothing about it. That is, apart from more than occasional bouts of highly educated self-abuse.

Norman went into the kitchen and decided that he couldn't face cooking himself something to eat for the evening. Plain-chocolate Hobnobs and a mug of hot chocolate would just have to suffice. Then he would wash everything up together in one fell swoop. He was just thinking what an inadequate diet that was for a man of his apparent maturity and good sense, and, by the bye, inadvertently spilling chocolate powder all over his kitchen surfaces, when there was a barrage of bravura knocking at the main house door.

He went through and, pulling aside the heavy green baize curtain, opened it. Out there in the gathering dusk, looking like some sort an apologetic alien, stood a figure lacquered from head to toe in black gloss – punkish zips, anonymous helmet, killer gloves, bovver boots. Little Miss Shakespeare had returned. For one split second he thought she looked uncomfortably like some sort of angel of death.

From an explanatory finger there hung her khaki-green cardigan. 'Didn't want you to freak,' she said. 'I realised I'd dumped this by your little hut and I came back for it. Didn't want to trouble you, Norman, but thought you might flip if you happened to spy an intruder lurking about your undergrowths.'

Could he ask her in? Should he? 'Thank you,' was what he

actually managed to say. She gave him one of her luminous wall-to-wall smiles. That was enough. He had a terrible urge to pick her up and carry her off. All he was able to do was to hiccup along on automatic pilot saying: 'I was just about to make a hot chocolate.'

'Kicking. Yeah, let's live a little. Me and Cadbury's chocolate's a match made in heaven.'

'Would you like a mug?' He seemed to think she was saying that she thought it was a good idea.

'Cool,' she said. She was already in the house.

He was so pleased. 'Ticketyboo,' he said and instantly knew how ridiculous it sounded. He ushered her slight figure into the kitchen and allowed himself just one brief squint at her leather-encased backside. Neat, tight and invitingly heart-shaped. And all very much there and available, less than half a yard away. He felt absurdly happy that she had come back. Even if only for one brief Cadbury's hot chocolatey moment.

She unceremoniously dumped her leather gauntlets on to the kitchen table and slid her gigantic helmet up and away. Once out of the helmet she was properly in the room with him. He could smell warm leather – warm leather and petrol. Leather warmed by the run of her blood. She shook her hair free and grinned unabashed. She had an inordinately hungry face.

'Cool,' she repeated.

'Yes, it is,' he said. 'Make yourself comfortable.' He sounded absurdly English and formal. But then he *was* absurdly English and formal. And none the worse for that. She might take her jacket off if he was hospitable enough. He would like that. He knew it was banal dealing with her, in his head, just like some kind of exquisite, sexy artefact. But that was all she could be to him. He had no idea what she was like as a person – only how she appealed to him because of how she looked. And, anyway, that was how Norman dealt with women – raging appetites completely disguised by unfailing courtesy. He turned away to the fridge to get the milk. He promised himself that if she did take any of her clothes off he wouldn't watch her doing it. Honest, God, he wouldn't. A tight feeling of reluctant anticipation evaporated as he heard the zip of her jacket sliding efficiently down behind him. Seconds later she had hung it on the back of a chair and had hauled her bum up to sit herself on the white formica working-surface over the washing machine, her big boots threatening his Hoovermatic's little round window. As there were three quite adequate kitchen chairs in the room to sit on, he did wonder why she had elected to sit up there. But that was how they were, these kids: give them the luxury of a sofa and they go and sit slam-bang next to it, all over the carpet.

Amy crossed one leg on the other, the ankle of one fearsome metalled boot perched on a sharp knee. He couldn't help but enjoy the way the words 'Hullo Girls!' undulated across the front of her T-shirt. He was brought up short with the sudden thought that she might be lesbian. Would that be the reason why she had contacted punkish little Frannie again after all that time? Oh God, he hoped not.

Amy enthusiastically rubbed the tip of her nose with the knuckle of a crooked first finger and looked at him with great grey eyes. 'Are you afraid of dying?' she asked. It completely stopped him short. It was more than just a bit of a facer. How could he tell her that the idea of his mortality haunted at least part of his every day?

'Golly, what makes you ask?' he parried.

'Well, you're quite old. Isn't it more and more of a preoccupation? After all, we're all going to have to book our holiday with Club Dead eventually. It's just that you're, well, further up near the counter than I am.'

'Doesn't bother me. Never think about it,' he lied. Well, why should he let this rude girl know anything that went on in his head?

'No, I'm interested. Most guys like me don't give squit about death. We're all bloody immortal, us. It'll never happen. But it still kind of bugs me though. In a dead positive, proactive way.' Norman didn't want to talk about dying. He had a sudden flash of an image of his brother Jonathan's

24

coffin, the centre of that brief meaningless ceremony in Golders Green, all those years ago. He eternally carried a grotesque image in his head of his father's face in Coombe churchyard, pressed about with wet earth. But even in spite of this, and almost against his will, he found himself asking her: 'Proactive, how?'

'You need to clean down this bench,' she said sucking deeply on a long wet third finger and dragging it through his spilled chocolate powder. 'I'll do it for you if you like.'

'"Bench"?'

'This,' she said, rapping the formica where she sat with sharp knuckles.

'That's not a bench.'

'What do you call it then?'

'Oh.' And he thought to himself, what the hell *did* he call it? 'I don't know – "the working surface", "the side"?'

'"The side"? What kind of a hell of a name is that, Norman, eh? New Zealanders call it a bench, for Chrissakes.'

'No. A bench is something you sit on.'

'Proves my point,' she said, laughing. The milk was beginning to bubble. Norman found mugs and spoons.

'It's such a razor part of the country.' Amy's remark was so cruelly conversation-making that Norman had to glance at her to see if she was sending him up. 'Oxfordshire,' she said, looking over her shoulder, at the dusk beginning to gather on Bargate Hill. 'Love-it-love-it-love-it. I was in Oxford last week,' she went on, 'at the Playhouse. I've a mate who's a wardrobe designer. She did the cossies for *Faust* there. Dead nifty. In my view. That old guy Mephisto poses a real mean question, doesn't he?'

'Goethe's *Faust*?'

'No, the other one. Henley. No, not Henley, um, Marlowe. Christopher Marlowe. Yep.'

'*Dr Faustus*, then.'

'Too right,' she said, not registering the distinction. 'Now then, here's a question: for what pleasures would you bargain your soul away, Norman? If old Mephisto-pants turned up one day and asked? You'd have to read the small print, wouldn't you? Like, I reckon old Fausty-baby got a pretty shit deal. As far as I could make out, all that was on offer as far as wicked Kit Marlowe was concerned, was shitting on the Pope and a quick gander at Helen of Troy in the raw. Not much of a heyho there, wouldn't you say?' She rubbed her nose energetically with a knuckle again and grinned at him with a sudden honesty. 'That was one of the things I came back meaning to say actually. Sorry about the swim and everything. In the punt. I was out of order, guv'nor. Totally out of order. I do just get these wild moments. You're dealing with a right drongo here. Didn't want to embarrass you.'

'I can't imagine what you mean. I noticed nothing amiss.' They smiled at each other, suddenly, delightfully, in collusion.

'That's all right then.' She put the subject away again. 'So,' she said, 'if I was to offer you anything in the world in return for your soul, what would you go for? Wildest dream time. You can choose anything. Answer in full. Be imaginative. Do not write on both sides of the paper at the same time.'

He couldn't think. Well, certainly, he could think of nothing that he could say out loud in mixed company, in any company. 'Someone to wash up the tea things?' he offered.

'Right you are. You're on. Amy of Troy at your service.' And she jumped down and addressed the crowded sink with a noisy alacrity, turning on both taps and splashing water all over the shop. He doubted he'd have many pieces of unbroken china left by the end of it all.

'How old are you?' she asked busying herself with the Fairy Liquid.

'You're impossible, Amy,' he said, selecting a new drying-up cloth.

'What?'

'How old are you?' he asked her.

'Twenty-four.'

He smiled. 'I'm sixty-nine.'

'Arthur's picnic! Half a century eh? Between us. Almost. The shit you'll have done. The shit you'll have seen, eh?'

'That's as maybe,' he said doubtfully. He had a shrewd suspicion that Amy, for all her youth, might very well have done more of the things he had hankered after all his life, than he had managed even to imagine. He guessed that she would have had more men (or, perhaps, God help him, more women) and done more interestingly unusual things with them in the past seven years or so than he had even contemplated in the last fifty. Why was it that, as far as he was concerned, oral sex seemed to have been invented only about the time of Kennedy's assassination – and too late for him? In the last thirty years, from all you could read in the magazines and in the racy airport novels, it had clearly become a regular part of the core curriculum for every lusting young bride on her wedding night. They all, to a woman, licked their way willingly to work, down over their grooms' honed pectorals and flat stomachs to the matter in hand. And he had never known it.

He poured out two carefully judged mugs of deeply traditional hot drinking chocolate. Amy of Troy had finished her task admirably and had wiped down the sink. Somehow or other there had not been a single breakage. Amy's wet fingers briefly touched his as she took the Morris Motors Centenary mug from him. She leaned back against the wall behind her, cradling the mug, dropping her chin into her collarbone.

'What would you like to do next, eh?' she asked. Kiss you, put my tongue down your throat, have you unzip my fly, he thought. But what he actually said was: 'How do you mean?'

'Got any plans? I mean, the clock's ticking, you must be running out of time. I mean, shit, aren't you?' There was nothing he could say. She motored on: 'That's why I think Old Father Death is such a turn-on. In my view. It's always on the thread to remind you that this lady-life is a terminal condition. That you'd better get on and do the lot. Do everything you've ever dreamed of doing, 'cos next Thursday, or whatever – too fucking soon anyway – bingo it's "hullo nothingness". Yabadabadoo. That's my story anyway. Particularly, I'm afraid, when deciding whether to plastic-out on expensive clothing-and-shit when, the truth is, I'm in debit desert.' She snorted at her own self-delusion. 'What I'm saying is: do it now or life just becomes what happens to you when you're busy making other plans.' She slurped piping-hot chocolate. She must have an asbestos mouth. 'John said that.'

'Boyfriend?' Norman pounced.

'Lennon.'

'Oh. Right. So, is that why you bought the big motorbike?'

'It was a present,' she said shortly.

'Boyfriend?'

'Your plans, Norman your plans? While you've still got time, health, the dosh, all your capacities.' She shot him a quick and what seemed like a keen look and laughed. 'I suppose you *have* got all your capacities?'

'You are a very rude young woman.' But he knew he sounded friendly.

'Yep. Yep, that's me. A rude colonial with no sense of proportion-and-shit. A really bad hat.' She pushed the dark mop of her hair from the back of her neck on to the top of her head. If it hadn't been so absent-minded, it would have been calculatedly sexy. 'That's me, dedicated to the business of – what do you ex-public-schoolboys call it? – debagging, what – pomposity? And, um, Englishness? Traditions? Double hot chocolate at dusk? Des says I'm mortally dangerous. That I mess with people's minds. Well, he's right. Or at any rate I am, at least, working at it.' Calmly holding his eye all the while, she sucked down the last of her drink and, having finished it, put out a long red tongue and licked her lips. Sensually.

'Des?'

'Boyfriend?' She echoed his earlier enquiries. 'No, I work for Des. Des Wright, location manager, Reach For My Gun, the film company. He reckons I'm "wilful, wicked and wise." I wish the last were true.'

'Are the others?'

'That's for you to know and for me to find out.' All her pronouncements culminated in a tweak up the octave. Along

28

with so many of her nation, she adopted a speech pattern that turned everything she said into a question. She slipped down off her perch and washed out her mug under a running cold tap. She was leaving nothing unwashed that evening. Norman could not help but watch the way her clipped flat pelvis pressed hard against the side of the white porcelain as she reached for the tap. He wouldn't have minded being a white porcelain sink at that moment.

God, these young women today, how lucky were their generation of menfolk to have such exciting foils to match them – young sexy kids who could take the battle to the men in a way his own limp war-torn generation of women never knew. He thought of his wife Grace, motionless on her side of their bed or with her arms dragging on his neck, letting him do what he required of her because it was only right that a husband should be able to take his pleasure. This young woman would grab what sex she needed with both hands and never think twice about it. The thought began to give him a small reaction and made him feel a mite bolder. And he would need to summon up some modest courage or else the girl would be gone again.

'Now, um, Amy, what was that exhibition all about, this afternoon, that spectacle you performed all over my summerhouse?'

'You saw that? I expect that was me goofing off. As per usual.'

'Of course I did. I could hardly help it. I suspect you got red paint all over my summerhouse roof.' It was meant to be jovial but it came out grumpy.

'I did not,' she yelped. 'I wiped everything down. Totalled the whole joint. Got it all over my arm too.' She raised one long naked arm to his face and indeed there was blood-red paint down the inside of it. 'Wasn't it just so *very*? I was bringing a little culture to your ducks.'

'God knows what it was all about. It was certainly amazingly successful in breaking my concentration.'

'It was? Arthur's picnic! Yeah, I think I thought I was trying to dilute the angst. Give you something else to think about. From what I'd managed to gather from the pre-match battle-plan, Fran's mum had come down to Oxford with this shitload of attitude. I'd reckoned you were about to be fiscally gang-banged by your whole famdamily, and I reckoned you'd get a blast from knowing you had someone in your corner. I was in your corner, Norman. Rooting, as t'were.'

She was sitting on the table now, in front of him, her boots dangling. She had taken hold of the button-hole of his jacket with a long finger and thumb and held his gaze firmly with grave translucent eyes. Unlike earlier in the day, now she was looking at him closely all the time, challenging his eyes to slide away. He could feel the blood running in his neck. Is this, he wondered, why they called it 'button-holing'?

'No,' she said. 'That's so much garbage, I'm afraid.' She made a face and let loose his jacket. She spoke slowly in a deep sad voice, as if trying to reveal to him what was in her soul. 'I get this torrid buzz out of performance-and-shit, that's all – disguise, dressing up, role-playing, acting the fool, impersonating, pretending, camping about, playing around, lying, oh yeah, every kind of deceit.'

She stopped and considered what she had said. She shrugged. 'It makes me wetter than sex.'

Norman must have looked shocked. She went on: 'It's about a kind of power. Power's cool as fuck. In my view. People get off on power, don't they? Often more than they get off on sex. Probably because it's easier, that's why. It's well-powerful pretending to be someone else and only you in the whole wide world world knows the honest, boring truth. I reckon it must be the main buzz that gets transvestites going, wouldn't you say?' Amy lightly punched his arm with a lightly clenched fist. 'Sorry,' she said. 'I don't think you need to know me. I'm not very nice. A bit fucked in the head, I'm sorry to say. And I think you are probably a very nice man.' She sounded like the old television commercial for the AA as she repeated: '"A-very, *very* nice man." Handsome even. Definitely handsome.'

'I could be a bit, er, messed up in the head too. I expect

everybody is. A little,' he ventured. And then he felt terribly embarrassed by what he had said.

'Uh-uh.' She shook her dark head, denying it.

He sensed that she was getting herself into exit mode. He hurried on: 'So that's why you do this cabaret routine, is it? To, um, enjoy performing. To enjoy the power of performing?'

'Quentin and me? Spot on.'

'Quentin?'

'Quentin,' she confirmed. 'And me.'

'What do you do? What kind of show is it?'

'Oh I think you don't need to know.' Norman felt excited. Joan had obviously been right. It was probably a bit blue. All of a sudden he needed to know very badly indeed. 'Oh I think you can tell me,' he said with a very poor attempt at studied nonchalance.

'OK, OK, Mr Man. "Hard-up and Flummoxed", we're called.' She threw her arms wide and sang a fanfare: 'Dud-DAH! It's a "tricky, sicky, flirty, thirty minutes of tickling an audience's fancy". Based around some fairly ordinary stand-ard illusions. But well beefed-up for pissed-solid, half-arsed punters with more money than sense, that's for sure. Adult parties, stag nights. City johnnies. Very rude, Norman, very, very rude. Sorry. But funny too, I like to think. Quentin says it's sophisticated but I think we could just be kidding ourselves. Here, I think I've got some of our literature.'

Amy pulled a small folded leaflet out of one of her pockets. It was primarily a glossy black-and-white image of two full-length naked backs standing side by side. It was not very difficult to recognise that the neat and downright feminine back of the two was Amy's. In the picture her hand had sneaked around and was pinching the man's naked posterior. For the second time that day Norman found himself trying not to contemplate Amy's naked bottom for too long at a time.

She took the leaflet back, but not before it seemed to Norman that, when printed, the act's name was punctuated in such a way as to be called something different. On the paper the act was entitled 'Hard, Up and Flummoxed'.

'Ah yes,' he said with supreme eloquence.

'Are you sleeping with anybody?' She gave the question about the same stress as asking if he took sugar. For a moment he had to rerun his hearing recall actually to make sure that those were the words he had heard.

'That's my business,' he replied with about as much dignity as he could muster. The phrase emerged reeking of pomposity and outrage but there was nothing he could do about it, once the words were out.

'So you're not, eh?'

'I think that's my affair,' he said choosing his words badly.

'Right. Yeah. Absolutely. You said it. It's your lady-life. But it *is* what people must ask about you, isn't it? You living here on your own. In this solitary, sexy luxury. Freedom City. No ties. Time to kill. Dapper fella. You could be ploughing your way through half the married female population of Oxford, I'd've thought. All those dons' wives gagging for it.'

'Why married?' He wouldn't allow himself to be flattered by 'dapper fella', whatever she meant by that. Why was she doing this? What did she want? Money?

''Cos it's the married ones who can't get enough.' If only, he thought, if only. Were they? Were those Summertown Christmas sherry parties that he occasionally found himself attending a hotbed of available libido and he had never picked up any of the clues? He doubted it. This girl had a serious fantasy dislocation. 'Listen I think this conversation has gone far enough.'

'Too right. It's just that I get mine. I wondered if you get yours.'

'Well, it's my business.'

'So, anyway, you don't.'

'What?' But he knew perfectly well.

'Tread the light fantastic.'

'As I said, it's actually none of your business.'

'Nuff respec'. OK – Sinless City.' She gave him her best grave, soul-searching smile and it turned what could have so easily been a taunt into a companionable intimacy.

'I didn't say that, either.' But he knew his voice had gone

up about fourteen octaves in a kind of ruffled defensiveness. He wanted to stop this conversation and he badly wanted it to go on as well. He was enjoying what seemed like the most frank conversation he had ever had. He thought he had better fertilise it just a little or it might get mislaid for lack of encouragement. 'I've had my moments,' he lied.

'Tell me one. Tell me a good one.' She was standing in front of him, looking up, close enough to embrace. He could feel the warmth of her body across the space between them.

'No, absolutely not. It's private and an area of trust. And I don't know you, little madam, from, from—'

'"Eve",' she finished for him. 'Why not? Why not? You'd tell me about splendid meals you've had. Or happy holidays or great concerts, or brilliant shopping. But not about torrid shagging, eh? It's so repressed, so fetidly English that people never ever talk about great moments in sex. In my view.' And she proclaimed it like a newspaper headline, describing the words in the air with her long fingers: 'Great. Moments. In. Sex.'

'Would *you*?'

'Yep. If you asked me.'

'All right,' he said. His throat instantly dried up. 'I ask.'

'When did I last have sex?'

'If you like.' He found it difficult to get the words out.

'Apart from touching myself up a bit in the loo when we got back from all those moist punts?' He was already in shock. She went on: 'Camden lock. This morning. Friend of mine. Obviously. I was returning a video of *Les Enfants du Paradis*. May weekend. So he hadn't got up. So I got down. And it was a very-very-nice, very-very-quick quickie. Wham-bang-thank-you-man kind of number. Me on top shouting, holding on to the bedhead – all that. Lovely, actually. Sorted me out for the day. Afterwards we did some illegal substances and then I bombed on up here. I was only in there thirty minutes. I didn't want to be late for you, you see.' She grinned innocently. 'All right?' she asked. 'You see, that wasn't very difficult, was it? Gives the jump a touch of credit, being able to talk about it. Now you.'

But no, no, it wasn't all right. He wanted more. He wanted so much more. But he couldn't ask her the questions. He wanted to ask her a thousand things about her casual 'quickie'. Did she use a condom? Had she been to bed with the boy before? Had she been to bed with the boy often? Who was he? Did she climax? Did she do this kind of thing absolutely all the time? What illegal substances? Was any of it true?

The idea of this spare, smoothly articulated vision with X-ray eyes turning up in the midst of one's morning slumbers, crawling under one's rumpled duvet and giving herself to one and then disappearing into the morning heat-haze made him erect. He was embarrassed by it. And mortifyingly pleased as well.

Could she tell what was happening to his cock? Probably. She was standing very close to him. For a mere child she seemed to know just about everything that happened between men and women. Presumably this was her goal – trying to get him all excited with this graphic chat. Why, in heaven's name? Did she fancy him? He could hardly believe that. Was it just some evil challenge? A bet? A tease? He cleared his throat. He wanted to turn away from her, hide his condition.

'Well,' he said, playing for time, 'you young people.' A really sound, deeply intelligent contribution to the debate, that . . . Then, out of the blue, he thought of Bertram and found his escape. 'My only real sin I suppose, is what I've got in the barn. My only real indulgence. Bertram. Well, the only one I'm prepared to bring out into the open,' he said coyly.

'Bertram? Oh, gay, are you?'

'I'll show you.' He led her out of the bright kitchen into the darkness of the yard. Yes, she was just a tease, this one. A dirty-minded little girl trying to get a bit of a rise out of someone old enough to be her grandfather. Perhaps she had an idea she could tease him into attacking her and then have him up for assault. He suddenly had the thought that she might be tape-recording all this. After all, it was a disgraceful way to behave. He ought just to send her packing, rather than indulging her. But the trouble was, as well as abhoring the grubbiness, he liked it. Very much indeed.

He flipped on the lights in the barn and went across to the car and threw off its covers. Even for Norman, who had owned the thing for some fifteen years, it was a thrill each time he showed it to someone new. Amy was suitably impressed. 'Arthur's picnic! Norman, it's the dog's bollocks,' she breathed, walking around it almost in a trance, holding her hands out to touch it, but not actually laying a finger on it anywhere. 'Norman it's stonking transcendental,' she whispered. 'Knockout. Totally knockout.' She murmured the words in almost voiceless awe as she circled the vehicle at a respectful distance. 'It's just so *very*.'

People were usually decently impressed by Bertram but Norman couldn't ever remember anybody giving their appreciation quite such quasi-religious fervour before. He himself, of course, could easily understand her feelings, but a lot of people never felt quite the same wonderment as he did when first they were allowed to look upon it. Norman saw his pride and joy afresh through Amy's eyes – the massive size of its open, four-seated, black-and-silver interior, the bold practicality of the instrument panelling, the folded canopy, like so many Mrs Gamps, resting in readiness at the rear, the upright formality of its windscreens, the unapologetic size of its wire-spoked wheels, the thrust of its enormous engine-housing, the bravura of its monumental, silver-plated headlamps – the whole splendid grandiloquence of that glorious seventy-year-old machine spoke volumes about privilege in a different age.

'What is it?' she asked him finally when she had ceased prowling around.

'It's a motor car, Amy.'

'Thanks, Norman, that helps. What kind, Mr Man?'

'It's what they used to call a Bullnose, because of the shape of the bonnet. It's the original Morris Oxford. Four-cylinder, eighteen hundred cc, thirteen point nine horsepower, twenty-eight brake-horsepower. Built just down the road, in Oxford, in about 1923. They say it was Britain's best selling car in the twenties. In 1921, old man William Morris, whose Cowley factory made these things, decided to slash his prices and the result was that he cornered the market. In two years they found themselves at the cutting edge of popular motoring. Popular motoring for the very first time in the history of the world. Easy to drive, economic to run and pretty reliable. The Ford Fiestas of the roaring twenties, I suppose.

'Adding seventy years has now made them unique. They sold some hundred and fifty thousand of them. There are still quite a few around. Jeffrey Archer's got one. At the peak they were selling as many as a thousand a week. They stopped making them in '26.' He was going on a bit. But it was his greatest enthusiasm. He probably loved Bertram more than he had loved anything in his life. Which was pretty damned strange, when you thought about it. Sorry, Francesca. Sorry, Grace.

'What did it cost?' Norman registered how quickly the value of the thing came up. Money was important with this young woman.

'New, three hundred and eighty.'

'And for you?'

'Oh I bought it years and years ago. And I've had a deal of work done on it since then. I suppose it's worth something like ten grand now – twelve perhaps if it wasn't for this recession. I don't really know. I don't keep up with these things. I just like having it.'

'Don't we all? Yeah, too right. Kicking. How fast did it go?'

'Top speed: fifty-five miles an hour.'

'Gonkyfilarious! Does it still go?'

'Good God, yes. I give it the odd airing.' He felt absurdly more proud of it than ever. It was so great to be able to impress this Amy. He loved the rampant enthusiasm of this beautiful, beautiful girl. He warmed to her for allowing him to have such a good time over his car.

'Start it.'

'Now?'

'Scared you can't?'

'No. No, not at all. Ignition's not a problem. They weren't difficult to start. Mark you, it doesn't always go first time,' he warned her cautiously. He would die if it was one of those rare days when Bertram turned from an old and trusted companion into an lump of unforgiving, useless metal. He opened the big latches at the side of the bonnet, switched on the petrol supply, adjusted the carb for slow running and retarded the magneto. He then went around to the cockpit to switch the vehicle on.

'Why "Bertram"?' she asked, following him closely, watching what he was doing.

'I used to go to the Christmas Bertram Mills Circuses at Olympia in the years after the war. They had a crazy car-and-clown act I liked a lot – explosions, bits falling off, water spurting everywhere. A bit like your washing-up, I suppose. Anyway, it needed a name. So . . .'

He finished adjusting the oil supply by putting the metal indicator just to one side of its usual position, halfway between where the words 'weak' and 'rich' were etched by some long-dead hand. The day had been very warm but it was still cool in the barn. He returned to the front of the motor car and put on the old leather glove that he usually used with the starting handle. He carefully bound his fingers around the thing, placing his thumb on the same side as his fingers. How many times had he heard of well-loved engines back-firing and breaking their owners' imprudently placed thumbs?

He allowed himself a quick silent prayer to the god of all petrol-driven engines and, with some expertise, cranked the handle. The first engine cough sounded pretty fruitful. Bertram was clearly in obliging mood. Third pull and the engine coughed profitably again, kicked and then burbled into life. The barn was suddenly filled with its considerable throb. Smoke and the smell of burnt fuel drifted into the empty, beamed roof-space.

Norman felt ecstatic. He couldn't hear anything that the girl was saying. No doubt she was going on about Alfred's picnic, or something. She was aglow with excitement, her washed-out grey eyes burning bright. He went back to the cab to adjust the mixture. The noise of the engine slackened and became less obtrusive.

Amy gazed at the machine in awe. 'It's like some stonking galactic motorised yacht,' she yelled. Then with her tongue protruding thoughtfully into her cheek, she slowly closed with the machine, carefully laying herself across its shaking bonnet cover, embracing it with long, outstretched arms. She closed her eyes and placed her cheek on the shiny black metal, pressing her T-shirt with her unfettered breasts to its warming surface and locking her flat sharp pelvis to its side. Her fluid lips took on a dreamy glazed kind of smile. Then she said something but he couldn't make out what it was. He had finished buzzing about ensuring that all was in order. He began to wipe his hands. Amy repeated herself louder and opened her eyes to see what he thought. He shouted that he couldn't hear and went and switched off the petrol supply. Bertram suffocated into quiet. The silence seemed to ring in their ears. And their voices seemed unnaturally loud.

For the third time she said it, looking happy enough: 'It makes a totally orbital vibrator. Better than the spin cycle on a washing machine, anyway.' She would bring everything back down to that. He said nothing, busying himself about, unconnecting the car, getting it ready to sleep again. It might look as if he hadn't heard. He just got on. The tart familiar whiff of burnt petrol in the barn was his very favourite smell. It was so lovely to be able to share the feeling with someone. Very few people had ever really understood about Bertram.

Not much later, he stood with Amy in the light of the yard as she zipped her body tidily away into her leather jacket. 'Well, big man, your Bertram's just totally the business,' she said. 'You're lucky to have a love like that. It's a lot better than bonking – I tell you, you're missing nothing.' She was silent for a moment. 'Don't take too much notice of me, please,' she said, almost softening. 'Well, there's a thing, you won't have to, will you?' She laughed. The dour, black, space-age helmet slid back on over her head, hiding her almost completely from view. 'Have a good life,' she said placing a gauntlet on his arm. 'You know what I think is a brilliant motto for a totally happening life? In my view?'

'No, what is a brilliant motto for a totally happening life?' he asked, surprised by how sorry he was that she was going.

'Some fine fella has put up in these ginormous red letters outside where I live in London. If you crane out of my bedroom window and look hard to the right – towards Westminster, I mean – there it is: three words – a knockout principle for Life At One Thousand Percent – this whopping great sign: "Do it all", it says. "DO. IT. ALL". And, bloody hell, don't I try to?' She put on her gauntlets. 'Even if it kills me.' She felled him with another of her laser smiles. 'There you go. There's a thought, eh? I offer you that free, gratis and for knickers.'

'"Do it" – the motto of the City of Mahogany.'

'Oh?'

'It's an opera – Brecht and Weill. *The Rise and Fall of the City of Mahogany.*'

'Right.' Then she asked: 'Singing furniture?'

'No. No, not really. Singing capitalism, I suppose.'

She obviously didn't understand any of this. She gunned the Ducati into life, waved a careless hand and was suddenly not there any more.

Finally, once he could no longer hear the bike's engine, Norman found himself going back into the barn. He dragged the covers back over Bertram's beautiful, burnished body and then went into the next stall where there was a whole pile of cardboard boxes. Denis Clarke had piled them up quite neatly against the one wall. Norman pulled some of them aside. Half hidden was a misty, flecked mirror-glass about three foot six by three foot six. Norman had had it tucked away in there for about eighteen months now. He had been so thrilled when he had first found it. After that, of course, he had funked the whole thing. Typical.

That girl had been absolutely right. He ought to get on. 'Do. It. All.' she would say. 'I. Do. Nothing.' he said out loud to the emptiness of the barn. With every day, there was less and less time available to change any of that.

He felt fit and well now, but, in the long run, only frailty beckoned. There was every kind of known and unknown sickness lurking out there in the future for him – cancer, Alzheimer's, motor-neurone, dicky ticker, clogged carburettor. The list was endless. He had never really taken enough exercise, never looked after himself all that well, never eaten properly, had probably drunk too much alcohol. His work had often been very stressful. He had never played squash as Gilbert did every week with fixated and sweaty single-mindedness. A round of golf every fortnight or walking the grouse moors for six days each year didn't count for much. He had smoked until he was fifty.

Were anything ever to go wrong, where would he go? The Aviary was already miles too big for him. Gilbert and Mary's? No, that would be unbearable. He was sure that, however full of bonhomie and hail-brother-well-met, Gilbert, when the chips were down, wouldn't want him around.

Norman had a sudden vision of himself in one of the Chandos House residential hotels on the south coast – Gilbert dubbed them 'crem-queuing'. There he was, among the other 'guests', sitting in cold morning sunshine on one of the narrow, easy-wipe, leatherette-covered armchairs with the angular wooden arms in one of the worn public rooms. He was there with his back to the wall trying to avoid watching *Richard & Judy* on daytime television.

So, yes, he had better get on. Thank you Amy Shakespeare. He had had the thing for almost two years now. And done nothing about it. Prevarication had been the watchword of his retirement. He tapped the metalled glass with an experimental knuckle. It seemed to ring true. Its potential for devilment was colossal. 'Total', 'Galactic' or 'Finger-licking', as that little sex-bomb might describe it.

That little sex-bomb (was that what they were called now? – 'sex-kitten', perhaps?) seemed, furthermore, to have a uncanny instinct. For example, it was almost psychic that she had picked on his thoughts about dying as a topic for conversation. How the devil had she guessed that it had always been one of his uppermost concerns? That one Norman Broderick Matthew Ranburn MBE had never ever been able to come to terms with his own mortality? And yet he had communicated this to others only on the rarest occasions. Normally he kept this particularly dread card very close to his chest. He remembered once absurdly confessing his fears to, of all people, his darling granddaughter Francesca.

It had been a cold Boxing Day afternoon and the two of them had been walking along the top of Bargate Hill as the last of the grey light dropped from the sky. The Christmas before last, it was – or the one before that. The trouble had been that he had been nicely buoyed up with post-prandial brandies. It had been quite wrong to confide in her. But she hadn't seemed all that bothered. She had, no doubt, thought it no more than grandfatherly burblings. Could she have mentioned the conversation to Amy? He rather doubted it. No, it was probably no more than the girl's innate killer instinct. He guessed Amy had a natural instinct for the jugular.

Death and sex tended to get muddled in his brain. Always had. He remembered his housemaster, over fifty years ago, Saul Troughton, giving one of his little sixth-form chats about the great wide world outside that they were all about to troop off into. Saul would go on about honour and about morals and about loyalty and about temptation and, inevitably, about sex and death. One thing he said had struck the over-confident Ranburn major pretty forcibly one of those evenings: it was that, before sex had entered the scheme of things, there was no death. Before sex, propagation was effected by cells, amoebas and plants and whatever dividing into halves in order to further their species. At that time there was no need for anything to die. Everything could just keep growing and growing and dividing and dividing. Only with sex came death.

He was getting depressed again. Tomorrow he would take his life (and his wonderfully wicked stolen mirror) into his hands and perhaps begin to put his oft-delayed and deeply aberrant scheme into effect. Or perhaps he wouldn't.

No, but he would.

He switched off the light and left the barn. All evening long he had been puzzled as to why the girl had come back to talk to him. She hadn't forgotten her cardigan, had she? It had just been an excuse.

Funny that.

CHAPTER TWO

For now we see through a glass, darkly

I CORINTHIANS 13:12

MONDAY 3 JULY

'What would you like?' the waitress asked Norman, without much sign of genuine interest. She had some sort of foreign accent – German? Dutch? Flemish possibly. She was a little blonde in a lacy white blouse that popped its buttons at the front, as they do. Her black tights were the focus of attention for most of the solitary businessmen scattered about the Charing Cross Hotel's George Stephenson Lounge. Her legs clearly had something of the same unremitting fascination for them all as a television screen with the sound turned down.

To put my hand up your skirt, was his head's answer; but the advantage of silver-haired maturity and respectable suiting is that it entirely allays suspicion in others. A prosperous, elderly, civilised face is the most perfect security system. He gave her his most gracious smile and ordered a coffee. She took her exquisite buttocks away to her Cona coffee machines, carefully observed by thirteen disparate, desperate men.

Norman had become dolefully aware that, since that young woman Amy had spurred him on to action, resulting in his bringing about the realisation of a two-year-old fantasy, something of a beast had been released to maraud heavy-booted about in his consciousness. Scheming corrupts. Effecting one's scheming corrupts absolutely. He was surprised by how turned on he seemed to be by that corruption. He was getting to be a lost soul. Well, it was something to do.

He had done what he had set out to do. He hadn't done it brilliantly but it was perfectly adequate. No one would ever be able to guess. She had a lot to answer for, that stunning girl who had turned up one day and teased him and got him all excited. The evidence of his endeavours was printed in the magazine there on the table in front of him. For all the world to see. He was on his way. That creature had come into his life for just one brief, dry-mouthed, intricately remembered afternoon six weeks before, and, ever since, he had become a man possessed with carrying through his dream.

He might be elderly, but for the first time in a long while he felt he had a direction. He felt he was living his life.

He didn't feel elderly of course. But presumably he had to accept that he was.

There had never been a particular door through which Norman had stepped one day from 'middle-aged' to 'elderly'. He doubted if very many people actually ever thought of themselves as 'old'. He guessed that most people tended to feel much the same as when they were about twenty-eight or so – just not playing quite so much golf. 'Elderly' would always seem to be an idea lodged mainly in the eye of the beholder.

Nevertheless, if he was honest, a time had arrived when he realised that he had begun to think differently from those of lesser years. And by this he was not thinking just of brother Gilbert alone. A period had arrived when, for example, he alone in the universe seemed to think that the Internet was nothing more than an electronic lavatory wall for the world to scribble on. All wired up and nowhere to go. A time had arrived when it seemed as if he and he alone mourned the death of the adverb – he was always hearing Boycott and those other media acolytes giving airtime to sentences like 'Ambrose was bowling really quick before lunch'. The word was 'quickly', Geoff, 'quickly'. Sometimes one of the commentators would even commit the crime of saying: 'He was batting real steady.' The total double-adverb loss.

This was probably all at about the same time that, to his astonishment, all the young men in the entire world, nation after nation, decided, for reasons of no practicality whatsoever, to wear their baseball hats back to front. When people dispensed with drinking-glasses and decided to drink beer straight from the bottle, with the bottle necks frequently now impeded with lumps of lime. Or, equally, when nearly all the women in the western world decided to wear their sweaters around their buttocks like surrogate skirts, tied at the waist by their sleeves, like so many urban hill-walkers.

'Elderly' seemed to have arrived concomitantly with that same monstrous regiment of womenfolk dividing itself in an irrevocable schism – those under thirty who, to a woman, wore big black hobnail army boots, and those above who remained properly loyal to decent ladies' footwear. This must also have been about the time when every business, no matter how large or how small, had to have a 'mission statement'. When, all of a sudden, the pronunciation of the name of the firm Nestlés shifted overnight from the happily and universally accepted 'Nessells' to something more along the lines of 'Nestlay'. And when the young entirely took against the idea of tucking in their shirts. It must have been about the same time that city streets became full of arrogant young black men who crossed the road in front of one's car without so much as a glance or a thought as to whether one might be about to run them down.

And what in hell's name was this damned word 'cheers'? In modern parlance, it seemed to have replaced just about every mode of communication. Nowadays, apparently, it did just fine for 'hello', 'goodbye', 'thank you', 'after you', 'mud in your eye', 'don't mind me', 'how do you do', 'here's your change', 'back soon', 'excuse me'; but never ever got an outing as that touching and traditional threesome of celebration – as in 'Three cheers for matron for doing the sandwiches'.

Yes, and whatever happened to the AA man's salute?

Norman sipped his coffee and flicked open the pages of the magazine. Every time he looked at his advertisement in print it made him feel short of breath. Still, in spite of himself, he found that he tended to glance about to see if there might be anyone around who could guess at its appalling – and delightful – subtext.

He knew the words by heart, but time and time again over the past three weeks he had not been able to resist the idea of rehearsing, in his head, the thought of some unsuspecting and innocent stranger reading the thing. There it was, again, shouting at him from among the usual discreet gentility of the rest of its content. The words appeared to him positively to shriek his carefully camouflaged needs. *The Lady* magazine featured it under its vast array of 'SITUATIONS AND APPOINTMENTS' in a black double-ruled box:

OXFORDSHIRE AREA

Young, married couple are offered an opportunity of comfortable accommodation and a reasonable annual stipend in return for general housekeeping and caretaking of an elderly retired businessman's small Oxfordshire estate. The owner is often away on business and needs to return to home comforts. Please write to Norman Ranburn, The Aviary, Coombe, Oxon OX5 3BY. All letters will receive a reply – any photos returned. Interviews at the beginning of July.

Interviews that very day, in fact, at the Charing Cross Hotel. Interviews to begin in half an hour, to be precise.

He was going mad.

Well, he was certainly not in control any more. Take last Saturday and Susan Davidson. Norman bought a good many of his provisions in the Coombe village shop, on the green. They needed the trade these days now that they were in competition with the supermarkets and those shoplifting emporia, the hypermarkets. At home, at the Aviary, his Mrs Clark kept the freezer nicely filled but Norman enjoyed doing the bits and pieces for himself. Once a week or so, he had patronised Mrs Thomas's grocery shop between the Blenheim Arms and the church. And Susan Davidson, their Saturday girl, always served him.

That was the point.

Norman could have spent the entire day in there, buying up all their bizarre stock, just to remain in close proximity to the nicely rounded, peaches-and-cream nubility of the blonde seventeen-year-old Miss Davidson. She would attend his bidding, bending and stretching, ducking and smiling, edging his sugar and his Branflakes and his Rich Teas and his Ariel into useful cardboard boxes with fair, young fingers.

The sunlight would catch the light down on her forearms and he could not but help noticing the way her buttoned shirt strained across her generous young breasts. He would stand benignly over her, friend to all the village, the reasonably well-to-do, good-natured surrogate squire of Coombe and concentrate on not allowing anyone to guess that he was watching her. He was watching the way Susan's rounded pelvis flicked backwards and forwards as Mrs Thomas edged past her, behind the counter, on her way to the till. His secret eye learned every part of the girl's rounded body off by heart until, regrettably, his box would be full and it was time to carry it out to the boot of his car. Of course, one disadvantage of this obsession with Susan Davidson's physiognomy was that the larder at the Aviary probably had the biggest stockpile of packets of unopened Kelloggs Branflakes in the whole of the United Kingdom.

Since he had begun to work on the cottage – his secret and solitary labour – the worst parts of Norman's imagination had become infected in a way he had never experienced before. He had begun to indulge himself in practices that had heretofore been entirely alien to him. Last weekend – Norman shuddered at the dreadfully titillating memory – Susan had been window-dressing Mrs Thomas's main shop window. It had been very late one soaking wet June Saturday afternoon. Most of the village were, no doubt, ensconced in front of their televisions waiting for them to roll back the covers at Wimbledon.

Norman had sat at the wheel of his car for the whole of an intense, shameful, wonderful hour watching Susan, across the other side of the road, squirming about in the narrow space of the window, going about her business. She had adjusted the calendars, dropped drawing-pins, hung aloft skeins of wool and displayed the tins of time-honoured stodge that the citizens of Coombe were wont to consume. Under Mrs Thomas's garish window spotlights, it was, of course, Susan herself who was very much on display. Her nicely covered, youthful limbs took up any and every configuration a gentleman might dream of, as she endeavoured to reach the items she needed. Now she was crouching, now she was on tiptoe, with her shirt escaping its waistband. Then she was squatting again with her chin thoughtfully pressed to her knee, unknowingly emulating Amy Shakespeare's pose at lunch on the riverbank that golden day six weeks before. Susan's face was pink with effort and the warmth of the shop and her grand little bum imprinted a neat heart-shaped miniskirt on to the outward window-pane behind her. She was totally unaware how very much on show she was.

Norman had remained sitting in his parked car, quietly hidden by a curtain of drenching rain. Breathing steadily, he slowly allowed himself to conjure up the imagined experience of holding that young elastic bottom in his cupped palm. After a little while, he could almost feel the damp of her naked skin against his warm, work-roughened hands, the rasp of her wiry secret hair as it accommodated his big thumb, the oily sensation of her body being pleased by its invasion.

Eventually he was obliged to tuck those self-same fingers deftly into his lap below his steering wheel and there, plumb in the centre of the village, to the rattle of incessant rain on the roof of the car, he had delightfully and shamefully brought himself off.

Immediately afterwards – and it occurred without fail, every time – a deep and savage melancholy swamped him as he sorted things out with a faithful Kleenex. What a pathetic old sod he was. What a sad and reviled figure he would be, should anyone ever discover what he was really like. But no one would be able to find out. However much he loathed the minutes after he had allowed himself to indulge himself, he knew, of old, that it would be but a short-lived tristesse. Twenty-seven minutes, to be exact. He knew the exact timing from many occasions in the past. For the whole of twenty-seven minutes he would vow with such fervent determination never ever to pander to himself like that again. Then, just twenty-seven brief minutes later, it did not seem to be such a terrible thing any more. Quite magically, a wicked, maddening little glint would begin to return to his sad old reviled libido. And after all, it damaged no one, did it? It wasn't as if he wanted to carry off young women in his car, or breathe filth down phone lines into unsuspecting female ears, or ever to do anything dangerous or frightening like that. Norman would never be able to hurt anybody, thank God. He would always keep himself to himself.

He finished his coffee in the bright sunshine of the George Stephenson Lounge, allowed himself one last grave consideration of his waitress's tights and all that they contained and took himself aloft to the interview room that the hotel had set aside for him. The rains of June had departed and July was being remarkably bright and sunny. It seemed like a good omen. The sky above the busy Strand outside seemed almost extra-luminous as if with nervous tension and the traffic lights down by St Martin-in-the-Fields flicked from red to red and amber, to green and back with an almost pent-up shortness of breath. As Norman looked out of the window every couple he saw looked as if they could be prospective candidates heading for their crucial interview with him. Until they passed the station by.

His interview room had a hat stand, a desk and a pair of high-backed mock-Queen-Anne chairs. Norman began by adjusting the furniture a little. He edged the desk around

49

until its back was square to the window. This wasn't particularly easy to do, because the carpet got rucked up underneath it, and the desk was rather more than one person could easily manage. Eventually he was satisfied. He would have all the advantage of the midday light. He would be able to look at his guests, without their necessarily being aware precisely where he himself was looking. He moved the various chairs about too, and by sitting behind the desk a few times and checking his line of vision, he was able to put them as close to the desk as he could, without losing the full-length view of his intended victims. He was ready.

He had selected five couples to see. Eleven days ago he had taken up his silver paper-knife and carefully tipped the contents of the large brown envelope on to his writing desk. The big envelope was full of little envelopes. The pulse in his throat had blipped away tensely as he straightened them into neat stacks of the same size. His study felt very quiet. He poured himself a large gin and tonic and then, delicately slitting the top of each of the smaller envelopes, he began to organise their contents across the red leather of his desktop. The mute piles of envelopes seemed to promise every kind of possibility. He solemnly counted the applications. There were fifty-seven.

Inevitably, he thought later, when he had skimmed his way through them all, the end result in no way matched the anticipation. But, then, what did? Anticipation was so often the very best part of any event. Some of the letters were, frankly, appallingly ill-written muddles from simpletons and the uneducated. The majority maintained a steadfast seriousness which made his heart sink. None of them were exactly overburdened with sheaves of references or photocopies of certificates. Only fourteen of the letters had taken note of the fact that photographic evidence might be of value. He placed these traces of gold-dust in a special pile all of their own, taking great care not to muddle the inch-square photo-booth likenesses one with another.

He didn't bother to read the applications that were without photographs. Given his purpose, it wasn't worth bothering to take the risk. After all, he was not on the lookout, first and foremost, for a talent to caretake and housekeep, was he? Mrs Clarke would still come in from time to time on an *ad hoc* basis, to keep an eye on things, even though her hubby, having reached retirement age, had now bowed out. She had decided that it was time for her to do less. But she would still keep the jolly old ship running smoothly when he needed her to.

Thus it was only the ones with photographs attached that he examined with any real concentration. And then, to be honest, it was only the women that he scrutinised carefully. His father's massive old magnifying glass had been useful here. With studious, gently breathing gaze, Norman Ranburn studied these specimens of human beings up for sale. There were five of them that he might want to look at in the flesh. The others were no-hopers.

He realised that he would need to apply his every wit of management science and personnel know-how to pick out which of these pairs of possibilities would be the ones to go about their business with a fair degree of casual uninhibitedness. Not easy, but essential if the scheme was to work and he was, at last, to feel at ease.

He imagined that this was what those casting-couch characters in the film world felt like. It was like playing God. Yes, of course, he had taken on people for employment for the best part of his working life, but it had been employment based upon skills, employment records, ability to do the job, on references and on recommendations. In those circumstances, if the candidate was a personable young woman, it would perhaps slightly enhance her chances, boost his spirit and cue gentlemen on the interviewing board to voice the odd appreciative remark after she had left the room. But, with Chandos House, on the whole, one was obliged, finally, to stick to the dictum of choosing the best person for the job.

But this very personal personnel selection procedure would be the first time when purely sexual considerations were to be of uppermost concern. And the idea of this quickened his pulse. It was possible that his sex life, for want of a better expression, might turn out to have an element of satisfaction at long long last.

It would be about time.

For someone of his power and capacity, Norman always thought that it was indeed odd that he had so radically missed out on what many thought of as the main event of the twentieth century – the sexual revolution. When he came to consider it, he would put it down, to some degree, to circumstances. But primarily he would simply have to blame a lifetime of paralysing, terminal shyness. These two elements had combined to immobilise him, as far as the female of the species was concerned, for most of his adult life. And then, in the last ten years or so, when he was, perhaps, finally, in the position to summon up the freedom, the time, the money and possibly the courage to try to surmount these things, AIDS had arrived exactly on cue to incapacitate even those meagre efforts. That was, of course, typical of the practical jokes that fate had played on him in the course of his personal life.

He had married in the mid-fifties, part of a generation that appeared to believe that sex was only about avoiding reproduction. It had been a time when knowledge about the 'facts of life' was gleaned from books written by forbidding forties oracles like Eustace Chesser, passed around by furtive damp hands in boys' dormitories. Chesser, while at least honestly explaining the basic functions, managed to do so in much the same way as one might explain the mysteries of the petrol-driven combustion-engine, or the mediaeval siege-engine. Chesser certainly never dared to touch upon the notion of fun, or pleasure, or lust, or delight, or need as having any valuable part in the whole damned complicated rigmarole.

Indeed, for the youthful Norman Ranburn, the magic of the two-stroke engine appeared rather more appealing and definitely less demanding. Norman's virgin bride, Grace, was a fine, worthy, slightly wary woman who did her duty by him. Grace had been a quite exceptional match for an up-and-coming businessman, the middle daughter of one of the finest families in Dorset. They had met during the formal procedures of a hunt ball in Dorchester, a town in which, as a young man, Norman had spent a year managing the grand old Wessex Hotel for his father.

Outwardly they were a happy and fairly handsome pair, and then a satisfactory trio – Norman and Grace and little Joan – gaining in prosperity and admired by the business community. In 1966, on the death of Magnus, Norman, at the age of forty, took over as chief executive of Chandos House and they all moved into the Aviary. It was the early culmination of an outwardly glittering and successful life.

For many years, however, although he hardly admitted it to himself, there was the difficulty of sex. On Saturdays, on occasional Saturdays, in the dark, under the blankets, Grace used to allow him to do things to her, which clearly gave her no pleasure and of which – of course – they never spoke. They became for him occasions of mute, dark, needful pain. And he would, at the end of those brief minutes, fervently promise himself never to repeat them.

But he remained resolutely faithful to her throughout their marriage. At first, this was because Norman genuinely believed men should be faithful to their wives. Later in the story, it was because he felt incapable of doing anything radical about it at all. He didn't seem to be able to summon up the audacity, the style, the deceit or even the basic know-how. On every side, all around him, colleagues and friends seemed to have taken what were later to be called the Swinging Sixties completely in their stride. In their middle-age, with a fervour that sometimes verged on the ridiculous, they embraced a world of freedom that lapped all around them. They certainly embraced the culture of the pill and the young women who consumed it.

Norman was suddenly aware of legions of elderly and functionless sperm released upon the various orifices of a population of willing and attractive young women. Trusted associates, whose wives were familiar, tired faces at countless dinner-parties and social gatherings, dropped in and out of extraordinary extramarital moments with many and all kinds of lady associates.

Sometimes it was grotesque and sometimes, apparantly, it was sublime. Flats were set up for girls, his daughter's age, in unlikely places like Marsden and Headington and Northolt. Photographs were brought back from what were then thought of as wildly exotic locations like Tenerife and Majorca, full of delectably glamorous, beehive-haired, bikini'd, sunbathing and, no doubt passionately accommodating, 'cousins'.

Norman would find himself, alone at his desk at the Witney offices of the company, imagining the world of his friend Gordon Driscoll. Wrinkled, bald, stooping but fit and tanned from hours on the sunbed, Gordon regularly took vigorous blonde 'birds' some third his age to his villa in the Dordogne, while the world (and his family) thought him at conferences in Vienna or Geneva. Driscoll would aver that the world had taken a turn for the better with the institution of European direct dialling. 'You can promise your nearest and dearest that you're more or less anywhere you like,' he would crow. He would report in salacious detail to Norman, when they met for occasional dinners at the Reform Club, his efficient rogering of various delectable females. 'Sets you up for the winter, doesn't it?' Gordon would ask rhetorically. Norman would have to agree that presumably it did.

Such stories, even if only one-quarter true, nurtured in Norman a steadily increasing longing. But he remained too inexperienced and too appallingly reticent to do anything much about it. The changing times had filled the streets of the capitals of Europe with free spirits in their braless, miniskirted ecstasy, bodies honed by a masculine God, with hip movements the quality of the finest engine oil.

Yet Norman never had even so much as a taste of it. It seemed that desire was entirely a one-way street – while he was possessed of the most extreme craving to prostrate himself before these wayward, infinitely lickable iconic creatures, they in their turn would always be entirely untouched by the slightest awareness of ever noticing, let alone wanting, any such as he.

He hadn't been entirely pusillanimous, though. He had made meek inroads to put his situation to rights with the

odd attempt to do something about 'companionship'. But that
had only resulted in such events as the disaster of Caroline
Oakley, or the awfulness of the Munich Pussycat Club.

Some little time before his retirement, Norman had found
himself increasingly obsessed by the small advertisements
that appeared each week in the personal columns of *The
Times* under the title of 'Rendezvous', in which men and
women announced that they 'WLTM' ('Would Like To Meet')
others for theatre, dining, friendship and 'maybe more'. Most
of the advertisements seemed to have been inserted by the
younger set but, even so, Norman enjoyed the *frisson* of
reading what were, at bottom, straightforward applications,
in the Top Paper, for sex. They were appeals for good old-
fashioned middle-class sex from the divorced, the widowed
and the alone – from the not-young-things-anymore. Yes,
of course, for all that they were dressed up as requests for
potential opera-going companionship, for would-be wining-
and-dining chums, for bridge-playing partners or for those
who also enjoyed 'those cosy evenings in', their universal
hidden agenda rang as clear as any bell. They might, every
man jack of them, be seeking a 'GSOH', but beside that
universally sought 'Good Sense Of Humour' they were all
applying, at the end of the day, Norman guessed, for orgasm.
He liked that.

On occasion, there were a number of advertisements from
those of more mature years. Norman never saw himself as
ever getting around to making a written communication with
such persons. But then, some three years before he took his
retirement, the service began to offer the possibility of hearing
such personal appeals for friendship in recorded voices over
the telephone. It worked quite simply – one rang and heard
the advertiser herself describe her character and interests
on what, of course, they had to call her 'voice-box'. If one
wished and felt bold enough one was then in a position to
leave a reply and one's phone number on the appropriate
piece of recording tape. Norman found himself virtually
obsessed, week after week, with the business of listening to
mouthwatering self-descriptions in many and varied female

voices from 'young thirty-year-olds' who were allegedly 'attractive' and ever 'fun-loving' who, while claiming to have a GSOH and 'a wonderful circle of good close friends', were looking for 'that special person', 'Mr Right'.

In the end he succumbed. Knocking a neat eight years from his age, Norman, in oddly secretive tones, left a mangled description of himself at the door of the voice-box of a lady who called herself Caroline. He had been particularly moved to do so by a passing claim, in her county-toned discourse, of being enamoured of classic vintage cars. And she lived near Woodstock, a mere ten miles away – it seemed as if, were they to meet, their juncture might be predestined in the attentive heavens.

Sadly, the very reverse turned out to be true. Norman had a series of teatimes at the Randolph Hotel in Oxford where, amidst the clack and chatter of salubrious afternoon tea-taking, he quickly learned that Caroline Oakley was not greatly to his taste. She, too, had, it seemed, been disposed to dispense with some of her years in her own personal description and, while neat and birdlike in appearance and nicely attired, was volubly neurotic about almost everything – starting with whether she could remember where she had parked her car and finishing with concern about the state of the Randolph flunkey's fingernails.

Norman quickly came to the conclusion that she was more in need of someone to help her fill up her insurance claim for a fallen bathroom ceiling, or organise carol-singing for the blind, than a friend. And, while she tried with some energy to hide the fact, Caroline was interested only in herself and the condition of her own life and found it difficult to show more than a polite concern about the existence and difficulties of her provider of numerous teas, scones and Black Forest gateaux.

For, regrettably, it had become serial tea-taking rather than just a one-off, because of what happened on the very first day that he and she found themselves nervously greeting each other over the signpost of his carnation buttonhole. Her only son, a man of thirty-five or so and, thought Norman, probably well able to care for himself, had taken it upon himself to disappear.

And it was almost Christmas. She seemed to have no one else to turn to. Norman felt one could not abandon the lady to her despair at that particular time of universal familial Yuletide joy, so he found himself ringing her almost daily during that year's festive season and joining with her over more pots of Earl Grey at the Randolph than he would have wished for. There was never the remote chance that he could ever have summoned up any sexual desire for her. He would as soon have gone to bed with his mother. Caroline Oakley became an irksome, needless responsibility that he hated himself for having taken on. He doubted at times that she actually had a son called Florian, even when the young man announced some weeks later that he was alive and well and living in Balham with a checkout girl whom he had met at the St Ebbes Sainsbury's.

One plus that resulted from that nightmare was that Norman stopped resorting to voice-boxes altogether. By February of that year he lied to the Caroline woman that he was going to be out of the country for three months. Unfortunately, whenever he was obliged to drop into Oxford during that time he found he had to fight a very real desire to slip anonymously from doorway to doorway, just in case he should run into the dratted woman.

His other troubling attempt to seek some sort of sexual response or contact with a woman came about almost by chance. It did, at least, involve someone considerably younger than himself. And a damned attractive woman at that. She was, indeed, someone with whom he would most happily have had congress had it been feasible. But it was never on the cards. And the whole event was so distressingly public that he still squirmed, some five years later, from embarrassment at the memory.

He was at the annual BPA conference in Munich. He had managed, one evening, after three previously self-aborted attempts, to summon up sufficient courage to enter and buy a solitary ticket for a place that called itself the Pussycat Club, off the Ecke Platz. Even on that final evening, Norman had managed to gain access only after a countless number of pathetic wanderings up and down the streets surrounding the club. He would brave himself for the onslaught on its lurid entrance, only to funk the issue at the final moment. A whole hour had been spent persuading himself that surely no one would ever recognise him in a foreign town, and, additionally, a visit to such a show could not be a truly outrageous act. The Pussycat Club had an upmarket reputation. And Norman was a citizen of the world, wasn't he? Gordon Driscoll once referred to the performances at the Pussycat as 'art' – 'erotic ballet, Norman,' he had said, 'erotic ballet; Covent Garden without benefit of knickers'. Even so, for three nights in a row, Norman had been obliged to rehearse for himself various explanations of how he had become lost in the backstreets around the cathedral, to use should anyone who knew him, by some evil miracle, come along.

Eventually, after what seemed like a lifetime of prevarication, Norman found himself sitting at his own table in the shadows of a smart enough revue bar as part of a small audience.

They played raucous European pop music of various sorts and a number of reasonably pretty, thin girls came on and removed their clothing, each of them in a quite carefully and artistically arranged performance over a period of about fifteen minutes. It seemed to Norman that they got to a state of undress more quickly than he would have liked. Someone had obviously informed them that their audience first and foremost wanted strip and that they need not be very clever about the business of tease. At the end of each episode there were long minutes of rather crude naked bumping and grinding. To Norman's surprise he discovered that watching even the best-hung young lady disport herself clad much as she would be in the privacy of her own bathroom, striding around to hefty drumming and whining guitars, very quickly palled. He tended to want to look away.

Even so, he was just beginning to find it was possible to settle down and enjoy the whole experience with a little less of his usual nervousness when with much to-do they heralded, in three indecipherable languages, the veritable climax of the evening. This, as far as he could ascertain, was to be a performer who rejoiced in the name of Berenice. A tall, striking-looking woman appeared in much less elaborate clothing than the other girls had been togged up in. She wore a lacy underwear panty thing and a white T-shirt – and that was the sum of it. While genuinely very attractive, she had a mannish quality with short cropped hair and Norman began by preparing himself for the possibility that the show might finish up with some kind of cross-dressing transsexual job. But this Berenice turned out to be all woman. They had more of their noisy rock-and-roll music. Berenice rocked and rolled about on a sort of plinth or bed tricked out to look like a Mars bar or something.

In spite of the young woman's being much less elaborately dressed, what she did with herself was so much more fetching than the routines that had preceded her. While the earlier girls seemed to have simulated desire and lust quite effectively, it had very definitely been simulation. This Berenice woman appeared to be genuinely excited by what she was doing. As she stroked and handled her breasts under her T-shirt, and as her fingers worked their way energetically down inside her knickers, it was as if what she was up to was as much fun for her as it was for Norman and the various Japanese and Bavarian gentlemen who were sitting stock-still pretending not to watch too carefully. And, from what he could see of her body, that too seemed to register genuine stimulation – the peaks of her nipples stood out like thimbles high on her marvellous breasts, holding the cloth of her short white T-shirt away from the flat lean body below like two miniature tent pegs.

Norman had just settled into secretly hugging himself with his enjoyment, and promising himself to return the following evening, when things took a serious turn for the worse.

The girl had finished up sprawled akimbo on the bed arrangement, quite beautifully starkers, suggestively unwrapping a bar of chocolate with a lot of delightfully rude tongue stuff and much appreciative smacking of her lips. The music continued to bang away appropriately as she pressed the chocolate bar deep into the back of her mouth. Then, after that, raising her hips off the bed with all the suitable preliminaries, the young woman began to push the now well-sucked chocolate bar into her pussy. To start with it was so very surprising – quite an eye-opener. He could not really believe what he was seeing. And for the very first time during the show he began to be aware of his own physical response to all these astonishing goings-on.

All this eventually came crashing to a halt when, after some more shenanigans on the bed, the girl changed directions and, illuminated by one of their moving spotlights, left the stage and descended into the auditorium with not so much as a stitch on and the chocolate bar half in and half out of her body for all the world to see.

She stalked through the audience, dragging a lazy arm over the hunched shoulders of various men. Norman suddenly realised that she was heading directly for him. His immediate instinct was to leave the room like a rocket, but there was no way he could do that without appearing ridiculous. He busied himself with looking away, hoping she might pick on someone else. Then, doomfully, he felt her arm around his shoulders and suddenly could smell a mixture of overpowering but attractive perfume and the tang of sweat from her skin. And there was so much well-honed skin to hand.

She draped a long thigh over his lap and settled some of her weight on his body. Her tits brushed his chest, their nipples still raised like sentinels inches below his downcast eyes. Her fingers patted his hair, caressed his cheek, stroked his moustache and removed his glasses. Her breasts were so much more immense and firmly pointed when seen at close range.

The music seemed to have got inside his head. To his surprise, he realised that his hand was steadying her firm, damp back. His glance briefly registered the very real shock of her stage make-up when seen close to. He could smell the lacquer in her hair. The light seemed to explode around him. He could see nothing further away than eighteen inches, but he knew that everyone must be staring at him and he wanted to curl up and die. And, all the time, he knew he was smiling wanly. Smiling wanly in a well-behaved, kindly, properly English way.

The girl took his hand and gently placed it on the protruding chocolate bar and indicated that he should remove it. Aware of his heart thumping in an abject agony of embarrassment, he took the messy thing from her.

And then, for God's sake, she made him put it into his mouth. Her hand led his up past her body, up to his face. And then the sticky, warm chocolate was between his teeth.

Seconds later, she was gone. He was alone again in the pitch darkness, feeling for his glasses. Berenice was back on stage, accepting a spattering of applause to further excited, celebratory exit music.

Almost immediately, Norman was back out in the street, gagging on the chocolate taste in his mouth, promising himself that he would stop this mad, obsessed pursuit of the erotic. He had enough fun watching cricket and listening to music, for heaven's sake. He must stop thinking about young women. It brought him naught but ill.

Back in the hotel that night, reliving the experience for the sake of his penis, he realised two things: first, that the girl had murmured 'Thanks love' in a proper West Yorkshire accent as she had departed from his lap, and, secondly, that it had been about the closest his fingers had been to a naked female cunt for about fourteen years.

So since then he had been reduced to just looking. He developed, over the years, a kind of wary skill of looking at women – women in the street, women in Club Class, women in restaurants. Women talking animatedly to other men. Always talking to other men. He knew that his cautious strategy of 'looking' was a sad and lowly form of existence, but he comforted himself with the fact that no one else would ever really know the depths of his situation. And it would never expose him to the kind of Berenice/Caroline ghastlinesses that real contact could provoke. At times he even quite prided himself on his developed skills of looking. He could stare abstractedly in quite the opposite direction to his quarry, before suddenly turning to allow his eye to peruse delectable limbs, pert bosoms, luxurious lips, knowing eyes. He knew that he was possibly kidding himself when he assumed that the girls themselves didn't really notice this routine, but he persevered. What else was there?

Well, there was inhaling them. Breathing women in. He found that, if he was able to take a deep breath during the three seconds after a fine-looking totty had walked past him, if he inhaled as the air closed about her departing form, he could be totally consumed, from head to toe, by the aromas of her body, her perfumes, her personal parts, her very being. It wasn't enough, of course, but it had to do.

Yes, Norman had to accept that his elderly lust would probably never now be assuaged. Or, at least, it had seemed like that until, one bizarre night on a balcony in Cardiff, he discovered the truth about the secret of his own particular personal sexual trigger.

Norman was abruptly brought back to the present by the Charing Cross Hotel's swarthy bellhop announcing the first of his quintet of interviewees. He shook the images of the Castle Arms Hotel, Cardiff, out of his head and settled down to the business in hand.

By lunchtime, he had seen his first two pairs of applicants and he was immersed in gloom. He had so looked forward to this day as one of private erotic electricity, but the past hour had proved about as arousing as a dose of influenza. The people he had seen and with whom he had spent pointless, painstaking question-and-answer sessions, had proved totally useless – stupid unattractive, ill-educated wastes of time. Pairs of people you would avoid watching in Sainsbury's together, let alone for what he had in mind. The photo-machine likenesses seemed to have lied to him extravagantly. One pair had been part of the black-clad workshy, the world-owes-me-a-living generation – white-faced, sullen and doubtless on drugs. The other couple had been cosy suburban folk with a homely cheerfulness that would most likely have driven him witless within a week.

Norman stood and watched the traffic filling entering and leaving the Strand. It was warm out there and there were lots of young men in shorts and girls in thin summer cotton. What was it about the average working-class Englishman that, given half an hour of even modest summer sunshine, he suddenly felt the need to remove most of his clothing and expose his belly to the ultra-violet? Norman watched the busy crowds going about their lunchtime purposes. There were so many fine-looking girls and boys out there who would have done him so extraordinarily well, but how could he ever entice them up there into his little room?

Somewhere out there, too, lost and gone for good, was Amy Shakespeare, the progenitor of all this.

Even so, he smiled to himself. He liked watching people through windows, unobserved.

About three years before, at his usual room in the Castle Arms Hotel in Cardiff, on a warm wet September evening, Norman Ranburn had stumbled upon the truth of his own personal physical nature and decoded his own intimate sexual riddle. From that moment on, everything fell into place. It was a secret that, of course, he must have known all along, without ever realising that he knew it.

Norman had always loved the Castle Arms, in St David's Street, just opposite the castle. It was good and solid and Victorian. Gilbert had sold it now, of course, as part of the whole downsizing operation. It had become part of the Forte group. On a final nostalgic trip, two months before the transfer, Norman had crossed the Severn Bridge for one last time to spend a night at 'The Arms'. In the fifties and sixties, it had been one of the jewels in the Chandos House crown.

It had been a warm and humid evening, in spite of the heavy Welsh rain which had fallen most of the afternoon, washing the streets a glossy black. Norman had had a fairly social staff meeting in the afternoon and, after a walk down to the Arms Park, had gone to bed early. For once, he had been unable to sleep. It was a great labour, but he dressed himself once again and took himself downstairs to the bar for a late sundowner. He trawled his way blankly through the daily papers.

It was late, therefore, when he returned to his room and had changed back into his pyjamas. Another steady downpour had started. At last, the atmosphere felt lighter. He had just decided not to face another session of late-night television, when he heard a groan.

It appeared to come from the direction of the rain beyond his open windows, where an ornate wrought-iron balcony stretched the length of the face of the old hotel. Norman switched off the overhead light in the room and opened the tall casement window a mite further. He looked out into the rain, and listened. There it was again.

Barefoot, he stepped out on to the narrow balcony, high above the street, and concentrated. Then he tentatively peered forward. His vision was both assisted and hampered by the flashing neon sign announcing the name of the hotel, suspended high above him. There was certainly no one on the balcony. It ran in both directions, away from him, servicing, probably only symbolically in recent times, all the rooms on that floor.

The groan came again. The voice was that of a woman, and it appeared to come from the open windows of the rooms next to his. The woman might be in trouble. He knew, of course, that she wasn't. He had had enough experience of hotel management all his life to guess pretty precisely what might be causing the strange noises that he had heard.

One got used to the idea that hotels generally reeked of it. But, even so, half his mind continued to persuade him that what he was hearing could be the sound of a woman who might be in need of assistance.

He edged along the wet balcony towards the open window to his left, one inch at a time. With each additional inch, another foot of the neighbouring room was revealed to him in the intermittent red-and-green lights that burst above his head. He could now see half the bed and that was enough. The layout of the bedroom was identical to his own. At one moment, the end of the bed was clearly lit, and then an instant later it was plunged into darkness again. But his mind was already adjusting itself for the image to be replaced equally quickly. It was like a juddering, touching, dirty home movie.

On the top of the bed's quilt was a lattice of human legs – a woman's and a man's, her feet thin and lean, his energetically digging into the surface of the bedclothes. Their limbs opened and closed; the two bodies swayed and strained at each other. High above the quietening Cardiff street, Norman stood on his narrow ledge, with his pyjama shoulders soaking up the wet, transfixed by the sight of what they were doing and by the noises they were making as they gave little bits of ecstasy to each other.

Suddenly he was ashamed and frightened, too, that he might be discovered. He was so appallingly close to them. They would sense his being there. He took two steps back, and he was in his own room again, cold and breathing hard. For a moment he stood there undecided. Then he crossed the room and abruptly switched off the bedside reading lamp. Now he was in complete darkness too. The room filled with and then emptied of reflected light from outside. By carefully tuning his listening, he could distinguish the noises the woman made from the quiet background sounds of the city and the languid fall of the rain.

She went on and on. Is that what it could be like? Endless gasping and panting and words – pleasuring, indistinct, dirty words. A foul mouth on a beautiful woman. He had never really thought it could last like that, except in the imagination of the directors of more explicit movies.

It seemed as if her wanton noise, and what he now realised was her deep and satisfied chuckling, was urgently calling to him. He found himself standing in the dark, shaking his head with anger at his behaviour. He was disgusting.

But no one would ever know. With his heart beating unusually strongly, he pushed on his leather slippers, quietly put his coat around his shoulders, placed his hat upon his head and stepped, as quietly as he knew how, out on to the balcony again.

For twenty extraordinary minutes, he experienced the most profound ecstatic pleasure. He found himself poised on the very pinnacle of fear, and lust, and envy – and wicked, wicked intrusion. He was desperately nervous about his situation. He stood in the pouring rain with his back against his window shutter, his slippers gathering the wet at his feet. He kept his chin pressed tight into his left collarbone as he stared hard over his shoulder into their room.

Were any passer-by to see him from the pavements on the other side of the road, by the castle wall, they would never be able to confirm his identity, hidden as he was by the brim of his hat. But if any member of staff should by chance look up they would recognise him, only too readily. The occasional car continued to swish by below him, adding a mundane counterpoint to the cries, the words and the rasping breathing of the two on the bed. No wonder he had heard them – she was very noisily at it, coaxing and crying and laughing and apparently coming all the time.

Her legs were so long and strong and young. She raised them high above the thrusting, eager, needful, twisting backside of her lover and then enfolded his thighs with them, clamping him to her, matching him thrust for thrust. She seemed to be wearing nothing but a satin wrap that the man had pulled aside in his embrace, but astonishingly, her hands were encased in a pair of fingerless black lace gloves as they scratched up and down the man's back, both inside and outside his white shirt.

Later, towards the end, he could see her moist face, raised eagerly to watch the activity at the very source of their mutual pleasure. Then as her teeth embedded themselves in the man's exposed shoulder, her hands cupped his busy rump with both her palms parting his rear slit. She seemed, to Norman, to insert her finger ends into the cavity hidden away within.

Norman realised that he just loved to watch.

What was occurring in the bedroom amid the absurdly

flashing and dramatic lighting was stimulating not only the participants. He had never felt such satisfying sexual intensity. Standing in all his ridiculousness, out there, above the street, with the water running off the front of the brim of his hat, he took hold of himself with an experienced hand. He had no responsibility here. No one was expecting anything of him. All he needed to do was to watch and not get caught. He was doing no one any harm in doing this – apart from his own personal but secret humiliation. It was complete and absolute paradise. Nothing could ever be as good as watching those two anonymous bodies rutting away, seeking out their pleasures with such abandon. All he had to do was to see that he, himself, did not finish too quickly. In this he had had some practice. They all three finished together, his own spending flying with the incessant rain into the empty street below.

Suddenly he felt cold and exhausted. And he felt stupid and exposed and vulnerable. But, for one of the first and only times, not depressed and saddened by what he had allowed himself to do. Back in his room, he peeled off wet clothing and realised that he felt a certain wry satisfaction about it all. It made a wonderful change from the usual despair and self-loathing that tended to swamp him at these times. By God, he was suddenly very tired.

Well – what a thing – he had discovered that, probably best of all, he just liked to watch.

He slept in his bed with no clothes on. He had never done that before, either.

And now, here today, in London, at the Charing Cross Hotel, he was in the process of making sure that such a show might always be available for him – with no threat of discovery, no risk or danger and without anyone ever knowing.

If he could find the right people.

And then, first thing after lunch, he did. They were from Kingston-upon-Thames. Lesley-Anne Ridgeway and her fiancé, Terence Miller.

There was a knock on the door and the little bellhop was followed into the room by a fine-looking dark-haired woman in a black dress. She was carrying a scarlet coat and looked natural and attractive in the kind of intelligent way that Norman thought was just fine. Terence Miller seemed a little older than Lesley-Anne. But, no matter – he was quite smartly turned out and fit-looking. In fact he was quite personable. And as for her? Well, good God Almighty, that was more like it. 'Arthur's picnic!' as someone he'd once met might have put it.

Norman was transported by the idea of these two and found himself talking far too quickly and effusively. He needed these two to be it. His cool businesslike questions ran into each other as he sat them down and Lesley-Anne crossed her legs, sat back and looked damnably confident. Norman's eyes were almost magnetically dragged back time and time again to the legs. They were shown off by a mesh of delicate nylon and a pair of black patent-leather shoes with acceptably high heels. This interview was all that he had ever anticipated. Even in his more advanced and hopeful imaginings.

So this is what crazy people feel like, he thought. Concentratedly fighting off unsociable behaviour, he went out of the room, ostensibly to order the pair some coffee. This strategy allowed him to walk around her and get a further perspective of her body. Her dress had buttons up the front. She had a milky pair of collarbones set off by a light silver chain. She had luxuriant, shoulder-length, dark-brown hair that shone in the sunlight. Oh, how much he would have given to have been able to touch the exquisite and apparent perfection of all that hid below the modest neckline.

He returned with his two black coffees and kept his eyes modestly under control as they accepted them. Back to his questions.

They didn't smoke. They were going to get married in the spring when Terence's divorce came through. They had not really done any of this kind of work before. They wanted to get away to live in the proper countryside. They had had enough of London. They thought it sounded challenging and interesting, and a varied kind of job. He had been a teacher and she worked at the French Tourist Office at the moment. She had read French at Brighton University. She was twenty-eight and he was seven years older. She thought that she was probably not a bad cook.

The answers came quite quickly and quite pat. It felt as if they had thought about what kinds of things he might ask them. Norman liked them for that.

From the way they communicated with each other, as they talked with him, the two seemed to be very close, very much in love. Norman had always imagined that the early days (and nights) of a loving relationship would ensure, once the doors of privacy were secured, that the participants would screw enthusiastically and with some originality for many hours. Lesley-Anne and Terence must doubtless be at it all the time, just at the moment. Norman was suddenly so overwhelmed with the notion, he lost his train of thought. The hidden agenda of his conversation with them was encouraging an astonishing leeway in his fantasy. He found himself wanting her to take all her clothes off for him, then and there. He allowed himself to speculate idly on the style of underwear she might wear. He liked to think that it might be delicate and classy. She said her father was in the civil service – in the Ministry of Agriculture, Fisheries and Food. That didn't necessarily guarantee wondrous lingerie style, of course, but the auguries were good.

So good were they that Norman completely ran out of things to say to them. The thought that, if all went well, he would be able to see her take her clothes off, any time he wanted, was arousingly affecting. A long silence hung in the tiny interviewing room as they waited expectantly for him to quiz them further.

Norman had to pull himself together. He was just a horrible, sad, scurvy, twisted old fellow, that's all there was to it. But enjoying himself enormously. And his guests, of course, saw him as just so much old-world charm and courtesy.

Norman dredged up some particles of conversation. They stirred coffee and talked of the weather and the present cricket season and places abroad and the price of English apples, and

Norman Ranburn's eyes took off on small secret journeys suckling their way all over Lesley-Anne Ridgeway's body. Norman could just imagine her long pink tongue feeding upon that of her man, their teeth clashing in their eagerness as their hands worked diligently and, with high spirits, excited each other's secret places.

He would have kept them with him longer had not some other unlikely candidates turned up and obliged him to let them go. He could feel Lesley-Anne's light farewell handshake on his hand for the whole of the next hour during his now completely pointless afternoon.

He had Gordon Driscoll to thank for this whole nerve-racking, joyful, awful business. It had been a year or so after Norman had returned from his revelatory trip to the hotel in Cardiff that he'd come face to face with the intriguing and fanciful possibility of the mirror. For weeks, he had run and rerun his internal video of that pair of welcoming and uplifted female legs. He had found himself less able to concentrate on anything very much apart from the sweet knowledge that he had been party to an incredible dream of actually seeing the bloody thing going in and out. And he had spent the time ruefully acknowledging that it would never be like that again. It was then that he tripped across the idea that perhaps it could. If he could be clever and resourceful enough.

He had tumbled across this unlikely project in the very unusual location of an upstairs room in the derelict carcass of what was once called the Duchess of Wapping. This was a boarded-up and gutted public house in Moxsom Street in the wilderness that is Docklands, on the Isle of Dogs, in the East End of London.

Norman's chum Gordon Driscoll was on some sort of residual sub-committee of the embattled London Docklands Development Board. Gordon used to pick up a lot of these little numbers from which he would collect spending money for the occasional attendance at meetings where he could give forth of his not inconsiderable wisdom. He continued to enjoy being almost part of that eighties vision, the Docklands Development, in spite of the fact it had become – as a vast, unattractive mix-'n'-match industrial estate – something of a nineties joke. Truth to tell, however, if the empty docks had just been left to rot in the care of the local community, they would, in any case, have presumably deteriorated into a concrete desert of empty graffiti, racist crime and the occasional Pakistani mini-supermarket.

Gordon seemed to be interested in pressing Norman into involving himself on some kind of business consultancy deal. Gordon inveigled Norman into joining him on a tour of part of his luckless domain. They had driven in the Driscoll Volvo down the red-surfaced roads that led to what the locals rather pathetically called 'the island'. Here a sliver of municipal gardens overlooked the river and the sweep of Greenwich Park over on the far side of the Thames. Then they had cruised down the short streets of crumbling back-to-backs, so reviled in the seventies as slums. In the late eighties, of course, they had gained a sudden surprising new lease of life, particularly in the pinker prints as 'the backbone of the infrastructure of life in London's East End' or some such jolly jargon. If Norman knew anything about it, most East Enders worth their salt wanted to get out as soon as possible. They wanted to be able to buy up their palatial bungalows with swimming pool and snooker room attached, on the fringes of Romford or Basildon and forget these pinched, damp streets. They didn't want to remain in the East End. Only the no-hopers remained there, and the old. So places like the collapsed and reeking Duchess of Wapping all had to go.

It stood on the corner of a triangle of so-called housing. Once, it had probably been a fairly splendid late-Victorian edifice – a huge and popular drinking palace. The years since the war had concealed its particular brand of brazen vulgarity behind a formica-clad, pool-table-and-jukebox-ridden veneer – no doubt with the bloody telly turned on full blast all the time, entertaining no one.

Driscoll had a key for the padlock on the boarded corner doors. Inside, it stank of urine and was completely vandalised. All that remained were a few broken tables, the sad, oddly unused beer mat and the broken coloured glass of the windows scattered across the floor among the pigeon droppings. Pinpoints of light barrelled across the huge rooms picking out scarred mahogany bar counters and what remained of some gigantic, wrecked pendant lamps. Driscoll seemed to have some specific mischievous notion for wanting to bring Norman into this piteous cadaver of a place. The old man's eyes were twinkling deviously as he led Norman up some wide stairs to where there was slightly more light from the grey winter afternoon.

'Something to show you, Norman. You wouldn't credit it.' They found themselves in a long hall of a room, above the main bar, with a high, dark-brown, plastered ceiling and a raised dais at one end. A few torn and handwritten day-glo posters seemed to suggest that they had used the place for music towards the end. Now it just stank.

'Oh, sod and set fire to it, they've taken it down.' Gordon's voice echoed strangely from the next room, behind the stage. He sounded disappointed. Norman crunched across the floor to join him. The two adjoining rooms were divided by a wall with a small window between them – like a serving hatch but rather larger. On the floor there was a mirror, exactly the same size as the internal window-frame – about three foot square.

'It used to be fitted in the hole. Bloody miracle it's not broken.' Driscol moved the mirror away from the wall where it was leaning. 'Spyhole. Used to watch the whores fucking, I reckon. Doubled your money, didn't it. Charge the fellow getting laid and charge his chums to have a butcher's. Can't see it very well in this light, but it works. See-through mirror – talk about Christine Keeler! Those Edwardians knew a thing or two.' Even in the gathering gloom, Norman could see that while, one way, the glass rectangle worked as a mirror, from the other side you could see straight through the glass.

He felt his scalp prickle.

'What d'you think about that, Norman?' Gordon asked him again. Norman wasn't listening. 'They tell me, in the twenties, they'd put some virgin lad in there with the choicest whore of the week and then, unknown to him, pack the paying customers in the back here. That's the sort of commercial instinct those buggers had in those days. Before the sodding welfare state softened their brains.' Gordon laughed and leaned the glass back in its place on the floor before heading back down to the ground floor.

Norman was virtually incoherent. All that now filled his mind was the dim impression of his own reflection in that trick mirror. What an opportunity. It was as if God knew what he wanted so very badly and had placed it almost within his grasp. He wanted it so very much. He could not afford to lose it. He had the quite astonishing clarity of everything dropping exactly into place. The devil was on his side. There was a God.

As they left, Norman was very careful not to latch the Yale lock on the inside of the door. And then he firmly took the padlock from Gordon's hands and took over the business of snapping it back into place on the hasp. In the early-evening gloom, it was not too difficult to make the padlock appear as if it was securing the battered double doors once more.

The two of them left the site, stepping between the corrugated-iron sheets that enclosed the premises. Gordon took him back to his car. Norman sidestepped invitations to go and have a drink and sup. He had much to do. Minutes later he had been dropped at his own car and the two vehicles droned out of the Isle of Dogs and lost each other in the traffic of the Commercial Road.

Ten minutes later, again in the darkness of the early evening, Norman was back in that macabre, dead house of entertainment. It was a arduous struggle to get the thing down the stairs. It was an awkward shape and the bricks underfoot threatened to make him stumble. To break it, now that he had found it, would be a terrible irony. Outside, he did nearly let it slip as he waded out between the waist-high nettles and grass. He had guessed correctly – it fitted into the boot of the car easily. It lay there like an icy eye and showed him a picture of himself, silhouetted against the dull evening sky. He shut the boot carefully and made sure he locked his secret away from the world.

But, in the cold light of another day, Norman found he had lost either conviction, or courage – it didn't matter which. Had he really thought he might be capable of building himself such a spyhole? It was a madcap, foolish scheme, perverse and corrupting. The sort of thing that often seemed feasible when contemplated at four in the morning but turned out to be pure crack-brained fancy by breakfast time. And probably very difficult to put into effect, anyway. So he tucked the thing away in the barn. He occasionally found himself thinking that he might tackle it in a few months' time. But he didn't. He did nothing. Until that balmy Whit Sunday when little Miss Shakespeare turned up.

Amy Shakespeare sat on his kitchen table with thighs lacquered with brush-on leather trouser, looked up into his face with a kind of blank determination, held on to his jacket lapel with one long hand and offered him her mundane but nonetheless surprisingly engaging philosophy: 'Do it all. You only live once.'

From the day following their meeting, Norman became builder, architect, labourer and all-round evil schemer. And obsessive. For six weeks, ten hours a day, he studied *The Practical Builder*, purchased yards of cement, sawed up hardboard and fiddled apprehensively with electrical wiring. Given his total lack of any previous practical experience, he found some of it difficult to do and rather tiring but often surprisingly satisfying. There were many days, of course, when things would just not go right at all. Days when he almost wept at the frustration and complexity of it. But it kept him lively and active. He had an interest. Good God Almighty, did he have an interest! It bloody kept him awake at night.

Finally, six exhausting weeks later, to his considerable surprise, it was finished. He had completed it. And it didn't look half bad.

The Aviary at Coombe was originally part of an Oxfordshire farm with medium-sized, late-Georgian stone buildings, linked at the back to a substantial barn, stables and a cowshed. Some of these outhouses had been turned into living accommodation by the former owners – the Simmondses

– in the early thirties, well before Norman's father had purchased the property. They had joined the two main domestic dwellings with a small doorway opening into what Norman was now pleased to call his study. Norman's Herculean building works had primarily been concerned with the annihilation of this small linking doorway. At the same time, he had renovated the stable-yard cottage and made it a completely separate independent place, in which a young carefree caretaking couple might live together in marital and occupational bliss.

When all was complete, it was no longer possible to see where the connecting doorway from the study to the cottage had once been. It was obscured by a huge and beautiful hanging carpet, all the way from Kayseri in Turkey. If this was held to one side, and the door hidden behind it was surreptitiously unlocked, it was possible to step down into a small secret antechamber – a space for which Norman had coined for himself the title 'the viewing room'. It was a tiny room about as big as a phone-box and it contained just one comfortable leather swivel-chair, which faced a neatly constructed window. The room had been soundproofed with a double thickness of plasterboard wall, stuffed full of irritative, deadening glass-wool filler. Through the observation window, it was possible to see the whole of the comfortable double bedroom of his ancillary caretaker's cottage, with the bathroom beyond.

If one was to go round and enter what Norman in his secret heart had taken to calling 'Onan Cottage', if one stood in the cottage bedroom itself and looked at the mirror, one would see nothing but one's own reflection. No matter what lighting prevailed, that expansive area of reflective glass, with its occasional brown fleck, revealed nothing of its secret. Norman had tested it at the dead of night and in the broadest daylight. Furthermore one could play a portable radio, placed centrally in the 'viewing chair', and one would not be able to hear a sound (well, anyway, nothing to speak of) in the Onan Cottage bedroom. However if one was in the viewing room itself and wanted to hear what was going on next door, it was simplicity itself to switch on the Mothercare baby-alarm system that Norman had fallen upon with severely hidden ecstasy, one heavenly day in the Cornmarket. The device, which was intended to allow fond parents to listen to the mewling and puking of their distant offspring, transmitted the gentlest sounds from the room beyond with the greatest success and clarity.

Norman was astounded by his achievement. It made him so very happy. He spent long periods of time, sitting in the confines of his viewing room, watching a deserted bedroom, switching on and off his sound system, imagining the joys that might lurk for him there. No one could ever begin to guess, even for a split second, that he was quite, quite mad. And looking forward to it all, quite, quite madly.

And now he had constructed this little pleasuring machine with his own fair hands, he felt less acutely embarrassed by his madness. He had just had the – the what? – the wherewithal and the imagination to make voyeurism a science, that was all. Because, finally, everybody used it as an amateur hobby, didn't they? One only had to look at the films they made these days, look at what sold the popular newspapers, look at what sold the most volumes at the airport news-stands, look at the multitude of suspect videos that popped up in the corner newsagent's.

They all sold second-hand experiences of the intimate, to stimulate first-hand handwork. What men did with women to pleasure themselves was so private and unspoken that it would always be the great taboo that everyone wished, in his secret soul, in some way or other, to break. And he, Norman Ranburn, had made a machine that would assuredly plunder that taboo time and time again, whenever he so wished.

At the end of the week of his interviews, Norman received a letter. In spite of the fact that there was a very sharp wind whipping down off Bargate Hill that morning, Norman was desperate to know. He stood by the gate where Barrington, the local postie, had given him his mail and, dropping various bills on to the driveway, ripped his way into the envelope from Kingston-upon-Thames. Within a moment, he knew that everything was going to be all right. Much more than all right. The most private intimate moments of Miss Lesley-Anne Ridgeway were soon to be his.

Dear Mr Ranburn,

Thank you very much for your kind letter of 4 July. Terence and I are very flattered that you should have chosen us for the job, or jobs, should I say? I promise we will do everything in our power to make it work. I don't really think that it need depend upon our seeing the cottage. From all you told us, it sounds fantastic! The thing is, we are really in need of a quick move as our accommodation here is running out anyway. So, if it's all right with you, we'd like to come up and start 'learning the ropes' as soon as possible. The only problem might be that Terence and I can't get wed until his divorce is through and this might take another couple of months or so. Will this matter? I do hope not, as we are really very keen to take up the opportunity that you have offered us. To put it bluntly, no one need know that the official ceremony has not yet taken place. I answer to 'Mrs Miller' quite effectively already!

Anyway, we'll have to leave this to you. We don't want to tread on anyone's toes and will quite understand it if you think, on balance, that our moving in together into the cottage, before the wedding, is not suitable. Of course, we do hope that it will be all right. We could even be with you at the weekend, if you wished. We wouldn't have to move a lot of our belongings, and could bring up an advance guard on Saturday (8 July), in Terence's car. Perhaps you could give us a ring here, to let us know what you think.

With best wishes,
Yours sincerely,
Lesley-Anne Miller.

Norman was completely unaware that he was freezing cold until after he had completed the phone call.

They would be living in sin, under his roof. He couldn't wait.

Then he noticed that there was another personal letter for

him in the same post. It was from Joan. It was clear that she was still terribly furious with him. She had even dispensed with her normal 'Dear Daddy' opening.

I just don't get it Daddy. I've fought and fought with myself over the past few weeks not to write this letter but I've finally had to because I am so fed up with your lack of support for this exciting project of Frannie's. I don't want to go through the arguments all over again but I just want to say that I am really shocked how little you seem to care for her, for both of us really. The poor kid has been crying her eyes out, night after night, with disappointment,

You could pretty easily find the cash for this investment, Daddy – you know that and so do I. That's what makes it so hurtful. And the ridiculous thing is that it would probably pay you back rather well in the long run. And anyway why do you need to hold on so tightly to all that money? It doesn't seem to me you do much with it. You drift from the club to the cricket, keep the Clarkes employed. But you don't go on holiday, don't travel the world – you can hardly be said to live a riotous social life. I can't believe you're really going to invest in another ancient motor car – you hardly do anything with Bertram as it is, as far as I can see.

I just don't get it. Don't you care about us? Has living on your own turned you into such a mean old hermit? I can't believe this is my father. Mum would certainly try to help if she could, but she can't, as what money she has is all tied up in Fraser's new yacht.

I'm giving you one more chance to see if you can get yourself together to be a really great grandfather.

Joan (your daughter – remember?).

It sounded rather like a threat.

CHAPTER THREE

For whatsoever a man soweth, that shall
he also reap.

GALATIANS 6:7

SATURDAY 8 JULY

Norman reflected that they did not seem to have brought
very much luggage with them. Lesley-Anne said that Terence
would go back down to Kingston before August and fetch
some more of her possessions. Only two rather smart leather
suitcases and a couple of zippered bags came out of their
Renault.

Norman stood welcomingly in the warmth of the afternoon
as they busied themselves, ducking in and out of their car.
Fit young people, they were. They were enraptured by the
cottage. Lesley-Anne exclaimed at the kitchen and certainly
did not seem to notice the rather poor finish he had achieved
on some of the doors of the units in there. Even Norman,
seeing the place afresh through the eyes of strangers, was
impressed by the living room. Then, finally, all three of them
stood in the bedroom together and Norman was aware of

how careful they were being not to show what they were all doubtless thinking. It must be the universal hidden agenda when standing in bedrooms with their occupants – the notion of the two of them, in there, at it.

Lesley-Anne touched her hair and casually surveyed herself in Norman's large and particular mirror. She was in an all-enveloping black sweater which entirely denied her shape, and jeans with flat shoes. All perfectly nice and workmanlike, but he would have preferred a nice little cocktail number. She wore less make-up than before, at the interview. He could not have everything.

They walked around the stable yard and the garden and he toiled with them breathlessly up to the top of the field to look at the Aviary's view of the village below them. Norman courteously allowed them to go before him, as he picked his way slowly up the hill. He was careful not to let them see him use this opportunity to observe the compactness of her posterior and the neat slimness of her legs. He did not want to arouse in them any suspicions about their landlord at this particular juncture, when the pair might be at their most watchful. After all, he would be able to examine her parts at his will, whenever the mood took him. But it was difficult not to be marginally interested.

They sat in the living room of the main house and sipped an afternoon sherry. He had planned most carefully how he would tackle this section of their induction. He had asked his erstwhile secretary, Mrs Pettit at Chandos House, to prepare some schedules and an information pack of local contacts and other matters concerning the running of the buildings – central heating, waste-disposal, car-servicing dates and the like. The two of them appeared to be excited about the prospects of the tasks ahead. Norman explained that he would let them have time to settle in, during the rest of the weekend. He would then ask them to begin providing him with service from the Monday. They were not to know, of course, that they would, prior to that, be servicing a number of his more private needs very adequately.

He was to expect an evening meal five nights a week and

on Sunday he would require them also to prepare luncheon. He had the idea of inviting a few people over on Sunday week for a noontide drink. He rather wanted Gordon Driscoll to run an appraising and hopefully envious eye over his new staff. Would Lesley-Anne very kindly wait on drinks? Wearing something, er, smart. And short, he would very much like to have added. Maybe she got the message anyway. Lesley-Anne and her partner nodded and smiled and sipped their drinks and said that it all sounded excellent.

Eventually his briefing came to an end. He dismissed them so that they could go and settle in. He found that he was quite dry in the mouth as they went off to explore their new domain. He managed to repeat, affably enough, that they had the rest of Saturday and all of Sunday to get to know the place and spend time together. He would not need to see them until Monday morning.

He wished them well and they left and walked around past the stables, to the entrance of the cottage. As soon as Norman lost sight of them through the window, he began to hurry. He locked his front door, went through to his study, switched the television on to some old Ealing comedy rubbish, and then, with a certain shortness of breath and a racing pulse, he slid, with the greatest possible care, behind his hanging carpet. He unlocked his secret door and for the first time entered his viewing room with the sure potential of something to view.

Six hard-working weeks had been the prelude to this moment. It was enough to make the old ticker turn a somersault. That would be a joke, wouldn't it – for him to drop dead before it began? Particularly if it happened while he was tucked away in his wickedly secret chamber.

His heart was beating so hard that it felt as if they must surely hear it in the cottage. He was hot and found himself panting in short careful breaths. Facing reality was a deal more taxing than he had imagined. He lowered himself silently into the viewing chair where he had so often, before now, sat in practice. He could feel the tension in his face as he reached to his side and switched on the listening device.

Ready for action. At last. This was going to be beauteous, darling Lesley-Anne Ridgeway's very special moment.

The familiar picture of the bedroom looked much the same as ever. It was like a small theatre stage before any of the actors have arrived. The bedroom door to the rest of the cottage was closed. The only evidence that his guests were in residence at last was a small pile of bags and suitcases by the dressing table. He could hear the murmur of gentle conversation from the direction of their kitchen and some music from their radio. For a very long while nothing happened.

He could wait. He had rather hoped, of course, that in their youthful passion, they would tear into the bedroom just as soon as they were released from his presence, in order to try out their new facilities. He was certainly hoping that, in the delicate privacy that he was offering them, they would be more demonstrative than they had proved to be in public. He would have been hard-pressed, so far, to know that they were intimate at all, so decorous and proper were they, in front of him. They were probably shy. Sometimes, he had heard it said that it was the quiet ones who went at it like rabbits.

One thing that puzzled him was the car that they had driven up in – a Renault Clio. Norman would have expected some kind of ten-year-old Sierra, but here they were in this very smart two-year-old Clio. What was it that Terence Miller had been doing before this? He had been told, but his head had been so filled with imagined visions of Lesley-Anne that he had failed to take it in. Export–import, he thought. But, in truth, he had not employed them on the basis of their previous track-record and experience.

Half an hour passed and, finally, Norman had to leave to replenish his glass and use the toilet. It was quite lunatic for a man of his gravity to spend an hour anxiously watching an empty room. Thank the Lord no one would ever know. When he thought about it with cold rationality, he realised that the whole thing was quite hideous, pathetic, brain-dead, perverted and a waste of energy. But sexy too.

He was furious when he returned to his vigil. He had missed something. The bedroom door was open and one of the bedside lamps had been switched on. Two of their bags had been moved and were now open. There was a small vase of flowers on the table in the window. That augured well. A few things had been placed on the bed – a dressing gown – hers? There were now some bottles on the dressing table. This was better. Norman Ranburn's private peep-show was about to get under way.

But it wasn't. Nothing happened for the whole of the next hour and a half. Norman took to popping in and out, as it became tedious just to sit watching nothing, even in his state of heightened expectation. *Passport to Pimlico* on the telly was considerably more entertaining.

Then, at about ten o'clock, the most frightening thing happened. He was back in the viewing chair for about the hundredth time. Lesley-Anne walked quickly into the room. She was dressed exactly as before. Without looking about or hesitating, she went directly to his mirror window and looked him straight in the eye. Norman flinched and almost cried out at the shock of it. Could she see him? Had he made some dreadful grievous error? Did the mirror not work? There she was, no more than twenty-four inches away from him on the other side of the glass, looking straight at him. Norman flinched from her gaze and felt close to fainting. He had stopped breathing and remained completely transfixed.

Then he realised that she was looking at herself in the mirror. At her reflection. Norman had never had the opportunity of having a real, live person under his microscope before, so he had no idea what it might be like. It was, in fact, alarming and would take a deal of getting used to.

Lesley-Anne touched her face and craned her head closer to the glass. Norman found himself urgently praying that the mirror, when closely examined, would not allow her to see, in the shadow cast upon the surface of the glass, the terrified frozen face of her employer staring right back at her, inches away.

Then the whole crazy scheme began to deliver the goods.

Norman went instantly from a determination never to enter his viewing room again, to a warm delight that told him that he could at last settle back and enjoy himself. Ecstasy was about to be his and his alone. He felt suddenly overwhelmed by a flood of such heavenly relief. If the world of men knew, they would be so very jealous. They'd all want to have one of these. But, then, they would have to be as wicked, and as secretive, and as clever, and as sick as he, to achieve such a treat. And most men just wouldn't have the balls. With a bit of luck he would be able to unzip his fly yet. And do what was required to his own.

Lesley-Anne. Beautiful. Brown. Tall. Mysterious. Strange. Lovely Lesley-Anne Ridgeway was going to become so much less a stranger. He was about to take ownership of her naked image for himself alone. No one in the world would ever have the face, nor the opportunity, to study her as unashamedly as he would now. In her completely private unguarded moments.

Without the slightest hesitation, in the privacy of her new bedroom, Lesley-Anne began to unclothe herself. Life instantly began to fall into place for an innocent, kindly and benevolent gentleman who would never wish anybody harm.

Even so, it was no alluring striptease. She removed her clothing in a perfectly matter-of-fact way, at speed. But Norman's mind was able to fasten, to record, to photograph each movement into his sharpest consciousness. She tucked her glossy chocolate-brown hair into a black grip, shaped like a paper fastener, crossed her arms across her body and then, in one glorious natural movement, swept her sweater off over her head. Paradise. Her breasts were all that a gentleman of taste and decorum could wish in one so feminine. They totally filled a beribboned and laced white top which was held aloft by the thinnest and tautest of shoulder straps. They were frankly gorgeous. Brilliant, round, peaked, cleavaged, firm, elastic, honey-coloured perfection.

The delight that Norman felt at her bralessness began, at last, to tweak his old cock blessedly into life. Her long thin hands flicked to the zipper of her jeans and, looking critically and interestedly at her body in his mirror, she tugged, and opened the tight silver teeth down to the very centre of her body. She peeled the denim off over her rump and arched her frame as she stepped out of her trousers. Now he would be able to discover the secrets of what she wore next to herself.

Her legs were enhanced by a pair of dark, ribbed tights. In the minimal back light of the bedside lamp, he could not distinguish the colour. The woman, Lesley-Anne, the centre of his very own, living fantasy, was almost in silhouette. Under her tights, joy of joys, she wore a tiny pair of what he thought they called bikini briefs. So tiny was this garment that her pubic hair clambered intently upwards to escape from the taut waistline. The white cotton showed the clearest profile of the indentation that must surely indicate the entrance to her vagina.

He loved it. He loved it. He loved it.

It seemed to Norman that her body was sheer sexual perfection. The tension of playing Peeping Tom and the disgracefully elating sordidness of owning her, like some graceful sexy zoo animal, had him rock-like in both his hands. Not bad for an old chap, eh? Well, he had deserved it. He had laboured, he had worked hard all his life, he had paid his dutiful family dues. Now he was collecting on his investment. And it was magnificent. What infinite pleasure. Gordon Driscoll, he thought, eat your heart out. Gordon would never have had the acute joy of such a beast as this.

Within seconds, she had undressed and was covered by the brown towelling dressing gown. It was huge and made her look suddenly vulnerable and much younger. She went into the bathroom. This was *it*. This was *it*. The overture had been frightening but it had been everything that he could have wished for. Now the main performance was about to take place. He must not get over-excited. It would give him the deepest chagrin to have to face his twenty-seven minutes of self-loathing post-onanistic tristesse too damned early.

Five minutes passed. She returned, now clad in a fairly baggy set of striped pyjamas. These were presumably some clothing of her lover's. Norman would have preferred some touch of silk and lace, some frills – 'baby doll', wasn't that the name? Even so, it would be enjoyable to see young Terence Miller retrieve his nightwear.

Oh God, it had all been worthwhile, after all. The battered hands from mixing plaster, the weary legs, the Polyfilla hardened like concrete in his best cereal bowl, the paint-splattered spectacles, the endless frustration of having to do it all himself and failing to get it as right as he would have liked – it had all been worthwhile. Of this he was now sure.

Lesley-Anne slipped under the duvet and put on a pair of horn-rimmed glasses. Their very formality increased the bizarre sexuality of the situation. It was as if he was about to see one of the more haughty, distant and inaccessible Chandos House secretaries violated. She sat in bed and read a stiff-covered book – a novel or something. All Norman now needed was the second player in his hot little bedroom scene.

He did not have to wait long. Terence came in, drying his hands on a drying-up cloth.

'Finished,' he said.

'You could have left that in the kitchen.' She hardly looked up at him.

'Beg pardon, Piggy,' he said, with mock servility, and gave her a tiny deferential bow. He took off his shirt and dumped it on the little easy chair. 'Which side?' She continued to read her book.

'Don't mind,' she answered. 'I'm OK here.' She shifted over very slightly towards the left side of the bed. Terence went into the bathroom and the door partially closed behind him. Norman could hear taps running and the sound of teeth being brushed at length. Well, Terence was clearly in no urgent mood to fall upon his wife-to-be with instant lasciviousness. Maybe they were so practised that they had no need of the added stimulation of a new environment. In the bedroom, nothing happened apart from the flick of Lesley-Anne's book pages as they turned. Then Terence returned clad in a white towelling dressing gown. He looked, to Norman, like a bronzed playboy. He certainly had an air of confidence. She, no doubt, found him a really good lover. Norman hoped that he would, as well.

Terence turned back the duvet and sat next to her in the bed. She was slightly obscured. She continued to read, her tortoiseshell-rimmed glasses focused on the book. He looked across at her, grinning.

'Quite like old times, eh?' Lesley-Anne hardly seemed to acknowledge his remark. Then the man removed his dressing gown while sitting upright among the pillows. He appeared to be naked.

'Haven't you got a T-shirt or something?' she asked slightly touchily.

'Nope. Turn you on, do I?'

'Fuck off, Tel.'

Terence yawned and rubbed his eyes lazily. He peered at the radio-alarm on the bedside: 'What time?'

'Leave it. Sunday morning tomorrow,' she said. 'The old boy doesn't want us till Monday.' He settled down, pulling the covers around his shoulders. She read on. What, in heaven's name, was so special about her bloody book? Why wasn't the fellow clawing at her delectably adjacent, totally available body with an avalanche of pent-up frustrated lust?

'We all right here, Piggy?'

'We're as OK as we'll ever be, Tel,' she sighed.

'Don't be like that.'

'I'm not. You know what I think.' She was reprimanding him. Then she relented: 'It'll be OK. Vanishing act.'

'God, I hope so.' He closed his eyes. For what seemed a very long part of eternity, nothing happened. Then Lesley-Anne put a tube ticket into her book to mark the place and closed it quietly. The cover was white and said 'Mary Wesley' in large black letters. She put it on the bedside table. Norman had purchased this stick of furniture as part of a package of different bits and pieces at a Bicester clearance warehouse. He remembered dryly imagining, when he selected it, the animalistic writhings that he assumed it would witness even more closely than he would himself.

He had amused himself with the idea of that bedside table being thrust suddenly into the rabid sexual culture of the nineties, so far removed from its previous life in some musty old Victorian mansion. It appeared that he had severely miscalculated. So far, these two were about as sexually active as a pot of yoghurt. The light in the bedroom snapped out. She, too, pulled the duvet around her. The two of them appeared to lie back to back. Hopeless.

'Night, Piggy,' he said.

'G'night,' she said shortly. Not even a single kiss. They had hardly touched. They had not touched at all. Norman was suddenly terribly depressed. He could recall occasional Christmases, as a child, when the gifts in his pillowcase had by no means matched his wilder anticipations – the worst disappointments are those heralded by the greatest expectations.

The man stirred in the bed and rubbed his nose. 'What about old man Ranburn, then?' he said quietly.

'Nice enough old guy,' she said without moving. 'Bit sad, I think.'

'Fancies you.'

'Tel!'

'Well, he does.'

'Doubt it. Bit past all that, I should think,' she giggled.

'Don't you believe it. It's these old guys you have to watch out for. You think, if we play our cards right he'll leave us the place when he pops his clogs?'

'You and your dreams, Tel,' she muttered wearily.

'Sorry,' he said, amused.

'G'night,' she said.

Nothing else happened. They didn't quietly turn into each other's arms and begin a long hour of unmitigated pleasuring. They just lay there quietly going to sleep. Norman sat, profoundly disappointed, and watched the silent motionless figures, lying in the bed, illuminated by the cunning light of the stable yard. Shortly, it appeared that the two of them were indeed fast asleep.

After a further half-hour of fruitless vigil, Norman carefully switched off his listening device and edged his big frame out of the viewing room and back into the reality of night time in his study.

It had been about as interesting as watching the lawn grow. It was an appalling frustration. Norman adjusted his dress, standing by his desk, realising that he was now dog-tired and had very cold feet. After all the tension and the fear, any energy that had built up had now evaporated, leaving him feeling like a damp squib.

He trailed on up to his own bedroom and hauled on his own striped pyjamas. There, in splendid and solitary state, he sat on the edge of his redundant double bed and thought about what he had seen. Huh. Thought about what he had *not* seen. Two actionless double beds in one set of buildings. What was the man playing at? The woman was a quite remarkable specimen, in the very peak of her sexual prime. She seemed absolutely right for extravagant devilry. Given a clear, strong, dominant, masculine will, Norman had thought, what would she not want to do?

Oh God, to have that power. To be in that place. To touch, to hold, to smell, to feel that bountiful woman. What would he not do?

Norman lay back poleaxed across the centre of his duvet and drank in, once more, the brief memory of that matter-of-fact removal of clothing – the grace of her turned back, the considered calm of her pleased and careful self-appraisal in his mirror, the revealed secret of the hair between her legs, the ripple of indentations as the shadows picked out the minute undulations of her spine. But it had all gone for nothing. They had done nothing. Nothing at all. Less indeed than he himself might do now. And he fell to thinking of the fullness of her welcoming smile, the invitation in her eyes, the arrogance of her cheekbones, the breathtaking swell of her breasts. All that, and her ignorance of his watching eyes, ultimately, did, eventually, and after much hard work, bring a limpish climax to what, that evening, he felt was his cheated and depressed penis.

Later, he lay under his unpleasantly warm duvet, face down in the pillow, in the direst distress. He was unable to sleep. What had gone wrong with him? Why was he so sick in the head? Maybe many men had similar yearnings and toyed with similar lusts but, surely, no one ever proceeded to do anything about it. Why was he like this? What was it that made a perfectly ordinary, quite intelligent and successful person like himself into this insatiably devious lecher? He could not bear himself. Norman lay stock-still and found himself screwing his face, in the pillow, into a grotesque mask of dry weeping. His empty bedroom echoed to the sound of his choking, painful sobs. At this stage in his life he should be giving the young a kindly, paternal helping hand, chairing charity projects, adding to the portfolio that would perhaps secure him an advance on his MBE, maybe even his K. Instead he found himself feeding upon their youth and their privacy and twisting their God-given attributes and activities to service an unspeakable depth of sordid evil.

It had to stop. Or else he would not be able to face himself any more. He would seal up the secret room tomorrow and never set foot in there ever again. Nail it up. He would be a changed man. It had to stop. He began to feel a sense of relief. It had to stop before he found himself actually doing anyone any damage.

As ever, the due number of minutes later, a certain strength of perspective began to readjust his view of his behaviour. Once again he was able to tell himself how little anyone was hurt by his secret. He was able to remind himself how his actions had given him a real reason for living. It could hardly be counted as much of a sin, in a world where all manner of horrors occurred daily.

WEDNESDAY 12 JULY

Lesley-Anne leaned across to clear Norman's plate from the

table. She had served a deftly seasoned goulash which he had eaten in his usual solitary splendour in the dining room. In the last three days, he and Lesley-Anne had developed a nicely informal ritual for these meals. He found, to his surprise, that he had begun to live each day, buoyed up by the promise of these meaningless exchanges with the girl. At the end of each course, she would return and remain for a short while, making conversation, while he helped himself to the various delicacies that she had provided. She was never going to be a great chef, but her cooking was perfectly satisfactory. Then she would excuse herself with the formula 'Well, I must get on.' And she would leave him to eat.

Of the whole procedure, Norman enjoyed the next episode best. Lesley-Anne's timing was impeccable. She would return to clear the course, just at the precise moment he wondered if, this time, she had forgotten him. She would reach across, her body swaying and bending as she swooped the bowls and plates on to her tray. It was the closest together that the two of them ever came. It would have been so simple to raise his hand off the table and touch her. Instead, he sufficed himself with the secret glimpses that he got of the shadows between her breasts.

And he would catch the smell of her. He was good at inhaling women. He would fill his lungs to capacity with Lesley-Anne. Tuesday had been a day of celebration for Norman, as she had worn a blouse and his eye had been able to travel further. His probably not-so-cunning glances had been able to wander almost at will down the tanned skin of her neck, to the recesses that teased him below.

And he was able to remind himself, as she moved quietly around him, talking about Terence's initial Trojan efforts with the upper orchard, that below the nicely tailored flared skirt and the loose sweater she wore a pair of pink laced briefs and a brassiere of pristine white. He had gazed at her, that very morning, as she had slipped them on, covering her intimate parts, in the closeted privacy of her own bedroom. The brassiere moulded her fine brown breasts into the stereotyped female vision that he so loved and so lusted after. He had been so moved by her loveliness, and by what had happened before that, that he had sat in the viewing room with tears in his eyes well after she had finally left the room to get on with her working day.

Even so, no matter how much he loved knowing this woman's most private secrets, his labours and scheming had, by no means, delivered. Terence and Lesley-Anne had the sex life of plankton. Indeed, until that very morning he had had to assume that they had absolutely no sexual being whatsoever. Or perhaps such things mattered to other people so much less. Norman Ranburn was finding it difficult to think of anything else during these feverish scorching July days.

Each of the four mornings so far, Norman's radio-alarm had awoken him in time for him to arrange to see his lodgers greet the day. Each night he witnessed their retirement. And on a couple of occasions on the Tuesday, when the two of them seemed to have disappeared from view around the buildings during the daytime, imagining that they might have resorted to their bedroom together, Norman had hastened yet again to his little room behind the carpet. They never had.

The two of them seemed very close, very fond, and clearly knew each other well. He called her 'Piggy', she called him 'Tel'. Their conversation covered a wide variety of topics. They had similar leanings to the political left and a typical scoffing attitude towards the government and royalty. Her language in private was, at times, surprisingly earthy. She had apparently worked in advertising for a few months at one stage, which probably explained this. They never talked much of Terence's history, although sometimes the name Eric came up and its mention seemed something of a difficulty for the man. But they never touched or kissed or hugged, or did any of the things that one might assume two healthy, young, about-to-be-married people might do.

It was so frustrating. He had not been able to understand it at all. It was sickening.

But that very morning, just when the overall disappointment of his venture had persuaded him never to return to the room, just when he had determined to lock it and never open the door again, a delicate private sparkle had entered his life. Certainly it had been something that would indicate that, whatever the situation between Lesley-Anne and her husband-to-be, the woman herself was, indeed, still in touch with her sexuality.

Norman had dozed a little, that morning, in his viewing chair. Terence Miller had got up quite early and had bathed and had gone out after a brief discussion with his recumbent fiancée about posting a letter in the village. The name Eric cropped up yet again: 'Eric'll be looking for us by now.'

Then nothing happened for what seemed a very long time. Lesley-Anne remained in the bed and failed even to sip from the mug of tea that Terence had brought her. She occasionally shifted in the bed as she dozed. As far as her responsibilities to Norman were concerned, she had no duties that morning so it was probably a pleasant idea to laze in bed for a while. He admired the slim length of her, curled under the pink-and-grey duvet. He would have left her to it if it had not been for the fact his recent long vigils had made him dog-tired.

Suddenly he was properly awake and aware of something unusual. It was difficult to know exactly what it was. Lesley-Anne was lying absolutely motionless on her back. Her eyes were closed. Her feet were spreadeagled wide apart under the duvet. She was incredibly still. She did not appear to be breathing. Her fine strong profile, with the slightly haughty, subtly hooked nose, was etched in outline against the dark background of the bedside cupboard. Her chin seemed to just unnaturally high for comfort. There was a kind of deathly silence. She looked as if she could be dead. How was it possible?

Norman stared at her and searched her whole form for a sign of life. Nothing. She lay completely still and quite stiffly, almost arched against the mattress. Was it this, the odd way she was lying, that had caught his attention? All he could really see was her face, with the duvet tucked right up to her chin, as it lay in a thick pool of her silky, black hair. What could he do? He could not suddenly rush around and raid the cottage. What on earth had happened? He willed her to move. He was as immobile as she. He had no idea how to proceed.

Then Lesley-Anne, the light of his life, and flavour of his wildest dreams, took a great hiccuping gulp of air and held her body even more rigid as she once again ceased breathing. A minute, or a minute and a half later – it seemed like a lifetime – it happened again. And as it occurred he realised with a sudden clarity what she was about. There was the slightest indecipherable motion at the centre of her body, at her crotch, like the smallest kitten, under the duvet, getting more comfortable in its sleep.

And then it all happened. There was a gasping, churning, shuddering lift of all the covers on the bed as Lesley-Anne squeezed out the words 'Oh Christ!' to her empty bedroom. Eyes tightly closed, her body bucked and moved once, twice, three times again, her head lifting right off the pillow, and then her being came to rest once again. She sighed massively and seemed, momentarily, to smile to herself. She let forth a heartfelt 'Oh' and, finally, turned luxuriously on to her side, curling up a little. Very soon she was asleep. Norman was transfixed. And so excited. And, at last, had a modicum of happiness. It had not been the most graphic of experiences. It by no means matched his fantasies. But it boded a little better for the future. If the woman consented to come, on her own, she could yet come with the reluctant Terence Miller.

THURSDAY 13 JULY

Afterwards, Norman could not believe that he had failed, at first, to recognise her distinctive accent. 'Hullo, Norman,' said the dark female voice: 'How you doing? How's it going?'

'Who's this?' he said. Yes, he had actually said: 'Who's this?' to Amy Shakespeare.

'It's Amy,' she said. 'Who else? Your friendly tame puppeteer and hot chocolate aficionado.' He was suddenly short of breath. 'Amy,' he said, contriving to sound cool and collected. Then he dared: 'Nothing so very tame about you, Miss Shakespeare, as I remember. Where are you?'

'I'm at Reach For My Gun. They run it from a bloody broom cupboard in Wardour Street. Film City, Norman, Film City. Well, Film Broom Cupboard, I suppose.'

'So, Amy, what can I do for you?'

'I'm after your body,' she said, teasing him.

'What?'

'Body. After. I am.' She spoke in capital letters 'No, truthfully, Norman, I wanted to ask if we might be able to steal a borrow of your brilliant stable yard.' He had a sudden mad instant vision of his stable block and the barn being carried off in the back of various pantechnicons. 'Just for a five-day shoot,' she went on quickly. 'You'd barely notice we were around. Oh shit,' she said on reflection, 'that's probably a complete bloody lie. We'd fairly total the place and you'll loathe the whole caboodle but it'd only be five days and there'd be a fee of course. And fame, I suppose. No, not much fame, but it would be a good giggle. Not much of a fee, either, when I come to think about it. But hefty giggles we can offer. We're epic at shit like that – crossed Is and dotted Ts, believe you me. Giggles-R-us. And stardom too – like it's starring Craig Luft and this year's young man's wet dream, *dud-dud-DAH!*' – she sang a fanfare at him – 'Georgina Lewis!'

'Georgina who?'

'Lewis. You know – *You Can't Do Much Without A Screwdriver.*'

She'd lost him completely. 'A film?'

'No, Norman, a dog show. Yes, my darling man, they're filum stars,' she said patronising him good-naturedly, 'folk who appear on the silver screen. For money. Professional movie actors. So they would have us believe. When they're not being professional wankers. *A Seduction of Consequence,* it's called. Graham Moorehead McPhee.'

'Graham Moorehead McPhee? What does that mean? Moorehead McPhee – what's that? You're not making a lot of sense, Amy. Why must you always talk in riddles?'

'He's the director. He's well famous, Norman. Renowned. In my view. In the view of quite a few people actually. Won the Golden Bear at Berlin the year before last. Where've you been?'

'I don't think I've been to the pictures since *Sound of Music*.'

'Poor thing. Deprived. Well, you must have, at least, heard of *Burlington Bertie*. That was his. *The Importance of Bunting, You Can't Do Much Without A Screwdriver* – all his.' She had said that last bit to him twice. It must be significant. Did she want to borrow his tools? No, they were all film titles, that was clear enough. She was rabbiting on: 'We're in week three already and the place we were going to shoot has had this blazerama.'

'"Blazerama"?'

'Conflagration. Fire. Nothing to do with me, Norman, absolutely nothing to do with the mad world of celluloid. We hadn't even arrived there yet. Give us a chance. We were scheduled to raze the place in two weeks' time. Poor guy lost his whole fucking wine cellar in the fire. He was crying on the phone when he told us about it.'

'I'm not surprised.'

'What do you think?'

'What do I think about what?'

'What do you think about it as an idea, Normski?'

'My name is Norman.' God, he could be so pompous.

'You'll always be Mr Ranburn to me,' she said, without a glimmer of sincerity.

He laughed: 'You have no shame, have you Amy? Never beset by English sensitivity, are you? Fearless.'

'Oh I like "beset", Normski, um, Norman. No, I'm silicone, non-stick,' she said. 'Nothing touches me.' Then she laughed, too, as if she didn't believe herself. 'Back home in New Zealand we're taught early that life is a bungee jump without the rubber band. It's on the school syllabus, down under – spunk. In the nursery – A for audacity, B for boldness, C for courage, D for daring, um, er, E for elan. Help, help, I'm running out of letters, Norman. Anyway it's why New

Zealand produces the All-Blacks. QED. Now then, er, nice Mr Ranburn, can we film in your stable yard for five days, eh? Please-please-please-please. We'd leave everything exactly as if no one had ever been there. And pay you lots of money. Well, not much money – but money nevertheless. What more could a man of grace, dignity and style and beauty and understanding, oh and, um, generosity ask?'

'When would this be?' His brain was doing tiny somersaults at the idea of seeing that awful little girl again. That awful little girl with the tight little body. That awful little girl who had no respect at all for older members of society. That awful little girl whom he would very much like to eat. Considering the saddening Lesley-Anne situation, the prospect would perk up his morale. It would be fun just to see her bum again. And her mouth. And, oh, lots of parts of her. All of her. It was such a turn-up for the books, her ringing like that. Amy Shakespeare could be guaranteed to be more than a little bit rude. And he sort of liked Amy being more than a little bit rude. When he wasn't feeling shell-shocked by it. No, he probably rather liked being shell-shocked by it as well.

'A five-day shoot from Monday the thirty-first.'

'Which month?'

'July. Now. This July.'

'Good God. That's two weeks' time, Amy.'

'Too right, Norm. Got it in one. You can read a calendar too. Oh, we don't do things by halves here – we are one-hundred-per- cent professional at creating a really good fuck-up. I said it was an emergency, Normski, sorry, Norman. Norman please, please help us. If you do, I promise you I'll come down there and do rude things to you, all over your body.' She wasn't serious. Girls didn't actually say that sort of thing if they truly meant it. 'And I'd arrange to bring my own supply of drinking chocolate,' she added helpfully.

'Well.'

'And, yeah, even, yeah, *dud-DAH*! – Plain Chocolate Hobnob Biscuits!' And she made luscious eating noises down the phone at him.

'Well,' he said again, as if he felt unsure. He wasn't, but he didn't need her to know that. Was that the reason why she had returned that Whit Sunday night to seek him out again – just so that she could check out his property as potential location fodder? 'What's in it for me?'

'Arthur's picnic! You are such a darling. You are just so *very*. A big wet kiss is in it for you. A full-scale antipodean tongue number. Oh yes, endless washing-up of the tea things is in it for you. All that. Oh and a fee. Dosh, a wedge, the readies. We could talk about that when we come down. I'd have to come down with Des – that's my boss. And Graham and Sue Smith. She's the designer.'

'When do you want to come down?'

'Tomorrow week? Friday, it's – what? – the twenty-first? In the morning? We're going over to Wormell Water first. We're filming there at the beginning of August. After you.'

'The twenty-first? That's the day before Lord's.'

'What?'

'I'm going to see the World Cup at Lord's on the Saturday. Cricket, Amy, cricket.'

'I know about cricket, Norman. New Zealanders know about cricket. That's their thing. It's in the blood. You got a ticket? Euphoria! Stonking galactic! Orbital!'

'I'm a member of the MCC. I don't *need* a ticket. I'll be in the pavilion.'

'Finger-licking!' she said excitedly. He would have felt cheated if she hadn't.

FRIDAY 14 JULY

'Well, I really don't know.' Norman stood alone in the Onan Cottage bedroom and peered at the clutter on Lesley-Anne's dressing table. He had got used to the fact that he often spoke out loud to himself. He supposed it came from being on his own so frequently. The words would barely be articulated but they would just about be audible to anyone who was around. He tried to convince himself that the rhetorical remarks were silent but the response in the street from the very occasional, startled passer-by was proof enough.

He was able to trespass in the cottage because Lesley-Anne and her less-than-potent Terence had taken themselves away for the weekend. She had confided to him that Terence had to wind up some old business arrangements. Very anonymous, she had kept it. 'Nothing special,' she had said. And she said that she was anxious to pick up a few more of her belongings – she had mentioned an ironing board. As she had, for once, consented to sit down in his house and had crossed her legs for him, he had had no choice but to suggest that he could manage perfectly well for the weekend on his own. He hadn't got around to organising invitations for his little Sunday drinks party, anyway.

So now he had taken their absence as a modest opportunity to explore their domain. It might be worthwhile discovering a little more about these two people to whom he had so casually attached himself. He had taken them on, like a silly old fart, with scant consideration just because he had liked the cant of her bosom and the promise of her smile. It seemed as if he was becoming two separate persons. One, the public man, resourceful, charming, intelligent and admired. Two, the private man, a sick and silly old idiot. 'Useless and impotent,' he heard himself say out loud to the empty bedroom. It made him angry.

There was nothing to be found in the cottage of any significance. Breakfast things stood uncleared on the kitchen table. The two of them read a great many newspapers. He was surprised by the number of wine and spirit bottles there were clustered around the plastic dustbin in the kitchen. On the whole the cottage seemed remarkably anonymous. It was as if there was but a light scurf of inhabitation spread through those unremarkable rooms.

Norman returned to the bedroom, smiled at his reflection in his favourite wall mirror and slid open the fitted cupboard that contained their clothes. Her things hung at one end of it. Not all that many hangers. Dresses he already knew quite well. He stepped into the cupboard and plunged his arms around her clothes. He drew all her dresses and skirts and hanging trousers to him and sank his face into his embrace. He inhaled Lesley-Anne. The scent of her completely consumed him. He moaned quietly as he took deep breath after deep breath. Then he felt deeply embarrassed at what he was doing and, looking around nervously, withdrew.

He moved to the dressing table again and opened her top drawer. He knew perfectly well what was here. He knew most of her underwear off by heart. It was so good to hold them gently between his fingers. He softly held up a slight pair of midnight-blue panties. Rolled up, they would fit in a matchbox with room to spare. There were one or two lovely items that he had not yet had the pleasure of experiencing on the model. He could wait. He held a mismatched bunch of lingerie to his cheek and felt very foolish.

At the bottom of the drawer was a British passport. He took it out. The photo was of Terence. A more youthful, darker young man. The pages revealed very little. An American visa for the previous year. Only then did Norman see the name. 'Terence Ridgeway,' it said quite clearly. 'Ridgeway'? He was called Terence Miller, wasn't he? 'Ridgeway' was *her* name. Could it be they were married after all? No, the name Ridgeway was hers.

And then, quite simply, he realised. The physical resemblance was startlingly clear once you knew. Terence and Lesley-Anne were brother and sister. Lesley-Anne had been lying to him.

SATURDAY 15 JULY

Even the following day, Norman found himself unable to shake off an overall feeling of torpor brought about by the gloomy events of Onan Cottage. He walked into the Chandos House building with a palpable sense of futility hanging about his shoulders. Since his retirement, going into the office had become a mixed blessing at the best of times. The ten familiar broad steps up to the front doors, off Moxsom Street, now felt as if they were featuring in an oddly disenfranchising dream. That was one of the reasons Norman preferred to make his trips to Witney on Saturdays – because the office always had a different atmosphere on a Saturday in any case.

Gilbert wanted to move the operation to Oxford, to a larger, cheaper sixties building in St Ebbes. Gilbert had always thought Witney was a backwater. The present building on Moxsom Street had been part of the local council offices until Norman had purchased it in '71. It had a certain Edwardian grandeur, even if it was not all that practical a building. The very centre of the main block, for example, was a fairly large meeting room that the company had little use for. It was an atrium with a jolly stained-glass, domed roof affair commemorating civic notables at the time of the First World War. When Joan had been a student at art college in Oxford in the mid-seventies, she had organised exhibitions in it. Norman remembered busy, excited and expensively wined gallery-launch evenings followed by weeks and weeks in which no one ever came to look at the exhibitions at all.

He met Gilbert in the atrium. It spared him having to see his brother in his own old familiar office.

'How're your new people?' Gilbert asked after they had dispensed with various pieces of Chandos House business for the next board meeting.

'The staff? Pretty good. Getting used to the way of things. He's done major works in the old orchard. It's never looked so good. He's found parts of the orchard I never knew existed.'

'Attractive woman, I hear.'

'Who said?'

'I spoke to that fellow of yours, Clarke. Met him in the Broad last week, in Oxford. Out shopping.'

'I suppose she is.'

'Lucky devil. Pretty woman cooking you your meals, flitting round with the duster. Wiggling her arse. Can't be bad.'

'Well, no, I suppose not. Didn't occur to me.'

'Oh yeah?' But then Gilbert unbuttoned his blazer and sat

elegantly next to him on the leather Chesterfield, changing the subject: 'What are we going to do about my niece Joan? She's been on the blower to me, going spare. She says she wrote you a note about it. You've not replied.'

'She knows what I think I'm able to do. It's perfectly fair. Why should Frannie have it all so easy? The whole thing dumped in her lap as it were – no struggle? I said I'd stand guarantor after all. That's fair. Business isn't easy. And, at the end of the day, to be honest, it does seem a rather half-baked notion.'

Gilbert looked at him, as he often did, with cynical, judging, raised eyebrows. 'Dad dumped the whole of this in your lap, no struggle,' he said quietly.

'God, no struggle? It was years of toil – you know that.'

'Yeah, afterwards. But at the start. And you had some pretty hare-brained schemes yourself, Norman. Wild notions.'

'Like what? Like what?' Defensive, knowing full well.

'This place, for example. Measly little rooms with ceilings so high that on a foggy day you can't see them. All these heavy doors that take such a lot of care and attention. A listed bloody building. A fortune to heat. Warped foundations in St Cuthbert's Street. No disabled access. Do you want me to go on?'

'I want us to stay here.'

'I know, I know, I know. But it'll cost. But you see what I mean? Just like you playing *Genevieve* with that old Bullnose of yours, this is yet one more jolly folly, a passion that, finally, we all finished up lumbered with. Well, Frannie's got her folly, too. Perhaps. And Frannie is family. It could be big, Norm.' Norman contributed one of his famous 'old-fashioned' looks. 'Well, it *could* be,' screeched Gilbert enthusiastically. 'And, quite frankly, at the end of the day, you can afford it.'

Everyone was suddenly calling him 'Norm'. Was he really being ungenerous? Had it really, in truth, all been too easy for him – Chandos House? No, at times it had been unbearable, gut-wrenchingly awful. He had earned every penny. Those years in the late sixties when they were extending too rapidly, when the cash-flow problems got completely out of hand and he awoke every morning at four o'clock with his ulcer giving him such gyp. Gilbert didn't know the half of it. Gilbert had been swanning about in Florida at the time working for Sargasso, living the high life. All this had been before Gilbert returned to the fold. It hadn't been easy. Norman had bloody earned it.

There had been lots of pressures. When he'd retired he had been so sad to leave, but he had also been exceptionally relieved. So much of the difficult times he would not miss. He would never again have to live through an episode like the Austin Peacock business for example. It had nearly killed him.

Austin had been chief accountant for Chandos House for nineteen years – since '73. He had shared the office on the first floor of that very building, right next to Norman. They had played golf together most weekends. Austin had been an able and supportive, rather formal colleague, with an endearing lisp. In his late fifties. A kind man. Traditional.

In the last year of Norman's regime it had slowly come to light that Austin – who had got into some severe personal financial difficulties over a middle-age separation from his wife – had been embezzling sums of money. For how long, no one would ever know. Norman guessed it had been only for about two years. Probably a total of four or five thousand pounds was involved in all, over the whole period – a tidy sum of money, but not really a massive major fraud.

Gilbert, who had never much liked Peacock, felt it was important, *pour encourager les autres*, to charge the man. Norman, who had worked alongside Austin for year after year, season after season, fought hard to try to find a way of gently jettisoning the man and arranging some sort of quiet payback scheme. But finally Norman lost the argument. A year later, six months before Norman's retirement, Austin Peacock, father of three, a man of erstwhile loyalty and endeavour, on remand in Canterbury Prison, killed himself two weeks prior to his case going to court. The shame had killed him. Norman could understand it – he might have done the same. Gilbert's only comment was, 'Well, he shouldn't have done it, should he? At the bottom line, it was theft.' Soft on some, hard on others – that was Gilbert. From then on for Norman, Chandos House had become a lot less than fun and the memory of his retirement was irretrievably bound up with the horror of Austin's son, Peter Peacock, screaming sickening grief-striken obscenities at him at the funeral.

'I'll stick with what I've told Joan,' said Norman, finishing his coffee, his attention returning to the here and now.

'Big mistake,' said Gilbert. 'Trouble with you, Norman, is you're too nice. Well, you've always been too nice to those you work with and not really nice enough to family. Family first. Always has been. And the devil take the hindmost. Dad thought that.' Norman didn't entirely agree. And if he had been 'too nice', then, all right, it was a big fault. But it was one of his best qualities as well.

Later, Norman played a solitary nine holes of golf into the evening. It was an attempt to get his life back into some sort of kilter. Then, after a drink, he felt much stronger and returned to Coombe just as dusk was beginning to fall. His headlights picked up the second car parked in the space by the barn just as soon as he swung into the drive. It was a Volvo. He parked in the barn and then went back and walked around the strange car, in the dusk. It was quite a new one. Smart. Terence and Lesley-Anne must have visitors. Norman never had visitors. Well, at any rate, never just out of the blue.

There were lights on all over the cottage illuminating the gathering mist as the last vestiges of daylight faded behind Bargate Hill. He hastened to his listening post to see if he could discover what was going on next door. Their bedroom was in darkness and their bedroom door was only just ajar. He stood and listened intently. He could hear voices in conversation. He was about to return to the land of reality when he was suddenly aware of the voices being heightened in anger. Men's voices. And a woman's voice, placating and reasoning.

Even so, it was difficult to make out more than that. He

left his secret room and took a turn around the garden and the buildings. In just one week Terence's work had already been considerable. The whole place looked so much smarter now. Norman took his stroll close to the cottage windows. Quite obviously, behind the illuminated curtains some kind of epic dispute was taking place.

He went back into the house and fixed himself a snack to eat while he watched the telly. He was angry about Joan. He was angry about Gilbert. He was angry about Lesley-Anne and Terence. They had taken him for a ride, those two. He had asked for a couple and they had therefore provided him with one. Not that there was very much he could do about it. He had, after all, been in the process of taking them for a ride as well. A wry case of the biter bit. He watched some damned awful serial on the box. Some stupid strident women sharing a flat – American, with irritating canned laughter.

At about ten o'clock, he heard the car leave, its engine whining as it tore its way up the hill to the main road. Half an hour later there was a knock and Lesley-Anne came in. She had never come into his house in trousers before. He had, of course, seen her into and out of her jeans half a dozen times in her own place. Very fetching, he reckoned. Her face was shiny. It seemed clear that she had been crying. She came straight to the point.

'I'm sorry to come and see you so late but I needed to talk to you tonight. I would never have got to sleep otherwise. Something's come up. I'm really very sorry but Terence has had these problems with winding up some business interests of his in Surrey and we're going to have to go down there to sort it all out properly.'

He got her a whisky and suggested she sit down. She at least gave him that pleasure. Even in distress she was a pleasing object to look at, perched uneasily on his settee, her thighs satisfactorily hugged by the denim. He was aware of an instinctive premonition. They were going to leave. He knew it. He would never scent her body across his breakfast table again. Or watch her select her knickers for the day, standing damply, well showered in the privacy of her bedroom. Well, she could go as far as he was concerned. Her remaining only made him feel depressed. How he had ached to see her wrought body suffused with pleasure, her whole being racked with intensity. All she had managed to supply him with was one solitary, anonymous, self-induced little gulp. It was no return for his enormous investment of time, money and humiliation.

'What's the problem?' he managed to say. He crossed and sat with her on the sofa. Her breasts were but a hand-span away from him.

'I'm afraid I'm really sorry but I've promised not to say. It's just that there are some outstanding debts which Terence had been promised would be sorted out. And, well, they haven't been. We've got to go down and look into it. We thought they might be able to give us a bit of breathing space.'

'Both of you going?'

'I'm afraid so. Yes.' Norman had one last despairing try – it wasn't worth it but he suddenly realised how very much he was going to miss his intimate moments with her: 'Can't he manage on his own?'

'I'm afraid not. I've promised him I'd help. Oh, it's so difficult. We were very happy here.'

He continued to press her but he knew he was now just being polite: 'Is there anything I can do to help?' She knew it wasn't a serious offer.

'I don't think so.' She caught his eyes properly for the only time in their time together. He was terrified at what she might say and desperate to hear it. Those great translucent brown eyes. 'I'd prefer it if you stayed,' he said.

'I'll get back just as soon as I can.'

Silence. She wasn't to be trusted. He decided to prove it to himself: 'When are you going to get married? Have you got the date planned yet?'

She didn't give a flicker. 'Just after Christmas, when Terence's brother is back from the States.' He could knock her around for telling him lies so confidently and with such arrogance. She was settling into it now. The whisky was no doubt touching up her daring. She thought she could do

106

anything with him. He stood up, and smiled at her with his usual sympathetic, old-world charm. In the cheating game, she didn't know it, but he had beaten her all ends up. But it was so sad that he had never had her under his secret microscope all ends up.

She rose to go. 'You've been so very good to us.' She suddenly held his arm with her hand and kissed him very quickly on the cheek. And left.

He stood there for a long time fastening her smell into the deepest cavity of his memory, holding the print of the touch of her hand on the surface of his skin beneath his jacket sleeve, recording for perpetuity the noise her lips had made in that intense, never-to-be-forgotten split second.

In the morning he let himself into the cottage and walked around. They must have been up all night. He had not bothered to watch them go. It was as clean as a whistle. Not a stitch of their belongings remained. In the kitchen on the table lay a scrap of paper with words in her handwriting, written hurriedly, which read: 'Dear Mr Ranburn, I'm sorry. L-A.' And there was a casual, thoughtless, half-hearted cross scrawled under her initials.

'We were very happy here,' she had said when they had talked the previous night. 'We *were* very happy here.'

They would not be back.

FRIDAY 21 JULY

Amy, of course, had been characteristically unclear about the precise time of arrival of the film party. Norman prepared himself for their visit absurdly early, and in something of a bate. He actually prepared for their inspection with even more care than he might have taken for a blessed AGM. He had a good hot bath and rejected at least three different ties before picking one that had an element of boldness about its design. He washed up and put away all his breakfast things. And then, being at a loss, he took to walking about the place – telling himself he was checking out his domain and looking at the work that Terence had done before he and Lesley-Anne had thoughtlessly taken off the week before.

This meant that, when the film folk finally did arrive, Norman had just got to the bottom of the main lawn and was standing, in a brown study, by the pond. They came down to him across the grass like four black crows. Leather-clad.

Well, when he looked a second time, Amy wasn't leather-clad. She was wearing a smart black suit with a shoulder bag at her hip on a long thin strap. It fitted her more exactly than ought to be legal, with a nipped-in black jacket hiding some skimpy silk vest thing. Her hair was caught up at the back of her head. She was so demurely orthodox that she wouldn't have looked out of place at Chandos House, or as a weather girl on the box.

Apart from introducing her three companions to him, she said virtually nothing during the hour they were at the Aviary. Norman found himself caught by the fact that sometimes she looked about thirteen years old, particularly when she smiled. At other moments she looked as ancient as days. Today, in her slight silky suit, she mostly looked just out of nappies. Efficient and pure.

In spite of the day already being warm, all three of her companions wore big leather jackets and seemed to bristle with mobile phones. They turned out to be perfectly ordinary and pleasant. They just looked terrifying. No, they were better than pleasant: they were exceptionally nice. They loved everything about the Aviary. All three did a lot of exclaiming about it.

Amy's boss, this man named Des, had hair sprouting from his chest, up his neck, out of his ears and on the back of his fingers, and had curling grey hair cascading over his ears. It looked as if his body hair was genuinely out of control. He smoked an endless chain of tiny black liquorice-papered roll-ups and sounded very – what Norman thought they called – 'street-cred'. When you cut your way past the argot, you suddenly discovered he was perfectly all right.

The director chappie, Moorehead McPhee, he of the *Lost Screwdriver* and *Bunting* fame, had his hair almost shaved to his scalp. He had developed a virtually American style of enthusing. It was dreadfully tiring. Everything Norman showed him was better than perfect. In some cases altogether too perfect. The designer woman, Sue Smith, wrote a pile of notes and managed a Filofax, a clipboard, several calls on her mobile phone and his proffered glass of wine all at the same time, with consummate ease. She was small with short blonde hair and bright perspicacious eyes. She complained of a hangover but showed no sign of it.

They finished up on the terrace with a typically splendid bottle of Château Cos d'Estournel, deuxième cru – never, of course, quite as subtle as Château Ducru-Beaucaillou, because the vineyards at St Estephe are higher and face more directly south, but excellent for all that. Norman at last felt relaxed. He realised that for some obscure reason he had been very keen for them to like his place. And they had given him the pleasure of absolutely adoring it.

Amy continued to say nothing. She took her glass of wine and hardly caught his eye. She was obviously a very junior member of this little coterie. He was surprised at the cut of her clothes. No matter how little he knew about women's clothing, even he could see her outfit had cost her a small fortune. Now she was sitting down, one could glimpse more of what she had on under her jacket – it was a sheer silk, light-pink vest job with lace along the top, held in place by two cobweb-thin straps. Smoothly filled, as far as one could see. Sitting on the brick terrace wall, she had crossed her legs and allowed herself to reveal an extensive vista of thigh. Silent woman, loquacious limbs. She sipped her wine and looked away from them, out across sunlit Bargate Hill, with grey eyes that could Brillo-pad one's soul. It was so hot.

Norman brought out his desk diary and checked on their dates. He sorted out with them exactly how much of his premises was going to be invaded. The fees mentioned were, it turned out, minuscule, but then he didn't really need the money. And he knew that he liked the idea of having Amy Shakespeare around the place for a few days, silent or no. So it was decided. In sixteen days' time they would arrive. There were going to be horses, and wardrobe trucks and dressing-room trailers and location catering vans and lighting rigs and mobile generators. A lot of vehicles, but they could park along the side of the driveway.

Norman accompanied the party back to where they had parked, at the back of the barn. There were three vehicles.

Amy had a brand-new, white, open-topped, very expensive-looking Mazda. A neat little female sports car. Where the hell did she get the money?

'Where's your great big motorbike?' he asked her.

'Sold. The world out there thinks two wheels are smeggy. Police, other drivers, pot-holes, men – too many of my friends were getting whacked on bikes. So I got this instead.'

He could not help himself saying: 'Must have cost a pretty penny?'

'I'm up to my hock in neck,' she said lightheartedly.

There was a good deal of fiercely determined shaking of hands all round. Then Sue Smith got into her Golf and she and the other car, with Graham and Des in it, moved in procession up the drive with the odd casually waving arm. Amy would go now. But in two weeks she would be back for a little while again. That was something to look forward to. He gently patted the bonnet of the Mazda. And thought of it as Amy. 'Well,' he said. He was always so bloody eloquent.

The girl gave him the longest look that she had awarded him all morning and placing a hand on both hips slid the tight little funnel of her skirt up to her crotch. This girl had such long lovely legs. He could get obsessed with her legs. He *was* obsessed with her legs. And she had them displayed in high heels today. She extended one of those tormentingly desirable limbs over the door of her feisty-looking car and sank her bum on to the driver's seat. She articulated her legs away from view under the steering wheel. She must presumably know very precisely how attractive her body was to men, he thought. She did all this to tease him. It was just her special game – her you-can-look-but-you-can't-touch ruse. But then, again, it could just have been entirely innocent and unpremeditated.

She gunned the car into life. The usual throaty sports-car showing-off routine.

'Tell me about the film. What's the story?' he yelped, sweating at the boldness of quite clearly holding her from going. She shot him a long questioning look, looked away and then drilled her pale grave eyes at him once more. Then the engine died as she switched it off. 'You want to know about the film?' she asked, deadpan. She didn't believe he was interested in the film. He nodded. It was all he could muster.

'That's cool,' she concluded, and then suddenly she gave him the most massive grin. She opened the door of the car.

'I could do you some hot chocolate,' he said, trying a touch of chumminess.

'Wine's good,' she said and set off for the terrace again, sliding her skirt back down over her bum as she went. He followed, watching her. She seemed like a different person now that her bosses had gone. Funny that she should apparently be so much in awe of them and never much in awe of him. On the terrace she unpinned her hair, which tumbled like molasses about her shoulders, and settled down on the sun-lounger that the director Graham had used earlier. It felt as if she thought of herself as the one in charge now. Oh, she gave herself airs, this one. Her legs, when crossed neatly at the ankle, looked even longer in her sweet matt-black high heels.

The third bottle remained immersed on its bucket of, by now, melted ice. The day was reaching the zenith of its heat. Amy hid her face behind sunglasses and accepted his proffered glass.

Norman looked about. His garden looked more beautiful than ever on a day like this. And quiet. You could hear his father's dolphin fountain tinkling far away at the other end of the lawn. There was no breeze. The summer was being endlessly hot. He wondered if it would be impolite to remove his jacket. The only activity was a sudden swirl of ducks – five of them – making their way, with their usual inordinate effort, diagonally across the orchard, flying down towards the river by the bridge.

'Well?' he asked.

'*A Seduction of Consequence*? *Jackanory* time, eh?'

'Did they have *Jackanory* in New Zealand?'

'Yep, and refrigerators, and bacon, lettuce and tomato sandwiches, and traffic lights and Doc Martins. It's almost civilised, New Zealand. Mind you the traffic lights have a different sequence, I think – yellow-red, green, red. Yes, that's it: they go yellow before they go red. Or maybe it's before they go green. Oh God knows. Different anyway.'

'Yes, yes, yes, I've been to New Zealand. The film, Amy, the film.'

'Oh, right, the film-and-shit. As you say so rightly say, the film. Well, what to tell you? It's based on this finger-licking little novel by Marina Macdermot.'

'Where's "finger-licking" come from?'

'Finger-licking?'

'Finger-licking.'

'D'you know, I'm not sure. Colonel Saunders, I suppose. Kentucky Fried Sicken. Very sixties – I picked it up from my dad, I think.'

'Who was your dad?'

'Questions, questions, questions! He was my father, Norman,' she explained patiently.

'Yes, yes. I imagine he might well have been. But what was he? What did he do?'

'Oh yes, of course, Mr Man – identity through employment. He was the nation's assistant executioner. Mostly that meant that he only got to top a few weird women and dozens of children. And pets. And goldfish. OK, OK, *pax, pax,* sorry. OK.' She laughed apologetically. 'He was a poet. He is a poet. One of New Zealand's leading voices, they call him. I suppose that kind of means, er, he, um, writes poems. Daniel Shake, he's called.' He loved the way she said 'New Zealand' – she made it sound like one word: 'Nyzilann'.

'Good, the poems?' he asked.

'I reckon. In my view. Some, anyway.'

'So your real name isn't Shakespeare, it's Shake.'

'My real name is A. Shakespeare. That's what I wrote on the

front of my exercise books at school all those generations ago. Now, do you want to hear about the film, or what?' she said, flashing him an enrapturing smile and peering at him over the top of her sunglasses. Archetypal coquettish behaviour. But one could not help but like it. She went on: 'Now, you're not meant to interrupt storytellers, Norman. When they're in full flow.'

'You weren't in full flow. You hadn't started.'

'Well, yes, that might be true. But watch it, big Norm – once more and I'll have you sectioned.' She held out a straight arm for a refill and began: 'Apparently the book was a bestseller in the eighties. I can't say it was a bestseller with me. It's a nineteen-thirties arty-farty smock-ripper. As melodramatic as fuck, based around this liberal bohemian set. This bisexual artist called something like Duncan Clark lives in this farmhouse with his mistress who's married to someone else. The usual artsy thing. But acute about the difference between women and men.'

'Duncan Grant?'

'I'm sorry?'

'This Duncan Clark. Is he based on Duncan Grant?'

'Possibly. He might actually be called Duncan Grant. I can't remember. Anyway. Craig plays Duncan. This naive young thing gets to be sent to stay with them – that's Georgina Lewis. There's this big-number neighbour – the local mover and shaker. He finally seduces her. There's this and that. This, that and the other. There's coming and going. Going and coming. And then there's just a lot of coming. Fleur – that's the innocent party's name – Fleur's innocence is corrupted by this well-endowed landed gentry character and she becomes a fallen woman as apparently they were in them there days. There is public disgrace. There is pubic disgrace. And Mr Big, the landowner – what the smeg's he called? Mr Ranburn, I expect. No, no, wrong again – Max Woodford-Perry. He kills himself for love, shame and all that shit. Duncan grieves. Oh yeah, and he reflects deeply and he reflects artistically on life being a smeggy dung-heap. Produces his greatest work. End of story. The tramcar generation served up to titillate nostalgics of the nineties. Dead melodramatic. A bit on the sexy side. Muddy, sub-Merchant-Ivory, I suppose. *Lady Chat*, *Women In Love* – that kind of caper. Frocks and fucking. And the impending steamroller of the war. Usual stuff.'

'Bloomsbury?'

'What?'

'It sounds as if it's about the Bloomsbury set – Lytton Strachey, Maynard Keynes, Clive Bell, Vanessa Bell, Virginia Woolf – those people.'

'If you say so,' she said. The names didn't seem to mean very much to her. He didn't really know enough about films to ask her any more questions. He conjectured that 'will it be a long film?' might be thought a slightly inept question. He never went to the cinema himself and had no notion how highly regarded or famous her 'stars' might be. So his reason for keeping the girl there with him now was, all things being equal, over. But she didn't seem inclined to move. Maybe he could rustle up a bit of luncheon for them both.

He had this insane desire of wanting to show her the inside of Onan Cottage. At the back of his mind he had been formulating the idea of Amy Shakespeare and her Camden-Town-quickie boyfriend making use of the place. At the *back* of his mind? That was a joke. It had taken up full-time residence as an idea in the very forefront of every part of his consciousness – Amy and some redoubtable young stud fornicating the hours away under his watchful and attentive eye. Then he could banish Lesley-Anne from his mind for ever. Or maybe Amy together with her Des or that Graham or this Craig Luft or some other likely film hero could stay there while she was working in Coombe. He so wanted to show her around. God, he wanted to show her around. He so wanted to find a way of suggesting it.

She could apparently read his dirty mind. 'Do you fancy,' she said, carefully putting her glass aside, 'showing me around some more, Norm . . . man?' She made a tiny joke of finishing his name. She remembered their conversations. It made him feel ridiculously pleased.

They walked round the buildings once more, but this time

side by side, some eighteen inches apart. He so wanted to take her hand in his but was clever enough not to try. She felt tall next to him, pricking her heels over the stone-clad paths that linked the various buildings. Inside Onan Cottage it smelled musty. And seemed small. The girl, bless her heart, posed away for a few moments, her arms thrown every which way, her shoulder-pads riding up, show-business style, in front of his favourite mirror. Then she gave a tiny shriek and launched herself on to the double bed, squashing the duvet. Face down, bottom up, she had her arms thrown out sideways as though she was on the cross, her cheek resting on the duvet cover watching him. Dead. A little like when she had embraced his throbbing car, Bertram, that day in May.

So that was the moment when he asked her, his heart pounding: 'You could use this. It's empty. To stay. While filming.' Could he say it? Could he get the words out? He did: 'You could bring your boyfriend.'

'Or my girlfriend,' she said with mock seductiveness, laughing. It sounded as if she was only teasing him. 'Finger-licking,' she murmured. 'God, it would be good.' And then . . . did she actually do *that*? Did she raise her bum up off the surface of the bed in a tiny, rude, simulated carnal moment? Yes, she did. Of course she did. Her knees were slightly bent, holding her bottom cocked up in the air. Asking for it. Then slowly she sank back into the duvet again. 'No,' she said 'Smeg. Double-smeg. I'd have to stay with the unit. It'd do me no good staying here. It wouldn't do. Brilliant idea though. Thank you, Mr Man.'

Then they were outside again, and Amy secreted herself once more behind her dark glasses. In the shadow of the barn, summer midges were billowing about in a cloud by the old chestnut tree. Two magpies. Two for joy. Amy and he, the two of them were marooned alone in the Aviary's tiny valley where his house had stood for centuries. Was there a joy, a chemistry between them as they stood together there, slightly tipsy? If there was, he felt that he didn't ever want to puncture it. And so, he was, for an instant, too fearful to say anything. She stood looking at him, silent, waiting, wanting him to do something. But he couldn't tell what. They were pretty well two generations apart in age. What could he ever possibly do? The moment went on far too long. Eventually it was desperately important to break the silence. 'Righty-ho,' he said. Oh, very clever, Norman, he thought.

'Bertram,' she said. 'Show me Berty-Bertram again. I love it when you show me Bertram.'

As they went to the big doors of the barn, she caught up her shoulder bag from the front seat of the Mazda. It was cool in the barn. And always smelled wonderfully of ancient timber-work and dry straw, although there was no straw in there any more. It was an evocatively distinctive smell. A pigeon had got into the roof space and it flapped anxiously away to the other end, where it perched on one of the great big roof trusses.

'How old is this?' she asked, genuinely awed by the building.

'Middle of the fifteenth century. This is a collared-truss barn. You see the way they hold up the purlins. Which, in turn, hold up the rafters. Unfortunately it fell into terrible disrepair in the last century so a lot of what you see has been rebuilt. But the timbers are original. Well, most of them.' They both looked up at the vast cross-beams, so high above their heads underneath the sharply pitched roof.

'Middle of the fifteenth century? When's that?'

'About 1430, 1460. Something like that. Older than Shakespeare, anyway.' He groped around for someone else she might know who would give her a better idea of his veneration for the barn. 'Even a hundred years before Henry the Eighth in point of fact. Richard the Third, Wars of the Roses, Princes in the Tower. That sort of time.'

'Double-double-ancient, eh? Five hundred years? That's almost older than you, Norm-man.' He took no notice. He began to flick parts of the cover off the car. The sunlight filtered into the barn through thousands of minute openings, making a whole theatrical show of needles of light piercing the gloom. A cloud of dust rose from Bertram's tarpaulin, to assist the effect. Amy climbed into the car. Their eyes were getting used to the light. She gave herself an amused, reflective smile and turned to him.

'Start it,' she said.

'No. It's not very good to start Bertram and then not give him a good ride.'

'I'd like a good ride.'

'Not today.' Suddenly he couldn't face being seen out in the world with someone quite so young. He would feel obliged to take on a grandfatherly role. He didn't want that. There wouldn't, of course, be anything different in his demeanour here at the Aviary, but at least here he wouldn't have to think that everyone was assuming she was his grandchild, or, at best, his daughter. Perhaps it was simply that he didn't want the rest of the world to impinge upon this enclosed private bubble of time with just the two of them there. He gave the Bullnose an offhand, prevaricating polish. Amy, sitting in the passenger seat, was fiddling with her shoulder bag.

'What are you doing?' he asked. Funny, he already seemed to know.

'Skinning up.' He looked puzzled. She explained: 'A toke. Share one with me?'

'Is this marijuana? Good God, Amy, that's against the law. I won't have it. I won't have you doing this.'

'Get real, Norman, driving above seventy miles an hour on the motorway is against the law, but everyone does it. Everybody does this too.'

'They don't, my girl.'

'Well, there's a thing, my boy.' She was carefully tonguing the edge of various small pieces of white cigarette paper together in a complicated tissue raft. He was fascinated by the work of her deft fingers and the sideways flick of the very tip of her pink tongue on the papers. It felt like a ceremony. Her neat nails split open a cigarette and she tipped the contents on to her paper construction.

'So you've never done drugs?' she asked.

'Of course not. What do you take me for? I'm sixty-nine. I'm not one of your old sixties hippies. I served in the war. Just.' He tried to excuse his conservatism. 'It's dangerous.'

'Everything's dangerous.'
'That's simplistic. And not true.'
'What about alcohol?'
'What *about* alcohol?'
'Dangerous?'
'Yes. It can be.'
'So?'
'So, nothing.'

But he knew he couldn't stop her. In fact, he found he didn't want to. While she concentrated so resolutely on what she was doing, it allowed him the liberty of watching her hands neatly at work, poised on her knees. He could peer into her jacket, watch her jaw flex her cheek muscles, consider the curved line of her eyebrows, allow his eye to embrace her tumbling hair. She rummaged in her shoulder bag and brought out an absolutely tiny, red, enamelled tin with a hinged lid, out of which she took the smallest clingfilm-wrapped block. It wasn't quite as big as an Oxo cube but looked very much like one. 'Cannabis resin,' she explained. 'As rolled on the smouldering thighs of Moroccan farm workers. This stuff's fairly galactic. But then I've never known a dealer who didn't mention that his latest batch of blow was rather special.' She clipped her lighter into flame and played it underneath the unwrapped resin, crumbling the outcome along her waiting cigarette. 'Pot,' she said quietly. 'About as evil as Pot Noodles. Less probably. Your kids must do dope though, eh? Mustn't they, Norman?'

'Kid. There's only Joan. She wouldn't have. Of course not.' He was aware of the delicate silence of the barn, the two of them there, in that enormous, ancient, empty space, totally focused on the tiny ritual taking place on her sharp knees, at the behest of her fabulous fingers.

'No,' snorted Amy rudely, seemingly recalling his daughter. 'No, I suppose she wouldn't. What about Fran, though?' They were speaking very quietly.

'Who knows? She mixes with musicians, I suppose.'

'Well, you mix with film people now, Mr Ranburn. Watch out. Are you about to become corrupted? They do coke and everything. Des is always saying how hard he finds it trying to get those cans up his nose.' She had rolled the long white paper into a thin elegant cone. 'A spliff, Norman,' she explained, waving it about between her first two fingers. 'Now a little roach and it's camera, lights, action. God, that'll be cool.' She rolled a torn strip of her orange Rizla packet into a tiny column and pushed it gently into the end of her cigarette. The careful insertion of the cardboard with articulate finger ends was genuinely arousing. Norman found that he was hardly breathing.

'Come and sit up here,' she muttered, patting the driving seat next to her. She tucked away the various bits and pieces that she had been using and flicked the lighter into use again. Norman felt nervous of the flame so casually ignited inside his precious motorcar. But he also felt very strongly that he would like to sit beside her. She lit the thing, pursed her wicked lips and drew hard on it, the end glowing in the comparative gloom. She dropped her head back, her hair hanging down behind her seat. He felt absurd sitting there next to her, both of them contemplating the empty barn wall just ahead of them through the windscreen.

Amy released a cloud of smoke from her lungs into the air above their heads and smiled beatifically at him, the edges of her fluid mouth seeming as if they were trying to lick her earlobes. There was a strangely sweet smell, which must have been the burning of the resin. She murmured a gentle, comfortably sighing groan. 'That's so fucking dreamy,' she whispered. She held the thing upright, like a little smoking lighthouse, between her fingers and thumb, offering it to him.

'No thanks.' he said stiffly.

'Oh come on Norman, live a little.'

'No, I'm all right. I live fine, thank you.' She dragged on the thing again herself. 'Join the party,' she said without very much interest. She had sunk down in her seat, her knees up and her head thrown back, staring up into the distant rafters. The pigeon fluttered from one of the roof trusses to another. Outside, other pigeons were doing comfortable cooing. It was as if the two of them were in an enclosed capsule together. The world outside hardly existed.

Her jacket had fallen open and Norman could not stop himself from glancing sideways at the pink shift that hid her breasts. They were never going to be magnificent orbs like Lesley-Anne's but, nicely, they seemed to require no support. And, as before, on that astonishing day in May, in the punt, her smooth feminine curves were triumphantly surmounted by two of the sharpest pinnacles. They appeared to scratch urgently at the inside of her vest. For a good minute her chest was magnificently on view, arched out before him in the car, clearly delineated in every detail, inches away from him. Then Amy slowly brought her head back upright and, probably seeing where he had been looking, pulled her jacket together in front of her. 'Tell you what,' she said quite laboriously. Then there was a long silence as she considered what she might be going to say. 'I'll offer you a challenge. A, um, tit for a tat. I do something for you. You do something for me.'

'What?' he said, immediately wishing it hadn't sounded so peremptory.

'I'll walk one of your beams.'

'You'll what?'

'Your roof beams, Norman, your roof beams. Up there. They hold up the roof. Purlins, you said. Trusses. Whatever.' She pointed a long thin arm randomly above their heads at the shadows of the roof. 'Up that ladder, walk across the beam there.' She pointed at one of the collared trusses that stretched from one side of the barn to the other. 'A "tight-beam-walk", it'd be called. Walk one of your beams, Norman. All mega-history of them. All the jolly old Wars of the Roses of them. All the Princes in the Tower of them. Now. Just as I am. I do that. Then you do something. Well, better yet, you and I will do something. Together. You and I will share a joint. Simple. New experience for me. New experience for you. What do you say to that, Mr Ranburn? What do you say? Is it a deal? Do we have a deal? A galactic little challenge for you. And a galactic little challenge for me.'

The girl was nuts. But then he knew that already. Actually, the idea of the girl climbing the ladder in her itty-bitty skirt was pretty appealing. 'All right,' he said, surprised by how quickly he had reacted. He wouldn't have to inhale anyway. Bill Clinton hadn't.

Amy was out of Bertram in a flash. The aluminium extending ladder was, by chance, virtually in the right place for the beam in question. That had probably given her the idea. Norman stood by the car. She reached down to remove her shoes. He would never know what got into him: 'No,' he said firmly, 'in heels.' She looked back at him, over her shoulder, on one leg, her hand gripping the ladder. 'You said you'd do it as you were.' Why did he want that?

'Shoes on?' She stood there looking at him, the light of battle in her eye. 'That's cool. My, my, Mr Ranburn, there's an itsy bit of wickedness in there somewhere. You're something of a bad hat underneath it all, aren't you? OK. That's cool. But, in return, you make fucking sure you inhale.' She could read his mind. She seemed exceptionally pleased by his sudden surprising stipulation. It meant he was playing her game with her – taking part. She obviously adored a fight. That was why she was here in the barn with him. He was what she would no doubt regard as 'an old fogey' and she was amusing herself, with what? Turning him on? Wasn't that what they called it? She looked over her shoulder at him again. 'Jacket off all right?'

'Oh, I think so.' He knew so, he knew so. She dropped the jacket off her shoulders, folded it and laid it across the handles of one of the big motor lawnmowers. She turned to him briefly and dropped him a swift curtsy as if she knew she was partially displaying the upper parts of her body. The extended darknesses of her nipples showed clearly against the silk of her top. Her shoulders and upper arms seemed all the more startlingly naked for the brief scrap of material that they supported. Her collarbones looked positively sculptural. Her arms looked surprisingly strong.

She hitched at her skirt, assured herself that the ladder was firmly lodged at the top and climbed quickly up it on the toes of her shoes.

Was this being stupid? Could she manage it? It was quite high up but once up there it wasn't very far to the other side. Presumably, though, she would have to turn around and come back. And remount the ladder. And he had no idea how her judgment might have been affected by that roll up of hers.

When her hands reached the top of the ladder, she barely hesitated. She clambered up the remaining rungs of the ladder as far as they would go, while holding on to the top of it with both hands – her bottom sticking out into space. Norman began to think that if she fell now she would probably hurt herself. She was such an impetuous fool. And it would be entirely his fault, letting her do it. This was stupid – they were grown adults. What was going on here?

He had a sudden vision of them both in casualty at the Radcliffe Infirmary. Waiting dolefully. Embarrassed. The doctor saying: 'And you're a responsible adult, are you Mr Ranburn?'

Amy squeaked and hoicked one leg up sideways on to the main cross-beam, which was at about hip height. She took hold of the rafters above her head to get a better, higher purchase. Momentarily, to Norman, she looked just as she had when she had mounted her Mazda earlier in the day. It was difficult for him to see anything very clearly up there against the myriad pinpoints of sunshine.

Norman circumspectly moved one of the hand-mowers away from the area directly underneath the beam.

'What are you doing?' she squawked.

'Clearing things. Don't want you to hurt yourself.' He picked her jacket off the handle off the other mower and held it over his arm, like a second at a duel, at dawn. 'I'm sorted. Don't you panic, Mr R. Piece of piss.' He wasn't so sure. He brought the jacket up to his mouth and nose. All he was good for – inhaling women. She smelled of angels, musk, summer, youth, forget-me-nots, lust.

It was quite a step to get the whole of her spare frame up

on to the beam from the top of the ladder. It was all to do with the logistics of transferring her centre of gravity. Dust showered down. 'It's yucking dirty up here,' she gurgled. 'Don't you ever clean up. Smeggy bastard.' She was standing on the beam now, her hands supporting her body, on the roof struts, high above her head. She was wearing plain white knickers. He could see them quite clearly.

'The top of this beam is bloody curved. That wasn't part of the frigging deal.' Her muttered voice echoed dryly about the roof space. She sounded preoccupied and was talking more to herself than to him. She was going to have to let go with her hands to walk across to the other side. Perhaps he should tell her to come down now. She had done enough. He'd smoke her rotten drugs. In fact he was actually intrigued to see what might happen if he did.

But at that moment she was off, her sinewy white arms outstretched either side of her for balance, placing each high heel with precise deliberation out in front of her on the ancient timber. He was startled by the hair at her armpits – he hadn't noticed that before. Three quick steps and then a horrible hesitation two-thirds across before she was suddenly holding on to the roof rafters at the other end. Dirt continued to descend like a sooty snowfall. Amy looked thankful. But how, in heaven's name, would she turn around and get back?

Then he saw what she had probably noticed from the very beginning of the dare – there was an old rope hanging down, tied on, bundled up into the rafters. Probably rotten as hell. She pulled it out. Its end hung to about six foot above the floor. Norman shouted 'No!' just as she put all her weight on it and slid down with her kicking feet splayed out miles apart. She dropped off the end of the rope, and dusting the filth from her hands, demolished him with a gargantuan smile. 'How's about that then?'

'Arthur's picnic, I expect,' he said to her solemnly. 'God, Amy, look at your clothes. You're filthy.' She was – every part of her was wiped about with centuries of grime. 'You can have a bath. I'll get you something to wear. I've got some nice old-fashioned collarless shirts. Girls wear them now, don't they?'

'Oh no, no, no.' She stalked back to Bertram, sweaty and dishevelled, tucking her white underwear away under her skirt. 'Now we do drugs,' she said with frightening determination. He had no choice in the matter.

Once more Amy and he sat together, side by side, a foot apart, in Bertram's comfortable bucket seats, facing the blank wall. This time both of them would break the law. Once more, he watched her fascinated, as her grimy fingers went through their ritualistic task. When the thing was ready, she lit it and sucked long and hard on it. Her face was crusted with a rime of dry sweat and dust. She checked the burning end, tapped off some of the surplus ash and passed it over. He took it from her cold fingers and tried not to let his hand shake. Norman was probably as nervous of the tobacco that it contained as much as anything. He had managed, with the greatest possible difficulty, to give up smoking cigarettes some twenty years before. He didn't want to find himself tumbling back to that addiction all over again.

He liked the business of passing it backwards and forwards to her. He liked his lips feeling the damp of hers on its butt. He had decided that, if he was going to do this, he might as well inhale the smoke properly into his lungs and hold it there, and see what happened. After all, this was a one-off. But nothing did happen. It didn't seem to do anything for him at all. It felt relaxing and that was about all. Smoke billowed between them and sailed aloft like a half-hearted mirage. Norman was disappointed that he didn't experience any fabulous exploding hallucinatory moments. What was all the fuss about? Maybe for some people this cannabis stuff just didn't work.

They sat silently together in the open car, passing the thing backwards and forwards resolutely. Amy occasionally glanced at his face to see how he was doing. He could get to like the ritual of it. He liked the touch of her fingers and the manipulation between them of the diminishing joint. He liked the tiny journey of that thin red glow as he awaited his turn. The beam-walk had taken it out of her and Norman had nothing special that he wanted to say. When the joint was almost used up and she was squeezing the last puff out of the stub, holding it with the very tip of her fingers, she closed her eyes and looked blissful. 'It always goes straight to my clit,' she murmured to no one in particular. She was always so execrably rude, was Amy.

Then he said he would take her into the house to find her something clean to wear.

He had a great deal of trouble walking in a straight line.

She giggled at him and, marvellously, held on to his upper arm with both hands and walked him through the afternoon sunshine to his front door. He had an acute attack of the rubber legs. He suddenly felt totally out of touch with reality. Everything was nicely distant, like watching the telly without his glasses on.

They negotiated their way into the house under a blameless blue sky, to a background of her laughter. Norman was so taken up by a general feeling of wooziness and a severe need to sleep that he took absolutely no joy out of the fact that Amy was prancing about in his very own bedroom in her ruined suit. Having found her a shirt, he found he was lying on his bed, taking very little notice of anything that was going on around him. He had the vaguest notion that Amy had drifted along the corridor to his bathroom to give herself a bath. At one stage he thought she came back wrapped up in one of his big white towels – all bony brown shoulders and a shiny helmet of wet hair. He seemed to remember she just smiled at him peacefully, but didn't say anything. He realised at that moment that he loved her. He was such an old fool. Pathetic.

Half an hour later he felt peckish and found that his body was in reasonable working order again. Amy came down to the kitchen where he was making toast, looking adorable and about sixteen years old, dressed in a long, white, collarless, tailed shirt, bound at the waist with a chiffon scarf and not a single shirt-front stud to be seen. Delicious. She looked scrubbed squeaky clean with not a vestige of make-up, and had pinned her hair up again. Norman felt prodigiously happy. Life was worth living. Outside the kitchen window, the day was perfect. The sky had not one solitary cloud. There were still two magpies lurking in the big cherry tree on some nefarious, piratical raid of the orchard. Two for joy. Two for joy. His shirt looked suspiciously like the only piece of apparel Amy was wearing.

'"It looks even better on a man",' he quoted.

'What?' she said, unashamedly stealing one of his Marmite toast soldiers.

'Van Heusen. It used to be their advertising slogan. They make shirts. They would have posters of this very attractive girl looking as if butter wouldn't melt in her mouth. In a man's Van Heusen shirt. And they claimed that it looked even better on a man. Of course it didn't.'

'Turn you on, did it?'

'I expect so. I was younger then, you know.'

'You don't get turned on any more then?'

'All I'm saying is that I was younger then.'

'I suppose you might have been. In years. I think you're getting younger every day, at the moment. You'll be bloody bearable soon, Norman.' She was eating all his toast. What was going to happen next? Would she go away now? He badly wanted her to stay. He wanted them to revolve around each other a while more – always that careful half-yard apart – perhaps for the whole of the rest of that heavenly day. Could he ask her out to dinner? Men did ask young women out to dinner, didn't they? There were some lovely places to eat out in Oxford and in Woodstock. It might almost feel like a sort of a date.

But she probably had a boyfriend, or, oh God, a girlfriend, that she needed to rush off back to. Someone young. Someone her own generation. Yes, that would be it. That would be her game – get an old gentleman overexcited, teased, desperate, and then go off and chortle with your hirsute, dashing young man as you and he lasciviously screw the night away. Why else was she here? He was just a light diversion for her, nothing more. Maybe nothing was happening here between

126

him and Amy at all. Was this occurring only in his own head? Maybe he was entirely mistaken and, if the issue were ever to be raised, she would be appalled at the notion. For her, it was just a pleasant afternoon with a nice enough and apparently solitary old chap, nothing more, nothing less. She would say that he had just interpreted the signs all wrong.

Worse, she could possibly see him as the genuine pawn here. A kind of joke. Well, what else could it be? Why had she spent so long with him? What was all this about? Perhaps she genuinely liked him. How could she? Why?

Was she looking for her father? He had often heard that sometimes these young girls were looking for an acceptable father-figure.

Perhaps she had him marked down as a very useful sugar-daddy. 'I'll have to go and find myself a very old millionaire.' that's what you heard them say, these women – he had heard. Eartha Kitt, wasn't it?

'What are you doing tonight?' he said, sounding and feeling incredibly foolish.

'Why?'

'I wondered if you might like to have dinner with me? There are dozens of excellent places in Oxford. Places where buttonless shirts are absolutely *de rigeur*.'

'No thanks.' She said it quite cheerfully and turned to wash up the toast plate and the tea mugs. He wanted to ask her why. He wanted to ask if she was busy. He wanted to ask what she was doing. But instead he went and stood on the kitchen doorstep and looked across at the brilliance of his herbaceous border. And the hill behind. And the sunlight on those green, green leaves. The landscape seemed to glow less vibrantly now. Ah well, he thought, it had been fun. He was going to Lord's the following day. That was something to look forward to. Forget all this.

'Lord's tomorrow. Should keep fine,' he said, apropos of nothing. Apropos of everything. He always talked about the weather a lot more than it deserved.

'Oh yeah. You're getting your cricket fix tomorrow, aren't you? Who're you taking?' She was putting things away, wiping down surfaces, clicking drawers open and shut. A surprisingly busy little housewife.

'No one. I'll no doubt meet up with some of the regulars. Lots of familiar faces. Cricket, lovely cricket. I'm stupidly overfond of it. Always have been. It's, er, finger-licking – for me, anyway. Almost a way of life.'

'For sure. Easier than life – all you have to do is watch,' she scoffed.

'Yes, I think I like that.'

'I expect you do,' she said, almost significantly.

'You no like?'

'What? Cricket? Get a life. I'm a New Zealander. I've no choice in the matter. When I was nine, I used to recite the seasons's batting averages before I went to sleep at night.' Her head was in a cupboard. 'Can I come too, then?' His head sang with joy. But he kept so calm and realistic.

'What? To Lord's?'

'Yup, to your stupidly overfond cricket.'

Oh, how very much he would like that. To walk around the Lord's cricket ground, meeting various old cronies, with Amy on his arm. That would be paradise. But it wasn't practicable. It wasn't on. He would never be able to carry it off. And, what's more, the big treat for him about being at the match was watching from the members' pavilion – that's what he had looked forward to all year. He wasn't going to give that up now. He couldn't.

'No, I'll be in the pavilion. You'd have to be a member, I'm afraid. To get in there. Even if I could get you into the ground on a returned ticket.'

'Can't I join?'

'Nothing in this life is as simple as that, Amy. There's an infinite waiting-list. Twenty-eight years it is at the moment, I believe. Some fathers used to put their sons down on it at birth. They don't allow that any more. Apparently lots of the sons turned out to loathe the game. Wouldn't be seen dead there. And there's one minor detail that might mean that you don't qualify anyway.' He concentrated on where some of her hair was coming untucked from its clip and stroking the nape of her neck. He laughed. 'It's chaps only. In the pavilion. Men only. Apart from the Queen. You aren't a chap, are you Amy? Or the Queen. As far as I can make out.'

'I went out with Freddie Mercury a couple of times.' He had a vague idea what she meant by that – he was a singer, wasn't he? 'You could sort it though, couldn't you?' she went on. 'You'd know who to jump on from very high. One can always get on the guest list. We could blag our way in on the door.'

'I rather think not.'

'Smegaroony.' She wrinkled her nose disapprovingly. 'All right then, Norman, I get the general idea – I have to be one-hundred-per-cent male and I have to have a membership card?'

'Right enough. Sorry.'

'No prob then.' And she laughed. 'Tell you what. Shall I drive you down to the smoke – St John's Wood, isn't it? You'd love it in the Mazda.' His pulse started charging along once again. Did that mean she was thinking of staying at the Aviary overnight? Then she said: 'I could come and pick you up at the crack of sparrows.' He was briefly terribly disappointed. The idea of her sleeping under his roof, no matter how many rooms and how many firmly closed doors away from him, had appealed to him immensely.

'No, it's all right,' he said. In truth, it wasn't all that useful being driven down by someone else. There was nothing worse than coming out of Lord's at the end of a day's play and having no vehicle in which to escape back to Coombe. The idea of that grimmest of evening return journeys by rail was anathema.

Norman was still smarting from the fact that his dinner invitation had been turned down. He had had to steel himself to ask her. It had seemed as if there might be some vague sorcery in the air between them. He was hurt by how abruptly it had been made clear to him that he was wildly mistaken in this.

But. But. It suddenly turned out that he might not have been as mistaken as he had thought. 'I'd like to take you,

Norman,' she said very coolly, almost as if it meant something else. She had suddenly stopped being all useful and housewifely and was giving him her speciality, her third degree – the long slow grave eyeball-to-eyeball look. Lots of deadpan consideration. And it was smoulderingly sexy. Or just a touch vacant. He couldn't be sure. He took in the narrow centimetre strip of her body where the front edges of his shirt failed to meet properly. One could see straight down this brown curving pathway of skin, all the way from her sharp collarbones to the unseeing eye of her navel. She seemed to be pushing her tummy at him across the empty kitchen. 'No,' he said. But with very great difficulty.

'Right, this is what we'll do. I'll deliver you at your precious Lord's tomorrow morning in my neat new car, and then, in return, I'll let you take me out and spend vast quantities of dosh on dinner for me at the end of your ripping, gripping day. And I will wear the dress to die for. How's that? What about that? Like it?' The idea was terribly appealing. No matter how England did in the game, the day would have a treat in store for him.

'What's the "dress to die for"?'

'It's so fucking neat. It hides what it reveals as it reveals what it hides. In its presence, men have been known to pass away from excess of pleasure. But it is well smart and decorous. Vulgarity it ain't.' It sounded like paradise. And he deserved a touch of paradise. It would be just so lovely for people to observe him with this astonishing-looking lady – and in 'the dress to die for'. He would give it a go. He grinned sheepishly. 'Oh, all right. Do you really want to do that? I'd need to leave at quarter to nine in the morning. I wouldn't want to be late.'

'No, you certainly wouldn't. I can see that.' She so enjoyed patronising him. 'OK. I'll be here. It's cool. I'll go now.' In spite of her flip response, she looked very pleased that he had changed his mind. Now she was going – and fast.

'Are you sure? It's awfully early.'

'You betcha. I do something for you, you do something for me. It's how we operate. You and me.' It was very difficult to stop the last three words from thrilling him. Without knowing it, he seemed to have become part of something called 'you and me'. She assumed a hell of lot, did Amy. He loved that.

Five minutes later she had driven away with a cheery wave and gargantuan throttle noise, leaving a lot of rubber all over his stable yard. Norman made some more toast. He hadn't the heart to cook anything. He felt so tired by the day's events. Toast would have to do as an evening meal. Toast and peanut butter, toast and Marmite, toast and blackcurrant jelly – a veritable three-course meal.

He decided to have a bath. It would, of course, be the very bath in which presumably each bewitching limb of Amy's naked body had so very recently been immersed. He took his clothes off in his bedroom and solemnly looked at his tall, pale body in the mirror. It was very different from the example of eager perfection that had been his company all day. He had never understood how anyone could ever feel sexually excited by the prosaic dullness of the male body. Any male body really, even a fit young one.

How is it, God, he thought, that you managed to make the crook of a little finger, the crease at the corner of an eye, the turn of a neck or the down on a forearm of a woman not just aesthetically pleasing, but also devastatingly compulsive? Why is it that a young woman's not really half-hidden cleavage could be so undeniably attractive when, for example, the low-slung bottom-cleavage of the jolly male building worker so deeply repugnant? After all, the proportions, the shadows, the actual fleshy mounds are very much the same in quality and size. And also, how is it possible, God, for this young woman's shoulder or slender upper arm to provoke such urgent lust, while for some reason of alchemical wizardry, other women's similar proportions don't? What precisely is the psychochemistry at work here? Or is the whole rigmarole purely learned conditioning? Is it years of training that's made men want to follow that beautiful girl's *louche*, oil-slick hip movements down the street while giving that other female's less archetypical femininity scant attention?

And when that woman's eager energetic smile or that other girl's crossed thighs develop a 'want' in their observer, what really is that 'want'? To own her? To place one's hand upon her? To have her around for daily observation? To possess her? To destroy her? To screw her? To please her? To run one's stiffened penis against the part of her that turned one on the most?

No, God, it must be the need to communicate with her, mustn't it? For ever. Or, at least, for as long as that supernatural chemistry continues to appertain.

God had set up all these infinite little lust traps for the male and thus life around women would always be about running the gauntlet of those triggers without allowing oneself to be shot dead by them. And that had never seemed fair. His invention of Onan Cottage had been an attempt to thwart God in his trickery. Onan Cottage had been intended for Norman to be able to relax and enjoy the sexual ambushes that God had set up in women for man's psyche without ever making a fool of himself and without ever damaging anyone.

Pity it hadn't worked. Or he might not have got so damned obsessed with this dratted twenty-four-year-old. A twenty-four-year-old who could out-stare the Sphinx.

In the evening, he decided he ought finally to respond to his daughter's angry letter. He had neglected it for about two weeks. He had been very preoccupied. He called her up. Well, he wasn't going to start writing Joan business letters.

'Grandad!' Francesca answered the echoing phone in the hall in deepest Cheadle Hulme. It didn't sound as if she was exactly laid low with unhappiness at his intransigence. She even sounded quite perky.

'Is your mother there?'

'No she's out at aqua-aerobics still.'

'Aqua-aerobics?'

'It's where they all bounce around together standing in the shallow end of the baths. It looks a bit loopy. She says it does her good.'

'She wrote me this letter about your Synchromesh thing.'

'Did she? I didn't know.' He couldn't be sure if that was true. 'Could you say I rang?' he said. He hesitated over whether he should involve his granddaughter directly in these conversations about money. 'You know, Fran, I just want to say that I'm sorry I can't be more forthcoming about the studio. I was going to say to your mother that I've thought about it a lot but that I still don't think I can very easily come up with precisely what she wants – what you both want, I suppose. As you know I will always stand as guarantor for you at the bank. It's almost as good.'

He could virtually hear Francesca considering what she could say to him about this. She had two mangled attempts at a sentence and finished up embarrassedly: 'Look, it's OK Gramps. Mum just gets in such a state about it, that's all. Particularly, well, particularly since Dad went off with the Dutch Crap. Whoops, sorry Grandad. Anyway she's giving Dad just as much grief about it as you. I think she's just awfully upset. And won't say. It's probably, like, her way of coping with it. You know what I mean?'

'Displacement activity.'

'What?'

'Nothing. Are you all right, Francesca? Are you in reasonably fine fettle? In spite of everything?'

'It's fine. Yes, I'm fine.' She sounded tired. 'I've been doing a lot of nights helping down at the Red House.'

'What?'

'It's the studio. It's very good experience, though I don't get paid at the moment. But they're talking about it.'

'Right. Do you hear from your friend, Amy?'

'Amy Shakespeare?'

'Yes.'

'No, not a word. Least, not since we had the picnic. But I'm not surprised – that's usual. I mean, I hadn't heard from her for absolutely yonks before we all met up that day.'

'She was a good chum though?'

'Of mine? No, I wouldn't say that. That's why I was surprised when she rang out of the blue. She was one of the tearaways at school. Frightened me. You know me, Gramps

– at school I wouldn't say boo to a goose. I'm a good bit different now.'

'So it was a surprise, hearing from her?'

'I suppose so. Yes, she suddenly turned up like that, said she'd keep in touch and then disappeared all over again, in a puff of smoke. Fairly typical, I'd say. Why this interest, Grandad?'

'I just wondered, that's all. What's her social situation?'

'How do you mean, "social situation"?'

'I just wondered, you know, where she lives? Boyfriend or whatever?'

'Hundreds I should think. She's spit-makingly attractive, don't you think?'

'I hadn't given it much thought. I suppose she is, yes. I wondered where she got all her money?'

'God knows. She said she was massively in debt. She's still working on a film, I think. She liked you, Gramps. Asked me lots of questions about you.'

'Oh yes? What sort of things?'

'I can't really remember. Stuff about your garden. When you split up with Grandma. About *your* social life, actually. Isn't that funny?'

'Social life?'

'About friends – you know – um, companions. That sort of thing.'

'What did you say?'

'I said I didn't know really. Told her about cricket. And Bertram.'

'Righty-ho. Thanks, Fran. Well' – he had a thought – 'have you got her number?'

'Amy?'

'Yes.'

'Think so.'

'Do me a favour, will you Francesca? Give her a ring. Try and get together with her. And report back. But don't say I said.'

'Why?' Francesca was suddenly fascinated.

'Nothing really.' He would have to lie fairly imaginatively

now. 'Well, her company – the film people – they're coming to film here later in the month. So I met them, to talk it all through. And they mentioned this cabaret show she does. With a friend. I promised to find out more about what it entailed – for a colleague of mine, Gordon Driscoll, Straker Oil. You met him, ages ago. He wants to know. It would be useful to get an unbiased account – straight from the horse's mouth, as it were. If you were to see her again you could discreetly find out about it – anything about her, really,' he said airily. There was a silence on the line as Francesca considered this. Where did her loyalties lie? Not with Amy, apparently, as she finally said 'OK' quite chirpily.

'Thanks. It's not important, but it would be interesting to know more about her. To know how some of you young people fare in the big wide world.'

'I want to drop down to London soon.' Fran sounded marginally suspicious still. 'I'll give her a bell, see what's what.'

'OK. Great. That's lovely.'

'All right, then, lots of love, Gramps.' She wanted to get off the line now, and think this all through. 'I'll tell Mum you called.'

'Yes,' he said, hoping he hadn't mismanaged it.

CHAPTER FOUR

There is neither male nor female: for ye are
all one

GALATIANS 3:28

SATURDAY 22 JULY

About ten minutes before he was expecting Amy to arrive
to pick him up, a young man appeared at Norman's door.
He was a slim and well-dressed fellow in his mid to late
thirties. He wore a beautifully cut, Horlicks-coloured, linen
suit, very good brown shoes, a neat short back and sides, a
dark, clipped moustache and, surprisingly on one so young,
an MCC tie. The man was perched nonchalantly against the
terrace wall, hands in pockets, looking distantly amused
behind dark glasses. Norman had the strangest feeling that
he must have met the man before because he fancied he knew
him. Perhaps Amy had not been able to make the journey and
had sent a friend instead.

Then he saw that the young man was Amy. Well, possibly.

'Good Lord,' he said. 'Amy?' He still wasn't sure. The

young man had a distant shadow from where he had shaved that morning and the moustache looked real enough. But he had Amy's cheekbones and quite definitely her mouth. Yet if it *was* the girl, where had all her lovely hair gone? In fact, where had her exquisite body disappeared to?

'How do you do? Lovely day for the match, eh? The name's Dick,' the young man said in a voice that was a deeper version of Amy's, but with ineffably English public-school tones. For a brief flicker, Norman's brain went into reverse again and it struck him that Amy might, in some strange way, have a older ex-Etonian brother in the Guards or something. And then he realised he was just being a fool.

'Dick,' the young man repeated. 'Not wholly appropriate, I'm afraid. I imagine that's why I chose it. Has a definitely classy ring to it though – Dick Shakespeare. Pleased to meet you.' And lazily picking himself off the wall he came forward and firmly shook Norman's hand. 'What do you think? Hugh Grant, eat your heart out. Orbital, wouldn't you say, eh?' said Amy's own voice.

'Good God,' he stuttered, beginning to see where all this might be leading. 'How did you do it?' he asked, still astonished. 'Why did you do it? Where's your hair?'

'I have this friend called Quentin. As you know. He can do anything – make-up, hair-cutting, all that. Oh, and probably forgery, bank-robbery, lino-laying, president of the United States, plum-tree-grafting, opening for England – you name it, he's probably done it. He's an awfully useful contact and altogether a jolly good chap, don't you know, when not trying to wriggle out of performing with me.' Amy's New Zealand accent had entirely disappeared. She spoke pure and distilled Guildford. Vowel-crunching sounds to T-cut one's ear-drums. 'We've been grafting all night. Launching this fabulous surprise – just for you-hoo. So there you have it – safe, sealed and deceitful – one masculine member of the MCC. Well, no actual member, of course, but at least I've got the tie. I'm a fraction bushed actually, don't you know, what.'

'Oh God, Amy, what did you do all that for? Your hair. It's

of no earthly use. You have to have a membership card too. Oh, you are so stupid. It's all a completely pointless exercise. Good God, Amy, you do really go at it, don't you?'

'As ever. Lemming at a clifftop, me.' Her hand reached into the inside pocket of her jacket and she produced a small, red, fabric-covered booklet. Norman recognised it only too well – it looked something like a fifties driving licence. It was the precious, hallowed MCC membership card. He took it from her. It was made out in the name of Richard A. Shakespeare. It wasn't all that wonderfully done but, for all that, it was still an achievement. Norman wondered how the devil this Quentin character could know what such a membership document might look like. Amy was defensive about his workmanship. 'Yeah, all right, it was a bit of a rush job. We had to get a lot done. It'll be all right if the place is sufficiently rushed and crowded.'

'You've got another think coming, Amy,' he said. 'It's no good at all. You're altogether much much too young. You'd stick out like a sore thumb – excellent disguise or no. No one would ever believe for a moment that you're old enough to be a member. You'd have to be old enough to have wanted to become a member for the best part of quarter of a century. There aren't any members younger than about fifty.'

'I'm a player-member.'

'What?'

'I'm a player-member. Player-members get in younger. Quentin looked it up. I know they'll be suspicious of anybody under the age of a hundred and ninety-four, but they could think I'm a player-member. I think you have to have played in two hundred games.'

'Two hundred first-class games?' Amy grinned expansively at the thought. 'And I still haven't the first notion about bowling a maiden over.' She shrugged. 'But I'm willing to learn. Bring me the maiden, and I will apply myself diligently. Sounds like a spanking good laugh, what.'

Her accent was impeccable. It was just that what she had to say was so nerve-rackingly over the top. Norman found he was sweating at the very idea of it.

'Well, it's out of the question, Amy. Nice try and every-thing, and I congratulate you on your masquerade. It certainly took me in, but I'm not risking my status at Lord's by trying to smuggle you in. If we got caught, I'd be a laughing-stock. It might even get in the newspapers, for God's sake. They're always looking for a bit of tittle-tattle about old institutions like the MCC – particularly at the World Cup. It's just absurd, my dear. Sorry, Amy. Good game – but not on.'

'You don't have to smuggle me in. I'll get in of my own accord. You wouldn't have to be anywhere near me.'

'Well, it's outrageous. It's a scandal. I won't be party to it. I'm just not doing it. That's all there is to it.'

'That's the whole point – outrage. Outrage can be fun. Outrage can be a way of life. In my view. Seize the morning, Norman *carpe diem* – all that. Isn't that what they say at all the best public school dormitories?'

'*Matinam.*'

'What?'

''Seize the morning' – *carpe matinam*. I think.'

'Seize something anyway. Oh, come on, we've been through all this.' Amy man extracted car keys from her pocket and tossed them lightly in the air. 'Right, whatever happens, we've got to go now, or you'll be late for kick-off. We're going to have to motor. Let's do it, Norman. It'll be finger-licking. Fun. And, as they say, girls just want to have fun. Don't wimp out on me, Norman.'

He turned grumpily away from her. So now this bloody girl was jeopardising his day at the cricket. Was there no end to her mischief? Why had he allowed himself to get entangled with her like this? Because, in his darker heart, he actually adored it? He didn't, did he? She sat on the terrace table – an attractive, muscular young 'man', coruscating grey eyes lost behind sunglasses. Her voice softened: 'Norman, Norman,' she said, 'you will have your reward. I'm just so *very* when I've hyped myself up and succeeded in something like this. So stick around, Mr Ranburn – you might be in for a touch of torrid.'

140

'Shut up, Amy.' But he couldn't help smiling at her effrontery. For Norman did find it exciting. He decided to stall. He would think about it on the drive down. Whatever happened, he didn't want to miss the start of play. What she had done was an enormous undertaking and had been carried out with great skill and, no doubt, considerable expense. She had presumably spent the whole night doing all this. It felt like a sort of signal. To do all that she must like him, well, rather a lot. What a delight. What a disgrace. What a disgraceful delight. It did make him feel sexy, though. And young. Well, younger. Finally that's what Amy did – she made one feel excited. And frightened. And younger. And she liked him. That was the best bit.

She sped along the M40 with the top down. Much much too fast. But then certain things are a given and he would never have expected anything less. Norman surreptitiously held on to his seat base with both hands and concentrated on keeping an unflinching gaze forward. He wondered if she was trying to balance the statistics of illegality between smoking cannabis and speeding on motorways.

He enjoyed being in the small enclosed space of the Mazda with her. She smelled more like a young woman than a man.

They were going too fast for him to be able to think very much about what was going to happen when they arrived. As they whirled past the BBC at White City, he shouted: 'You're going to lose your licence.'

'What licence?' she yelled cheerfully. 'What makes you think I've got a licence?' But then she gave him one of her young-man grins and he hoped she was teasing him.

She parked in the minutest space behind the Hilton. The game was due to start in about a quarter of an hour. Around the ground, St John's Wood was seething with folk carrying cool-boxes and wearing odd-looking hats; fathers and sons; game, supportive womenfolk; crazy mad old gentlemen with shooting-sticks; hurrying sporting-media stars. Every kind of Panama hat.

'I'll meet you in the pavilion,' she said. 'I'm going to put the hood back up.'

141

He had an overwhelming feeling of relief that she didn't require him to run the gauntlet with her. He had stopped thinking about the risks. It would be her funeral. He would deny her thrice, if it came to the crunch. He checked with her. 'Do you know where it is and everything?'

She gave him one of her arch drop-dead looks. 'Worry not, Norman, the benevolent Richie Benaud – the man with no ears – watcheth over me. I'll see you in the bar.' He looked at her. She went on: 'Well, there must be a bar in your celestial pavilion in the clouds somewhere, mustn't there?' She added: 'Old chap?'

'What shall I do if you don't get in?'

'I'll get in, even if I have to sleep with all the ball-boys.'

'Amy.'

'What? Don't they have ball-boys? What kind of a game is this? What a frost. What are you taking me to, Norman? What am I taking you to?'

Norman walked through the Grace Gate, past the bustle of newspaper salesmen and ticket-touts and souvenir vendors. He had diametrically opposed emotions. He adored walking in there on one of these major cricketing occasions. For him, nothing could ever match that air of expectancy and tradition. It had style and grace and smacked of everything English that he loved. His very spirit worshipped that virtually unchanging world of blazers, cravats, flannels, flowery dresses, decent standards, courtesy, trust and confidence. As ever, the day promised so many great things. Yet, at the same time, Norman was wretched with fear about what might happen concerning Amy's madcap scheme. Could it reflect on him? Could anybody know? Would she say he had colluded with her? And, if she genuinely couldn't bring it off and failed to materialise, how the devil would he know and what should he do about it? He could see himself in half an hour's time, while Atherton was dashing towards his first half century, scouring the streets of St John's Wood looking for the dratted girl – or, rather, for a distinctly tiresome young man.

Passing by the Lord's Real Tennis court, Norman flashed

his own mercifully genuine membership card as he filtered through the barrage of stewards at the pavilion doors. There was a massive throng of people about. There was such a mêlée that, indeed, she/he might very well manage to gain access. If she did get herself into any trouble he would just keep his head down. Cowardly it might be, but it had been she who had invented the game and she who would have to abide by the outcome.

He adored this building. It was one of his favourite places on earth. Sydney Opera House and the Taj Mahal were knee-high to it. He loved the red-bricked Gothic grandeur of it – it was like a terracotta wedding cake decorated by an unhinged crossword puzzle addict. He doted on the formal exclusiveness of it and its Edwardian eccentricity and its grace. His heart always surged with ecstasy when he reached the top of the four steps beyond the entrance, and there, straight ahead of him, so very close, just the other side of the further glass doors, sloping unerringly down to the right, was the turf on which geniuses like Bradman, Hutton, Compton, Sobers, Gooch and Botham had all made magic. And at its centre, the pitch itself, lying green and rolled and mowed and sparkling and patiently waiting in the glorious sunshine. Two sets of stumps were already set up. Two sets of stumps looking oddly bereft and naked as they awaited the embellishment of the players. England had won the toss and had put the West Indies in to bat. The theory was that during the morning session, the English bowlers would make what use they could of the moisture in the pitch. And, of course, it is often easier for a team to chase a target than to set one up, in the one-day game.

His brother Gilbert thought Norman's love of the game verged on the possessed, but quite apart from the comforting familiarity and the feeling of security afforded by submerging oneself in the game's culture, Norman found in it a compelling metaphor for life itself. For most people, its certainties were welcomed in the same way as performances of D'Oyly Carte Opera in Gilbert and Sullivan used to be. Norman's pleasure, however, was gained from the ineffable way the game seemed to be a allegory of the life struggle, the career pattern, the relationship history.

A cricket match Norman mused, trundles along ball after ball, stroke after stroke, over after over, in what appears to be a fairly repetitive way – there are occasional flurries of activity and, of course, a constant state of intense expectation; but it would appear, to the uninitiated, to offer pretty constant and even dull replication. Yet, at the end of the day, everything has totally changed. So the overall fascination of the state of play never departs – once one knows what's really up.

In this, it seemed to Norman, it was so like one's life – day after day, it trundles along, from toothpaste time to the bedtime chocolate – every day seeming already to be yet another Friday. Surely, it can't, already, once more, be four weeks to Christmas? But, daily, in the course of that apparently unvarying pattern of behaviour, the minutest individual decisions are made and those tiny moments of choice or happenstance can be seen, in the end, to have entirely altered everything one has ever known. A small flick to leg off the last ball before tea from a tired batsman whose concentration has been tripped by the brief thought of his teatime cheese-and-pickle sandwich allows leg slip to steal a low catch.

Suddenly, after an hour and a half of the dourest struggle, the side is two hundred and sixteen for five, instead of two hundred and sixteen for four. In the earlier case, the future looked rosy, all things were possible, the prospects seemed good. Then, seconds later, with no recognised batsmen to follow, the side's expectations suddenly appear pretty dim – everything looks as if it is going to be a struggle. And this is all the result of one fleeting micro-second. In an instant, the whole outlook of the game has massively changed, and everybody watching knows it.

Cricket's possibilities of sudden death could be endless. Rather like life. Watching it could be as bloodthirsty an activity as any in the sporting world. It was a team game with all the one-to-one aggression of the boxing ring. And yet all hedged about with the traditions, manners, style and grace of a sporting Bolshoi Ballet. Norman found it very much to his taste. He might have sadomasochistic tendencies.

Norman looked to his right into the revered Long Room, only to see all his favourite leather Chesterfields already occupied, as were most of the taller viewing chairs. Some of the older members were already asleep. He ducked back into the crowded bar and ordered a sherry.

'Wow, talk about Blazer City!' A familiar young man and rabid motorway driver stood at his elbow. 'And Moustache Heaven.' She had got in. 'Thank God, I didn't shave my moustache off,' she laughed. 'I reckon you're only allowed in if your top lip is discreetly well covered.' She briefly stroked her own with the fingers of both hands and grinned up at him unashamedly. She looked ridiculously young in there among all the tummies and baggy trousers and the heavy percentage of blazers. Norman loved the olive green of the official MCC blazer but there were lots of others too – mostly in smart if positively prehistoric navy blue. 'Sherry?' She declined disdainfully. 'I'd rather have a Pimm's,' she said and, as if with effortless habit, her hand went to her hip pocket and she produced a worn, very masculine-looking wallet. 'What's yours, Norman, old fellow?' said his young man friend. The greying temples had been beautifully done. The hair looked genuinely grey. Norman was horrified by the savage loss of her shoulder-length hair. As they stood together trying to catch the eye of one of the bar staff, he glanced down. Dick Shakespeare had a flat young man's chest tucked behind his MCC tie. How had she done that?

'How the devil did you do it?'

'Simplicity itself, dear Mr Ranburn. The Grace Gate was well easy. There was the dickens of a scrum. They were just taking tickets and merely *glancing* at Chairman Mao's little red books. The pavilion wasn't quite so cushy. I hung around by the souvenir shop until there was a great pack of old gentlemen trundling head down for the pavilion doors and then I burrowed into the middle of the bunch, waved my forgery in the air and, just as I passed the guys in the green battledress, I turned away and said to the nearest old codger: 'Great day for the match, Major Armitage.' It kept my face away from the geek on the door and the guy I addressed was so surprised he upped and died on me forthwith.'

Norman reckoned that a couple of members nearest them, at the bar, were already more interested in the youthfulness of his companion than he would like. Dark glasses tended to be rather frowned upon by some of these chaps. They used to get more than a little exercised when Ian Botham first wore them on the field of play. And Norman's friend Dick clearly wasn't removing his sunglasses for anyone. Norman came to the conclusion that he would be safest if he arranged for them both to take seats outside at the front of the pavilion on the white slatted benches close to the field of play. There, amid the usual burgeoning of gold and crimson neck-wear, other members would be able to see only the backs of their heads. That was unless some wicked TV camera sought them out in the crowd. They might just still get away with all this.

Norman followed his slim-hipped and elegant companion out of the main doors of the pavilion to the seating at the front, not long after Atherton had led his men out through the crowded Long Room and on to the pitch for the start of the day's play. For a while, Amy was absorbed by the cricket and from her boyish appreciation of activity clearly knew rather more about the subtleties of the game than she had allowed herself to admit. Norman slowly began to relax a little. All he had to do now was to keep a low profile and then at some stage in the afternoon they could make their escape. He would be all right. He might not get found out. He even had to acknowledge in himself a marginal enjoyment at the deceit of it all. It was almost enjoyable knowing they were taking all these sniffy officials for a ride.

And he ruefully had to confess to himself he liked being able to spend all this time with her – in spite of the godawful circumstances. Yes, maybe he *was* a closet masochist and had never realised it. Certainly he loved the opportunity of contemplating Amy's sharp knees tightening the oatmeal linen of her suit trousers. He spent almost more time watching her long, fearfully female fingers holding the so far unblemished scorecard than he did the cricket. And toying with the idea of what she must do with those fingers to the men in her life. Or, as she would herself doubtlessly add, if she knew, to the women.

The ground was full to bursting. The stands looked like overflowing multicoloured peanut bowls full of every kind of T-shirt, sun-hat, summer blouse and pinkish torso. At this early point in the day when no one was overheated, sunburnt or drunk, the concentration of the vast majority of the crowd was still very much on the game and its detail. Later on, in the better-oiled afternoon, the crowd might get into the hideous mindlessness of one of their 'Mexican waves'. But for now, moments of applause, appreciation and surprise rolled around the stands with one voice.

Over to his right, beyond where the late lamented tavern was no more, stood the eccentric edifice of the Mound Stand with its tented summits looking more like something delivered on an elephant's howdah than a seating stand in west London. Already the heat of the day was beginning to burn into the crucible of the ground. Norman realised that he would soon have to face the need of relieving his bladder but there was no way that he felt able to leave 'Dick' unaccompanied. There was no knowing what the young madam might get up to in his absence. Norman decided he had better grin and bear it.

At the end of the first hour the West Indian openers had scored twenty-nine for no wicket. Pretty evenly balanced. Not entirely grim from a West Indian standpoint and equivalently encouraging for England. But in the heat, the wicket would be drying out and the going would get easier. And, after all, the visitors had not yet lost any wickets.

However, even the most dedicated crowd needs a bit of easy excitement to conjure with and after the first hour there was a moderate outbreak of barracking about the slowness of the game. 'Sounds like the House of Commons at question time,' murmured Norman's companion. 'They don't reckon on being denied their twenty quids' worth of blood and heroics, do they?' Both Norman and his companion fell to watching other aspects of the day around them – Old Father Time, the wind-vane, forever removing the bails for the end of the day's play, swinging gently at the sober call of a light breeze, the constant ripple in the crowds as tray after tray of lager-filled pint glasses were fastidiously delivered to eager friends and colleagues. Amy was intrigued by the hospitality boxes, crowded with the great and the good, already two or three bottles into the Veuve Cliquot.

'They're all sitting with their backs to the game,' she breathed mystified. 'Prefer their canapés to their cricket, do they?'

'No, they're watching it on their televisions,' Norman told her. Amy was dumbfounded. 'Christ! Really? Smeggy bastards. Why bother to trail all the way up here then? Might just as well have stayed in Sofa City, back in Esher, or Morden, or bloody Braintree, or wherever they dig these jokers up from.' Norman was pleased. He tended to agree. But wouldn't have put it quite like that.

And then, what Norman had feared above all happened.

It was the thing he had been dreading most since they had set out that morning. And it had been inevitable. Before the end of the day, someone who knew him would turn up, looking for a chat. Today's someone turned out to be Gordon Driscoll. Norman knew for certain that Gordon could hardly fail to notice something a bit odd about Dick – after all, just for starters, the delicacy of the young man's wrists alone spoke volumes. Gordon hailed Norman as loud as one dared in that environment and shuffled his wizened frame along the row of benches towards them, while the bowlers changed ends. As he approached them, Norman could feel sweat gathering on his chest. And his heart began to pound. Why had he allowed himself to fall in with Amy's lunatic scheme? He was about to be revealed as a bloody stupid old fool.

Gordon Driscoll would always claim that he had eyes that could root out the very best-looking, most screwable female in any stand at Lord's in two minutes flat. But today, to Norman's intense relief, the man hardly seemed to take Dick in at all. The boy stood and on being introduced, gave

Gordon a firm brusque handshake and then sat back down to watch the cricket, his head marginally inclined away from them. Thank God, not a single pert comment passed his lips. He was a picture of ex-Guards politesse. Gordon, anyway, entirely failed to notice the feminine frame of the young man, hijacked as he was by fizzing concerns all of his own. He had arrived determined to pass on to Norman some uncomfortable news.

It appeared that Gordon's sister-in-law, Jane, had an elderly mother who was in permanent residence at Cowsdown House, one of the Chandos House residential hotels for the elderly and infirm. It stood outside Budleigh Salterton on the South Coast and had been one of Gilbert's earliest conversions of use. Norman had a fond regard for the time when, as the Luttrell Arms Hotel, it had stood proudly amid rolling countryside and guests had strolled in the luxurious rose gardens and played croquet on the clifftop lawns. Now it was full, all year round, with the better-off class of the gaga, not many of whom would ever themselves have the energy to get out to look at the roses, let alone pick up a croquet mallet. But, Norman had to admit that the place was seeing an infinitely better annual profit margin.

Gordon clearly enjoyed explaining that his wretched sister-in-law was deep in the throes of some violent dispute with Chandos House over staffing levels and the quality of care down at Cowsdown House. She was of the opinion that the promised ratio of care-assistant to 'guest' was – during those times when it was not being inspected by newcomers sorting out where they would like their rich elderly parents to get used to dying – severely less than advertised. Worse, this Jane was of the opinion, apparently, that many of the less *compos mentis* residents suffered from some actual neglect – even, Gordon suggested, with hardly feigned mischief, locked away in their rooms for good parts of the day. Norman, of course, knew nothing of this and felt at a disadvantage. He couldn't believe it was true but promised he would look into the whole business with his brother on Monday.

Norman could imagine only too well exactly what Amy

might make of this doleful rumour of perfunctoriness and omission. His distress at what he was being told, together with a desperate need to keep Amy's identity hidden well away from Gordon, meant that Norman found himself almost completely inarticulate. Indeed, Gordon, even asked him if he was all right. And, of course, he wasn't.

Dick's dark-brown public-school voice broke into their conversation from beside them: 'Drunk again, I'd say, wouldn't you, Gordon? It's that kind of time of day.' And they all three laughed in good measure at the young man's brazen jocularity.

At the end of the following over, Gordon took himself away, reminding Norman that he was expecting to see him in a week's time, at his grandson's wedding. Obviously he thought some candid research into the Cowsdown House scenario could usefully be undertaken by then. After all, his sister-in-law, the redoubtable Jane, would be at Charles's marriage and would be more than eager to 'have a word' about her concerns.

Then Sherwin Campbell was out, caught behind. Jack Russell had done his stuff. But it was three-quarters of an hour to lunch and the West Indies, improving, were sixty-four for one. The morning's attrition had virtually petered out and the balance of advantage was beginning to swing away from England. Brian Lara came in first wicket down. He began setting about his task with consummate abandon and at lunch the score was one hundred and twenty-one for one.

Norman had been bothering himself about how to handle the luncheon interval from the moment play had commenced. He had absolutely no desire to parade his 'friend' Dick around the place. It would ultimately lead to all sorts of difficulties and a multitude of unanswerable questions. But could they just remain sitting in their places all the way through the lunch break? Norman himself couldn't, anyway. He badly needed to go to the gents'. He muttered to Dick that he should stay there and stalked quickly off through the Long Room to the toilets. He would be able to return very shortly.

Thankfully unzipping his fly at one of the big urinals, he realised that he had been joined in the adjacent stall by the man he would least want to meet in the entire world – Peter Peacock. This was being a perfectly beastly day. Peter – tall, fair, better-looking than his lamented father but with the same hooked aristocratic nose. White linen jacket, rimless spectacles – something of the look of a fanatic, Norman always thought. Peter Peacock loathed him. And with every good reason. Austin, his father, was the accountant who had killed himself with sleeping pills in Canterbury Prison. Norman loathed himself about Austin too.

'Norman Ranburn,' Peter said significantly.

'Oh. Yes. Hullo Peter,' Norman replied with more confusion than he would have liked.

'Very good morning's play.' They stood shoulder to shoulder ridding themselves of their breakfast coffees. Peter didn't have his father's engaging lisp. There wasn't much that was engaging about Peter.

'Yes it was. Yes it was.' They adjusted their dress as unobtrusively as possible and moved away from the urinals. Then, again in macabre unison, they stood washing hands at the great gushers that passed for taps in the pavilion lavatories. Another man had slipped into the gents'. Otherwise they were alone.

Norman had not clapped eyes on Peter since the appalling business over his father about three and a half years before, at the time of Norman's retirement. Etched in his memory was the vision, in front of twenty or so sadly depleted mourners, in the cloister of Eltham Green Crematorium, of this same young man screaming foul disgusting abuse at him. Surrounded by damp wreaths, wind-blown flowers and the bitterest tears, Austin's son had yelled that the death of his father had all been Norman's fault. It had been one of the most completely awful moments of Norman's entire life.

Now, astonishingly, the man was being almost affable to him.

Then the third person in the toilet spoke. 'Aren't you going to introduce me, Norman?' Amy's masculine figure turned away from the section where, presumably, 'Dick Shakespeare' had been pretending to relieve himself. Norman froze. And could not help but shoot a glance down at Dick's well-adjusted fly. 'Yes,' said Norman, 'Dick, yes, meet Peter.' Actually he did it with some aplomb. Then he did it less well: 'Dick Shakespeare, a colleague, um, friend of Joan's. Peter Peacock, Lefevre Carnegie. Peter's father was a – a treasured colleague of mine. Many years.'

Amy did her solemn 'how do you do?' routine and smirked away behind her dark glasses, which looked frankly absurd in the shadows of the toilet. 'Cork bowled rather well, didn't he?' Norman's young friend gurgled, as Norman himself died all over again. Dick Shakespeare was clearly finding straight-facedness an almost impossible task. 'He' turned to the basins and did much splendid business with soap and taps. Norman felt obliged to continue to show some interest in life. 'How are you doing, Peter?' It was verging on a croak.

'Good. Good. Made a tiny bit of a killing last year. The Diefenbaker business, you know. Very good. Can't complain anyway. You?'

'Retired now. My time's my own. Life shuffles along, you know. Cricket and stuff. Very pleasant, very pleasant.' He embellished the truth a touch.

'I'm sure it is.' Was there a touch of sarcasm in Peter's voice? It was impossible to tell. There must be, surely. All Norman knew for certain was that he had to get them out of there. Dick had finished elaborate hand-washing and now, for Christ's sake, had produced a comb and was combing his hair in front of the mirror. Men just didn't do that, Norman realised. Certainly not when there were other men about in the room to see them. Well, car salesmen might perhaps, and telly people. Not real men. But then Dick wasn't, was he?

The boy finished his ablutions and stood there mutely contemplating the result in the mirror, hands on hips. Again, his whole posture hollered his obvious femininity. Men hardly ever allowed themselves hands-on-hips poses. Norman wondered why that was. Why did men so rarely cock their clenched fists on their pelvic bone like that? Women did it all the time. Dick's body language seemed to be entirely concentrated on announcing: 'I'm a girl, I'm a girl. You've got a randy, evil little girl in here with you, strutting her stuff in the gentlemen's pavilion toilet at Lord's.' And the awful thing was, if he were truthful, the idea of it excited Norman terribly. Excited him and terrified him all at the same time.

'Well, nice to meet you, Dick,' said Peter. Did he slightly emphasise the name? No, probably not. 'I must go now. Back to the evil round. Have a good afternoon, Norman.' And, with a flounce of his fair hair, he was gone. Norman was astonished. The man had been perfectly civil to him. And yet, by all accounts, Peacock abhorred him. It was such an amazing turnaround. Could it be true? Was that whole Peacock episode over now? Could Norman sleep easily in his bed at night, and try to forget all about it?

Amy was drying her hands. 'God what a gonkyfilarious little bum *he* had. For an old guy. Is he het?' she said of Peter. Dear Lord, thought Norman, if Peter was 'an old guy' what did that make Norman? But he didn't respond. 'With bums like that around,' Amy chortled, 'I could gladly lurk about in the loo here all day. But they're mostly going to be your dead average, third-age backsides, aren't they?'

Norman wasn't really listening to his companion's musings about the quality of the members' bottoms. He had been completely taken aback by this most encouraging turn of events with his old enemy. So much so that when Dick informed him they were going to the bar to have a lunchtime bevy, he went along with it. Obviously they could do anything, Amy and he. The bar was absolutely packed. Dick insisted on buying. Nothing untoward happened. Maybe Norman had stopped noticing, but it didn't seem as if his companion was the centre of attention any more. For Norman, things suddenly seemed to have improved. Could Amy be his very special shaman, bringing him nothing but good fortune? And a new acute sharpness of experience? A great shadow seemed to have been lifted from where it had hung about his shoulders for the last couple of years. He felt almost carefree. And, later, a little bit half-cut.

They returned to their seats in the front of the pavilion before play started again. Yes, Norman felt inebriated. He hadn't eaten a thing all day, thus far. So silly. He was stupid about food these days.

He and Dick sat, once more side by side, watching the whole kaleidoscopic panoply of Lord's Cricket Ground in full-scale luncheon mode.

Norman felt a gentle touch on his knee. He looked down. Amy had placed a small capsule there – like something one might take for flu.

'What's that?' he said.

'A Dennis. A Dennis the Menace.' It was black and red. He remembered Joan getting the *Beano* every week when she was little. Dennis the Menace had been a ghastly urchin in a red and black sweater – devilry incarnate. Oh bugger, he thought doomfully, what's she up to now? The two umpires were walking back down the steps of the pavilion followed by the England players. The afternoon's play was about to begin.

'E,' she said.

He knew what that meant. 'Ecstasy?' he asked.

'Just one tab. Kicking. Take it. The afternoon'll sing.'

'Stop it, Amy,' he whispered, virtually imploring her. It had been all right until now. But he didn't want it to get out of hand. So far so good. But no more. This might be getting worse than ridiculous. Let's stop now, Amy, he thought. He'd enjoyed being in the bar with her. He had actually been tickled her masquerade – getting into the pavilion and everything. That had been all right. Once it had been achieved. It had been almost kinky being there with her, surrounded by the grey-haired and balding old codgers who always populated the place, knowing that only he and she in the whole wide world were aware that hidden deliciously beneath her suave suiting there lurked the only pussy in the place. Now it was all going to get out of hand. He was sure of it.

'No, sorry, Amy,' he whispered firmly. She dug a discreet

elbow into his ribs. '"Richard" if you're being all grundyish. "Dick" when you're being my friend.'

'I'm not being your friend. You're dreadful. You are a terrible, terrible menace. I don't know why I put up with any of this.'

'Because you love it. Turns you on. Turns me on, too.' Norman dropped the pill into his jacket pocket. 'Uh-uh,' she said, shaking her head minutely. 'Pop it in. Pop it in. I'm already going. It's kicking stuff. Come fly with me, Normski. Thousands of kids do it every night.'

'Absolutely not.'

'You always say that, Norman. And then I persuade you.'

'You'll never persuade me.'

'Try me.' There was a grumpy silence between them. Then, with them both looking straight out at the game, she started to whisper to him in darkly secret tones: 'You've dug this, actually. I know you. You've liked what we've been doing. You've adored it. I saw you, in there, at the bar, among all those smeggy straights – randy for it. And I've liked doing it with you. It's been Scam City. Don't duck and run on me, now, soldier. It's harmless enough. Have one afternoon of different perspectives, of radically inverted proportions, of proportionately inverted spectacles.' And she giggled quietly. Something was clearly already happening to her own perceptions. 'I've done something for you, you do something for me. All for one and one for all. Awful one.' She wasn't making as much sense any more.

'Sorry, no,' he said very firmly. He hoped there was no touch of regret in his voice.

'That's cool,' she said wearily. 'OK, I'll tell you what's next on the agenda. If you haven't got friend Dennis past your tonsils by the end of the next over, the very next time Mr Lara plays one down the hill to this side of the pavilion here, exactly at the moment the telly has picked us up in the crowd, I promise you, I will take off my jacket, buff up my nipples and rip off this incredibly uncomfortable moustache and go into overdrive flaunting in front of the whole merry derry world.' She let the import of what she had to say filter though. 'I fucking will, too, you know,' she whispered dourly.

'Yes, I know. Yes, I expect you will.' He was sweating.

'Sticks and carrots though,' she said. 'If you can – tonsil the Dennis, I mean. If you stay with the team – us two – then, well, what then?' She considered: 'Yep. OK. I know. We'll do kissing. I'd like to let you kiss me. And I promise I'll kiss you back. The big wet tongue-sandwich job.' It sounded disgusting. Yet, at the same time, the thought of her hard tongue flicking on his had a dreadful appeal. He felt like a young teenager facing the Christmas mistletoe. 'Can't say fairer than that, can I?' she finished, whispering brightly.

Lara clubbed a four down to the Nursery End and reached another quick fifty. The West Indies were starting to look invulnerable – one hundred and sixty-seven for one. And England were now beginning to toil in the sunshine. It was the usual depressing English cricket story.

Her awful drugs might take his mind off it. Or do nothing at all – like that joint thing she had made him smoke the day before. Oh God, he was falling apart with her, losing every standard of decency. Amy laughed gently and added dreamily: 'If your feeble old heart's up to doing snogging, that is, Mr Man.' He couldn't reply. How could he reply? Why did she keep on moving the goalposts? Asking more of him? What did she want from him? What was in it for her?

He made putting the little capsule in his mouth serve as his response. 'Finger-licking,' she breathed. Well, she would, wouldn't she?

As with the marijuana, nothing happened at all. A big fat zero, as Gilbert was so fond of saying. It was simply nothing like what it was cracked up to be. Perhaps it wasn't so scary after all. This was a doddle, he thought. What a relief. He just felt warm towards her. Nicely warm. But then he felt warm to her quite a lot of the time. Without toying with drugs. Even when she was behaving like shit towards him, he liked her more than one might expect. When she was being kind to him, he was totally overwhelmed with feelings of goodwill. She was just a silly mixed-up kid. She was often quite kind.

So he felt warm towards her. Warm. And warm towards the cricket, whoever won.

There must be a better word than 'warm'. But he couldn't think of one. He felt warm to the blessed velvet green Englishness of the vast expanses of grass stretching away in front of him, warm to the piles of jolly colourful peanuts heaped on all sides, warm to the flannelled fools at play at the best game, the best ballet, in all the known universe. God, and how very warm he felt towards the sepulchrally beautiful corner of that single chocolate-brown eyebrow of hers that he could just glimpse at his side. And warm towards all that was joyous and festive and undeniably wonderfully English about the extraordinary place where they were so fortunate to be, surrounded by kind, warm, friendly fellow-feeling, lovely people – warm, warm, warm, warm – proper, nice, kind, English, English, English, polite people that you would like to spend time with, if you had the choice. And he was so lucky because he had the choice. He was the luckiest fellow in the whole wide world, here, now. Here now with Amy. Sorry, with Dick. And the sexy, enchanting, libidinous crook of her astonishingly sleek little finger.

'Libidinousness'. Now there was a word. A much better word than 'warm'. Better than 'sexy'. Better than 'erotic'. Better, incidentally, than 'toothbrush' or 'gerbil' or 'numbskull'. And certainly better than her obscene-sounding 'tongue-sandwich'. 'Libidinousness'. Difficult to pronounce though, even in your head: 'libidinousness', 'libidinousness', 'libidinousness'. 'Libidinousness' and 'Lara'. Two of the most beautifully expressive words in the whole wide work-basket. No, not 'work-basket' – he meant 'world' – 'whole wide world-basket'.

Brian Lara, a man of such charm and delight and smiles and such ravishing inexpressible, ineffable talent. The young black god grabbed the spinner Illingworth by the scruff of his neck and launched the ball in one magnificent disorientating parabola right over the pavilion roof. Right over the whole wide world. Right over the moon. And on all sides men and women of such great good humour stood on their hind legs and cheered to the heavens.

Oh brave new work-basket that had such people in it. How rarely had anyone hit the roof, let alone lost the ball of play somewhere over the rainbow like that? Over the rainbow, over the brainbell. The ground exploded in an incandescent display of colour and light and joy and togetherness, with every single one of some thirty-eight thousand people standing on their hindmost in the blazing, God-given sunlight, roaring their approval at that display of burnished virtuosity.

Music played and lions roared and trumpets blew and angels wept and Norman dribbled man-sized tears down crusty cheeks into the wiry grey jungle of his very own moustache. Just to be there. Just to be there at that moment. He removed his spectacles and clutched his young friend's shoulders to him in the awestruck intoxication of just being there and she turned her head briefly and in the confusion and spaghetti of the excitement planted a neat, dry, chaste kiss on his cheek. And with eyes sparkling, smiled at him with a very complete joy, the edges of her mouth so wide they actually met and tied neat little reef-knots around the back of her neck.

Norman struggled away from her to vouchsafe himself the freedom of a visit to the toiletries and found himself a blessed island of peace in the rhetorical roulade of the Long Room, imbibing the very smell, the very essence of the history of a hundred and fifty years of everlasting cricketing legend, of Victorians caught and bowled, of 'leg-befores' disputed, of 'googlies' and 'wrong 'uns', of Jessop, of Ranjitsinhji, of Truman and Statham, of C.B. Fry, of Dennis Compton, of Learie Constantine, of 'bodyline' and Bradman, of a thousand schoolboy heroes tangled together in his mind deep in the wiry grey jungle of the very own beard of that great, grumpy, giant Doctor W. G. Grace.

He stood in the middle of the Long Room, as enraptured crowds celebrated one of the finest hundreds ever seen on that ground. As Lara's bat was raised aloft looking as broad and as wide and as massive as one of the great collared trusses of his very own barn at Coombe – one of the blessedly walkable collared trusses with skimpy white panties on show for him and him alone – he realised that he had as concrete a hard-on as he could ever remember. It was a tower, a cricket stump, a walking talking desire to make love to the pavilion, to the game, to the moment, to Amy.

Oh God, how he wanted to fuck that girl. And he wanted to tell everyone about it. About that extraordinarily beautiful sylph of a woman dressed as a man. And about the peace he had made with Peter Peacock, and about the overwhelming love he felt for the crook of her little finger and for the arched teasing eyebrow of the most beautiful boy in the whole wide work-basket.

And then Dick was standing there next to him in the gossip, the fervour, the excitement and the rolling rallentando of that famous room.

'Kissing time,' said his handsome, forty-year-old friend with the neat black moustache and the greying temples. 'A wager is a wager is a wager. Yeah?'

'God, not here.' Norman was suddenly very panicky.

'Got it in one. Course not here, Mr Man. They'll all want one. But I've got the very place. Private, discreet, secure, hot and cold running water. Follow me, nice Mr Ranburn. A very-very-nice-man.' And she was gone.

The next thing Norman was aware of was that he and she were closeted together, secured in one of the cubicles of the gents'. He had virtually no remembrance of how the devil he had arrived there. All he knew for certain was that Amy's bleached grey eyes had emerged like two full moons from behind her sunglasses for the very first time that day. Was she a hypnotist? They raked his face gravely as she gravely took his head between her two thin cool hands. She smiled abstrectly at him. She, too, wasn't entirely present. She ran a neat pink tongue along ready lips. 'Enjoy, enjoy,' she mumbled.

Yes, she seemed a little half cut herself – definitely vague, anyway. But vaguely definite too. She raised herself up on to her toes. Their moustaches joined. Her serpent tongue flickered and burrowed stiffly in between his pursed lips and sought out his own. Her lips puckered, worried and nuzzled at him. It was almost as if they spoke to him. Her paradise mouth was his and his alone. Her lips nibbled and opened and closed and chewed and massaged his big tongue in a way that he could not ever remember.

He stopped breathing and felt faint with the heat, shut up there in that tiny space, the lavatory seat cutting into the side of his leg, his back against the cubicle wall. He was so terribly hot, and thirsty – the sweat was running off him in rivers. Her arms were locked like steel cables around his neck and he tried desperately to gather a margin of concentration because then he might be able to sense the shape of her breast pushing against his solar plexus.

Then, finally, eventually, after an eternity, she broke away from him. 'Swanky-doodle. Better than Postman's Knock-and-shit, eh? Knee-tremble City,' she murmured. He stood there, embarrassment washing through him like a river. 'All right?' she whispered solicitously. He assented with a nod. 'Cool?' she breathed to his jacket lapel where her forehead was resting, her hands lightly on his hips.

'Yes,' he muttered inaudibly.

But cool was the very last thing he felt. God he loved this wickedness, this secret – even the crazy absurdity of it. But he was so very confused. Why now? At this late stage in his blameless life? What was it between them? Where was it all heading? And why? Was she just playing with him? Building up to some big humiliation? Perhaps she was up for some macabre bet. In all honest truth, she could hardly find him genuinely attractive, could she? Young Peter Peacock of the 'neat bum' perhaps, but not an old fellow like himself. And, put like that, it actually began to sound somehow obscene. There was something he couldn't fathom here.

Above all, emotionally, he felt demolished by it. Disorientated. Distanced. 'It was that thing,' he muttered in her ear and he raised a hand to give her short hair a reassuring stroke. 'The pill thing.'

'Yeah. Feel the rush.' He could feel her moist breath on his cheek. He wouldn't mind kissing her again. Could he? 'Yeah. You're orbital, Mr R.' Then she grinned wickedly. 'Better than orbital, my friend. My big friend.' And the brazen little hussy wiped a palm across the front of him, seeking out the material about his fly and briefly pushing his erection back up at his belly. She was so appallingly graphic and unashamed. So rude. Her face telegraphed mock apology at his obvious disquiet. 'You are such a lovely, decent, straight man, Norman Ranburn.' She spoke almost voicelessly, the damp of her mouthed words settling on his ear in the darkness of the cubicle. 'Pity,' she added. At least, he thought that's what she said.

Then they were both suddenly aware of the main door of the lavatory opening and men outside, using the urinals. They stood facing each other, frozen, inches apart, her hand on his hip, her nose tilted up, her eyes seeking out his reaction to this new circumstance.

The automatic flushing mechanism in the urinals squished noisily into life. Norman's face must have registered his heart-stopping surprise. Amy's face sparkled with merriment and she reached her lips up to his ear for a moment. 'Cool as fuck,' she mouthed. And then taking his big hand with both of hers, watching his eyes with a kind of droll amusement, she carefully pulled the flap of her jacket to one side and placed it on her shirt, MCC tie and all. He could feel the smooth, warm swell of her breast and, surmounting it, the firm steeple of her nipple nudging at the centre of his big palm.

Then she gave forth to sudden, noisy, mock-orgasmic panting.

The whole of the room was filled with her raucous, obscene breathing. Norman stood there paralysed. He could almost palpably feel the outraged reaction of the members outside, in the body of the toilet. Please let him die now. She was a stinking, hideous, evil degenerate. He was completely mortified. Then, thank the good Lord above, she stopped. She looked triumphant. He gave her a look of such consummate loathing. She stuck her tongue out at him and continued,

God rot her, to look shiny-eyed with amusement. Outside they could hear a muttered exchange and a half-heard off-colour comment about what might be going on in their cubicle. Norman was about to be caught behaving lewdly in a lavatory with . . . with . . . well, with a young man.

So that was her game – his complete humiliation and disgrace.

They heard the toilet door open and close as people came and went, some to use the facilities and others to summon help. This was the end. It was all over for him. He hated this corrupting bitch. She was entirely off her rocker.

A steward's voice came from outside the cubicle: 'Are you all right sir? Anything I can do to help?' Norman prayed: oh dear God, please let me die. They would now have absolutely no option but to exit from their tiny cubicle and face the music. One perverted elderly gentleman and one uncommonly young, remarkably feminine-looking man who would then prove actually not to be a member at all. Norman prevaricated pathetically: 'It's all right. Out in a moment. I'm all right.' Nothing was all right. Everything was insanely wrong. He had been led into a trap, set up and now was burning alive. It would probably reach the papers. Everybody would know. He would have to face sickening public humiliation in front of everyone: friends, colleagues, old associates, family – Francesca, Joan, Gilbert . . .

'Thanks, Dad. You're a star. I feel lots better now. God, I felt so ill. It must have been those boquerones.' Amy suddenly started chatting noisily away like some mad thing. But in a carefully masculine forty-five-year-old voice. A dutiful masculine grown-up son's voice.

She shot back the toilet bolt. Adjusting her tie, she stepped out into the lavatory to face three gentlemen – an MCC official in his green blazer, a white-coated bar-steward and another red-faced old gentleman whose expression was already moving swiftly from blind outrage to intense relief. Amy patted at her mouth with a folded white handkerchief and said in her best old-Etonian voice: 'Oh, I'm so very sorry gentlemen. Meet my father. Came to help me. God, how awful, I have been so very sick. You just don't want to know. Come on, Dad. A breath of fresh air should do the trick now. Thank you so much, Dad. Thank you, gentlemen. A father in a million, I'd say.'

'That's all's well as maybe, Richard. You just eat much too quickly. You always have done. Wait till I tell your mother.' Norman was astonished by his garbled but not wholly unworthy improvisation. He could get good at this. Relief flooded through him. Talk about a rush.

The two of them strode quickly out of the toilet, out of the pavilion and out of the ground. To freedom. You could get away with anything if you had a sufficiently public-school accent.

They walked stolidly on until they were well out of sight of the ground. For Norman, it seemed as if the MCC membership secretary had binoculars trained on the back of his neck all the way – checking his actions for suspected impropriety. They reached a quiet, narrow set of garages called Walker's Mews. Here Amy sat precariously on the edge of a skip, ripped off her moustache and howled with hiccuping, obsessed, ungovernable laughter. Over and over again, she yelped, imitating his gruff tones: '"You eat too quickly, Dickly", "You eat too dickly, quickly", "Just you wait until I tell your mama".' And tears of almost soundless, hysterical laughter coursed down her cheeks. Norman stood alongside her, as limp as a piece of string, both hands grasping the skip's sides. His whole being was entirely flooded with feelings of sheepishness, shock, relief and astonishment. As well as the tiniest touch of pride. He had, after all, done it.

Eventually, Amy tucked her now unengaged moustache carefully into a folded handkerchief and pocketed it. She jumped down, disrobed herself of her jacket and the famous tie and untucked her big white shirt so that it now hung fashionably mid-thigh. She clipped a large, beautifully curling copper fish to each ear-lobe. The young man evaporated and was replaced by a bob-haired, bony young girl whom Norman felt he would like to kiss again. Would he ever get the opportunity?

What seemed moments later, they were sliding through the Soho traffic in her tiny, white, open-topped chariot looking for tea – a granddaughter showing off her pride and joy to an elderly relative. The brief cross-section of narrow cosmopolitan streets that made up Soho was awash, in the sunlight, with tables and chairs and thousands of people, men mostly, and tourists looking lost. The place felt more like the centre of a small provincial French town than prosaic, no-fun, puritan old London. Old Compton Street had entirely changed since Norman had last seen it.

'The power of the pink pound,' she yelped. The place was vibrant with colours and smiles and Viva Zapata moustaches and closely shaved heads. Amy sang to him obscurely as she roared away up Frith Street looking for somewhere to park: 'Isn't it rich? Are we a pair?'

He couldn't grasp what she meant. He sought clarification: 'I'm sorry?'

'Send in the clones,' she shouted, explaining. And it still wasn't entirely clear what she was on about.

She suddenly turned left behind Berwick Street vegetable market, bumped up over a tiny pedestrianised pavement area and sought out a piece of roadway off Wardour Street of which she and a pair of Palladin dustbins alone seemed to be aware. They were parked. She pointed out three grimy windows, above a shop selling drums and big square speakers with 'Marshall' emblazoned all over them, as the offices where she worked.

Then somehow they finished up in a thriving little place he thought was called Patisserie Valerie, eating creamy cakes as if they were going out of fashion and pouring down gallons of Earl Grey tea, squashed together at tables the size of stamp albums.

And he talked to her. Talked at her. Like a dam breaking. He found that he had a tremendous desire to talk, to tell her everything and anything. About his concerns over affairs at Chandos House, about the Cowsdown House rumours, about his uncomfortable feelings *vis-à-vis* Gilbert, about Grace and Fraser, about Joan, about the awfulness of Austin's appalling suicide, about his fear of Peter Peacock, about Fran's putative investment. Endless tributaries of information and worry gushed forth, probably boring the pants off the little lady. But she stickily held his one solid hand among the tea things across the table and listened intently, her eyes glowing as they fastened upon his. About them, the busy crush of people whirled oblivious – waitresses with their little notebooks, actors with dog-eared scripts, foreign students perusing small advertisements, customers unable to find a free table. As far as they were concerned, he and Amy were just two more unexceptional weirdos.

Then he just needed, very badly, to sleep. He had promised to take the girl to the Dorchester or to the Ritz or perhaps Le Caprice for dinner. That had been the deal. But now he was feeling so exhausted he just wanted to lie down instead. Amy said that it was cool with her. He wasn't to forget, she reminded him, that she had been up all night. She was 'zonked' too.

She delivered him to his club. The Reform would have accommodation for him for the night. They were never over-busy at the weekend. The two of them sat briefly together in the car in Pall Mall outside its magnificent Barry-designed edifice. It was late teatime and he was strangely, and prematurely, ready for his bed.

'Where can I reach you?' he asked hesitantly. She smiled mysteriously, looking forward over the steering wheel, suddenly stony-faced, an enigma again: 'You don't call me, Dad, I call you.'

And then she was gone. He didn't remember a solitary thing after that until the porter called him in the morning.

CHAPTER FIVE

But evil men and seducers shall wax worse
and worse, deceiving and being deceived

I TIMOTHY 3:13

SUNDAY 23 JULY

'Sorry to disturb you, sir.' The voice of Clarence, the club porter, broke unapologetically into Norman's slumber from the bedside telephone. 'There's a young lady at the front desk. Asking for you.' Clarence was clearly intrigued by the idea of her. You could hear it in the man's voice. Norman's heart leapt. And plunged. She was back. She must be. He didn't know any other young ladies. Apart from Fran. And it couldn't possibly be her, could it? He gabbled that he would be down in a few minutes. He wished he had a change of shirt. It was quarter to ten. He felt as if he had slept for a week. No toothbrush, either.

She was sitting as far into the Reform Club as any young woman would be allowed on a Sunday morning – something like eighteen inches inside the heavy front doors, under

Clarence's watchful eye. She was flicking idly through some Sunday tabloid.

She had transfigured herself into a vision of flowing white. No wonder the hall porter had been fascinated. She was wearing a floating dress of the most diaphanous texture, covering her completely, all the way from her throat to her ankles. It made her look to Norman's eyes like some kind of virgin bride. God, she so loved being a chameleon. Her face was meticulously made up and, in spite of the woefully short black skullcap of her hair, looked almost wilfully feminine after yesterday, with generously tricked-out eyelashes and scarlet lips. The girl seemed to be able to transmute herself into any image she wanted – Dracula's bride, the devil incarnate, anything.

'Hullo, Dad,' she said, putting the paper aside as he reached her. 'This place,' she whispered, awed, looking up into the towering majesty of what they called 'the saloon'. 'It's a smegging palace and then some.'

'Sir Charles Barry.' She had no idea what he meant. 'The architect. Did this – went home, had tea, and then designed the Houses of Parliament.'

'Orbital.' But she wasn't really interested. 'Come outside,' she said. 'I need to say something to you. Privately.' And she shot the porter one of her fulsome array of rabbit-punch looks.

Outside, it was almost as fine as the day before. Fresher, with a delicately pale-blue sky. Pall Mall was still fairly deserted at that time of day. Her Mazda, with the top now in place, was parked at a characteristically bravura angle, on the double yellow lines. They stood a couple of yards apart on the broad pavement.

'I've prepared what I want to say,' she said. 'It's a speech.' She cleared her throat theatrically, smiled at him and stepped carefully on to the first and lowest step, using it as a tiny stage. 'Norman, I want to say to you that I'm really sorry. I treat you so badly. You don't deserve it. Period. And I don't always want to. Truth is, there's this grundy old banshee lurking inside of me and it gets out of control. Well, it gets *in* control,

I suppose I mean. As I say, you don't deserve it, Dad. You're totally straight – good, kind, tolerant, all that. Halo City. In my view. And I'm sorry if I'm a half-arsed domineering little bitch sometimes. So I've come specially to say that I'm sorry. I ruined your cricket for you yesterday. And that was right drongo of me. But underneath it all, on top of it all, I truly am your friend. Yeah, OK, OK, I know like we're some kind of bizarre collision between *The Remains of the Day* and *Tank Girl* – Mayhem City, all that – but, well, fundamentally, I really think you're just terrific. In my book.' She smiled genuinely at him and went on slowly: 'Kind. Long-suffering. Smart. Funny. All that. In my view.'

She finished. God alone knew what she meant by *Tank Girl*, but he got the general idea. He was pleased, however, that she had read the Ishiguro. And he was very moved by her stumbling declaration. He considered making a little joke about her little tricks making him 'smart' a little, but he rejected it as soon as thought. She clearly wasn't into jokes that morning. Particularly not one of his more abject ones. Something different was in the air as far as she was concerned. As an apt example of this, the next thing she said surprised him.

'Do you like me?' she asked almost imploringly.

'Of course I like you. I'm much more concerned as to how you could possibly like *me*. Surely everybody likes you. You must be, well, one of the most thrilling, original, attractive—'

'Shut up, Dad,' she interrupted him firmly. 'And thanks.' She came off her step and opened the car door for him. They seemed to be going for a ride. When she spoke again, it was grave. 'I'm much more sodding vulnerable than I give out, Dad. People think I'm as old and as secure as the hills. Fact is, I'm younger than the hills.'

The flow of traffic was starting to build up as it hurried down Pall Mall towards St James's Palace and points west. Norman began to feel absurd standing by her car under the curious eye of Clarence above them at the top of the steps.

He got into the car. There didn't seem to be a lot of choice in the matter. Could all this poignant vulnerability be just one more disorientating ploy? Another role for the quicksilver Miss Shakespeare to explore? She was either as changeable as the breeze or as severely calculating as a witch. Or just a muddled young girl. But so effortlessly beautiful that he was thrilled to be in the car with her again. She smelled of summertime and he hugged himself with the thought that, for the rest of the day, Clarence might be sneakingly envious of one of his more established members.

'Where are we going?'

'Church, of course,' she said. 'It's Sunday.' And, the next moment, all that remained of them in Pall Mall was the smell of burnt petrol and rubber. She always thought she was driving Formula One. Badly.

Once they had settled into the first chicane, he asked her about calling him 'Dad'.

'I like it. It's a groove. Hi, Dad.' She grinned and reached across a bony hand and squeezed his knee. Briefly. 'You no like?'

'I'm not sure. I thought it was just part of your oh-so-wondrously diverting practical joke yesterday, in the toilet.'

She snorted. 'Heart-attack City, yeah?' She decided to show willing as far as some red lights were concerned and they came to a shuddering halt halfway across a T-junction. 'It's swanky-doodle – calling you Dad. It suits you.'

'Thank you.' He couldn't help sounding miffed.

'Better than "Grandpa", anyway. Wouldn't you say?' Amy threw her vehicle into a neat four-wheel drift around Eros the god of love and hurried on up Shaftesbury Avenue. For the moment, Norman concentrated primarily on remaining in the car. 'I've never had a full-time dad,' she bellowed.

'You think of me a surrogate father, then, do you? Is that what this is all about?'

'It's cool. I can't handle Normski as a name. I've got this generational block about it. A Normski-Tebbit-panic-alert situation.' They were now heading for Oxford Street. Astonishingly enough, without a single solitary police car on their tail. 'And I guess I reckon it reminds you that you're going around with someone young enough to be your daughter. That's potential Gloat City, I'd've thought.'

'Am I "going around" with you?'

'That's for you to know and me to find out.'

He guessed that she had picked on All Saints', Margaret Street. He hoped so. From Barry to Butterfield in five minutes flat and – if they lived to tell the tale – a Sunday-morning tour of the great Victorian architects. But there seemed little point in sharing the notion with his speeding chauffeuse – architecture didn't seem to be her thing. He wondered what was.

What might be her thing? What was the catch in all this? Because there must be a catch, mustn't there? Because this girl was an absolute stunner – every man's wildest fantasy, he imagined. In normal everyday circumstances, he imagined that a young woman like Amy wouldn't notice him at all. In normal circumstances, she would be fighting off the attentions, and choosing the choicest, of the most talented, good-looking young men of the nation. That was the way of these things. Like mated with like.

Not, of course, that there was any mating going on here. But there had been some heart-stopping kissing. And, for one wondrous moment, her hand had reached for his trenchant cock. He might be her surrogate Dad but that didn't mean that she was being a hundred per cent daughterly.

Amy had another attack of seriously random parking in the deserted rag-trade streets around the back of Oxford Street, where not a soul apparently ventured on the sabbath. The whole place had an air of severely untidy, empty neglect – an area recovering from the wreck of a week of toil.

He hadn't been in the church since he had been an undergraduate almost fifty years before. Very High Church, of course. Eighteen candles probably. He couldn't remember. All that golden ritual would appeal massively to Amy's love of excess. She'd mop it up. It struck him that, in her floating, white, layered apparel, she looked pretty much like a child up for her first communion. She always needed to play her parts to the fullest extent possible. 'Over the top' – wasn't that what they called it? 'God, I always think this is just such a dead sexy church,' she said as they approached the place and, as if to astonish him completely, she looped one of the flowing veils of her dress over her head like some kind of casual floating wimple. She looked like a very innocent and a very knowing child bride. Or like one of those sexy Scottish Widow adverts, but in white.

An architect friend of his father's had told him what an achievement the very plan of the place was. He remembered, years ago, this man explaining how, because of the surrounding buildings, the light source reached the building from one side only. The site was very restricted yet the place still somehow managed to contain a presbytery, a choir school, a tiny courtyard with a tinkling fountain and this magnificently lofty, square church. The whole conglomeration was constructed in crazy geometric patterns of red and black brick – there was something of the Lord's pavilion about the brickwork. Inside, the church teemed with portraits of medieval knights and their ladies, Chaucerian saints and pilgrims and the Holy Family in every possible and impossible configuration of their story. And, filling all the available space in between these, like a kind of overpowering, sculpted, woven, painted, carved obsession, romped endless intricately patterned leaves and branches and ivy and flowers and bouquets of reeds and grasses. It would be a hayfever-sufferer's nightmare.

Incense hit them like a wall as they entered the place. Norman picked up a leaflet and they filed into the nearest available pew. He glanced at it as Amy sank to her knees beside him and closed her eyes over devoutly entwined fingers. About the abundant display, the brief guide informed him wryly that 'there is evidence that the secret of knowing where to stop in decorative work had still to be acquired.' As Amy would doubtless have put it, he'd go along with that.

It was a modest congregation – two dozen solitary men, some pairs of older ladies and hardly any family groups at all. This was inner-city society at prayer. Amy knew and sang the hymns with a pop-song lustiness that he quickly realised he should have expected from her. Her voice had the cut and curve of a Vera Lynn. And the fervour of a Joan of Arc.

The sermon was given by an absurdly young priest with an abundance of tightly curly hair, a shiny complexion and what Norman assumed were thought of as trendy spectacles. He drew out for inspection the unoriginal notion that, in the twentieth century, people had become vastly overindulgent and, in a world where there was so much poverty and unhappiness, perhaps the Christian will should be bent more to alleviate and less to indulge. As a message, it seemed to Norman, a bit rich to promulgate in the particular environs of this most indulgently ornate setting, wedged, as it was, into the backside of London's Celestial City of Shopping.

But Amy was apparently entirely transfixed by the tidings. Out of the corner of his eye, he could see her eyes moist with concentration, her hands clasped together on her lap in reverent modesty. What mutability. Those were the very same articulate fingers that the previous afternoon had flirted playfully with his most personal part. He was amazed by the extraordinary dichotomy of her character. And of his own too – for he was enjoying being there in the cool and calm of the church. Yet he was the very same N.B.M. Ranburn who had spent two long laborious months disgustingly seeking to invade lovely Lesley-Anne's most intimate privacy. He was, in his own way, as sick and mixed up as Amy. He could not be her judge.

The organ thundered out some towering and enveloping Bach as the congregation slowly filed up to the altar rail to receive the Eucharist. Amy made no move. Clandestinely, Norman watched her as, oblivious of the world about her, her eyes fastened upon the carved toga'd saints arrayed above the altar screen, many of whom were incongruously armed to the teeth with every kind of sword and cutlass. She seemed awfully alone, next to him. And she wept softly.

Eventually she caught his eye and brushed the tears from her cheek with the back of a hand. 'Wet, wet, wet,' she said, and she grinned sheepishly. 'Every orifice.' It briefly crossed

his mind that she might have breakfasted on some passing
stimulant.

They left the church and walked back out into the blinding
midday sunshine, surrounded by tall office blocks and the
backs of department stores. They sat on the small wooden
bench by the fountain in the courtyard. It had a plaque
dedicating it to the memory of a Mrs Eleanor Harvey of
that parish.

Once the young priest and his various acolytes had stopped
shaking hands with anything that moved and smiling inanely
at every one of their departing flock, they disappeared,
the cleric giving the two of them a puzzled wave. Amy
produced her papers. Norman was taken aback by how
much he wanted her to roll a joint. It gave him a joyful
feeling of dark togetherness with her, a touchingly intimate
act. Probably to her it was nothing. But he just loved sitting
watching her clever fingers going about their deft business.
He wouldn't partake this time, but why shouldn't she? There
was a comfortable silence between the two of them. They
were in shadow but the day was exceptionally warm.

'Dad?' she said as she concentrated on fastening her
oblongs of white tissue together.

'Daughter?'

'Tell me about Gilbert. Is he a sexy younger brother?'

'I don't know what constitutes "a sexy younger brother".
To be honest, I shouldn't think so. He's had his moments, I
expect, but he and Mary seem fairly steady. He's not young.'
Norman almost added the word 'either'.

'He doesn't play the scene? In your view?'

'Amy, one day in the far distant future you will find out
that accursed middle age lumbers one with a vast multitude
of responsibilities. One can't live for the appetites alone,
however appealing that might be. You heard what the young
man in there had to say. His sermon seems to have had a
rather short-lived impact,' he observed wryly. Her lighter
flicked her construction into life.

'Would I find him sexy?' she asked, 'Gilbert?'

'I don't know what you find sexy, Miss Shakespeare.'

'You do, Mr Ranburn. Manipulating people I find sexy. Frightening the pants off people I find sexy. Screwing, I suppose, too. Sometimes.'

'Power?'

'Yep, probably.' Blue smoke rose above them in the court-yard, seeking the sun.

'Kissinger said power was the ultimate aphrodisiac.'

'Kissing who?'

'You don't know?'

'Sorry, Dad, should I?'

'He was Nixon's shuttle diplomatist. In the seventies. It seemed as if he was always in the air, flying here, flying there. Trying to bring about peace. Mostly in the Middle East.'

'Subtle diplomatist?'

'"Shuttle". I always had this idea of him in various editions of what they used to call Air Force One, um, well, in the throes of, well, I suppose—'

'Rutting?'

'Amy,' he sighed.

'Well that's what you mean, isn't it? Ruttle diplomacy. Giving it to various bimbette Texan air-hostesses, yeah? The mile-high club. All that.' She turned towards him and ran the flat palm of her skinny hand over the letters of the inscription on the bench. 'But old kissing-gate was right about it being a turn-on. Power. It is, isn't it?'

'I think he actually meant that someone who wears the mantle of power is found to have a vastly added sexual attraction. Mark you,' Norman snorted reflectively, 'I don't think it ever worked for me.'

'I think he meant if you've got power, if you're in charge, if you're doing the steering, it makes you feel dead randy all the time.'

'I don't think so, Amy.'

'Good God, I should know.'

'No, what I'm saying is that I don't think that is precisely what Kissinger meant.'

'You think Gilbert gets randy on power?'

'I think that's overstating it. Being in charge of Chandos

House isn't exactly Ghengis Khan territory.' He was amused by her posture, holding the glowing joint below the side of the seat, inadequately hiding the thing behind her hip, tapping it with a practised finger. If she offered it to him, he thought, he might allow himself another go. After all, he thought, only rarely did these opportunities ever arise.

'But you worry about him.'

'I worry about Chandos House. I think he cuts corners. He's very forceful in his ideas. Very bright,' he added loyally. 'But I don't really have the information, so I don't know what's happening any more. And I can't start prowling around behind Gilbert's back. Anyway if I turned up unannounced at one of the establishments no doubt there would be hell to pay.'

'You need to have someone go and have a look-see for you.'

'Are you offering?'

'I've got a job.'

'Yes I suppose you have – teasing me.'

'Got it in one. I get triple-double payments for every seriously successful torment.'

'Oh, from whom?'

'Big Brother. She Who Must Be Obeyed. The Inland Revenue. Chairman of Selectors. Greenpeace. The usual suspects.'

'But not little brother Gilbert?'

'I shouldn't think so.'

They were sharing the joint now, but Norman made sure he avoided inhaling too much. He had to get home to the Aviary in one piece that day. Eventually she trod the thing under her foot. 'I think I might like to light a candle.' She got up.

'For whom?'

'Never you mind. Some things are mega-private.'

They returned to the cool of the church where the organist had stopped playing and had at last departed. It was strangely quiet inside. Frozen in time. One couldn't even hear what little traffic noise there was. About two dozen candles remained guttering away on their stand, the flickering light making the place seem almost pagan. Amy paid for and lit her candle. They stood mutely together side by side at the altar rail. He felt so very big beside her.

Then suddenly the girl bent double and picking up the hem of her skirts, hauled them aloft, exposing, for an instant, a large expanse of brown thigh. Norman watched as she unclipped a large safety-pin from the edge of her underwear.

'Blood brothers,' she said. The skirts floated back down, hiding her legs once again.

'No,' he said awkwardly. He had been right all along – the girl was deranged. Or, anyway, dreadfully young.

She drew a sharp breath as she banged the point of the pin into her palm. The gasp echoed about the building. 'You?' she offered, holding it out to him. The thing was huge. It must have been a nappy pin and had a pink safety cap over its head.

'Absolutely not.' He was quite determined. He wasn't lancing his flesh for her on some childish whim. Not just because of AIDS, but because it was stupid.

'Grundy bugger,' she said amicably. Fascinated, she held her pierced palm up to her eyes and pressed bright red blood into a little bubble on her hand with her finger. When she was satisfied that she had enough for whatever it was she had planned, she firmly took his big hand in hers, wrapping her fingers between his.

They stood together at the altar steps, hand in hand, silent. Absurd. It struck him that with Amy in her white and he in his dark suit, they must look like an oddly aberrant bride and groom. She kept them standing there for a few minutes. He felt embarrassed but fortunately they were alone in the church. Her eyes were shining with moisture again. Certainly there was a funny feeling that some sort of pact had been made between them. God alone knew what it might be. And He was resolutely keeping it to Himself.

As they left the church, he surreptitiously glanced at his palm. There was a goodish smear of dull dried blood on it. Amy's blood. From deep inside her body. Blood that her heart had pumped around every moment of her every night and day. Blood that had been with her everywhere and knew everything that she did. Blood that presumably sometimes sped with adrenalin, or coasted quietly in sleep, or primed her clitoris, and which some thirteen times a year, evacuated her womb. He had the wild thought that he wouldn't easily want to wash it off.

Later, after another life-threatening journey through London's West End, they were sitting in her car in the covered taxi slip-road beside Paddington Station. He would catch the train back to Oxford. He was about to get out of the car when he realised that she was quietly weeping again, tears dripping on to her dress. She was awfully unstable today.

'What's the matter?' It came out much more brusquely and irritatedly than he had intended.

'I'm sorry.' Her face was wrought with silent crying. He could hardly make out the words. 'I hate it all. I can't bear it.'

'What?' But she just cried and snuffled and arched her head back in her misery, wiping her eyes and nose uselessly with wet fingers. 'What is it?' he said again, more kindly. He wanted to put his arm around her shoulders.

'This smegging need to fucking control. This endlessly itching . . . hunger to, I don't know, to – to manipulate. It's so bloody sick. Sick, Dad, sick. I'm full of shit – a great grundy fucking sickness.' And she cried piteously all over again, keening quietly, her forehead resting on her steering wheel.

He took her hand in one of his but knew there was nothing very useful he could say. After all, she did seem to have a problem. He couldn't say that she behaved like most other people of her age and that it was all right. Because, often, she didn't, and it wasn't. But he was startled by this show of vulnerability. There seemed no question that it was a real cry of despair. Amy wasn't playing any fancy role now. This was a very bothered lady. They sat together silently in the tiny hot car, her fist bunched up, swamped by his. She snuffled and heaved and slowly got herself back together.

She seemed to live so close to the edge of things, he thought, that she might not last all that long. This was a new idea and it shocked him very much. He found himself saying to her that whatever happened he would always be there for her. He did not really know what he meant by that. Finally, she began to mop herself up properly. In truth, she must have pretty well run out of tears by then.

'Could I give you a treat?' she announced, turning to him, eager again. What in heaven's name now? he thought, alarmed. But she was massaging his hand with both of hers and he liked that. 'What about the end of the week? Glyndebourne? You like opera, don't you? Just your scene, Dad. Dead classy – "Nessun Dorma" City.' She was suddenly madly cheerful again. 'I could get tickets. Least, I know a man who can.'

'Quentin?'

'How did you know? You know too much about me, storming Norman.'

'I know next to nothing about you, Amy.'

She hurried on: 'Next Friday. I don't know what's on. But it'd be a good laugh. It's bound to be good, isn't it? Glyndebourne? They're pretty good, yeah? And I've never copped any opera. I could dress up, the full gear, no sweat – the dress to die for. You'd dig that, at any rate. Cross my heart, or hope to die. Go on, say yes. Please, please, please, Dad. My shout. To say sorry about the cricket.'

'You've said sorry already.'

'I'm not one to be stingy with my sorrys. I'll say sorry again. And again. And again. Until it's all right. What about it, Dad? Opera? Gloomy songs and divas and all that shit?'

He was going to say 'no' but it came out as 'yes' instead. 'Give me a ring about it.' He doubted that she would be able to get tickets at this point in the season, whatever she said. But, given the chance, he would like to see the new opera house. 'See what you can do. Yes, I know: don't ring you, you'll ring me. Yes?'

'Got it in one, Daddio.' Suddenly misery had been cast aside again. 'It's a done deal. Piece of cake. No problemo.' She laughed, despair now quite forgotten in the throes of her latest enthusiasm. She kissed him chastely on the cheek and he got out of the car. He must look awful – he had totally forgotten to wash, let alone shave, when she had got him up in the morning.

As he walked away towards the trains, he heard her shouting to him. He turned around. She was standing by her car. She obviously had a thing about white. She ran a few steps towards him.

'Dad,' she called earnestly up the concourse to him. 'I forgot to say: the West Indies won with ten balls to spare. Cork made seventy-eight in just about half an hour or something. And still they didn't win. It must have been fucking galactic.'

She made him laugh so easily. He waved to her and ducked into the station.

On the train, Norman tried to read his *Sunday Telegraph* but found he couldn't concentrate. He took himself off to the toilet and found himself thinking of her all over again – her tears dampening the rise and fall of her dress where it covered her breasts, the flash of her bare legs under the eyes of all those bearded saints in the church, the proud insistence of her nipple under his hand yesterday, the firm dry pout of her lips on his grey stubbled cheek, her tongue going walkabout in his mouth in the lavatory, her desperate, clenched praying in the church. His brain was full to capacity with her – overloaded. He sighed and almost reluctantly unzipped his fly as he stood, feet apart, looking out of the tiny unfrosted part of the glass at the rushing Home Counties countryside. He had better just have her fuck him in his imagination. He guessed it would be the closest he would ever get to it.

He rested the side of his head against the window. He was making such a fool of himself with her. She would tease him on and tease him on until she got him in some really tight corner. There could never be anything genuine and proper between them. They came out of different boxes, different time zones. For him, she was like some kind of sexy Martian, a dangerous Medusa. And he for her? He still had no idea why she spent time with him. Money, he thought again, probably. He must stop allowing himself to be flattered into impending idiocy. She had kissed him once. And had allowed him to hold her breast. And that would be the sum total of it. It was over. After all, he hardly knew her. He could never ever trust her. She had so little to lose. He had so very much. Or did he?

It didn't matter that he might be in love with her. Love meant nothing at his age. Except, he discovered with some fascination, that he didn't want to besmirch and overlay his vision of her with a dirty wanker's fantasy.

So he put himself away, unspent, and zipped up his fly. And returned to his seat. Well, he thought, that was one for the record books. Bully for you, Amy Shakespeare.

MONDAY 24 JULY

She rang very briefly early in the afternoon. She had two tickets for Friday night. *The Marriage of Figaro*, she said. 'Any good, that one? Good numbers and everything?'

'They'll pass muster,' he replied. He promised to do the picnic. He thought he would drive down and meet her there. But before he could sort out any more details, she had gone, rung off, busy, rushing. But it sounded as if it was on. He thought he might just drive into Oxford to purchase some decent champagne from Russbridger's.

TUESDAY 25 JULY

By teatime on the following day he had changed his mind for the fiftieth time. He had to remind himself that, at heart, she was an illusionist. She had been honest about that. Was he just another more extreme example of handcuffs-at-the-top-of-the-Sherston-Oak? Would he finish up with his trousers around his ankles, manacled to the topmost branches? She was, after all, a sorceress, a nemesis, a games-player. She

181

could so easily be his downfall. So, after a day-long emotional struggle, he decided it would be best to call it a day. He found Reach for My Gun's Wardour Street number from directory enquiries and rang them to talk to her. He would let her down gently. It went though his mind as he listened to the dialling tone that she might not even work there at all. A bright engaging female voice told him that Amy was away sick. Did he want to leave a message? He didn't.

Promising himself that he would ring off abruptly if his daughter Joan answered the phone, Norman rang Francesca to see if she had been able to contact Amy and arrange a meeting. It would be interesting to get another perspective on the young woman – particularly from one of her own generation. He just got the answering machine. He left no message.

WEDNESDAY 26 JULY

Time seemed to be passing, on its hands and knees, very slowly. He rang Gilbert to see if he could talk over his concerns about Cowsdown House. Mrs Pettit informed him crisply that the whole family were spending the day at home at Abercrombie Hall doing an interview and photo-spread, for God's sake, for a magazine called *Hello!*

He found he couldn't get the big mower to start, so he tackled two of the smaller lawns with the Flymo. By the time he had brushed up all the cuttings, he was exhausted and had to promise himself to do the rest at another time. He felt irritated by these reverses and was grumpy with himself for most of the day. He thought about her a lot of the time. And that didn't help.

THURSDAY 27 JULY

He spent too much of a dull day willing Amy to ring him. She didn't. Several times he checked his phone for a dialling tone, to see if it was connected. He felt like a love sick thirteen-year-old. He was pathetic. He hated himself. He just needed to hear her voice saying the word 'Dad'.

He had so little to do. He watered the greenhouse. And worried about the state of the garden, which was getting out of hand. But he couldn't raise the level of his energy to do very much more than worry about it. He would finish mowing the lawns over the weekend. If he didn't he would lose control of them. Got to keep in control, or all was lost. Amy knew about that.

At five o'clock, he tried and failed to start the big mower. And managed to savage his forefinger in the process.

FRIDAY 28 JULY

She rang him just after midday. He'd given her up. It was too late by then anyway. She was on a mobile, breaking up. 'I'll see you there. In the car park at four p.m. It starts at four-fifty.'

'It's too late now. I'd never get there in time. You are such a trial, Amy. I thought you'd never ring.' He was shouting into his phone, standing in his hall, out of breath.

'Frightening, isn't it – life? Sorry, it's this smegging work. I've been up to my armpits. As I'll tell you. I never found a moment.'

'You've been off sick, actually, Amy.' There was a brief silence. 'Well I have and I haven't, nosy, if you really want to know,' she crackled at him. 'Now, drive like the fucking wind, Dad. Be there or be square, as they used to say back in the depths of time. I will be.' And the line went dead.

He had laid out his dinner-jacket and shirt and everything on the armchair in his bedroom two days before. The picnic was already prepared and in the cold-box, so it took him very little time to be on his way. But it was a long drive – over a hundred miles – with some potentially trying parts of the M25 about midway.

Even so, he felt youthfully excited as he drove the Daimler

too quickly down the M40 towards London. He was going to talk to her properly this evening. Ask her a few salient questions. Find out what the devil was going on between them. Would she allow him to hold her hand? And should he try? What would she be wearing? What was this dress from hell she spoke about? Oh, dear God, please make it something reasonably appropriate. If it wasn't, it would ruin the Mozart for him. Should he be feeling all these conflicting emotions? Was the whole thing an elaborate kinky game, a gavotte for the doomed, dedicated to consuming the elderly, the privileged and the archetypically English? Could he be an innocent performer in some kind of bizarre colonial revenge-scenario? He would find out tonight. He would pin her down. He would not come away until he had a few answers.

She was laminated in liquid silver. True, it wasn't a very great deal of liquid silver. She arrived at the very last minute, of course. She was dressed, if that was the right word for her state of nakedness, in a shining, sheer, silk sleeve which dropped to the floor from shoulder straps of thread. If it wasn't for the fact that everyone would spend the evening enraptured by the tanned shoulders, clavicles and the succulent bosoms of the woman, they might also have relished how the material clung fondly to every curve of her spare frame. She wore the most elaborately labyrinthian hairpiece filled with silver ribbons and black woven flowers. Complicated earrings the size of small budgerigar cages hung from her ears. Otherwise the whole outfit was simplicity itself. No doubt obscenely *costly* simplicity. As she must have been wearing heels the height of hollyhocks, Amy was almost as tall as he.

Apparently there was to be no problem that evening about physical contact. She shrieked elegantly when she first caught sight of him, stalked smoothly down the pathway beside the new auditorium, kissed both his cheeks warmly and interlocked one naked arm with his jacketed one.

'You're late,' he reprimanded her jokingly.

'Des couldn't remember where he'd parked the Bronco.'

'He gave you a lift down?'

'No, I materialised under a gooseberry bush.' She squeezed his arm.

'You look sensational.'

'You look pretty drop-dead gorgeous yourself. I adore a man in a black tie. It should be made compulsory for everyone – at least once a month.' They said the next phrase together: 'In my view', and laughed. 'You're my Mr Braun. You know?' She giggled. 'Mr Braun'? It's an anagram of your name – M-R-B-R-A-U-N.'

Norman was so touched and embarrassed that she should have found it in her to play anagrams with his name that he felt obliged to turn the subject away from himself: 'That dress, Amy, you should be a model!'

'Thank you, kind sir,' she said. 'Versace.' With this last, she was presumably imparting some information but it could just as well have been a summer sneeze. 'I waxed my armpits especially for you. The pain, my dear. It was exc . . . exc—'

'"Excruciating"?'

'No.'

'"Excoriating"?'

'No, um, no – exquisite.'

'Greater love hath no woman, eh?'

'Too right, Dad. In my view. She has to slap your arm to take your mind off the pain – as she yanks off the smegging wax—'

'Yes, yes, yes.' He certainly didn't need to hear any more about these depilatory processes. They walked into the beautiful cloisters that enclosed the new auditorium.

The new opera house was a wonderful thing. It was built from delicate honey-coloured brick, set next to John Christie's old house in the middle of the verdant burgeoning countryside. On every side, on the swooping Sussex downs and, closer by, in the garden itself, beautiful ancient trees and hedges stood bountiful with every hue of green. The sky was cloudy and the atmosphere close but it was as warm an evening as one could wish for.

The noise was tremendous. The audience, togged up in its

finest evening apparel, tucking away its cool-boxes and folding chairs under bench and bush, ready for the long interval,
chattered away like clouds of starlings coming home to roost.
There were, of course, the usual quota of bald heads ('Skin
City,' tittered his companion) and a goodly array of ghastly
floral bodices harking back to seventies hunt balls. But, on
the whole, the assembly made a pretty, privileged picture.
Inalienable, entrenched Englishness at its most handsome.
Norman loved it.

They briefly strolled through the open foyers together and
watched the people. Amy virtually enfolded herself about
him. If he died now he would be happy. She gazed up into
his eyes with rapt attention and her every physical gesture
confirmed to the throng their obvious mutual, endlessly
rampant, carnality. He felt almost as if he wanted to shout
to the watching eyes all around: 'Yes, she's with me. I get to
feel her hand in mine, her easy palm on my shoulder. I get to
mutter intimate somethings into her ear. And what a simple
pleasure it is for me, and me alone, to drop my glance into
the shadows of her cleavage.'

The fact that what the onlookers surmised was hardly true
in any particular mattered not at all that afternoon. He adored
them all, especially the men of course, watching him and Amy
together. Was he right, too, in thinking the women wanted to
kill her for her youth and him for their age difference? All
of them, he imagined, were fantasising about what she and
he were to each other. And what sport they might get up to
with each other, when in private.

He also guessed that many of the assembly might very well
not notice them at all.

'Tell me about this Figaro character, then. It sounds like
the show's about some kind of French newspaper merger,'
she said. But even she didn't really believe that.

She had secured them seats slap-bang in the middle of the
front row of the circle. 'House seats' she called them. The
auditorium was an exceptionally beautiful and traditional
horseshoe in pale timber, intimately focused upon an orchestra pit full of glowing lights and front curtains luminous with

promise. Norman quickly provided what narrative details he could remember of the feast ahead of them, touching upon the wandering eye of the count, the concerns of his crestfallen countess, plus additional swift character sketches of the revengeful Dr Bartolo, the urbane servant Figaro, Susanna his intended, the lusty lad Cherubino and the rest of the incestuous Almaviva household. 'It's right up your jolly old street, I'd've thought, Amy – scores of people dressing up, pretending to be people other than they are, plotting, deceiving, even a bit of what I think you call cross-dressing.'

'I've remembered: I saw it when it first came out,' she whispered mischievously.

'Amy, it's rather older than that,' he said.

'Yeah, it was absolutely ages ago. I was still at Sherston. It's the film where Tom Hulce gets them to reinstate the ballet music, isn't it?' She laughed. 'Sorry, sorry, I'm teasing again. I know about *Figaro*. It's about a count with attitude. He wants to fuck Susanna before the groom gets his sniff. 'Cause he's the boss. And that's what bosses do. In them days. In these days, too, I reckon.'

'Well, yes. I wouldn't put it quite like that.'

'Well of course you wouldn't. You'd say it was about the count wanting to exercise his *droit de seigneur* by taking the maidenhood of his vassal's bride.' He was astonished by some of the things she knew. Then he realised that she was squinting sideways, reading his programme notes.

The lights dimmed and the audience rolled out expectant applause as the young conductor Peter Friel entered the pit. He beckoned the orchestra to rise and acknowledge the reception.

'Why are they clapping?' she asked. 'They haven't done anything yet.'

'It's in expectation of what they *will* do,' he whispered.

'Can we take it back if they don't come up to scratch?' she asked but she was applauding energetically with everyone else.

As the familiar music of the overture engulfed him, Norman

knew that, for him, this was an evening in seventh heaven. Nothing in his life had ever been, or would ever be, as good as this. Her calm dry hand held his throughout the first half, occasionally stroking him with her thumb. He could smell her perfume and sense her quiet breathing. And her locked-on enjoyment.

The singers were young and powerful and beautiful. The orchestra played with a brightness that he thought was unparalleled and the production was often genuinely funny in an unstrained affectionate way that didn't deny the darker colours of the piece. How well, he thought, he could identify with young Cherubino's declaration: *'Non so piu cosa son, cosa faccio; or di foco, ora sono di ghiaccio'*. Because Norman, too, knew no longer what he was or what he was doing. He, too, was all fire. Or all ice. The heavenly music seemed to invade his very soul and dance mysteriously there, mixing ethereally with visions of Brian Lara's balletic cover-drives and with the colours of candles guttering in All Saints' church, and that very first moment with this girl – when she had unashamedly dropped her clothing into the bottom of his punt and he heard her shriek, that very first time, at the coldness of the water.

At the long interval they emerged, ready to seek out his St Michael's picnic, with Amy clinging lightly on to his arm. Instantly they ran into the Woodfordes: Nick, Barbara and their pretty daughters Emily and Kate, long-standing Ranburn family friends who lived in Brighton. Introductions were effected all around. Amy was terrific. She shook hands and smiled winningly and then, when some explanation of her presence seemed to be required, announced brightly in ringing tones that she was Norman's lover. Everybody laughed together with delightful understanding in order to indicate that they all knew, of course, that this was nothing more than a fetching piece of flattery and good humour. Indeed the whole incident passed satisfactorily.

The two of them settled on a wooden bench at the far end of a brick terrace under a flowery gazebo. All over the lawns, groups of elegant men and women pressed plastic plates and Tupperware boxes into service. The air was alive with the sound of popping corks. It looked as if the rain would hold off for a little while yet. Norman had brought along a small silver candelabra and a red checked tablecloth. Amy was elated by this touch. She carefully melted the bottoms of three red candles so that they would stand up properly in it. She allowed him the honour of pressing out their own champagne cork. She was like an eight-year-old at a birthday party – beaming and shiny-faced with pleasure.

Nevertheless, he was still determined to ask her a few probing questions. The time had come. He waited while they tucked into his smoked salmon and the various exotic middle-class, Middle Eastern salads that Marks and Spencer had decided were going to be the fashion that season.

'I'm going to have to ask you some questions.'

'Shoot,' she said with her mouth already full.

'I'm sorry, some of these are really quite personal but I feel I don't know anything about you at all. And that worries me. And I would so much like to know more about you.'

'What do you want to know, Dad? An open book, me. OK, let's see. Here goes. Twenty-four. Leo. On the cusp. Almost a Virgo, would you believe? Twenty-five on the twenty-third of August. Conceived and raised just outside Wellington – Summer's Creek, Wackenpateh. Only child. I was reckoned damned thin, too tomboyish, bloody unruly and a right pain in the proverbial. So I got transportation for life, eleven years ago, to get the shit kicked out of me at Sherston. My mother of a mother – Ursula – rich, lunatic, short-tempered, short-statured, bohemian, New Zealander, neurotic – famous for it. Dad – unfazed, dreamy, under-published – *hardly*-published – poet. An antipodean Seamus Heaney. Brilliant, I think, but then he is my dad. At Sherston I accumulated a seriously bad reputation and, to the sound of jaws hitting the deck on all sides, three – goddammit, *three* – finger-licking A-level results. Mrs Trenchard, my housemistress, was totally mortified. She just knew I was going to finish up in the gutter. Of course, nowadays, all I can remember is the third law of thermodynamics. What else? They thought I was going to be a heap-big cross-country runner for the whole of one Michaelmas term. So did I. But I got bored. Top of my faults list is a pretty instantaneous boredom factor. Sex life: virginity lost in the school swimming pool. Aged fifteen – itinerant French-master – isn't that just too grundy? It was a bet, of course. In at the deep end – ha ha ha. The swimming pool 'cause people could check on the action there. There was this underwater viewing hatch in the water-conditioning plant and someone stole the key to get in. I almost drowned. Turns out I'm a screamer. Mr Fleurant was categorically seen to have it away and Angela Baltao's CD player was mine. That's about it then. I'm a cabaret performer, film-world lackey, water-skiing instructor and professional cock-teaser. End of story. Oh, you'll want to know the usual: well the grand total, as of today, is nineteen. Men, that is – and I still know every one of their names, though I'm microscopically confused about two Spanish architects one night in a camper-van behind the Mormon Tabernacle in Salt Lake City. But that's still only about two and a half fellas a year, isn't it? See, I can take it or leave it, no prob. I can last almost thirty-six hours at a time if I want.' She giggled and rubbed the end of her nose with a crooked forefinger. 'So, no boyfriend – just a couple of guys I see regularly when I'm feeling horny. Which is most days.'

'Where do you get your money?'

'What money?'

'Well the car. I mean, Hands Across the Sea, or whatever they're called, can't pay you all that much.'

'Reach For My Gun. Yeah, too right. Got it in one. I've an allowance – my mother, guilt, only child. She wants me to be all right. And vast overdrafts – "Nat West – more than just a wank".' She turned her head away from him and splashed first-class champagne inaccurately into their two stainless-steel, stemmed goblets. He hesitated. It was very difficult to know how much he should ask her.

'What is this thing – between us?'

'How do you mean?'

'Why are you spending time with me?'

'Am I?'

'Amy.'

'Sorry, yep. Sorry. Why am I? I could be looking for a father, couldn't I? That's simple enough. It figures. But I don't think you'll buy that, Dad.' She stopped and contemplated him calmly, in mid-bite. 'I suppose I like talking dirty to older men. They like it too.'

'"They"? So I'm one of a clutch.'

'No, I think I'm doing the clutching.'

'Amy, be sensible. Why are you and I spending time together? I'm old enough to be—'

'Methuselah's grandpa. Yeah, OK.' She gulped down champagne. 'I like it. Spending time with you. Surprising you. Yeah, manipulating you, I expect. I told you what turns me on. No, I like you. It's no big deal though. Do you want to stop?'

'No. I like it too.'

'Well, I know that. So what's the big prob? You've got it covered. Stick with it, Dad.' She started to sing quietly under her breath as she spooned tzatziki on to her plate. '"If you're happy and you know it, cut the crap; if you're happy and you know it, get the clap; if you're happy and you know it and would like to have me blow it, if you're happy and you know it, take the rap." I'll have to get into this opera-writing malarkey myself.' And then once more she was eating as if she seriously hadn't seen food for weeks. 'I have to warn you, it may not last, Dad. I've a notoriously low boredom threshold. Hardly a threshold at all – more like a nodule.'

She stopped and raised her eyebrows and indicated something to him with her cool grave eyes: an elderly lady, florally decked out with powerfully pre-stressed-concrete, powder-blue hair who was making much of smelling some yellow roses close to them. This ploy seemed intended to allow her to overhear the more lurid bits of Amy's life story. Amy, raising her voice substantially to be of assistance to the woman's eavesdropping, announced noisily in best Guildford tones: 'Basically, Dad, I suppose I dig getting a rise out of older gentlemen almost as much as I adore banging smart young boys.'

191

Norman couldn't help smiling as the lady had a third-degree attack of the vapours and, clutching up her sequined satin skirting, hurried away.

'Don't you get frightened of AIDS – with all this, um, activity?'

'I don't do any, um, activity, Normy. I do fucking. And I've invested in a person-to-person, action-led, zip-coded, wholesale account with Mates Healthcare of Surbiton, Surrey,' she said chirpily. 'Oh yeah, Nonoxynol 9 is my telephone number. Anyway, the last thing I want cruising my ovaries are able semen.' Sometimes her wordplay felt as if it was rehearsed.

There was a silence. Then Amy was quieter again, almost ruminative. She sighed massively. 'I am either very, very sick. Or, Dad, maybe, as far as you are concerned, it's just that I think you ought to live a little. You are, aren't you? Living a little?'

'Why me, though?'

'Why not? You've got the nicest smile. The most potential, I think. You could be dead wicked, given half a chance. I'd like to be along for the ride when you are.' She looked rueful. 'I tell you, it's bugger awful sometimes, forever having to manage fit young studs sloshing with too much testosterone. I suppose you're a bit of a holiday.'

'I don't know why I put up with you.' But he did know. It was because of the way her silken skin undulated beneath her shoulder straps as she ate, because of the way her lean wrist flexed inside its plain, heavy, silver bangle, because of the way the taut silver material varnished her thighs and because of the way her nipples were never all that far from being noticeable. She saw him looking at her and glanced down at herself. 'See nipples, and die,' she said approvingly. He wondered how long she had been nursing *that* particular line, too.

'I think I might just love you, Amy Shakespeare.'

'Oh.'

'Well, is that all right?'

'Fuck knows, Dad. It's on my schedule as one of the greatest bores in all the world – love. Listen, I'm really fond of you.

Dead fond. But that's it. Period. No romantic shit. Good times. I thought you were lonely and needed good times. Before it was too late.'

'Oh. Charity?'

'No, of course it's not sodding charity. It's to do with honest bloody fondness. You are a nice, kind—'

'Shut up, Amy. I don't want to hear any more.' But what had he expected? What else could he have expected her to say? He felt suddenly terribly low. She pushed her glass back towards him for a fill up. There was a distant flash of lightning and a lugubrious roll of thunder. It would rain soon. 'I'll tell you how fond I am of you, bloody Mr Norman Ranburn, ex-steaming-ex-chief-executive of steaming Chandos House. I've just spent two and a half solid days working on your behalf.'

'What do you mean?'

'You wanted information. I went out and got it for you. Research they call it. You were right. Little brother Gilbert is cutting every corner he can find. The staff are revolting – no, that's the point, they're not – but they are deeply grundy about it all. But, the point is, He Who Must Be Obeyed implies the direst threats of dismissal if they cut up rough. He's slashed resources and tells them they'd better keep up appearances or they'll all get the chop.'

'How do you know this?' He didn't believe her. She was spinning him a yarn.

'Took two days off sick. God, I was poorly. I had a severe attack of Chandos House-itis. Took along a friend as a photographer.'

'The ubiquitous Quentin?'

'The very he. And I dressed up – not, of course, that that was any great hardship for me – as an over-the-top *Hello!* magazine hackette. Fortunately Gilbert didn't recognise me at all in my short back and sides and my eighties power shoulder pads. He was too busy pretending not to notice my other bits. Quentin flashed his Nikon. I flashed my fanny. Gilbert and Mary poured themselves into various spanking new outfits and sat around looking proprietorial by the pool on the lawn, or in their gorgeous three-acre lounge or in their preposterous bedroom – the one with the hanging tapestries and drapes that look like Andrex toilet tissue. I picked up lots of casual info which we used to wriggle our way next day into the matron's confidence at Cowsdown House. And we looked up a Mrs Peterson who is the kind of administrator at Aubrey Manor.'

It must be true. 'You saw Margaret Peterson at Aubrey Manor?'

'Sure as hell did. You betcha. Drank coffee from her Andalusian ceramic mugs. And nibbled on her plain chocolate Hobnob biscuits. She's a woman of taste and discrimination.'

'And she confirms all this?'

'Some of it. I think the situation at Cowsdown is worse than Aubrey Manor. But even Margaret's the equivalent of five full-time staff down.' Big drops of rain began to fall all around them, marking the brickwork of the terrace with large dark-brown circles. 'I'd better go and talk to Gilbert about this,' he said.

'Got it in one.' People were beginning to hurry from the lawns back into the opera house. All of a sudden it was as if all the water in the heavens was being dropped on their heads. They packed up their picnic with the delicacy of ram-raiders and took to their heels. They found themselves, having charged through the warm, soaking rain, in a corner of the foyer space looking bedraggled. In Amy's case, bedraggled and virtually naked. The rain had plastered her lamé to every nook and cranny of her body. Water dripped copiously from all parts of her beribboned head-dress. It was obvious and clear to see from the darkness at her crotch, and the small brown circles that now rather obviously surmounted her breasts, that under the silver clingfilm there was only Amy.

He took off his jacket and drapped it around her shoulders, more for decency than for warmth. The gentlemen with medals around their necks, who were moonlighting from being Something In the City to undertake the occasional

194

foray into front-of-house duty at Glyndebourne, began to hurry the audience back to their seats.

Norman and Amy found themselves in the middle of the front row again. She slipped his jacket off and placed it over their laps. No one could see her indecency once they were securely in their places at the front of the circle. They would be able to get good and dry during the second half.

As the music began again, Norman was in shock. Had the girl really gone traipsing around the south-west of England, asking questions about Chandos House? And would the staff have dared to impart that kind of information to a passing journalist? Why on earth had she bothered to do all that? She constantly amazed him. He constantly distrusted her. And yet he felt powerless to do anything about it. As the audience settled back to witness the ramifications of Count Almaviva's marital suspicions at the commencement of the second half, it struck Norman that the feisty little reporter at his side could only really have discovered Mrs Peterson's Andalusian connections, surely, by actually going down to Bath. So she must have done it. But why? She must like him very much. And want to be of service. God, he would so like her to be of service to him.

The darling girl held his left hand again. Now somewhat damply. Outwardly, her apparent composure seemed a thousand miles away from his own internal feelings of agitation and doubt. Amy was always casually lobbing one of her mind-bombs into his life and then sitting back as if she had done nothing at all.

He could sense the damp of his dinner-jacket folded in front of him. And he could smell Amy's wet body as well. He was now also shockingly aware of her virtual nakedness next to him. He had an easy wry sympathy with Figaro's disgust, on stage, at manipulating womankind: *Guardate queste femmine* – 'look at these women: they are thorned roses, alluring vixens, smiling she-bears, masters of deceit, who cheat and lie and feel no love.'

Amy didn't love him – she was just fond. That's what

she had said. How could she? What more could he have expected?

Her hand moved idly in his. And disengaged. As Figaro embraced Marcellina, whom he had thought he would be forced to marry that day very much against his will – only to discover she was his mother – Amy's hand moved subtly, under the cover of Norman's jacket, to rest lightly between Norman's legs in the damp of his trousers. This intimate gesture alarmed him and pleased him at the same time. He glanced sideways at her face. It was enigmatic. She was entirely absorbed in the action, the fabric of her dress still clasped to her. As he looked down, it seemed, in the reflection of the stage lights, as if she was more or less unclothed. Looking magnificent. She could be so alluring. A thorned rose.

He was going to get an erection. There was nothing he could do about it. With extreme distress and some degree of impish pleasure he knew that unless he got up and left the auditorium now, he would soon go hard under that hand. It was Lord's all over again. He concentrated fiercely on the opera. Listen to the words, follow the story, he told himself urgently. Appreciate it. But his main thought continued to be one of great potential embarrassment. Would Amy be embarrassed? He thought not. Maybe she had wanted this. Of course this was what she wanted. She loved this. It was like the panting in the toilet last weekend.

Alone on stage, the countess in sad rejection sang her aria: 'Umil stato fatale io son ridotta' – 'To what humiliation am I reduced.' Amy's hand was nestling gently in the fabric of his trousers – moving ever so gently. He was reminded of watching Lesley-Anne's own hand at work, one heart-stopping moment, a thousand years before. Amy must now surely be all too aware of the thing that she had engendered. Her face seemed entirely oblivious. It was as if that hand of hers had a completely independent life of its own.

The pleasure that suffused his whole body, but centred upon that rock-hard piece of flesh, was getting impossible to deny. It was just wonderful. Dirty. Wicked. Evil. Lovely. It was appalling. And so appealing. He found, to his astonishment, that he had marginally pressed his bottom forward on his seat, presenting himself more availably to his assailant. He realised that his knees had crept a touch further apart. He was, as Amy might coin it, 'really getting into it'. It was dreadful. Her hand had taken his virtually imperceptible movements as a cue to enclose his penis under his trouser material with long knowing fingers.

They began to stroke stealthily up and down. On stage, the plot to ensnare the count continued its inexorable progress but, apart from the gorgeous swell and caress of the voices, Norman's concentration was now much closer at hand. And what a lovely beneficent hand it was, too.

What was happening was wholly delightful and also deeply, deeply worrying. Down there at the front of the circle, he and Amy were under the watchful gaze of two or three hundred people sitting behind them. Norman had a nice old boy from Weston-super-Mare sitting on his right, with his elbow firmly embedded in Norman's own. It seemed to Norman as if the eyes of the world must surely all be focused on the back of Amy's and his own motionless heads. The folded jacket on their laps made no move. The only clue that anyone might have picked up was that, when the entrance of the chorus of village girls was completed and everyone applauded, his companion did not. One of her hands was busily engaged elsewhere. Norman surprised himself by using his own applause to settle a few more centimetres forward in his seat, his knees further splayed.

And Amy took the opportunity of the action in the auditorium to disengage a few of his fly buttons. She could do anything with her fingers, this girl. For crying out loud, she had the beast right out now, under his jacket. Out and as hard as rock. Up and down, up and down went her educated fingers, toying with the tip – her fingers' ends giving him what amounted to tiny, nipping kisses. Then she was hardly touching him. Next, her whole hand wrapped around him, she was squeezing him hard. Norman closed his eyes and, listening to the music, allowed himself to be carried away into a world where he and Amy were entirely alone – not surrounded by hundreds and hundreds of decent folk having a properly cultural evening out.

Alluring vixen, smiling she-bear, witch, siren, night-owl. Heaven.

And it went on for ever. He could not remember, not in his entire life, being up and hard for so long. She could do it so well. The opera's action moved into the final scenes in the garden. He wanted more, stronger, he wanted what? What did he want? Everything. Nothing. Stop. Go on. This was so awful, so gorgeous.

He had turned his head surreptitiously to his left so that he could monitor any movement that might be a give-away. As the characters assembled in the darkness of the garden, the countess disguised as Susanna and she as the countess, as the whole charade began to untangle towards the finale, all Norman was conscious of was the action of a teasing, tantalising, disembodied hand. He found himself gripping the arm-rests and bracing his shoes against the balcony balustrade in front of him in order to keep the whole thing imperceptible.

She was getting quicker. He was finding it hard not to pant just a little. Sweat poured off him, mingling with the remnants of the damp of the rain. He was suddenly aware that the naked muscle in her left shoulder was now flexing visibly. There was a concave shadow on her skin tweaking away rhythmically in time with the action of her fingers. The whole audience must by now surely be totally agog at that tiny portion of reflective brown female shoulder as it swooped and flicked, swooped and flicked. That minute piece of evidence of her busy-ness added to his now more frequent movements must surely give the game away. This was madness. This was sick. And he was trapped there. There was nothing he could do. Or wanted to do. The Weston-super-Mare man seemed to glance at him once. Amy's nipples were as clearly erect as his cock.

The disagreements and confusions of *la folle journée*, of

Figaro's marriage day – the 'crazy day' – were resolving themselves on stage with all voices raised in celebration – 'In dancing and pleasure', they sang, *'Corriam tutti a festieggiar'* – 'Let's hasten to the revelry.' Eight singers in full voice. Magnificent. Wonderful. Overpowering. God-given. The front curtain descended like God's hand. This was it. This was it. This was it. The auditorium exploded in thunderous applause.

And he came. Massively.

With such a groan that he was obliged to turn it into a severe attack of coughing. Amy withdrew her hot little hand and, glancing evilly sideways, at him, tongued her fingers briefly before joining in applauding the endless curtain calls.

It was quite the most disgusting thing that he had ever been involved in. She was a sick tart. He loathed her.

Ten minutes later, he was telling her so in the car park, in the continuing drizzle, as people fought their way to their cars and took no notice of an old gentleman shouting horribly at a beautiful but now very bedraggled young woman. 'Stinking', 'nauseating', 'loathsome', 'poisonous' were just some of the epithets he threw at her.

She was fearfully calm. 'Oh no, Dad,' she said quite quietly. 'No. I know you now. You loved it. You adored it. And now you owe me two favours. You owe me, Dad.'

He was so infuriated by her lack of guilt or shame or concern or friendliness that he threw himself into the driving seat of the Daimler, and seeing a sudden gap in the line of cars, shot away from her. Leave the sick little bitch there, he thought. He owed her nothing. She was quite wrong.

He briefly caught sight of her in his rear-view mirror, illuminated by someone's headlights – bereft, soaked, make-up running, stranded.

No, no, no, no. It was over, the games.

'Leave her,' he said out loud to himself. So he did.

As he reached the bottom end of the M23 in the pouring rain, Norman suddenly snorted to himself – 'Mr Braun'! It wasn't an anagram of his name at all. She'd been lying. She had taken one of the 'n's out of 'Ranburn' and replaced it with an 'm'. She even cheated at anagrams. Typical of her. No one cheated at anagrams, for God's sake.

CHAPTER SIX

Woe to him that is alone when he falleth,
for he hath not another to help him up.

ECCLESIASTES 4:10

SATURDAY 29 JULY

It was just after midnight when he drove back down the
drive to the Aviary. There was a light on in Onan Cottage.
The curtains were drawn.

Norman briefly flirted with the idea that by some kind
of extraordinary, kinetic, supernatural means, Amy had got
to Coombe first and had set up house in the cottage. Then
he realised that he was being worse than stupid. It was
purely that he felt wretched about having deserted the girl
at Glyndebourne and was trying to wish it better.

It felt absurd knocking at one of his own front doors. But
what else was there to do?

It was Lesley-Anne Ridgeway who opened it.

His initial feeling of anger towards her was quickly swept
away when he saw how poorly she looked. She was profuse
in her apologies for what had happened. He allowed himself

to join her in the cottage kitchen where she made him a cup of tea and began to explain. Her defences were down. She tearfully confessed to him that she was terribly, terribly sorry, but she had lied to him. Terence was her brother. He had got himself into serious difficulty over the financial management of a company he had had charge of in Kingston-upon-Thames. He had appealed to her, his sister, for help. He had truly believed that, if he could disappear for a short while, the truth would come out and he would be seen not to have been party to fraud. Lesley-Anne had read Norman's advert in the *The Lady* and thought it might be a way of finding an ideal secret hideaway. Norman had required a 'couple' and so they had been obliged to masquerade as one.

'But two weeks ago, as you know now, they caught up with Terry. We went back down and he spent three days being interviewed by the fraud squad. Finally he was charged and he's now on remand. He's awaiting trial. There was no one who could afford bail. He's in Snapper Green Remand Centre. It's just outside Northampton.'

'Not too far away.'

Lesley-Anne's eyes filled up with tears again. 'I couldn't think of anywhere else to go. I didn't know what to do when you weren't here. Originally I had decided that I would come and tell you and see what you thought. Then, when you weren't here, I spent about an hour in the garden waiting, trying to decide what would be best. Then it began to get dark and it rained. I still had a key. So I let myself in. To wait.'

'How did you get here?'

'Train. Bus. Then I walked. They've impounded the car.' She was crying again.

'I still need help here.' And he did need help – though, to be honest, more in the grounds than in the house. But, since Lesley-Anne had left, he had partaken of a pretty inadequate diet for a grown man – toast and cups of coffee and bits and bobs. Not healthy at all. Marmite toast is not a totally adequate diet. And he hadn't been able to find new Hoover bags anywhere. He had been reduced to recycling an old one, repairing the holes in it with Sellotape and getting dust over everything.

Also, ill though she might look at the moment, Lesley-Anne was still a hell of a looker. So very full and womanly and mature and nicely dutiful. Not like the little minx he had abandoned in the rain among the departing cars of West Sussex. She would be much easier to deal with than that crazy, dangerous crackpot. To have Lesley-Anne back under the microscope would make up for the severing of his friendship with Amy. Golly, how often he found that he tended to land on his feet.

'I could do with the help,' he repeated. 'It's late now. I'll talk to you about money in the morning.' She managed to stop herself physically embracing him, but she was clearly inordinately relieved. And that felt like a good position for him to be in. Amy was probably right about the less virtuous sensations of power.

Norman left Lesley-Anne to it. He was round back behind the hanging carpet, in the viewing room, before you could say 'knife'. To think he had been sure he would never ever enter it again.

Maybe it was just because he was tired, but he found seeing Lesley-Anne briefly naked again no great pleasure at all. Maybe the day had already been too full of sexual jiggery-pokery. The bald fact was that to watch someone preparing for bed who was depressed and even rather unwell turned out to be about as exciting as watching *Celebrity Squares*. There was absolutely no chemistry at all. As soon as she switched out her bedside lamp, Norman left her to it and took himself off to his own bed. He was pleased that Lesley-Anne was back, but bothered by how little it had excited him. He fell asleep with the encouraging idea that, now that Lesley-Anne was in residence alone next door, she might perhaps find herself a lover. Bachelor girl and all that. That would be a bit of all right.

Norman awoke with but one thought in his head – that he didn't want ever again to have to face Amy Shakespeare. And yet her whole bloody film unit would arrive on Monday and he had agreed for them to be *in situ* for the best part of five days. And Amy Shakespeare would be present the whole time – no doubt with furiously accusing eyes. He didn't think he would be able to bear that. He'd best go away for the week. Or cancel the whole thing.

Even while he was on the telephone seeking out Des Wright's mobile number, he knew in his heart of hearts that cancellation was not on. Des confirmed this only too emphatically: 'Good God, sir, it's all set up. It's all taken care of. This is an enormous investment in time, logistics and money, Mr Ranburn. I can't believe that you really want to pull out on us now. We have an agreement with you. We shook on it, sir. I couldn't possibly pull the plug now. The whole bang shoot arrives with you in forty-eight hours' time. It is only for five days. Once we've gone, I promise you, you won't know we've been there.'

Norman already knew he was wavering. 'If you say so,' he said warily. After all, the man was right. What was more, the damned man had the cheek to make yet a further request: 'I was going to call you today anyway, Mr Ranburn. Amy – you remember, my assistant who made our initial introduction – she tells me you've got a grand old Bullnose Morris in the barn: 1920s job.'

'Actually, 1923. Well. Yes?'

'Absolutely ideal. Spot on. I wondered if we could use it for three days. For dressing, when we're over at Wormell Water, the following week. Just for dressing, if you get my meaning – no one would have to drive it or anything. Sue Smith, the designer, would give her eye-teeth. It would just be parked. It would look so bloody great, sir. I can't tell you. There'd be a fee, of course, and we have twenty-four-hour professional security on the set so it would be one hundred per cent safe. You have my word on that, sir, no problem. We'd just need it for the first three days of the week – Monday to Thursday. What say?'

'Oh, I don't know.' Lending his car would mean a possible extra three days of having to deal with run-ins with Miss Shakespeare.

'Think about it, Mr Ranburn,' said Des and then, thank God, his mobile cut out.

Norman was disgruntled by his complete lack of success with his appeal to Reach For My Gun. Using his overall feeling of irritation, he rang Mrs Pettit at Chandos House and left a message on her answering machine for her and Gilbert saying that he wanted to call an emergency meeting of the Chandos House board for Tuesday week – the 8th August. Leaving a recorded message meant that he wouldn't have to put up with any flak from Gilbert until Monday morning.

SUNDAY 30 JULY

On Sunday, life began to take on a more acceptable and manageable character once again. It was one of the hottest days of the year. Lesley-Anne served him a very pleasant salad luncheon on the terrace where he spent about an hour and a half sitting under the green garden umbrella in his Panama reading the *Telegraph* and imbibing the better half of a bottle of Haut-Medoc. He even smoked a cigar, which he did rarely nowadays. One of the nicer parts of his meal was that Lesley-Anne looked much better for her sleep and served him wearing, for his covert delectation, the briefest strip of a denim skirt that he had ever seen her wear. And a T-shirt with some futuristic scarecrow called Judge Dredd emblazoned upon it. It set her off a treat. He could get used to this.

In the afternoon he saw that she had taken herself off with a blanket to the top of the orchard. He caught the odd glimpse of her in the distance, wearing a chocolate-brown two-piece bathing costume, with her hair caught up in a clip, rubbing suntan oil all over her body. But when she lay down she entirely disappeared in the long grass. He spent a fruitless hour trying to think of cogent reasons for walking up to the top of the orchard but none came to mind. So he left it at that. But he felt a good bit more cheerful. He liked having her around. She was much easier to handle than that ball-breaker Shakespeare.

Even so, he felt so much calmer now about Amy, that he even allowed himself a stimulating half-hour reverie in the sun thinking about that wicked witch and that which she had undertaken with her shrewd fingers in the auditorium at Glyndebourne. It was odd how quickly outrage could become, in retrospect, a gratifying diversion.

At about six in the evening, the unit transport began to move in.

All through the long warm evening, various colossal generator trucks, lighting lorries, dressing-room trailers and location-catering vehicles lurched their way through Coombe village and finished up parking on the verges of his long drive. Whatever Des had said about leaving his property pristine, Norman couldn't see how it was not going to take a good few weeks for the verges to recover from this battering. Taciturn men popped up from all over the shop with mobile telephones, short-wave radios, clipboards, purchase orders, skimpy sleeveless vests and enormously baggy shorts covered with multitudes of capacious zippered pockets. Their attitude towards Norman was one of silent surprise, tempered with a modicum of acquiescence, that someone had been foolish enough to have allowed him to intrude his presence into what was now their own exclusive domain.

After about three hours of slow accumulation of more hardware than he could ever have imagined, the bulk of the men took themselves off for the evening to the hostelries of Oxfordshire. There was no sign of Amy. Indeed, there were no women at all involved in this cumbersome but ruthlessly efficient activity. The man Des strolled up to the terrace as the sun sank behind Bargate Hill, and shook Norman by the hand with a resolute firmness. 'Thanks about the car,' was the last thing he said as he sloped off. Norman hadn't the energy to interject that nothing had been decided about Bertram. But he supposed it probably had.

He fell asleep watching a film on the box about two people being in love but living either end of the United States, which made for difficulties in consummation. Obscurely, they seemed to finish up having it away on top of the Empire State Building. But he might have got that wrong. All he knew was that by the time he went through to check up on Lesley-Anne's all-over suntan for himself, he discovered her well tucked up and fast asleep. When alone, she slept with her knees pulled right up under her chin. Altogether less tense, he thought.

MONDAY 31 JULY

Since dawn, he had peered carefully out of various bedroom windows, standing well back so as not to be seen, watching the build-up of activity in and around the stable yard. The place seemed overrun by what appeared to be hundreds of people – young men and women, all of whom seemed to have remarkably little to do. And who did it with a concentration and seriousness that had to be seen to be believed. He had no idea what duties could possibly involve quite so many virtually identical-looking people. The basic idea seemed to be for them all to look as scruffy as the average lorry-driver, and a baseball hat was clearly indispensable. It was impossible to tell from their dress who were the bigwigs and who the mere serfs. They all looked the same – big knees, jutting bottoms and short-wave radios grafted to their ears.

It had all started up obscenely early. A few precious seconds after dawn, Norman had been summoned and the director chappie, Moorehead McPhee, had taken him around. Why, he wondered, did the man seem to require the use of two surnames when one was quite enough for most folk? He and Norman watched the horses being delivered and chatted to their groom. It appeared that they had come all the way from Letchworth. Funny, when there were so many horses within five miles of Coombe. Norman was also introduced to the leading man, who was a very short, very good-looking, well-built young fellow called Craig, of whom everyone seemed in awe. They kept on referring to him deferentially as 'Mr Luft'. Norman got the distinct impression that being allowed to meet this Craig character was deemed almost as valuable as the fee that he was receiving for the use of his premises. Norman had certainly never heard of him. But then Norman could hardly put a face to Clark Gable.

He also met the Lewis woman who was this Craig's opposite number in the film. While she seemed to be called 'Georgina' on all the written material he caught sight of – everyone around her called her 'Sam', which was a touch confusing. She was sitting in a caravan having something complicated done to her hair, reading a battered script in large sunglasses, although it was still much too early for the sun to have got up. She would be devastatingly pretty once out of her rollers, he imagined. Thin as a snake and about five foot nothing in her stockinged feet, but proportionately quite surprising in the bust area. Saying an embarrassed 'hullo' to her, Norman found himself inadvertently thinking about breast implants. They were damned prevalent these days, weren't they? She smelled very good and jutted out a long way for an anorexic. He could easily have spent longer in her caravan but they hustled him away.

All around the stable buildings and the barn there was the busy unloading and standing about of all manner of obscure technical equipment – colossal lamps on stands and enormous sheets of white, stiff, plastic board, pieces of what appeared to be a miniature railway and finally a great big, satisfyingly complex-looking camera. In various unlikely corners, small folding tables were set up with Thermos urns on them where expanded polystyrene cups and white plastic spoons swam gently in puddles of milk and where the coffee was making a determined bid to take up residence in the sugar bowls.

But no sight of Amy. And he couldn't possibly ask after her. Once he had been given the short royal tour, he was released. He was surprised that this double-barrelled McPhee had so much time for him, but it appeared that the man in charge, or, at any rate, the only man whose voice was allowed to be heard everywhere, was a chappie with the handle of 'production manager' who went by the name of

Harrison. Marty Harrison – a one-surname big gun. Aged about twelve.

And then, once they had begun their shoot, he twice saw Amy squatting on her haunches, on the steps of the barn, thoughtfully chewing the corner of her clipboard, surrounded by various animated young men, all of them vying not too stealthily for her attention. Clearly, Norman wasn't the only male in Oxfordshire that deemed her yearningly sexy. And all those fit young men – 'I adore banging smart young boys,' she'd said – were so much more suitable for her youthfulness and grace than his own ponderous decrepitude would ever be.

He felt eaten up with envy seeing her bestowing the very best of her liquid, all-embracing smiles on these young fellows. Her attention to them seemed so much more genuine and relaxed than the kind of manufactured response with which she tricked out her conversation with him. Did she sleep with any of these boys? Did she sleep with all of these boys? She must do. Why ever not? He wanted to groan out loud with the sharpness of his jealousy. And he thought of how it had been in that very barn, just behind her, that only two short weeks ago she had rolled him a joint and scaled his beams and nonchalantly allowed him to eye her underwear. When they had been some kind of friends.

Then his phone rang and he went to answer it.

'What the fucking hell are you up to Norman?' shouted his brother down the telephone at him. 'What, in fuck's name, are you doing, calling an emergency meeting without consulting me? What's the game? What the fuck are you up to?'

'I'm sorry you're taking it like that, Gilbert. I've received some information about some parts of the operation and I want to ask some questions about it, check it out, that's all. Seems reasonable enough to me.'

'What information? What information? This isn't how we do things, you and me – all this formal gubbins. Are you trying to give me a bad time, Norman? If so, say so, and we can have it out. Why couldn't we have sorted this out between us privately, eh? The last thing we want is Dorothy and Robert and Sir Bernard all getting their knickers in a twist because someone's blathering away about undermanning.'

'So you do know what it's about, then?'

'I can guess. I can guess. We've been doing some restructuring. Some of the managers find they've had their corns trodden on and start to make a fuss. I'm surprised you get taken in by that sort of thing. After all your experience. Who's running this outfit now, eh? Come in and talk to me about it.'

'Well I've got these film people here today. I'm not very keen to leave them to their own devices.'

'I want to talk to you before we go to the board, that's all. Come in and talk. I'll explain everything to you. Again. You know,' he sighed insultingly, 'we've been through all this before. You don't listen any more, Norman. You seem to have dropped out through a black hole into a world of your own. You've lost it. Have you left your business head out in the rain or something? Brace up, Norman. I'm trying to run a company here. It's not as easy as it was for you in the eighties, believe you me. And actually I think you know that. What's more, mate, it's a business that sees you all right, whatever happens. Bloody handsomely all right. So don't give me all this grief. Let's talk. Come in and see me. Right? You'll come in?'

Norman, still listening, thought he caught the sudden image of Amy walking past the two long windows at the front of his house. She might be looking for him. He could try to catch her when she came back. He told Gilbert he would go into Witney to see him prior to the meeting, rang off and rushed to the front door, out of which he strolled with studied nonchalance.

But these subterfuges didn't work. Over the next three days, as the filming seemed to move forward hardly at all, he was unable to exchange a single word with the girl. Every evening at what they bizarrely called their 'wrap,' the staff and crew would evaporate to hotels in Oxford – the Randolph for Mr Luft, the double-barrelled McPhee, the well-stacked 'Sam' Lewis and persons of that ilk, while hoipolloi like

Amy and her myriad cohorts were accommodated at lesser establishments, he suspected. And what went on at night in those particular places? he wondered. Well, he knew pretty well and it didn't make for long hours asleep on his own, back on his tod, at the Aviary along with the horses, the overnight security guards and the solitary Lesley-Anne Ridgeway.

There were so many odd things about Amy that didn't add up. On the Thursday, Norman had endeavoured to escape some of the pain of the whole thing by driving into Oxford. That afternoon he had drifted, on a vague whim, into the reference library of the Oxford Public Library in the Cornmarket. He'd looked up Daniel Shake, the New Zealand poet, and Amy's putative father.

There was a Daniel Shake who had died in 1967, aged fifty-four. As Amy had presumably been born in the early seventies, that made being her father a tall order for this Mr Shake. Moreover, in an obituary which Norman chanced upon, it said that Dan Shake had been a much-reviled, leading light of a nascent gay-rights movement. Dead homosexuals didn't, in general, father little girls, however exceptional a progeny they might turn out to be. Would Norman ever get the opportunity of questioning the little lady about this odd fact? Or did he just have to get used to the fact that Amy Shakespeare (or whatever she was called) was nothing more than a deceitful little cat – for whom lying was her daily bread?

Whatever, on the set, in his busy stable yard, this figment of her own imagination was scarcely to be seen. Or, if she was, it was in the constant company of one of her admiring young men.

She was never more than a hundred yards away from Norman all day, all week long and, as far as he was concerned, she might as well have been in Timbuktu.

Just once, on the Wednesday afternoon, she hurried around a corner by the old pigsties and almost bumped into him. She smiled a distant smile and said 'Hi.' But, as she had one of her disciples in tow, there was no way in which he could introduce any topic of personal significance. There was, naturally, not the slightest hint of any intimacy between them. Did he imagine it or did she give a snort of derision to her young companion as the two young people departed? Certainly, it was as if she hardly knew him at all. He felt jealous and sad beyond belief and, time and time again, cursed his stupid, thoughtless behaviour at Glyndebourne. If only, if only . . . Not that her occupied air necessarily stemmed entirely from his behaviour that evening. Some of it, he felt sure, was because she was busy working with the unit on a very tight schedule. After all, she was doing a job there. It was just that she did seem to have time to stop and talk and be friendly to other people. And it hurt very much seeing her laughing, bright-eyed and so at ease with the rest of the world, in his very own garden.

However much he contrived to be in the right place to run into her, however much he found himself crossing the car-park field when they were 'wrapping up' and going home, their paths didn't cross again. At times he felt she might be hiding from him as he found himself meeting just about every other person time after time. He felt sadder than at any period since Grace left. And furious with himself for being sad, because any thought of a proper relationship between them was ridiculous. But it did not stop him from dry-crying into his pillow sometimes when he couldn't get to sleep at night. More from anger than from anything else. And he would reflect that, at precisely the same time, the 'deceitful little cat' was doubtless opening her legs for Des or Quentin or Craig or, God knows, any of a dozen young men near her own age in a seventh heaven of all-night-long *Kama Sutra* pleasuring. When he was younger he had always imagined that this kind of heartache was the provenance only of the under-twenty-year-old. How wrong he'd been.

He did discover, though, that she appeared to have struck up a friendship with Lesley-Anne.

He spied her ducking into the cottage doorway during the Thursday lunch-break. He made swift tracks to his viewing room and switched on his trusty Mothercare system. They were in the kitchen and all he could hear was that they were talking. Unfortunately, Lesley-Anne had the radio on and most of what they were saying was obscured by it. From a careful consideration of the tone of their voices and the length of what each had to say, it felt like some sort of gossipy female question-and-answer session. He could hear the dark voice of Amy putting the questions, and the higher-pitched tones of Lesley-Anne giving some longer answers.

Just once, Lesley-Anne came briefly into the bedroom to pick some hand cream off her dressing table, while continuing to talk. As she came and then left, rubbing cream into her hands, she spoke to Amy, who had remained in the kitchen: 'Haven't been here all the time. But as far as I know, he doesn't have many people come here. He talked about a Sunday lunch drinks thing but it never happened. Desperately lonely, I think. Certainly no women. You can tell that by the way he looks at you. But old chaps do, don't they? Nothing to lose, I suppose. But he's nice enough. Charming, really.' And then she had gone.

They were talking about him. There was no question about it. Amy was trying to find out more about him. Of course, Lesley-Anne knew no more than Amy did herself. But nevertheless Amy was interested. She hadn't quite forgotten he existed. If it was all over, she wouldn't mention his name at all, would she? It felt as if she was seeking out Lesley-Anne to see how the land lay with him. Maybe she was looking for a sign from him. It was all too complicated for an old chap.

He decided that he was torturing himself. It was unnecessary and immature. Tomorrow he would take himself off and play a round of golf and keep well out of the way. He really could not spend his whole life hanging around for the unlikely drop of little Miss Shakespeare's mascara'd eyelid. He had better start acting his age. This thing with Amy, whatever it had been (and it may not have been a thing at all), was well and truly over. He had better just get adjusted to that fact.

FRIDAY 4 AUGUST

It was pouring in the morning. Sheets of rain. It looked like November. The unit wrapped everything that didn't move in swathes of plastic and put everything that moved into the barn. There was a lot of standing about under large umbrellas looking at the direction of the prevailing weather. There had been a lot of weather during the summer. Mostly of the record-breakingly hot kind. Today was obviously an aberration. Good for the garden, though.

Norman decided to watch the Open on the box. At least it was nice and sunny up at St Andrews. Top of the leader board together, and six under par, were Lyon and Paschalides. Nick Faldo was having a much better second day.

Lesley-Anne made him a chicken salad for lunch and served it on a tray in the sitting room. She was wearing her promise of a denim skirt again, which cheered his recently damaged libido. She asked him if she could abandon him to go across to see Terence at Snapper Green the following day – the Saturday. He didn't see why not. It struck him that for the first time, that morning, he had not bothered to go and see her getting up. That whole voyeur thing obviously had a short shelflife of excitement. Lesley-Anne didn't matter to him in the way that she had. His head was full of his loss of Amy. His viewing room had just been a waste of effort. He would have to find a way of losing it altogether – barricading it. It would never do for anybody to find it. He would die if they did. It would have to be decommissioned. And quickly.

When Lesley-Anne had cleared away the lunch things, Norman found himself staring out of the front windows at the damp desolation outside. He couldn't see the top of Bargate Hill at all.

Down at the far edge of the lawn, sheltering on her own under the slightly projecting roof of his octagonal summerhouse, stood a disconsolate-looking Amy Shakespeare, arms folded, head sunken, alone.

Norman pulled one of his golfing umbrellas out of the rack and, opening it, squidged his way across the lawn to join her.

'Would this help?'

'Galactic,' she said but she didn't sound all that convinced. She wouldn't look at him. 'Smeggy weather,' she said wrinkling her nose. She seemed genuinely depressed.

'Yes. Horrid.' She took the handle of the umbrella from him in long fingers the exact shape and characteristics of which seemed to be engraved on his heart. Then, surprise, surprise, she pulled herself together enough to grin at him. 'Thanks,' she said. And she shot him a look.

'You all right?' he said tentatively.

'Overdosing on weather, aren't we?' She was wearing plimsolls and they heavily exuded water.

'Well,' he said hopelessly. There wasn't much else that he could think of to say. She wouldn't be interested in the fact that it would be good for the garden.

'I'd better escort you back to the house. Otherwise,' she added sinisterly in her best Gestapo, 've hef vays of meking you vet.' They began to walk together under the big umbrella back to his front door, three inches apart physically and a long mile and a half apart in spirit. Her elbow touched his briefly.

Then one of the catering flunkies down in the stable yard dropped and smashed a milk bottle. He had just put a new urn of hot water on to the table under the big projecting roof. A patch of white spread slowly across the York stone paving.

'Want a coffee?' she asked dully.

'Righty ho,' he replied. They joined a small group of damp technicians by the polystyrene cups and polystyrene sugar. Norman held the umbrella shelter as Amy did the honours. The other men went back into the barn. Amy and he each held an all-important symbolic peacemaking quantity of warm fluid. It wasn't easy but he managed to say: 'I would very much like to have the opportunity of having a brief talk with you.' It came out so formally – he could have kicked himself.

'You betcha.'

'Well?'

'If we wrap on schedule today, I'll come and find you, if you like.'

'Will you?'

'What? Come and find you?'

'Get it finished?'

'It's only one sequence. But all this wet needs to bugger off.' Then her name was called from the darkness of the stable entrance and she took herself away.

Norman spent the afternoon cursing the good fortune of St Andrews for having such fine summer sunshine and praying for a change in the Oxfordshire skies. But his devotion did not seem to pay off. Nothing had changed by teatime and, when Lesley-Anne came in to offer him a choice of teas, she mentioned that she had heard the unit were thinking of calling it a day.

While she took her neat, round, meagerly clad backside away to brew him up a little Earl Grey, Norman sat back on his sofa and screwed up his eyes, concentrating on the living room's compact central chandelier. He found he was trying to get the small chandelier to go out of focus in his distorted sight. He found himself imagining that, if he could manage to get the chandelier to dissolve entirely in his vision, then, concomitantly, it might, by some magic of psychic vibration, very well stop raining. To his embarrassment, he was still indulging in this infantile procedure when Lesley-Anne returned with the tray.

She poured him his tea. 'There's a girl on the unit. She's interested in you. A young girl – one of the runners.'

'She's on the location staff.' He wasn't having Amy's status – lowly as it might be – any further denigrated than need be.

'Yes, that's it. She's very nice, actually. Attractive too. She should be a model. God, what I'd give to be as thin as that. She was very keen to know private things, I think, about you. I wondered why.'

'What sort of things?'

'Oh, things. Friends, oh, I don't know, partners. Secrets, I think. Funny, I thought. Gossip, I suppose it was. Very keen to know about your relationship with your brother.'

'Gilbert?'

'Yes.'

'What did you tell her?'

'Nothing. There's nothing to tell. We just had a few cups of coffee together.'

'I know her slightly. Amy Shakespeare.'

'That's right, Amy. Manic streak, I reckon.'

'Manic?'

'I don't know. Fired up. The crew don't like her very much. She's a bit possessed, I thought. Do you know what I mean?'

'I suppose so.'

Outside it suddenly wasn't raining any more. The gods of defocused chandeliers seemed to have done their stuff.

In forty short minutes, the last sequences were set up. Puddles were brushed away from the stable yard, straw was scattered. The man Harrison's voice boomed again. One of their miniature camera railways was laid all the way up to the barn doors. Actors appeared from nowhere, blinking in the light like moles, in full make-up and 1930s costume, followed by anxious women with combs and brushes tweaking at their hair. Dozens of people flooded the yard again, appearing from nowhere.

Finally, an elderly actor whom Norman had not seen before was filmed riding into the yard on one of the Letchworth stallions. The actress 'Sam' appeared, running out to greet him looking lovely and dishevelled with her salient attributes well to the fore.

Norman stood close in the crowd but still could not hear a single syllable of their dialogue. They seemed to play the whole thing very close to tiny Georgina Lewis's magnificent chest. But it was obviously the most charged of highly dramatic screen moments. A charge added to by the fact that the elderly actor was in serious danger of falling off his horse with each entrance that they filmed. He seemed to be trying to find more and more ingenious ways of sliding off. He spent more time apologising to the crew than acting out the scene. Much to Miss Lewis's fury. The famous bosom rose and fell in the most attractive high dudgeon.

Everyone watched the sky with mounting concern. Clapperboards clacked. Harrison sounded so deadly calm of voice that it was clear their schedule was in the most serious jeopardy. For her trouble, the actress then got her face resoundingly slapped by the elderly actor. But this appeared to be part of the story as she then took to kissing him with enormous passion before being bundled back into the stables for all manner of high jinks to come. If only relationships were that simple, Norman thought.

The light was just beginning to fade properly when Harrison announced the traditional mantra: 'That's a wrap.' There was a universally audible sigh and hundreds of pairs of hands fell to ripping apart everything that they had so carefully created.

Amy appeared at his elbow: 'Seven-thirty in the summerhouse?'

'Come in and have a cup of tea.'

'Nope. Summerhouse. Seven-thirty. No man's land.' And she was gone in a squelch of a gym shoe. He would have to face yet another tense ninety-five minutes before he and she could talk.

He found it impossible not to leave for the summerhouse five minutes early. It was sheeting down with rain again. Vehicles were hauling themselves away up the drive and out of his life for ever. The unit was moving on. Wormell Water next week, wasn't it?

The summerhouse was full of old garden furniture, garden tools, sacks of compost and, stored to one side, a very old ping-pong table that had belonged to his father. Norman reckoned that he hadn't entered the place for a couple of years. More, probably. It smelled of dead deckchair canvas and cricket bat oil.

She was in a bright yellow oilskin coat when she arrived – water running off it, soaking her knees. Her shoes made a squelching noise on the wooden floor. She looked like a tiny deep-sea trawlerman. Matted hair, dirty face, pink, smiling.

'Hi, Dad,' she said. 'Saved by the sun, eh?' Instantly, he began to feel better. She got out her cigarette papers and her other illegal bits and pieces. Well, it was the end of the day. It appeared that she seemed to feel quite different towards him again. He just so liked seeing her roll one of her joint things.

He had practised his speech endlessly: 'I'm sorry about Glyndebourne. It was an unforgivable thing to do. I don't know why I did it. I don't always know how best to handle things any more.'

'You get depressed when you've come, that's all. Happens to most guys. Paradise flips out in one half millisecond and you suddenly discover you've been consorting with a smelly tart. That's cool. Men go from ecstasy to instant snap-on puritanism in one single solitary squirt, I find. It figures. I got a lift with a viola-player who was into fossils and cyberspace and thought I should take off my dress.'

'Did you?'

'Well, it *was* smegging wet.'

'Oh.'

'"Oh" nothing, Dad. Just you thank your lucky stars there was someone on the second viola desk who took pity on a sodden customer and only wanted a bit of oral by way of compensation.'

'Amy, you're disgraceful.' He didn't believe her. 'I don't believe you.'

'And in that, you are right, Mr Man. He had a big woolly tartan car-rug into which I nestled, a goodly wife called Natalie, who was waiting up with supper because it was her birthday, and they have twin progeny called Daffy and Donald—'

'Amy?'

'All right, all right, I don't know their names. But they were very recent and much-celebrated birthlings. Weighed down by responsibilities of fatherhood, this Roger drove at just under twenty miles an hour all the way back to London. It took fourteen weeks. He did not place a hand upon my person throughout that whole period of time. Nor I, his. More's the pity.'

'I thought you were furious with me.'

'Furious? Furious? I wasn't furious. "Furious" could never summon up the heights of tantrumania to which I ascended. I was cataclysmic. Mega-galactically-cataclysmic. Middle finger, Norman Ranburn, middle finger!'

'I'm sorry.'

'Sorry's no good. You owe me, Norman, you owe me. You left me in the sodding lurch, Dad. And I had gone right out of my way to give you the best time – I'd blagged the Versace off of Donna, I'd spent every single second of an hour and a quarter on my hair and make-up, I'd got Des to drive me fifty miles out of his way, I'd worried myself sick about why that Figaro should have gone and left it till the morning of his wedding day to measure up his room to see if the bed would fit, I'd rolled you one of my bestest spliffs, and I'd given you my most careful attention in terms of a supremely elegant knuckle-shuffle—'

'Yes, well, that was it.'

'I'm sure it was. Er, *what* was it?'

'The – um . . .'

'"The um"? do you mean the J Arthur? The Sherman? The Nat-West?'

'I suppose so.'

'You adored it. Gonkyfilarious, you thought it was. Fandabbidozy, you thought it was. Until, of course, it terminated.'

'The point is, Amy, at my age and with my background, that sort of outrageous – I don't know – that sort of unusual activity, in public, well, it's not something that I find very easy to deal with. My generation tended on the whole to think of sex as happening very occasionally, very quietly, very privately, in the dark. What you do is the reverse of that. Why are you always trying to go out on the furthest limb of propriety? Can you never behave properly? Just ordinarily?'

Amy seemed to give this puzzled assessment. She dragged on the joint and passed it, their enmity over, to him. They were like two colleagues trying to solve a problem of logistics.

Amy perched herself on the side of a deck-chair. She was never happy unless perched. It was gloomy in the shed. Her oilskin continued to drip solemnly on to the floor. The glow of her cigarette end illuminated her face. Her eyes sparkled. 'I *can* do ordinary shit,' she began warily. 'I think. Yeah. No prob.' It was as if she had been offered an impossible challenge. 'It'd be quite intriguing doing "ordinary"'. I could even go for the full gold-medal "boring" as well, if you like.'

'I'd like to see you try.'

'Have faith, Norman, you just have to have faith.'

'All right.'

'You're on. You owe me two favours already, anyway. I'll do your smegging "ordinary". And you do my, um, less smegging "ordinary". Two such in fact.'

'Must I?'

'A deal is a deal is a deal.' She puffed on the joint. 'Is a deal,' she added for good measure. 'You want "ordinary", you have to pay.'

His head had got rather vague. 'I know,' he quoted her: '"You do something for me, I do something for you."'

'That's the ticket.'

'What do I have to do for you?'

'You'll see.'

'What?' He was terrified.

'Well, actually, I've no idea, at the moment.'

'Well, I've got an idea.' He was so excited by this turn of events. They were back on joshing terms again. It was a good feeling. He wanted to capitalise on it. Very badly. 'Are you free tomorrow? I'm going to Gordon Driscoll's grandson's wedding in London tomorrow afternoon. The Goodman Club for the reception, anyway. A society do. Posh. If you could do a really good "ordinary", you could come along. It would be an absolutely marvellous place, well, to try it. I expect you'd find it a bit of a laugh. The Driscolls are tremendously "County". I'd be very glad to take you along. You could be my young cousin. My young, *female* cousin.'

'It's a tall order, Daddio.'

'You can do it.' He was nicely disorientated by the joint.

He was getting better at this marijuana stuff. He felt so happy again.

'Samantha Glottalstop.'

'What?'

'That's what I'll be called.'

'Amy.'

'Well Samantha anyway – like gorgeous Ms Georgina Lewis. Bet you were creaming yourself to polish that pair of knockers, Dad.'

'You are just incorrigible.'

'Yeah, great isn't it? But not tomorrow afternoon. Tomorrow afternoon, I'll be the very reverse of incorrigible. Tomorrow I'm going all out for the "Dull As Dishwater Award".'

He hoped he hadn't made another horrible mistake. But he couldn't leave her alone, could he? They emerged from the summerhouse. The buildings were almost clear. But there were still a number of people around. They had agreed to meet at Sharpe & Williams, the costume and dress-hire people in Jermyn Street, the following morning. He would hire her something dreary for her to wear at the Driscoll event. And a hat, he thought. And gloves. The very idea of it made him smile.

SATURDAY 5 AUGUST

They met at ten outside Sharpe & Williams. Amy was uncharacteristically punctual. She pressed hard lips to his cheek in a way that suggested that bygones were indeed bygones. Impressed, no doubt, by Norman's morning coat and top hat, a multitude of at least five assistants of the dress-hire shop danced attendance upon Miss Shakespeare, who was very quickly transformed from jean-rigged woman of the nineties to florally bedecked woman of the Festival of Britain era. Within ten minutes she was looking like a queen of the coffee-morning and flower-arranging set and hailed from somewhere elegantly repressed like Godalming, Chichester or Henley-on-Thames.

Amy, who reckoned she would not start her bash at being 'ordinary' until the reception itself, entertained the hour with much and varied dashing about the changing-cubicle curtains in multifarious states of charming dishabille, while Norman sat on the largest pouffe he had ever seen. He pretended that his eyes were glued to *The Times* and never rose from the page to light upon the various visible bits of Amy, clad in only bra and pants. He consumed quantities of good coffee, and felt like a Sultan. Well, pouffes do that. And one-woman harems.

At one stage, when the Sharpe & Williams handmaidens had taken themselves off to seek out yet further supplies of dress-pearls and dark-blue satin court shoes, Amy appeared in an outfit of such a large print design and so pink and navy that she looked almost beyond middle-aged. Seeing that she and Norman were alone, Amy lazily lifted her gloved hands behind her head and, growling out what he presumed was some raunchy 'stripper-music' from the side of her mouth, executed a number ludicrous bumps and grinds. Thrusting a carefully considered hip in the direction of El Sultan Ranburn she allowed her pelvis slowly and graphically to illustrate the activity of his dearest wish. Then the door opened and they were joined by a startled employee by the name of Melanie whom Amy swiftly drew into the fullest inspection of an errant thread on the skirt's hem. Amy had adjusted her demeanour at such express speed that it was difficult for Norman not to guffaw.

By eleven-thirty, they were out in Jermyn Street with Amy in white shoes, killer handbag and a dress of navy with white naval trimmings that would pass inspection at the most regal of royal garden parties. She wore a white straw hat the size of Yorkshire, with the biggest navy ribbon and bow seen this side of Ascot Ladies Day. The whole rig-out made her look as if she had left Cheltenham Ladies' College bereft of a single O level some time in the early 1970s.

But he couldn't help seeing that the skirt, however long, wrapped itself revealingly about her bottom. Amy noticed it too. 'They're not all fuckwits, these proper ladies, you see.

223

We may get all dolled up like Christmas in Oxford Street but we like to do a bit of discreet advertising as well. I could get a pull today, yet. You watch me go, Daddio.'

They went into Fortnum and Mason, the Piccadilly top persons' grocer's shop. In their wedding outfits, they fitted the decor, the produce and the style of the place to an absolute T. Amy lightly took the crook of his arm as they strolled the counters and watched the tourists, most of whom were tickled pink at being served with a hundred different sorts of mustard by staff in tails and starched collars.

'OK, then, Mr Man,' said his companion, her cat's-eyes grilling him coolly from the shadows of her flying-saucer hat, 'Gentleman's Relish.' And indeed they were standing in front of a lavish display of small, circular, white china boxes which contained the spread known as the 'Gentleman's Relish' or 'Patum Perparium' as they called it. The design printed on the lid was of the famous Fortnum and Mason clock, which was high up on the building's facia above Piccadilly, outside. The price was a modest six pounds ninety-five – 'the anchovy spread for toast or biscuits'.

'Do you want some?' he asked.

'Oh, do I? I'll say,' she grunted, making it sound almost orgasmic with need. He reached for his money. She laid a single white-gloved finger on the hand in his trouser pocket. 'No, no, my dear.' Her poised English accent again. 'You owe me a game, Normanello. You owe me two games actually. This is game number one. Come with me.' And she led him firmly back out on to the pavement.

'This is it. Now don't be an anorak. This is a well easy one just for starters. You go back into the shop. Nick the relish. Meet me outside the Royal Academy building across the other side of the road. With said relish. In five minutes.'

'Nick it?'

'Steal, shoplift, pilfer, snitch, knock off, filch. Where've you been since the war? This is your test for today Mr Ranburn. You chicken?'

'Yes. I'm not going to start stealing things. What kind of a game is that?'

224

'A good game. You're happy enough when I do stuff for you. This is just a one-way street, is it, Norman? They won't notice. They can afford it. There are vast crowds in there. Whip in, dip the goods, slide out and you've got it made. And, in addition you'll get the Big A – an adrenalin rush as good as E. Better, in fact, for you. Then we can go off and spend the afternoon being mega-ordinary. And you'll have the satisfaction of having a big round hard thing filling your trouser pocket all afternoon. With a slightly tangy salty taste inside. For your toast. To go with your world-famous hot chocolate.'

'No.'

'Oh, you and your noes. You're pathetic, you are.' She stalked off away from him, down Piccadilly, past the intriguing window displays that Fortnum's delight in. If he didn't get himself together, she'd be gone. It shouldn't be too difficult. It could be worse. It wasn't as if she had asked him to abscond with a full picnic hamper or anything. 'All right, Amy,' he called to her among the throngs on the pavement. 'I'll see you opposite. As you say, five minutes.' Without turning, she waved a white, lacy-gloved hand over her shoulder and kept on walking. She would be the death of him.

He returned to the shop. Moments before, he had been drifting around it in the jolliest frame of mind. Now he could feel the blood thumping in his throat and a shortness of breath. He didn't have to do this. But if he didn't, would he ever have the opportunity of watching the ghastly, gorgeous Amy tumbling in and out of her clothes as she had done for him that morning? He thought not. This was his last opportunity to show that he wasn't just a dull old fart. She thought he was so straight. That's what she called it, 'straight'. Little did she know. He was about the most perverted man she had ever spent time with. If she were to know about his viewing room – well, that would be a thing. Little did she know how disgusting he really was, in his heart of hearts.

He edged the longest way through the throngs in the shop heading for their neat stacks of Gentleman's Relish pots, looking myopically at every single item of the goods on display on the way. At the same time he was peering, in an obviously suspicious manner, at the way the staff were distributed around the busy shop floor. What the hell was he doing, in there, setting about breaking the law? What, in Christ's name, was he doing, trying to break the kind of decency code that he had always tried to lead his life by? Well, at least, his public life. Hanging on to Amy, he supposed.

She was right: it really shouldn't be too difficult to do. He picked up one of the little disk-shaped boxes and made much of reading the description on its lid. He read all the words twice. And carefully examined the design of the clock on the lid of it as well. Then, blushing furiously, he set off for the cash-till holding the little pot very obviously out in front of him as one does when one has picked up goods in a service shop but, as yet, has not been able to pay for them.

As he turned around the end of the fixture, where they were showing a magnificent range of fancy olive oils, he surreptitiously dropped the thing into his side jacket pocket. He couldn't stop his head from whizzing about in every direction, to check which of the staff had seen this clumsy prestidigitation. In spite of the fact he was staring about with the eyes of a maddened horse, no one seemed to be looking his way. On all sides there was bustle and hustle and wrapping and queuing and buying and guessing at the value of things in yen and in dollars. No one was looking at the most flamboyantly dressed man in the shop stealing almost seven pounds' worth of traditional gentlemen's anchovy spread for cheese and biscuits.

He left the shop, desperately trying not to let himself run. Once outside he slowed to a magnificent dawdle and even, with enormous courage, allowed himself casually to stop and admire one of the windows, which was entirely filled with an enormous straw hat tricked out with marquees and sculling eights to look like the Henley Regatta. There was no adrenalin rush. She was wrong about that. Perhaps that would occur only once he had truly got away with

226

it. At the moment he was in mid-crime and he just felt terribly sick.

He crossed Piccadilly and found himself on the big traffic island waiting to cross to the Royal Academy side. He couldn't see where the hell Amy had got to.

'Excuse me, sir.'

It was one of the men from the shop. In tails and collar and everything. Norman died. 'Yes?' is what he actually said. He took the briefest possible relief from the fact that he managed not to stutter. But he was dying all the same.

'Would you be kind enough to step back into the store with me, sir?' The tone of icy politeness was almost insolent. The Gentleman's Relish felt so obviously resident in his pocket that it must surely be bleeping. Norman was aware of sweat breaking out in profusion all over his body. He could already see the magistrate's court and the small, sad, pathetic paragraphs in the newspapers.

'Why?' he asked.

'I think you know why, sir.'

'I'm sure I don't.' Could they search him? How long could he bluff this out? The man had only to stroke his pocket to feel the little china pot in there. Should he just try to run away? And thereby compound his guilt? Would there be hue-and-cry the length and breadth of Piccadilly? How far could he run before they caught him?

'I have to say to you, sir, that I have reason to believe that you may have left the shop without paying for something that you have about your person. If I am wrong, please believe me, you will have my fullest apologies. If you would step back into the store we can continue this discussion in private rather than out here among the multitudes.'

And the man's disdainful eye took in an increasingly interested crowd of passers-by that had accumulated on the now over-occupied traffic island. The spectators were not going to disperse until they saw the climax of this interesting incident – the arrest of a man in a top hat. If the number of people increased much more, a policeman would probably turn up and the whole thing would instantly become a court matter. And Norman would die of dread and embarrassment and shame. But he would kill Amy first.

'Come along, sir,' said the man, gesturing his way back towards the shop. Norman felt limp. He was just about to walk, heavy-hearted, back across the road to prison and execution and shame and death and misery, when a familiar voice cut into the scene – 'Dad!' And there was Amy's navy straw hat ducking, with the greatest difficulty, through the watchers. 'You forgot your receipt.' Amy had in her hand a small till receipt. It was for Gentleman's Relish. It was for six pounds ninety-five pence exactly. It was for 5th August, that day's very date. It was even timed for four minutes earlier.

'Hullo there,' she said brightly to the Fortnum's man with the archest of Roedean tones. Norman suddenly knew he was going to be all right. The weight of the world flew from his shoulders. The man took the receipt briefly between finger and thumb and shrugged. 'Left it on the counter. Silly Daddy,' said the girl.

'Sorry, sir,' he said. He could see that Amy clearly didn't have room about her – not even in her narrow white handbag – to hide a further pot of Gentleman's Relish. Unless she had it hidden in the crown of her hat. And the Fortnum's man wasn't about to start searching about in that. He was already too embarrassed. He disappeared with a little bow and an 'I'm truly sorry to have bothered you, sir.' Amy deftly presented a graphic, gloved, extended middle finger to his departing rear. But it was all right. The bulk of the onlookers had by now departed, in search of other top-hatted shoplifters being apprehended elsewhere.

'Galactic. Orbital. Finger-licking,' she murmured in his ear as she hung on to his arm and they finished the great crossing of Piccadilly. 'God, old man, you turn me on something horrible.' And she stuck her tongue firmly into his ear. And bit his earlobe. He did feel demonstrably wonderful. In answer to the girl's question, 'Is the Big A kicking in, now, then, Dad?' the answer had to be a palpable 'yes'. He was still in shock. Sweat continued to pour off him. But he couldn't help grinning. He couldn't help strutting. He couldn't help feeling immortal. He had done it, done it, done it. And got away with it. Just. Thanks to Amy.

It didn't mean that he didn't guess, at the same time, that Amy could have been the perpetrator of alerting the Fortnum's man to his misdemeanour. He was beginning to realise just how much she found his potential humiliation a mainspring for action. So far, she seemed to find saving him in the very nick of time an equally thrilling motivation. But how long would that last?

He was right, Amy played these games with him because of the crazy deviant kicks she got out of it. There didn't seem to be any other motive. He didn't think she was after his money – she never mentioned money. She seemed reasonably well provided for. And she had invested not a little herself in supporting these shenanigans. She had, after all, paid for the Glyndebourne tickets. Any secret agenda that there might be for her was purely that she liked elegantly deviant kicks. That was the long and the short of it. Little did she know, but it now appeared that so did he.

All right, Norman knew now for certain that his gorgeous escort was a deceitful little cat and one couldn't trust her as far as throw her. But he loved the way she was hanging on to his arm. He adored seeing her eyes flick up, like lasers, into his, from under her aircraft-hangar headgear and he wanted nothing better than to feel the soft press of her warm breast against his forearm as they walked along. It seemed there was a lot he would be prepared to put up with, to keep all that.

He remembered, at the end of his masturbatory sixties, reading Philip Roth's psychosexual novel *Portnoy's Complaint* and how it gave him such infinite comfort because it revealed that his own private, solitary shame of self-abuse was not unique. Norman remembered, too, scorning the eventual arrival, in the novel, of Portnoy's sexual wet dream of a girlfriend, the Monkey. To his understanding, that kind of sexual nemesis on legs never existed in real life – it was just a novelist's optimistic fantasy. And all the poorer for that. Now he knew how wrong he had been.

What had Roth said about parents? 'A Jewish man with

parents alive is a fifteen-year-old boy, and will remain a fifteen-year-old boy till they die.' That could not have been truer, also, about the intimidating Magnus and his oldest son.

In the meantime, as an extraordinary twosome, they were going off to enact the very reverse of Portnoy and the Monkey in darkest Anglican Mayfair. A gang of two, richer now by one pot of Gentleman's Relish and sharing the wicked secret of having undertaken a successful, if modest, heist, even though, truth to tell, she had finally paid for the thing.

But, could she do 'being ordinary'?

She could. She turned out to be the very mistress of it.

The Goodman Club was in Braithe Street, just off Old Bond Street. It was now a little dowdy, although in the thirties it had been at the very centre of sophisticated literary London. The walls were covered with cartoons of H. G. Wells, Priestley and Isherwood and framed menus signed by the Sitwells and Vaughan Williams. If you asked nicely the short and elderly doorman, who rejoiced in the name of Osian, would take you and show you exactly where, on his one and only visit to the club, some dread day in those masturbatory sixties, Brendan Behan had managed to throw up all over his brother Dominic. In the last ten years the place had been entirely superseded, as far as media and artistic attention went, by glitzier, less formally mannered, spritzer-serving watering-hell-holes like the Groucho Club, Green's and 2 Brydges Place.

The gentle, faded Georgian charm of the building with its high-ceilinged dining room was absolutely perfect, though, for the Driscoll reception. The assembly matched the building more exactly than it was possible to imagine.

Elderly wine-waiters circulated around a crowd of some two hundred of the most brightly chattering, brightly made-up, Maida Vale, Finchley and Home Counties set. Norman was suddenly aware that, in the same way that one sees one's own familiar residence afresh because one is escorting a stranger around it, he was seeing this gathering through entirely fresh eyes. And this was because he was seeing the throng through the jaundiced eye of his fearfully exceptional antipodean companion.

And it was Amy's cynical observation of such gatherings in the past that allowed her to fit into that milieu with such withering accuracy. She had lived alongside this society's children and grandchildren during her years at Sherston. She had heard their chatter, witnessed their privilege and enjoyed their patrimony on many a great festive day at the school. Days like Founder's Day, the Sherston Ceilidh Sunday and the Bulstrode Epigram Day. She could match it all exactly. Virtually disappear inside it.

Norman watched her in covert amazement as she took her new-found cut-glass accent around the room, comparing notes about Ascot with old man Driscoll himself, sharing a recipe for rhubarb crumble with the bride's mother, swapping chalet-maid names in St Moritz and Chamonix with the Sir Joshua Tibbotsons and bemoaning, with Gordon's daughter-in-law, the changes that the Al Fayeds had wrought upon the food halls at Harrods.

Amy and Norman moved around the room independently, he to feel more and more astonished by the grotesque hats, tights and skip-sized handbags of the women and more and more fascinated by the dyed-in-the-wool certainties of the men, she to work her own special brand of disguised magic on the assembled menfolk. Where there weren't hats, the ladies sported the universal candyfloss-hair look – spun sugar masquerading as softly waved helmets but with the tensile texture of whipped steel. The menfolk, for their part, provided a lunar landscape of pampered bald-patedness – endless pink boulders hovering just above shoulder height. Norman thanked the Lord for his virtually unique head of hair.

At one supreme moment, after the jollity of the speeches, and well into everyone's seventh glass of champagne, Norman spied his 'cousin, Samantha Glottalstop' holding court, a minute figure surrounded by at least seven well-upholstered gentlemen, all of whom were attempting to outbray each other in their appreciation of her doubtless unusual humour.

Samantha seemed even to be putting the bride in the shadows with her reprise of Eliza Doolittle at Ascot.

Later, Norman's heart lurched with jealousy as he watched her enrapturing both the groom and an attractive young man friend of his with tales of a totally fictitious Surrey childhood. For a while, then, she disappeared from view. She had probably retired to the toilet to regroup her exhausted 'ordinary' faculties, and probably, knowing her, to smoke some of her drugs. Norman circulated the throng as quickly as was practicable, but completely failed to spot his society companion. She hadn't left, had she?

Then, later, thank goodness, she popped up again, blithe and bonny, butter unmelted in a mouth flickering with amusement. They both joined a shrill crowd throwing rice about in Braithe Street as the happy couple set out on the first stage of their journey to honeymoon in Florida.

'I'm a mite pissed,' she giggled. Norman too had imbibed rather more champagne than he guessed at.

'I've been ever so good,' she went on. 'Ask the groom,' she said enigmatically. 'Made the people laugh, though.'

'You have been magnificent, my dear. Astonishing. I take my hat off to you. I so enjoyed your performance.'

'I had just one tiny slip, I'm afraid, Norman. Nothing to write home about though. Panic not. It's just that I found myself schmoozing that Charles, you know, the lovely groom, hitched now for evermore to stalking-horse Betjemania Frumpington-Bore or whatever her grace was called. Our fingers clashed over a platter of figgy puddings. Well, his eye was on the wander. Like blokes' eyes usually are. Particularly when they sense the gate has just slammed shut on them for ever.' Amy put on one of her most abject looks. 'Norman, I promise I tried to bite my tongue to stop the words coming out. I held on to my tongue with both fingers and thumb like this.' And she demonstrated. She pulled out the end of a bright pink tongue with a forefinger and thumb and waved it about in the Mayfair afternoon for Norman to examine where she may or may not have bitten it. 'But there was naught I could do. Naught, Norman. Against every grundy fibre of will in my body, out slipped a sudden, last-minute offer: 'Fancy a quick shag before they throw away the key?' I think I meant it as a touch of conversational biplay, a millijest, a nanoquip, if you get my meaning. But the guy took me well seriously. So *I* took me well seriously. And, do you know, Norman, it was a breeze. Ten vintage minutes of feral groin-grappling. The cubicles in the club loos in there are as big as a horse-box. Better than smegging old Lord's anyway. In my view.' Amy's eyes danced at him merrily. Was any of this true? 'I'm sorry, but don't worry – no one noticed. Oh, I suppose Charles noticed, but I doubt he'll mention it about. I told myself I was doing the bride a heap-big favour. I mean, he won't come anything like so quickly tonight.'

'Amy, you didn't.'

'If you say so.'

'You did?' She grinned at him and squeezed his hand and poured her plastic cup of celebratory dry rice down his starched shirt front. 'Whatever you like to think,' she breathed at him. 'Whatever's in your head. I did or I didn't.'

She hadn't, had she? No. Yes. No. Well, *had* she? He doubted it. She was watching his face as his brain ticked over. He decided to put it out of his mind. He changed the subject: 'Who was that fair-haired young man you were talking to?'

'Charlie's mucker? The hunky guy in the all-over tan? "How do you know it's all-over, Amy?" No, well, I don't, Norman, I don't. Jamie, he's called. A dealer. LIFFE. Aren't they all? But he plays bass in a band as well, so he's probably just about tolerable. More than tolerable, in fact. Did you get a feel of those shoulders?'

'No, Amy, actually, I can't say I did. Obviously I missed out on an opportunity of a lifetime there. Unlike your good self, I imagine.'

'Nothing good about me, Dad. Anyway, they're the dog's bollocks, I promise you. "Smitten" is the word I'd use. And he looked as if he might be grievously well-hung too.'

'Stop it, Amy. Your mind's an open sewer. You are a total disgrace.'

'For sure. Money on the ticket, there, Dad. Fun though, eh?'

They had got to that appalling time of a day in the life of a wedding guest when, slightly pickled, duty done, and not a single Ancient Mariner in sight, the evening stretches empty ahead like a post office queue on pension day. He would just have to drive back to Coombe now. He was tired. The day had been another emotional rollercoaster.

'Where did you park the car?' she asked. 'Do you fancy seeing where I live?'

Did he ever?

She lived in one of a group of tiny streets round the back of the Vauxhall interchange, just south of the river and virtually across from the Tate Gallery. He parked the car in a street full of skips, battered dustbins, pot-holes, unhinged cats and surreally abandoned furniture. Though he might be a bit tiddily, it felt like a useful opportunity for him to discover more about the girl. Maybe he could question her about her links with her poetically inclined so-called father.

She apparently shared her place with a costume designer called Donna who was away in Ireland working on a film.

They lived in a scout hut, for God's sake. With 'Be Prepared' carved in doomful letters over the door lintel. An apt aphorism, thought Norman, for all those who entered there. Amy explained that the place had been a tiny church hall once, and then a scout hut, before doing service as a carry-out pizza establishment and, in the last two years, as wardrobe store and Shakespearean residence.

It felt so intimate, being allowed into her home. He was thrilled, wary, fascinated and a touch randy.

It was unlike any place he had ever seen before, in which people actually lived. It was more like an enormous wardrobe than a home. More than half of the hall was taken up with rack upon rack of clothing, hanging in shining plastic bags, with shelves groaning under the weight of boxes, wigs and hats, and with cupboards and chests of drawers exploding with shirts, shoes, bags, collars, ties, padding, hoops, fans and shawls. Even the nearer half of the room had ropes slung right across from one wall to the other, with materials of every kind hanging from them, dyed in the most vibrantly extravagant colours. There were a number of Turkish and Indian rugs and carpets all over the floor of the 'living' part of the hall. They made the place look something like a mosque. Indeed, the whole place felt as if it hailed from the East – it was like a souk, a bazaar, but without the incessant noise. It smelled oddly of old socks covered by a masking of various sweet and musky essences. To one side hung a full-scale plastic skeleton. Well, of course. Norman imagined that these sorts of place always had to have at least one full-sized plastic human skeleton hanging about somewhere. He was just glad to have spotted it so early.

The windows had black roller-blinds pulled right down and the only light came from one ancient theatrical floodlight, which threw crimson light up above the costumes, into the rafter space. The room was full of shadows. There were dozens of unlit candles standing around on every surface. It wasn't wonderfully clean.

The whole focus of the room, standing there splendidly on a small, square, raised island, was an immense throne-like brass bedstead with heaps of unmade duvets and pillows scattered about on it in a random and colourful disorder. Norman had a feeling that this whole ragbag of an accommodation was designed to display this particular piece of intimate furniture, presenting it as a kind of hippy altar. There was no other furniture apart from a set of library steps, a secretarial swivel chair which addressed an extravagantly high-tech sewing machine and a bar stool which lurked alone in the quasi-kitchen area which stretched along one side of the room. The only occupant of the place seemed to be a cat – the largest tabby cat that Norman had ever seen. It entirely covered the top of a battered refrigerator. It was a perfect sphere and looked like a very fat, very furry toilet-seat cover.

One corner of the room was boxed off into a separate space and this was labelled with an arrow in big red spray-can letters, six foot by six foot, as 'BATHROOM – have bath now!'

The end wall, above where they had entered, had writing on it as well. Also printed in red letters, but smaller, it said: 'Faith, Sir, we are here today, and gone tomorrow' and 'Love ceases to be a pleasure, when it ceases to be a secret.' Both these quotations were neatly accredited to one Aphra Behn.

Intriguingly, he thought, there was but one bed. Amy, he assumed, must therefore sleep alongside, or on top of or possibly even underneath this Donna wardrobe-person. Funny lives these young people led. Unless, like Gilbert and Sullivan, they Coxed and Boxed it – one sleeping at night and the other during the daytime. Anything was possible with these folk.

'Can I use the toilet?' he asked and he took himself off to the bathroom.

Inside, he found himself facing the biggest, most daunting plate-glass mirror that he had ever seen. He was obliged to watch himself in magnificent detail as he set about jettisoning the afternoon's champagne. He turned to the sink and opened the bathroom cabinet that hung on the wall above it. The thing was chock-a-block with Lillets and Tampax. He shut it quickly. While washing his hands, he managed to drop his signet ring on to the floor and it rolled away under the side-panel of the bath. Grunting irritatedly, he knelt down to retrieve it. He then realised that the formica side-panel would come away, making it easier to retrieve his ring.

He found the absconding ring and pushed it back on to his finger. In the dust under one end of the bath, where the pipes went up to the taps, there was a shallow cardboard box lid. It looked as if it had been placed there specially. It had some strange things in it. He carefully drew it out. There was a small, beautifully dressed teddy bear lying spread-eagled on top of some papers. It was a leather-clad motorcycling teddy bear with biker's jacket and trousers and a peaked black leather cap sewn on to its head. And a lot of chrome metal studs. Around its neck was a small card luggage label and written on it in a neat green-inked hand were the words 'Please look after this bear. I'm Biker Bill. Amy, with fondest love. Yours ever, W.'

Why should anyone tuck such a beautifully dressed teddy bear in the dust under a bath? Particularly one that would seem to appeal so perfectly to its recipient? He had to presume that Amy had hidden these bits and pieces under there on purpose.

The papers in the box were press cuttings. Not many. All of them had been carefully snipped out and fastened together with paper-clips. Every one of them appeared to involve a retired judge in some way or another. A Lord Justice Boyd-Orr. A William Boyd-Orr. Norman vaguely recalled the name from the media. Most of the cuttings were newspaper obituaries. He had died some eighteen months earlier. No, he hadn't just died, he had committed suicide. The obituaries were not vastly forthcoming as to why this should have been. 'Depression' was a word that Norman picked out of two of the reports. Boyd-Orr's wife had died the previous year. There were a couple of newsprint photographs of some event or party – some celebration – both from different newspapers. One was of Amy, on her own, wearing the silver Glyndebourne dress, nicely caught by the light – which was presumably why the newspaper had featured it. The other photograph was of about seven people gathered together at the same event. At any rate, Amy was wearing the same dress and earrings. She was standing three from the left among the crowd, smiling like the cat who had got the cream. From what evidence one could glean from the photo she appeared to be accompanying a reasonably good-looking, tall, older man. It wasn't certain, but from the photographs accompanying the obituaries the man could well be this same William Boyd-Orr.

Norman hadn't much time, so he could only quickly scan the various clippings. It dawned on him that it looked as if he, Norman, must be one of a series of gentlemen as far as Miss Shakespeare was concerned. She must have some very strange kink for dreadful old men. Or she could just be plain batty. But clearly Norman wasn't the first.

He was hurrying to put the box back when he saw a small twist of tissue in its bottom. It was a tiny roll of toilet paper or kitchen roll. There was something hard wrapped up inside. He unwrapped it. It was round. It was a ring. A gold ring with green stones – six of them set in a cluster – like a small green rose. Even to Norman's unpractised eye, they looked as if they were probably large emeralds surrounded by a network of tiny diamonds. A valuable ring, by all accounts.

He rolled it thoughtfully on his palm. So this William Boyd-Orr character had got into a thing with Amy, given her presents, died, and she was unhappy and had hidden away the evidence? Something like that? But why would one hide away a bit of jewellery like this? It would be worth selling. Perhaps she just couldn't bring herself to do it. Maybe Boyd-Orr had really mattered. He stood silent in the bathroom considering. Was it just possible that he, Norman, mattered to her too? That she just had this mad power-crazy – well – craziness and a severely twisted brain which needed her to consort with men three times her age? Or, at any rate, chaps who were getting towards the end of their lives? Was it, as he had often wondered, about money? In the end, he would have to ask her.

Without thinking anything through, Norman found he had dropped the emerald ring into his side jacket pocket. It wasn't theft. It was just a bit of evidence. He would return it to her. And ask her a few questions. He quickly put everything else back under the bath and fitted the side-panel in place and went back into the main room.

Boyd-Orr had apparently overdosed on sleeping pills while the balance of his mind was disturbed. Amy was always thrusting pills into Norman's mouth. He had better watch it, he thought.

The vast room was now totally illuminated by dozens of scented candles and two great glowing Chinese paper lanterns. Terrible fire risks. The place jumped and swayed with shadows. It was magical. And it helped one not to notice the dust. The front door of the hall had clicked shut, cutting out the brightness of the late-afternoon sunshine. The room now looked as if it was set up for a seance. Or a black mass. The bed appeared to glow in the gloom.

'There you are then. Sit,' she commanded. She was bustling in and out of the pools of light, ducking under the hangings, scratching matches into life as she continued to light joss-sticks and other incendiary devices.

'Where?' he asked trying to maintain some joviality.

'Bed's good,' she said. 'Drugs?'

'I'm a bit squiffy from the party actually.' He lowered himself onto the edge of the bed, pushing some of its many lacy pillows aside to make a semblance of room. He felt reasonably comfortable but, given, what he might have just learned, he had better watch her carefully.

Amy's head popped up from behind a great hanging yellow sheet. She had abandoned the hat. 'Yeah, I'm a bit toasted too. All the better. I'll just release myself from this ayatollah of an outfit and I'll skin up.' Norman demurred. 'For God's sake, Dad,' she called out to him on her trip around the premises, 'you haven't broken a single solitary law since lunchtime. Brace up, you Englishman. This was not how your empire was established.'

'It's all right,' he said, but he knew it probably wasn't. He did so like seeing her going about her nefarious purposes with her papers and her matches and her funny-smelling accoutrements. He lay back among the pillows. He was beginning to feel like a sultan again. It wasn't a bad sort of feeling. He wondered if Boyd-Orr had ever lain there.

He may have snoozed briefly.

'Look,' she said. Norman looked. She was standing there in the dark with the light behind her, naked apart from a series of tight leather straps and buckles that laced her whole body. One of her legs, too, was encased, from crotch to ankle, entirely in thin strapping. She wore the tiniest black leather thong thing, the legs cut away high on the hip, which only inadequately hid her silky black pubic hair. Was that what they called a G-string? What did the 'G' stand for, he wondered, vaguely, waking up. 'Goatish'? 'Gross'? 'Gorgeous'? She had on heels like glass kitchen knives. 'It's without the face of course,' she said. 'Or the hair. Or the glitter.' As ever, her nipples stood to attention, entirely visible now, poking their way out strongly between the taut straps. They were seeking out his attention, moving gently with her breathing. He felt himself instantly hardening at the bravura of it, the unafraid quality of it – her, standing there, firm breasts in the ascendant, long brown legs challengingly apart, grinning mischievously.

'You like?' she asked, needlessly. 'Smegging better than this afternoon's Haslemere Carnival Queen outfit, anyway, wouldn't you say, Mr Man? It's my costume for *Hard-Up* – you know, the cabaret, *Hard-Up And Flummoxed*? Oh yeah, phew, yeah, I reckon I've picked up a new partner in crime for the show. Which is well useful as we've got a gig in two weeks' time. No, don't worry, it's not you – stop quaking, Dad.' Looking down at herself approvingly, she said: 'Brilliant, isn't it. Dead tacky. S and M with its tongue firmly in its lower fundament. Smegging uncomfy to wear though.' And, thrusting one of her fat, smoking, peculiar cigarettes at him, she disappeared behind the hangings once more.

Norman inhaled and lay back like the experienced substance-abuser he was. He watched the circles of smoke twisting like hallucinations into the distant roof space high above his head, catching the red light. The meandering vapours looked as if they belonged to a nineteen-sixties, French, new-wave film. He could get used to this – feeling woozy and having nubile women flaunting themselves at him. This was every bit as good and as easy as his viewing room. Infinitely better in fact. It didn't feel secretive and soiling. And it still demanded nothing from him. He sucked at the neatly made, nicotine-stained roll-up again. Her wicked joints had such an instant effect on him now. One never experienced that with alcohol. Already he knew that he would be unable to walk satisfactorily, should it be required of him. But it wouldn't be.

He kicked off his shoes and loosened his tie and collar. Would he be able to get home? He wasn't sure about where he had dumped his jacket. It was around somewhere. He wasn't sure about where he lived. He wasn't sure about very much. Hey ho. Except that he had to be watchful. He had to keep an eye on her. Not take any of her capsules. With two distinct, echoing clunks his shoes hit the deck and tumbled off the bed rostrum. He inhaled massively again. He was getting good at this. He had a long pile of ash poised on the end of the thing – a tiny, grey, fragile erection. Fascinating. Beautiful. Intricate.

Soft flute music began to filter about the place. Two flutes fighting with each other in an uneasy harmony. Flutes, but with an insistent determined drum-beat as well. A duet for Debussy and the Mau Mau. Then he heard a new voice, a hectoring voice, a button-holing voice. It was the sex-bomb in yet one more guise. She never stopped, that girl. She had much too much energy. Couldn't she – what did they call it – hang loose? No she couldn't. Her voice took charge: '"You are old, Father William, the young man said, and your hair has become very white; and yet you incessantly stand on your head – do you think, at your age, it is right?"'

Lewis Carroll, by all that's wonderful. Norman looked around and there, in the shadows of the hall to his left, high up, a caricatured young man's face appeared, wearing a big beret with a pair of preposterous staring eyes and floppy ears, apparently suspended in mid-air. It was hovering in the darkness, high above one of the over-burdened washing-lines. Befuddled as he was, he guessed how it was done – Amy was lying on her back at the top of the library steps. It was puppet-theatre time again. This crazy head was mounted on top of, or over, her foot. Thus the man had the longest most sinuous neck in the world – it was made out of Amy's calf and the back of her knee and her thigh. And, if Norman looked carefully enough, even in this odd stupor, he reckoned he could just make out her naked bottom. Her peach-like – oh no, what a terrible image – her smooth, heart-shaped – ugh, again – her God-given – oh, words, words, words – her Auguste Rodin of a bum, her very centre – the source of all her mystery, her ultimate heaven. Lawks, he couldn't get his brain around any of this.

Then there was such a commotion. Amy landed at his side on the bed, her head enclosed in the most hideous, rubberised white-haired old man's mask. The bed creaked and groaned and twanged as if it was possessed. She threw piles of scarves and ties and shirts all over him and clutched herself fervently to his shoulder. She could do this for ever – he didn't mind. Mad of course, but terrific, too. He could feel her warmth through the thin red gauze square that she had wrapped herself in. Her voice was shocking in his ear – a cackling old gentleman: '"In my youth, Father William replied to his son, I feared it might injure the brain; but now that I'm perfectly sure I have none, why, I do it again and again." You do the old man now, Dad.' She had the words on a greetings card that was tumbling about with them somewhere on the bed. She groped rumbustiously about, looking for it.

'I can't,' he snorted.

'You can, you can. You can do anything. Just a bit of make-up. That's all you need.' She was daubing away at his face with sticks of paint and damp stuff on sponges. This was so stupid. She was undoing his shirt. She would rip it if she wasn't careful. She had no sense of moderation at all, this one. What the hell must he look like? She was fiercely tucking coloured scarves around his neck, giggling away like some mad monkey, her hot garlicky breath on his face. She was bloody strong for a little one. It struck him that she may have taken something in addition to the marijuana. He often thought that. There had to be something to explain her behaviour.

Suddenly, she was sitting astride his chest.

She was sitting astride his chest, knees up in his armpits, covered by nothing more that this gauzy orange shawl. He wanted so much to touch her breasts. He almost did, but she laughed at his irresolute effort and, taking his wrists up behind his head, she tied them very quickly to the bedstead, one with a scarf and the other with the MCC tie. She seemed to think that this was a good game and giggled away like a car that wouldn't start. He would have protested more vehemently but at that moment his whole concentration was being applied to registering the touch of her naked crotch on his bare chest – she had her pussy firmly pressed down on to his body and seemed, in her manic activity, completely oblivious of it. Every iota of his blurred consciousness was directed at feeling the damp of her. And he could. At least he thought he could. Her wetness, her excitement, moist on his bare skin.

Hidden away, behind her back, in his trousers, he was rigid at the very thought of it.

And, during the process of this whole malarkey, she had tied him up.

Her fingers placed the joint between his lips and he sucked on it like a baby being given a bottle. Some burning ash fell on to his chest and burnt his skin. He cried out half in jest and half in reality. Amy continued to chortle like a possessed monkey and brushed his grey chest-hair with the flat palm of her hand. He could smell the tang of burning. This was getting out of hand. He must keep some sort of control here. He started to protest.

The grotesque old head on top of the nubile limbs took absolutely no notice. It jabbered on: '"You are old, said the youth; one would hardly suppose that your eye was as steady as ever; yet you balanced an eel on the end of your nose – what made you so awfully clever?"'

'Wrong head,' he roared. 'Wrong head.' Amy tore the rubberised mask from her overheated face and threw it to the floor. 'Smeg,' she laughed, tickling him with hard fingers, wrinkling her nose. 'Smeg.'

She bent forward and kissed him shortly on the lips. He could feel the brief soft touch of her breasts on his chest through the thin gauze material. Her hands were on his shoulders. His wrists, above his head, hurt where she had tied them.

'So what would you like, Daddio?' she asked teasingly. 'Old man Mephistopheles calling, Normski. Your wish is my command, oh master. What do you want? If you could have anything in the world happen to you, now, what would it be? Anything at all? Sexually. Go for it. Choose. Norman. Ranburn. This. Is. Your. Dream.'

It was so simple. All he would ever truly want was for her

to enclose his steeply reaching penis inside her body, right up inside her lovely body, and with some gentle adoration and not a little lust, bring him to a solitary climax. That's all. It was probably, in her eyes, such an incredibly dull desire. But that was everything he would ever need. However, he found even this impossible to say out loud. This in spite of the fact he was woozy from the drugs. Weren't they meant to make one feel less inhibited? 'I don't know. Someone to wash up the tea things?' is what he finally answered.

'You must know, Norman. Come on, Dad. You must know,' she shrilled at him. 'You must have some mad dream. Some weird unspoken something. Surely.' She was bullying him. Pummelling him with little fists in her exasperation. He was frightened. But he mustn't let her know. He didn't think he had any weird unspoken somethings. None that he would ever confess to, anyhow. He could never tell her about his dark need to watch. 'No,' is what he said.

'The straightest man in Christendom, aren't you? A regular goalless draw. Mr Normal Norman. Not "Mr Braun" at all.' He tried to lighten the mood, to get on bantering terms again – back to normality: 'That's not an anagram of "Ranburn" you know,' he countered. 'Not at all,' he went on. 'You cheated. Substituted an M for an N. Naughty. You are so naughty, Amy.'

'I cheat at everything. You know that. But I'm dead honest about the cheating. And I'm dead honest about what I like to do, too. No prob about telling you *my* unspoken somethings. Do you want to hear me speak the unspeakable?' she growled at him. 'I know what I like to do Norm-man.' She bent slowly forward and kissed him neatly on the nose. 'I like sitting up here, toying with you. Having you at my command. Being in charge. In control. What I say goes. Sergeant-major stuff. And that means I can do what I like with you.' She stroked his cheek tenderly. 'Cut your face. Light a bonfire on your chest. Suck your cock, very, very slowly. Pee on you. That'd be nice. Or worse – crap on you. Would you like that? Yes I can see you'd really dig that. That would be favourite with you. Or go off and watch *Brookside* – leave you here all tied up and impotent. The choice is all mine. And I like that so fucking bloody much. What's it to be? *Brookside*? Leave you here?'

She was laughing. 'Don't worry, my darling man, I don't mean any of it. I does it – aw shucks – I does it, 'cos I loves yer, Dad. And I'd like to give you a good time. 'Cos' – she stopped – 'cos I loves yer.' She seemed to have surprised herself.

She shook her head and brought herself back to the task in hand. Winking a glad eye at him, she produced, from nowhere, a pink bottle of baby lotion and squeezed great dollops of it on to his chest. It was shockingly cold. She began to rub it all over his body with a flat palm. At times she lifted her hands to her own body and, closing her eyes, massaged her breasts under the folds of material that hung from her shoulders. Her fingers tucked between her legs, smoothing the lotion in there as well. Then she spoke: 'But what really turns me on is to talk about fucking. Screwing someone you, Normal Norman, know only too well. Talk about it in detail. Someone you know terribly well, actually. That'd be a laugh. Turn us both on.' She giggled. 'Even more.'

She jumped from the bed and disappeared behind flailing curtains. He wondered what the hell was going to happen next. He wondered if he could release his wrists. They weren't very tightly tied but they weren't going to slip out all that easily. It was terribly hot. He didn't feel like doing very much, anyway. What was she talking about? 'Someone you know terribly well'? He might bring all this to a stop now. He would only have to say the words 'Boyd-Orr'. That would stop her in her tracks.

Amy returned to his field of vision. She posed. She was wearing a smart pillar-box-red suit. 'Duh-DUH, dud-DAH!' she trumpeted. '*Hello!* magazine hackette!' Her arms were thrown aloft, her pelvis thrust out, her eyes gleaming in the candlelight. He had seen her do this, in front of his mirror in the cottage, the day she had brought the film people to Coombe. 'I went to see little brother Gil in this,' she burbled. 'Your brother Gilbert. What do you think? What do you think? What do you think he thought?' The jacket was neatly fitted at her waist, the skirt was straight and narrow though the overall effect was not. But it was much too smart to be tarty. 'A real fuck-me suit, eh? And did he get the message? Do you have to ask?'

Had she gone to bed with Gilbert? God, no. He couldn't believe it. This was madness. His head was spinning.

She had stopped being raucous. Music stealthily filled the space between them and she was considering him. 'What have we got here, Mr Ranburn? What on earth have we got here? What the devil has got into you, Mr Ranburn? There seems to be an alien lurking in your trouser.' She teased him in her low, slow voice. Then she sounded like a shrill, manic headmistress. 'Jiminy Cricket, you're standing all to attention.' She saluted his trousers: 'Attention!' she shouted the command. 'Well-done-well-done.'

'Untie me, there's a love,' he said, pulling feebly at the hands above his head. God, it was hot. And this was all getting so out of hand. And embarrassing.

'No, no, you owe me dozens of tricks, Dad. Dozens. Lit-er-ral-ly dozens. It's ready-reckoning time for Norman and Amy.'

Sweat was running off him in rivulets. 'You randy old devil, Norman,' she cooed. 'You're quite a big boy, aren't you?'

'Untie me, now, Amy,' he said as firmly as he could.

'Lor, love a duck! I can do better than that, guv'nor,' she said in a mock cockney accent. She knelt on one knee on the bed beside him and reached over to his waist band. She was going to take his trousers off. She was bloody going to take his trousers off. He kicked his feet about protestingly. Feebly. Oh God, oh God, oh God, oh God, oh God, oh God. He twisted his head away from her and hauled at his wrists again. But this only seemed to make the knots tighter. He could feel her hands on his trouser buttons. He wasn't going to think about any of this. She was pulling his dress trousers down, under his buttocks, over his legs. He helped her, for God's sake, by lifting up his backside. Why did he do that? He could tell from the cool on the skin of his hips that she was removing his underwear, too.

'What have we here? Bejazus, Ranburn, begorrah, begorrah, what the devil have we got here?' It was the headmistress again. An Irish headmistress now.

'Amy, stop it,' he moaned. 'That's enough. Game over now. There's a dear.' She was away from him, at the bottom end of the bed, easing the clothing off over his ankles. This was awful. This was – this was – this was – awfully nice too. Awful and nice. Nice and awful. Then he realised that she had tied his ankles as well. She had attached him to the bottom of the bed. Spread-eagled, she had him. Oh God. What now?

'Finger-licking,' she said to herself. 'Fucking finger-licking.' She came to kneel at his waist. She was inspecting him. She was looking at his cock, his old, much-abused, tired, hard old cock. 'Well,' she murmured quietly. 'There's a thing.' Looking down he could see her hand in the candlelight making slow curving passes in the air around his erection, her long fingers carving the air like a tiny dancer, never to settle. Please settle, Amy. Please settle, Amy. He wanted it so.

She almost voiced his thoughts: 'What a smegging cock-teaser, eh? I took my Masters in it. Passed out top of the class. God,' she said. 'The power. Kissingit. Wasn't he the guy? Power – the ultimate thingy – the ultimate Afro-haircut, the big A. God,' she groaned long and low – a distant wolf howling on the moor. Her hand sought out her own crotch and she held her palm there. Her eyes closed. Her most thoughtful smile returned. 'To be in charge. To confirm or deny. Thumbs up or thumbs down. Depends on how I feel. Maybe. Maybe not. And you want it so much, eh? I just so love it. I may or may not deliver. It's up to me. Yes. Yes. Love-it-love-it-love-it. Wet, wet, wet, wet, fucking wet.'

Norman waited, wanting more than anything in the world for that hand to alight on him. But it didn't.

'Open wide,' she sang at him, leaning forward and stroking his cheek. Her hand was surprisingly cool and as firm as ever. He opened his mouth to speak and, oh God, she dropped some capsule, some tablet, into his mouth. He coughed and coughed, desperately trying to evacuate the tablet from his throat. She was going to kill him. 'Swallow, darleeng,' she sang. 'There's a love,' she cooed. His throat bucked and the thing, whatever it was, had gone down. Christ knew what was going to happen to his head now. He must be mad to let her do this. Mad or very stupid. Both.

The music was stroking him now as well, and Amy was talking in a whisper, kneeling on the bed with him, so near and yet so far away, blowing cool air from her wide-open mouth on to his disgraceful rigid, needful, preening thing. Her voice was growling softly: 'A fine specimen and that's for sure. Rather bigger than little brother Gilbert's, too.'

Had she said that? Did she mean that? How could she? Amy was standing by his side now. The room seemed to be coming and going. He was sweating again. She took his head in both her hands and turned it to look at her.

'Want to hear about little brother Gil?' she growled. 'This little hackette went to market, this little hackette had roast beef with the big executive and finished up – wee, wee, wee, wee, all the way home, you'd never guess where. He took this little hackette for a drink at the Randolph after work. Well, they do, don't they? Big execs?' She began to unbutton the front of the red jacket, her adept fingers crawling from button to button until she had undone them all. As usual, she had nothing on underneath it, but she wasn't going to let him see. She just grinned arrogantly at him and made tiny movements to flash one side of her jacket open and then the other, without actually showing him anything. 'Having a good time, Dad?' She grinned at him in her most friendly fashion. 'I am. Too. You. Are. Completely. In. My. Power. Nothing like debts being paid.' The room whirled slowly around and Amy seemed burnished, aglow with light. What was it she had stuffed down his throat? She was the very devil. Why had he got involved with this witch?

'Stop it,' he blurted out.

'Silence in court,' she snapped.

'No. That's absolutely enough. Amy, I mean it. Stop it now,' he groaned.

'I'm telling you special secrets, Daddikins. I will not be interrupted. Not nohow.' She stooped down and picked a roll of carpet tape from the floor. 'Not a squeak, Daddikins.' She ripped a short strip of the black tape from the roll with bright teeth. 'Right, some gaffer for the gaffer, eh?' she murmured. 'You'll like this. Just watch and listen. Watch and listen.' What was she going to do to him? There was no way he could stop her. She laid the gaffer-tape carefully across his lips. The adhesive caught at his cheeks. he struggled feebly on the bed, rolling his head from side to side.

Amy suddenly dropped completely out of character for a brief second and asked him: 'Can you breathe all right?' He found he had nodded obediently.

'Right. Where was I? Oh yes. Gilbert D. Ranburn and Randolph and this little hackette all got squiffy. That's the word you Ranburns use isn't it?' she laughed. 'Well squiffy we was. Well fucking squiffy.'

She turned to her side and, peering to examine the zip of her skirt at her hip, she lifted the zip toggle and peeled it down very slowly a tooth at a time – as if she was doing complicated brain surgery. 'Boom boom,' she whispered eventually as she carelessly dropped the expensive, lined, twelve-inch strip of woven material to the ground. 'My head's going too, Norman. Join the party.' She stepped a delicately heeled shoe out of the abandoned scrap of material. She could do this so well. She had done this before. She was just a sick little whore. He loathed her so much. He loved her so much. Loved it so much. Underneath she was wearing a wisp of lace, but not enough to fill a thimble. 'So, your brother, yes. We had to go and have a lie down upstairs. Gil took the honeymoon suite – which was pretty damned orbital and appropriate. And expensive. Shampoo, caviar, and we hit it with some imaginative cavorting.' She stepped delicately out of her panties. For a moment Norman just saw a flash of brown between her legs and then she had turned her back to him.

'Oh God, I did love it. He's brilliant, your brother. Knows his onions. Is that what you call them in the Home Counties? Well wised-up for a suburban Englishman. Positively wired.'

She dropped her jacket off her shining shoulders and it hid her little bum. She hummed her 'stripper' theme under her breath as very gradually the jacket, too, descended to the floor revealing more and more of that spare back of hers, shining with perspiration. 'There,' she said. 'Bloody hell. Yes. Yes. Man, is my motor running?' Her pelvis oscillated obscenely. 'You really need me to turn round don't you, Dad? That's what you require at this time. That is at the top of the hit-list of your schedule of priorities, isn't it? You're really desperate for me to turn around. Well, thing is, I may and I may not. 'Cos, as I have explained, at some drongo length, I am in charge here. And I love it. Great, living Jehosophat, I love it. And, honest injun, you like it too, nuncle, don't you? No responsibility. No decisions. Nothing. None. Just instructions to follow. And. You. Will. Follow. My. Instructions. To the hilt.'

Resolutely keeping her back to him, she perched her bum on the bed next to him and then swung her legs around on to it and placed her head on one of the pillows beside his head, covering her breasts almost modestly with a forearm. He could feel her breath on his face and her naked shoulder firmly wedged, hard and warm against his. 'You see,' she said, 'this is your absolutely classic see-but-not-touch pitch, ain't it? See, not touch, not speak but, yeah, OK, hear.' She impaled him with one of her favourite, cool, challenging stares, the unique washed-out grey of her eyes, inches from him. 'Sssh. Whisper who dares, tiny Gil Ranburn is going upstairs. So. Do you want to know what kind of a fuck your little brother is?' She mouthed this so quietly he could hardly hear her. But he could feel her breath on his face. Her hands were busy with herself elsewhere. 'God, he could do things with his prick to make a poor little girlie tingle. Dumped his wife and kids. Shot off to honeymoon it at the Randolph. How I loved it. How he loved it. Hours of fun. I screwed his soul away. Completely away.' She was beginning to pant. 'And at dawn, we had a replay. All the hits and then some.' There was a web of perspiration laid over her face. 'Oh God, I love this. This is right up my valley, Daddy.' She gave way to groaning. 'Nuncle-nuncle-nuncle.'

Norman thought he might be close to passing out. He was soaked, sopping with sweat. Unashamed now of his powerless, pathetic, exposed rigid body. He had other things to think about. He might be going to die. Yet he watched her nakedness like a hawk. As well as he could, out of the corner of his eyes. There she was, beyond his upturned elbow, sighing and giggling and shifting about on the bed with him – cushions and shawls and knees and shoulders and her head twisting sideways and backwards. Her sharp knees were drawn up now and lolling apart, her thigh touching and then not touching his hip, the frantic fingers of both her hands going about their private business. She was beginning to make a lot of noise.

Then coherency stopped being a strong point. She was off on some private journey all of her own. Inches from him. Both hands were flapping away nineteen to the dozen and her buttocks lifted time and time again to meet them. With one hand she seemed to hold herself ready while the other flashed to her mouth, returning to its work wet with spittle. Her head began to rock backwards and forwards and seemed no more in control. And, when she wasn't panting and screeching like an express train out of control, she was shouting. 'Yes,' she shouted. A lot. There were a great many yesess. There was much 'Yes, yes, yes, yes'. 'Gilbert,' she shouted. 'Do-it-do-it-do-it. Fuck me, fuck me,' she shouted. 'Right up, right up, Gilbert,' she yelled. It was degrading and riveting and wonderful and dirty and thrilling and animalistic and odious. Her body banged around on the bed, bucking sideways into Norman and tossing cushions and clothing off the bed. They were both drowning in sweat. The noise moderated only when she almost comically held her mouth closed with the fingers of her other hand.

For some minutes it seemed as if she wasn't going to get there. Twice she stopped breathing and held herself steady to receive what she sought. Twice it came to nothing and almost with irritation she began the violence all over again. Then it overtook her when she wasn't quite prepared for it. Her breathing hiccuped to a stop and for a long moment she tensed her whole body. She lifted herself up with only the soles of her feet and her shoulders touching the suddenly still mattress. He could see the whole glistening flank of her, raised up next to him – brown, firm, perfect – both hands motionless at last, her fingers clamped to her vulva.

Her screams doubtless broke windows in parts of Brixton and probably Brighton as well. Then, after a long gulping silence, with a great exhalation of breath, she collapsed back on to the bed, curled on her side and thrust her thumb in her mouth. They were both awash with sweat. She had reached the top of whatever mountain she had been trying to climb. She was momentarily exhausted.

But she didn't stay down for long. It couldn't have been more than half a minute or so. Her energy was unquenchable, insatiable.

She was up on one elbow, looking at him again. 'And what are we going to do about this little number?' she asked. Shamefully, astonishingly, he was still up and hard. Not bad for someone who was almost seventy. It must be the drugs. But, tied up as he was, there was very little he could do to hide it. It certainly felt absurd. And embarrassing still. But, to some degree, he seemed to have got over feeling shy. Once one had been around during a moment of such epic abandon as Amy's, normal modes of propriety suddenly slipped out of the window. That was probably helped by the drugs as well. He didn't feel bad. He felt appalled, he felt excited, but he didn't feel bad. He was still alive and less frightened. And he had been to heaven and back. And hell.

He felt tired. Old and tired. Odd and tired. Where he could glimpse it in the dark, this extraordinary store of people's clothing, each item with its own individual personal story, continued to revolve about his head, coming and going, light and dark, hot and cold, delightful and disgusting. He ought to sleep.

Amy had hung a T-shirt over her nakedness. He heard the huge refrigerator door clunk shut. She returned to the bed with a large, very sharp-looking kitchen knife. He was suddenly petrified all over again. What, in God's name, was she going to do with that? He made protesting noises at her through his gag. She laughed almost gaily.

She was also holding a large grapefruit. It was enormous and pink as well as yellow. Amy perched a hip on the bed. Norman watched the knife like a hawk. Not that there was very much he could do about it, whatever she was up to. He tried pulling gently at his wrists, but to no avail. Surely, surely she would do him no real damage. Well, not more than she had already done.

Amy began to cut her way into the grapefruit. The innards of the thing fell all over the bedclothes and the juice trickled on to him, too. Her tongue was clamped between carefully pursed lips as she concentrated on carving a narrow shaft right through the fruit. She didn't seem to mind about making a mess. When she had finished it to her own satisfaction, she peered closely through the hole in the fruit, up at the light glowing above their heads. 'Yep,' she said to herself. Then she turned back to him.

Once more she was panting cool breath on to the tip of his penis with pursed, kissable lips. Oh God, if only she would grab it. Grab it, Amy. Grab it in your long thin hand. "Erewego-'erewego-'erewego,' she breathed tunelessly. 'You'll dig this, Daddy. I reckon you may just really dig this. The original alternative breakfast . . .' she cradled the grapefruit in both her hands '. . . fruit,' she finished. 'Righty-ho,' she said, 'let's see how it ap-peals. Hohoho, rib-tickling word-play.' She impersonated a sort of telly ad: 'For that fresh early-morning jump start – Go. Fuck. A. Grapefruit.' And then, cackling insanely and without more ado, she firmly pressed the grapefruit down over his cock. It was wet and warm and tight. There was such a feeling of blessed relief. He felt as if he had come home. Oh, good god alive, what the hell was he doing feeling his life's resolution in a bloody old grapefruit? Amy began moving the great yellow thing up and down with both hands. Slowly at first and then more quickly – all the while breathing excitedly, chuckling, willing him on, chortling and delighted.

It didn't take very long. And it wasn't great. But it was

a blessed release. Almost the last thing he remembered was Amy idly flicking gobbits of his sperm from her forearm with her finger. And watching it interestedly as it caught the light in its arc to the floor. Then they were very suddenly joined on the bed by the largest tabby in the western world. 'Catus Interruptus,' giggled the girl. 'Oh, get down, get off, Towser, you're not wanted here.' She tore the tape painfully from his mouth. 'All right?' she asked him quietly, with concern. She kissed him briefly with closed dry lips.

Norman felt swamped by a feeling of totally abject humiliation. But it was short-lived because he must have fallen asleep immediately.

He awoke an eternity or thirty seconds later. He had a road-drill of a headache and was appallingly stiff and uncomfortable. But free. She seemed to have cut his fetters. They were still attached to his wrists and ankles but he had been cut free from the bed. She had even sliced her way through the MCC tie with her scissors. The girl had absolutely no conscience.

He felt damp. And physically and mentally filthy from the previous night. Because it *was* dawn. He always got so ashamed – afterwards. It was worse this morning. What had they done? More truthfully, what had *she* done? He had had no choice in the matter. The bed was full of squalid broken bits of grapefruit. He hated her. Detested her. He must get away.

There were just two candles left burning. In the gloom, Amy was lying on the bed, next to him, in her T-shirt – a tight ball with her back to him. He could just see where she had a pair of kitchen scissors still held in her sleeping hands. Her bum was exposed and looked neat and perfect, like a child's. Not sexy at all. It was five in the morning. She was breathing noisily. Bright early morning was out there beyond the closed Gothic blinds. The room looked considerably less than magical now. It looked disreputable and messy and smelled warm. He managed to collect his scattered clothing and his shoes, took a kitchen knife to the remnants of the fetters at his wrists and ankles, and dressed himself as silently as he could.

He stood by the kitchen sink and, watching the dim form of the silent girl for any movement, attempted to slake an absolutely raging thirst by drinking handful after handful of dull London tap-water. He had a meagre attempt at washing and tried to clean his teeth with his fingers. Finally, he finished putting rumpled dress clothing back on to his weary person and left.

He drove towards Oxford down empty dawn roads with his mind galloping feverishly from pillar to post. So the randy trollop had gone and bedded Gilbert. And had delighted in not actually bedding Norman. Norman had always suspected that Gilbert played fast and loose. Well, lucky bloody old Gilbert, eh? It made Norman feel sick with jealousy. If he allowed himself to think about it. But that was why she had done it. It was her twisted little notion of what constituted fun.

And William Boyd-Orr? Norman positively throbbed with theories and questions. Whatever the truth, Amy Shakespeare obviously had a thing for these grandfatherly characters. He wearily had to recognise that he was probably not the first that she had entertained with her grapefruit diet. Et cetera. The man under the bath had been seventy-three, for crying out loud. And he had killed himself.

Norman made the turning towards Thame and Coombe at about six-forty-five a.m. Almost immediately, he was pulled over on the deserted main road by two police officers in a squad car.

'Yes, officer?' Norman wound down his window. The young man seemed, for all his uniform, to be familiar. Norman thought that he lived close by, in Radleigh.

'Would you step out of the car please, sir?' The man was looking at Norman searchingly.

'Of course,' he replied and heaved himself out of the car. 'What's this all about?'

'We noticed that you were weaving about rather a lot on the main road, sir. Did you feel you were in control of the car?'

'Why yes. I own I'm a bit sleepy. But I haven't been drinking.'

'Not at all, sir?' He didn't sound as if he believed him.

'The last alcohol I had was at a reception yesterday afternoon.' He understated it: 'Just a couple of glasses of champagne. Wedding guest, you see.'

'Well, we'll have to ask you to blow into one of our little machines, if you would, sir.' The other policeman, having walked very carefully around the Daimler, had now joined them. He, too, was looking at Norman with a surprised expression. Norman wondered if it was possible to guess what had happened to him in the last twelve hours by just looking at him. When he was in his early teens he remembered thinking that his father could always tell if he had been 'indulging himself'. He had often imagined that Magnus could see it in a certain dullness in his son's eyes. These men were looking at him as if his fly-buttons were undone. Given what had occurred to his fly-buttons last night, they were something he was sure, this morning, were fastened with the greatest possible care. Indeed he might very well have his fly-buttons completely sewn up in the future. Double stitching. With carpet thread.

'Party, sir?' The second policeman spoke at last. He was obviously reading clues from Norman's tails.

'Reception. Wedding reception. The Goodman Club, Mayfair. Yesterday afternoon. Gordon Driscoll's grandson.' He was gabbling. He sounded about as sober as a brewer's dray.

'Children there?'

'Not really.'

'Oh.' The second policeman didn't seem very impressed with this reply. The first, Radleigh-based, policeman brought along his little device. And there, standing beside the hedge at the beginning of another peerless summer's day, Norman, dressed in his crumpled finery, tried to blow into their thing. It was surprisingly difficult to do.

'Just blow as hard as you can, sir.' Norman expected there to be some resistance. There wasn't any. It was like blowing into the air. The policeman finally seemed satisfied. He communed with the three mystic-coloured lights on the side of it. Norman fervently prayed that the device did not, in some magical way, also register drug abuse. It didn't. The machine said he had a residue of alcohol in his bloodstream but that he was nowhere near the limit. The boys in blue gave him a puzzled farewell. They then tailed Norman all the way through Coombe village. For which reason, he drove at about three miles per hour until he was able to tuck his way into the long drive to the Aviary – and safety.

Only when he had taken off his clothes and gone to run a bath did he realise why the police might have been taken aback by his appearance. Apart from being in serious need of a shave, his face was covered completely with blue, green and red make-up. He looked like Widow Twanky after a really bad night in the laundry. The make-up was terribly hard to remove and, in particular, the red hung about in his moustache for the best part of the next twenty-four hours, however hard he scrubbed at himself.

He put the emerald ring in his tooth-mug. He would have to try to think that one through. But then, he might not have to. He reckoned he wouldn't be seeing the bitch again.

Then, thank God, he slept. The sleep of the dead.

CHAPTER SEVEN

Who is she that looketh forth as the
morning, fair as the moon, clear as the sun
and terrible as an army with banners?

SONG OF SOLOMON 6:10

SUNDAY 6 AUGUST

'Have you ever heard of something which I believe they call,
um, "harloting"?' Lesley-Anne stood on the dining room
threshold. She had taken Norman's lunchtime tray away
when she hesitated and posed this obscure question. It was
quite out of the blue.

'I'm sorry, what do you mean?' Norman was still too tired
to concern himself with riddles.

'Yes, well, I'm sorry. It just intrigued me. It's something I
came across yesterday when I went to see Terry. I'd never
ever heard of it. Probably very few people have. But there's
a whisper going about that it does go on. It's known in certain
circles. As a rumour, anyway. Well, Terry seems to have got
some of this from the horse's mouth. Apparently.'

She was wearing an ankle-length dress with bare shoulders.

259

It completely hid and accentuated her figure both at the same time. But Norman would never bother to look at a woman's body with interest again. All that was over. From now on he would live a blameless non-sexual life. Lesley-Anne looked white-faced with tiredness. Or maybe it was just the endlessly hot and exhausting weather. The summer was the hottest since 1975. She had been to see her brother the previous day in Snapper Green. He had totally forgotten. She obviously wanted to talk about it.

'Yes, sorry, how was your trip?'

'Awful, Mr Ranburn. To see someone who's your flesh and blood locked up like that. It's such a grim place. And they say it's one of the better ones. It's quite wrong that he should be locked away. He's not been found guilty. And he won't be. Because he isn't. It was his partner, Eric Ware. Terence didn't do anything wrong, believe you me, Mr Ranburn.'

'Call me Norman,' he said, surprising himself.

'Oh,' she said. 'If that's all right.'

'I think it is, isn't it? I call you Lesley-Anne. You can probably return the compliment.'

'Thank you.' She put the tray down on the sideboard. She obviously needed to talk some more. What on earth had she asked him about? Something odd. 'What did you say?' he asked her. 'Something about a whisper? "Harlotry"?'

'Yes. Harloting. Have you ever heard of that? No? I didn't believe it, either, at first. I still don't, really. But, anyway, Terry's sharing a cell with this city solicitor – used to work for Harborne and Wise, would you believe – in the City. A man called Rajindra. He can't get bail either. They get hours and hours to talk. There's nothing else to do, is there? It just came up. This Rajindra mentioned to Terry something he'd heard about. It's called, well as I say, it's something called "harloting".'

'And?'

'Well it's such an extraordinary story. I don't know how much you can believe. But it seems that there's a man who runs a group, a stable if you like, of highly paid young women who are given targets to destroy. Men. And people

pay money to have it done, to have these men "taken out",
I suppose. Highly placed men, usually. And it works. I
suppose one can think of some well-publicised cases. People
in the Cabinet, the privatised national companies, loathed
headmasters, that sort of thing. I'm not sure how they do
it, completely. I think what happens is that for a vast fee
this syndicate can arrange to destroy a man publicly who
the, um, client, I suppose, wants to remove from office. It
can be revenge or just plain mischief or someone who wants
to undermine the enemy. You disagree with their policies, so
rather than fight them, you get them removed. Sounds like
a different world, doesn't it? These young women are paid
huge quantities of money to tangle with these men. Seduce
them, if you like. They're normally men past their middle
age – easy targets, willing, married. Men for whom that sort
of thing might seem to be over. They get flattered, excited,
caught up by it all and then the truth comes out and the
newspapers do the rest. The sleaze factor. Marriages over.
Careers aborted. Good name in shreds. That sort of thing.
This man Rajindra told Tel that they reckon they can go
from revelation, through the usual expression of confidence
by the Prime Minister, via the group family photograph
for the press with children and the little wife standing by
her man, all the way through to final resignation in about
eleven days. He said it works a treat. Well we all know that.
It does.'

'Good God.'

'Yes. You want to get someone removed from office or get
some kind of revenge. All you have to do is find the organiser,
pay the money, sit back and keep schtum. "Harloting" it's
called.'

'I don't believe it,' he said.

'Neither did I. But it happens. And, well, I'll tell you
what Terry said to me. I'm sorry about the language, Mr
Ranburn – Norman – these young women, um, mess with
men's brains.' Norman smiled inwardly, conjecturing that
Lesley-Anne might have been too shy to give him the original
four-letter verb. She went on: 'Apparently, if you can believe

it, when they get a result, they earn a small fortune, these girls – double the money.'

'And why are you telling me this?'

Lesley-Anne sat herself down in one of the Queen Anne chairs by the door. 'I don't know whether I should say this. What he said just struck a funny sort of chord with me. I could be quite wrong. But it was because of something I was told about one of the women working on the film crew here. We talked about her. Amy. It's just funny that their location manager, you know, Des Wright, used virtually the same phrase about her. And, yesterday, when Terry came up with the self-same words, it struck such a chord with me. "She messes with men's brains". Des said exactly the same, or words to that effect.'

Lesley-Anne was beginning to look bothered. She went on reluctantly: 'I really don't know whether I should say this. Forgive me but I'm trying to be, well, a friend I suppose.'

'What?'

'It's about her behaviour. As I told you, Amy spent a lot of time during last week seeking me out. Asking me questions. Asking me about you, mostly. And about your brother. Whether you had any areas of dispute with him. What your relationship was like. Fraternal jealousies, that sort of thing. She even asked me about some accountant person that you'd had to sack.'

'Austin Peacock?'

'Oh, I don't know. I can't remember the name. All I know is that it was important for her to find out. I told her she'd picked the wrong one in me. I mean I didn't know anything. But she did press on so. And that was what was so odd.'

'Yes, I suppose it was.'

'And,' Lesley-Anne continued, really embarrassed now, 'there was a rumour flying around the unit that Amy was—'

'What?'

'I don't know – a friend of yours?'

'Hardly a friend. She went to school with my grand-daughter Fran, that's all. She's only twenty-four or something.

It wouldn't be very likely that we'd actually be proper friends.'

'Yes, I know. I know this is just so absurd, but from what I heard people say I worried that she might be trying to get – I'm sorry, this is ridiculous – I shouldn't interfere –'

'No, go on.'

'I thought it seemed as if she might be trying to get her hooks into you. There, I've said it now. I'm sorry.'

'No, that's quite all right. Don't worry. I only know her very slightly,' Norman lied, and the very fact that he had had to lie made him think, in passing, that there might be something in what Lesley-Anne had to say. 'She's visited here just once before, with Fran.' Norman was thinking it through. He lied some more: 'If she is, as you say, trying to get what you call her hooks into me – well, she's not being very successful. I hardly ever see her.' His brain filled with an instant mind-picture of Amy's naked, tense body rising up in self-generated ecstasy a couple of inches away from his roped-up figure, only the night before. Could there be anything in what the woman was telling him?

Whatever the case, the next thought was at least true, and comforting: 'I wouldn't really be a very good target anyway. I'm single, retired – I have no position to be compromised, even if that were possible. I've no wife or young family to be scandalised. The newspapers wouldn't give a damn, even if there was anything to give a damn about. But thank you for worrying, Lesley-Anne. The whole thing sounds rather unlikely to me. The rumour mill can throw up some truly ridiculous ideas, can't it? It sounds like an urban myth to me. I suppose it might just be true. But not about me. And probably not about Amy Shakespeare. She wants to be a film director, not a Mata Hari.' He was beginning to bring this conversation to a close. 'Interesting, though.'

'She *is* attractive.'

Norman caught her drift and stupidly allowed himself to

react to it: 'You mean it would be a surprise for someone as beautiful as that to spend time with an old man.'

'No, of course I don't mean that. And, for goodness, sake, you're not an old man.'

Norman was regretting his outburst. 'Not, of course,' he said, 'that she does spend time with me.'

'No, it's me who should be sorry. But I feel better having told you about it. It's just that, from what Terry said –'

'I don't think there's anything else to say. Thank you for thinking of my welfare.' He cut her off and sent her on her way. For a moment she looked as if she was about to come to the crux of her rumour-mongering. But he didn't feel like hearing any more. It was absurd. The very idea. But, for his liking, it ventured a little too close to the madness of what had actually happened.

Norman had, of course, wondered incessantly if what had happened between him and Amy could possibly be part of a set-up for some kind of epic fall – the game in the toilet at Lord's, the thievery at Fortnum's, the bondage business last night – but in each case she had been party to saving him, to releasing him. Norman had come to the conclusion that she just adored the power of having him in her clutches, sweating and frightened, and for her alone to be in the position of freeing him. He was clearly right – there was no way that he could be disgraced in the public eye even should the most appalling behaviour come to light. He was of no interest whatsoever to the media. He had never had a particularly high profile when he was in charge of Chandos House and now, as a retired divorced gentleman, he would hardly rate half a paragraph. After all, there was nothing that he could ever resign from; he had no position to lose. The MCC? The Reform Club? No, it just wasn't even worth thinking about.

So he was all right.

But he didn't much like Lesley-Anne suggesting that Amy might be manipulating him. Amy did manipulate him, of course, but he'd prefer for it not to become common gossip, or for Lesley-Anne to have guessed at it. Maybe Lesley-Anne would have to go.

MONDAY 7 AUGUST

The film unit rang Norman at eight the following morning enquiring politely why he wasn't yet at Wormell Water with Bertram. He dragged himself from his bed and, twenty minutes after waking, was trundling down the five miles that led to the reservoir. He didn't feel he could let these film people down. And part of him liked the idea of Bertram being in a film. It would be for only two days, after all. He would deliver the car and duck out. Taxi back. He realised that he hadn't driven the motor car on the open road for about ten months. It was a shame. He should do it more. People always smiled so much as Bertram chugged by.

He felt better again by the time he drove down into the valley. Wormell Water was more beautiful than he remembered. As far as he could recall, he had not been there since Joan had grown up. To start with, one had to approach the lake from below the dam that formed the reservoir above. Once the impressively high, stained wall of concrete was behind him, Bertram laboured slowly up the twisting lane to the level of the lake. The place looked idyllic. One could almost be in the Alps. Very low Alps.

It was going to be yet another perfect day. A clear blue sky was reflected in a blue lake. The surrounding trees were every kind of green. There was a small rustic boathouse down at the water's edge. It was so beautiful. They were filming on the other side where, fascinatingly, they seemed to have constructed a gigantic Elizabethan mansion at the edge of the ancient Wormell woods that tumbled down to the shore. It was a daunting piece of construction and looked fabulous. There should always be an Elizabethan manor house just there.

One of the film johnnies popped up from nowhere, with hands full of short-wave radios, and told him that he needed Norman to drive the motor car over the dam to the location site proper on the other side. There was a curving roadway running along the top. It seemed very narrow but obviously some of the bigger location trucks had already managed the trip perfectly well. Norman drove with the greatest possible care towards where the film unit was working. The dam had been constructed some time in the forties and had an expressive curve to it. As he drove sedately across, to his left, the surface of the lake fluttered in the sunshine and a ragged trio of ducks splashed down on the waters, while, to his right, the valley plunged away hundreds of feet below. It was an awesome sight and he tried to keep his eyes averted from it.

The manor house, which looked so substantial from the other side of the water, could be seen, from the top of the dam, to be nothing more than a sham – pieces of cladding and scenery attached to a sizable scaffolding structure.

As soon as he arrived, he was motioned by another film-struck lackey to switch off his engine. They must have reached one of their moments when they were filming a little sequence and needed silence. As usual, thousands of people stood around looking important and not much seemed to happen. At the centre of a cluster of lights, cameras and crew and other vitally important hangers-on, Norman could just see the blonde curls of beauteous Georgina Lewis in conversation with two-names McPhee. Even from that distance, it was clear to Norman that all did not seem to be sweetness and light between the director and the minute star with the impressive features.

Then he saw Amy. She detached herself from part of the crowd and loped up the track towards him. She was wearing cut-off denim shorts and a white T-shirt cut extremely short with some useful information emblazoned on it: *'je suis comme je suis'*. Well, you couldn't argue with that. It was probably true of most people. There was a leanness about her bare, exposed ribcage that made him jettison all his good intentions about future dealings with her in about one and a half seconds flat.

On leaving the group, she briefly, in farewell, took hold of a young man's hand and kissed him – whether on the cheek or lips, Norman could not be sure. But he could definitely recognise that this young man was the boy James – Jamie – the

London International Financial Features Exchange character that Amy had met just last Saturday afternoon, two days ago, at the Driscoll wedding. What, in God's name, was he doing here? Why wasn't he at Cannon Bridge in one of those garish coloured jackets gesticulating away like a mad thing at all the other crude young men on the floor of the Exchange? The woman was unstoppable. She must have picked him up. Norman's heart suddenly felt leaden.

'I'll take you back in my car,' she called to him. She didn't even bother to say 'hullo'. She was dreadful. He was right, he was well out of this. She turned and hurried off to where the Mazda was parked in the shadow of some great black fir trees. It was hardly worth her wearing the cut-offs – they made scant effort to cover the cheeks of her backside. And they were tight enough to be able to read the raised credit card number in her hip pocket.

Their journey back to the Aviary in the open car was almost silent. Norman was thinking through the implications of the sudden appearance of this James. He also managed to claw back his determination that enough was enough. Amy, alongside him, was in 'film-crew mode' he guessed, hardly acknowledging his existence at all. And driving like a whirling dervish with the runs. He could begin to hate her quite easily. And perhaps it was better for them not to talk. He could feel a row coming on and he didn't want that, whatever he thought.

'Can I drop you here?' she said, pausing her whirlwind progress in a sandstorm of dust, at the top of his drive.

'Tickety-boo.' It seemed the best thing to say after her conversationless charge down the Oxfordshire lanes. He got out of the car and decided he would walk away from her without another word, however painful that might be. But she said softly: 'You are such a nice man. You don't deserve the way I treat you.'

'Yes, yes, you could say that.'

'I just have,' she laughed and, shading her eyes with her hand she looked at him searchingly. Suddenly her white shirt was doubly fine. She was almost his friend and conspirator once again. 'It might be better if we didn't do this any more,' she said. 'It could get to be bad news. I'm a really bad hat, I'm afraid. And not healthy for you. Sorry. I wish it could be different.' She was serious but genuinely friendly. 'What say?'

'Miss Shakespeare, you are the most changeable beast. One minute you are doing such things that my poor brain cannot even now encapsulate them in words – and with an intimacy impossible to believe – and the next it is as if you hardly remember who I am.'

'Too right. It sucks. But I get confused.' She climbed out of the car to remove a parking ticket that had been jammed under her windscreen-wiper. They were either side of her little white car. 'Sorry, Norman and stuff,' she said.

'*I* get confused, girl!'

'Join the club. I get so focused on this filming, on my work.'

'What? Totally focused? Centred, even?' he asked, teasing her.

She laughed: 'Yep. You've got it. Absolutely. In one.'

'But not so "totally zeroed in" that you don't have time to dally on set with the likes of that young James. You need to concentrate on him now, do you? What's he doing here?'

'Nothing. It's just easier for me to acknowledge him on location than to acknowledge you, that's all,' she said. And of course that was true. He was an unremitting forty-five years older than she was. 'However much I might want to,' she went on softly. Norman's heart did an almost complete back-flip somersault. Amy gave him so little verbal encouragement that, when a modest scraplet of comfort turned up, he was overwhelmed by it. It was the complete opposite of diminishing returns.

'You'd like to, then?'

'Natch.'

'Why?'

'You're a good bloke, Norman Ranburn. That's why.'

'And this James?'

'Oh, nothing. I've recruited him for the cabaret. We're going to be rehearsing. He's just a hunky guy, Norman.

Thick, beautiful, willing. Nothing special. Just a bit of fun. The usual.'

'The usual?'

'Yep.'

'Are you sleeping with him already?'

'There wasn't much sleeping going on. Got to get the guy sorted. It's a show with attitude, *Hard-Up And Flummoxed* – it's not Shy City, Norman. It's rude and you have to know one another. In my view.'

'You'd never sleep with me,' he muttered.

'You never asked.' But Norman had set off down the drive, seething with everything the green and yellow gods of jealousy could throw at him. Amy ran a few steps to catch up.

'I ask,' he grunted.

'Norman,' she said warningly.

'Too old?'

'Nothing like that. Too straight. Too nice. Nothing devious or complicated or twisted about you. You're just such a nice bloke.' They reached the little lawn where the sundial stood on its ancient brick pillar. 'Too decent,' she said gently, 'You'd believe cunnilingus was an Irish airline.' She smirked. 'Oh yes, it's the way I tell 'em,' she said deadpan.

He stopped, tired, sad, humiliated, puzzled. 'Is it just that you like humiliating me then? That's what's kept you around? Is that what this whole thing has been all about?'

'You dig it, too, Normy. You dote on it. Positively drooling buggins, you are. I know you. It's your very favouritest bit, I'd say.' She laughed. 'In my view.' She leaned forward to rest her forearms on the brass plate of the sundial but leapt back when her skin touched the sun-scorched metal. Norman made sure he didn't try to look down the front of her T-shirt. They must look so odd there, the two of them standing either side of his father's sundial. Across in the kitchen window of the cottage he caught sight of the blank face of Lesley-Anne steadily watching them.

Amy then, inadvertently, stumbled upon a fact that Norman had known for the best part of the last thirty years

– that one could lift the whole square brass plate of his father's sundial off its base. One could then settle it back down into its regular fixing holes but in the wrong position. It amused her, changing the top around. She tried it in a few different configurations. 'I've always dug different positions,' she gurgled irresistibly. This conversation was of no moment to her. Playing with the sundial was more congenial and as significant. Norman had been a passing fancy. She would probably term the whole thing 'a bit of fun with a wrinkly' – 'and stuff' – certainly nothing of note. Exactly like this James character she'd picked up now. Worthless. Of no moment. A bit of fun. The usual.

The shadow on the sundial was now telling them that it was not a quarter to twelve any more, but a quarter to six.

'So I'm one of the straights, am I? One of the moral majority, one of the suits, one of the grey men?' he asked gloomily. 'Amy, I've been behaving perfectly outrageously ever since I met you. God knows why, I'm sure *I* don't. You think about it – I've smoked your drugs, played your games, lots and lots of things. It's crazy – after a life of pedantic carefulness, I've seemed to have thrown caution to the winds with you. It's been tantamount to ridiculous. Don't I get any credit for that?'

'Following.'

'What do you mean "following"?'

'Follow my leader.'

'Yes.'

'I need someone as unscrupulously perverted as me, Norman,' she ruminated. 'Someone really kicking. Someone who comes back at me with something even better, even more twisted. Kink tennis is what I want. That would be intriguing – a challenge, a groove. No chance, though. They just don't exist. I'm on my own out here. Languishing, Dad.'

'Heaven preserve us if what you get up to is languishing, daughter.'

'No, but you get my meaning. Norman, you don't have a single solitary dark corner, do you? You're just a nice, nice man.' She quoted that tedious television advert again:

'"A-very-very-nice-man". And none the worse for that. But not for me. I think we ought to split. Call it a day. For both our sakes.'

He had the beginnings of an idea. 'You make me sound like an affliction.' Little did she know what he was truly like. God, if only she knew how really sick in the head he was. 'Straight'? It was enough to make a cat laugh. He was about as straight a corkscrew. But could he do it? Could he let her know? That would be a turn-up for the books. That would astonish her. 'All right,' he said, thinking hard. 'All right,' he said again, playing for time, considering. 'I'll astonish you. "Straight"? You must be joking. Come with me, my girl. I'll have you eating your words.' And with a thumping heart he strode smartly off, leading the girl down towards his front door by a limp wrist.

'It's your celebrated store of fifties wank magazines, is it?' she giggled as she tumbled along beside him, bouncing around like a young colt. 'Or your very own inflatable sex-toy?'

'Better than that.' To Norman's own astonishment, he found he had now firmly taken hold of Amy's left hand in his own and was marching her into his house. Let Lesley-Anne think what she would. He would show Amy something to knock the smug, perverted wind out of her sails.

'The study,' he said.

'Yes, cap'n. Six of the best is it? Flobadob. Let's hope so. You public-school boys sure know how to dish it out. I hope.'

It was cooler in the house. He had to leave go of her hand to lead the way up the six steps to his study. His brain was racing. Right, he would show her. This would surprise her. He could top every single one of her games with this. They underestimated the old, these youngsters. He strode behind the desk and tugged the carpet roughly aside. There was the door. This was it.

'What?' she said.

'Look,' he said, feeling a little like a conjuror who was about to surprise the children's party and even some of the adults. He unlocked the door with too hefty a clunk. Fool, the last thing he wanted was to alarm Lesley-Anne. It opened and they stood shoulder to shoulder looking down into the tiny space of the viewing room, with the solitary viewing chair and the Onan Cottage bedroom clearly visible through his secret window.

'You fucking scamp, Norman,' she whispered, overwhelmed by the wickedness of it. There was the longest silence. Then her reaction was all he could have wished for. 'Arthur's fucking picnic. God, I love your mind, Norman Ranburn. Massive. Orbital,' she whispered, awed. 'You're really wired, aren't you? Fan-dabbi-bloody-dozy.' She relished it. Her deep voice was suffused with sexual excitement. 'You're just so *very*, Dad. Aren't you? Fucking tempestuous. In my view. I absolutely fucking adore it. I *love* it. I love your wicked lovely brain.' He could not have asked for a better response. He was *in*. He had paid his dues, with a vengeance – joined the club. He was as sick as she was. She was positively intoxicated with excitement. There you are, my girl, he thought rapturously, what do you think of that? Got you going, eh? Surprise, surprise?

Amy stepped cautiously into the room peering carefully at his arrangements, his soundproofing, his doubtful handiwork. Her reaction was as if he had constructed the Ark of the Covenant in one quick half-hour after tea, single-handed. She was ecstatic. Her eyes shone. Her smile double-wrapped her cheeks. She adored it. He had really moved the trollop. Her eyes glowed with moisture. He squeezed down beside her and switched on the sound. The scratchy noise of Lesley-Anne's kitchen radio filled the tiny space. He pulled the study door to, behind them.

Was he just being stupid letting her know his secret? Did he really need to show off to her as badly as this? The pent-up thrill of, at last, revealing the room to another person began to evaporate almost as soon as Amy had reacted to it. Moments later he was once more beginning to recognise the basic sordidness of what he had done. It wouldn't take him long to be gloomy again. He had such mood swings at the moment.

He sat down in the chair to give them both a little bit more space in the room.

The bedroom door beyond the mirror swung open and Lesley-Anne walked quickly into the privacy of her bedroom, snapping the door shut behind her. She was wearing an enormous T-shirt and lycra shorts.

'Swanky-doodle,' hissed Amy with considerable reverence. She was so impressed. 'Neat, Norman, neat,' she whispered. 'Oh, I want to come,' she moaned in his ear.

Lesley-Anne had a bucket and a squeegee cloth with her. She wiped down the surfaces by the windows and then knelt on the floor to attack a large dull stain on the fitted carpet. 'She is such a smacker,' breathed Amy. 'You stonking brilliant scamp, you. Will she take her clothes off? Have you seen her fucking?' Lesley-Anne knelt up and tucked her hair into an elastic of some sort and once again tackled the carpet. They both watched her bottom wagging with the effort.

'Great bod.' Amy had her mouth virtually in his ear. Her breath made the side of his head damp. 'Eyeball the tush, would you.' There was nowhere else to look. 'Normski, you kill me. How you must get off on it in here. It's so well sordid it's completely exquisite. God, she has boom-booms to die for, hasn't she? No competition here.' She sighed, looking ruefully down at her scrap of a T-shirt.

Then, without more ado, Amy clambered on to his lap, in the viewing chair, her wide eyes locked on to Lesley-Anne's backside. Amy, in her nothing shirt and shorts, felt startlingly naked and warm and smelled of summertime. She was so strong and hard to the touch as well – muscular really. Short of breath with excitement, she kissed him. Unblinkingly watching Lesley-Anne over the back of his head, Amy applied herself to her kissing. It seemed like a resolution for her. It was as if she was inviting him to celebrate with her as well.

And he did.

Her sharp tongue nudged his lips open, her strong hands around the back of his head pulling him into her mouth. She kissed him with such rapt attention, almost as if it was a job she needed to do well and professionally but which was also, by lucky chance, one that she hugely enjoyed. Her tongue stroked and curled wetly, her teeth clashed with his and her body seemed to welcome the nervous intrusion of his great hands upon her finer features. Then she broke off, arms around his neck, laid her cheek on his forehead and twisted her head around to watch Lesley-Anne. Her left hand dropped to his trousers and she rocked her flat palm on the piece of solid flesh that had turned up under his fly.

Lesley-Anne had risen and almost went out of the room before she swung around and returned to the wall-mirror to fiddle with her hair. She pushed her long black curls about in a dissatisfied way, regarding herself in the mirror, inches away from them. Then, obviously feeling more and more critical of what she was seeing, she held the baggy T-shirt close to her body, at her rib cage, examining the profile that this gave to the figure beneath the material. She turned sideways and ran her hand briefly over both breasts, her fingers pausing at their peaks. Norman and Amy, their heads damply together, had stopped breathing. Lesley-Anne must surely be able to see them. It didn't seem possible that she couldn't.

'The dog's bollocks,' breathed Amy deliciously, her hand still hard on him.

Then, with a flurry of knees and elbows, Amy suddenly scrambled off his lap. 'Christ, shit, I'm meant to be working,' she muttered. And she had gone.

Norman was suddenly alone. He hauled himself out of his chair. Alone in her bedroom, Lesley-Anne had turned away from contemplating her faults in the mirror. She picked up her plastic bucket and left the room. Norman edged out of the little space and back into the fresher air of his study. The sunlight streaming through the windows hurt his eyes. He could hear some movement downstairs. Obviously Amy hadn't actually left yet. He went to the study door and was about to descend to see what was up, when there at the bottom of the stairs was his brother Gilbert. Had Gilbert seen Amy? Recognised her? He must have done.

'What's happened to you? You said you'd come and talk to me, sod you,' said Gilbert grimly. He put his hands in his pockets and looked pissed off. Norman realised that, behind him in the study, the viewing room door was probably ajar and the carpet was certainly pulled aside revealing all. 'You owe me an explanation about this meeting tomorrow. I've not had a sodding word from you. So I've had to trek all the way over here to sort it out. I've got better things to do than chase around the country looking for you.'

Norman had a flash of the image of Gilbert licking drying champagne off Amy's naked body in the Randolph Hotel, making her tingle. Gilbert had, indeed, so many, many better things to do, he thought. Gilbert began to mount the stairs. Norman blocked his path and suggested they go down and have coffee.

'No, let's sort this out, Norman. I'll have coffee with you when I've settled all this garbage with you.'

They stood face to face on the stairs, a step apart. Norman could not possibly let Gilbert enter his study. If Gilbert were to discover what evilness he had constructed in his study, Norman would just curl up and die. He felt frightened, ashamed, angry and frustrated and jealous. Sick in the head with it. This was the man who had pleasured himself with the woman that Norman most wanted in the whole wide world and would probably, now, never have. This was the man who was turning their revered family business into a rotten shoddy scam. This was the man who endlessly treated Norman with less than scant respect. This is the man who, were he to discover the sick secret lurking three yards from where they now stood, would despise him and hold him in utter contempt forever.

Gilbert, obviously thinking it was absurd for them to stand there chesting it out with each other on the stairs, endeavoured to shoulder his way past Norman. In his desperation, Norman found that he had grabbed Gilbert by the shoulders and was pushing him backwards down them again. They swayed about fruitlessly for a moment. Gilbert said: 'What is this? Are you all right?' He twisted sideways, lost his footing, stumbled, and then lurched back down the steps, crashing into a side-table at the bottom, spilling a vase and some irises on to the floor. 'What the fuck!' he roared.

Norman decided that it was time he grew up. He put aside various hurts about his brother's potency and vigour and about his own inadequate shamefulness, went past him into the kitchen and put the kettle on. They would have this damned coffee and try to get back on an even keel.

Gilbert came in and sat down, shaking his head in amazement. Norman had to ask him: 'Did you see the *Hello!* magazine girl?'

'Pardon?'

'The *Hello!* magazine girl?'

'Who?'

'The girl who interviewed you for the magazine. She was here. In her sportscar.'

'Oh yes, I parked next to it. I must have missed her. I thought I saw you in the garden. Do you know your sundial has its top on the wrong way round? She was here then?'

'Who?'

'The photographer.'

'The interviewer.'

'You're not making a lot of sense, Norman. What interviewer? I'm not following you. Are you all right? What the hell is this about the interview anyway?'

'She was here. I wondered if you saw her.'

'Who was here? What are you talking about? The interviewer was a man called Simpkins. I think. Thin man with a cut head. Diving accident. St Lucia. There was a girl photographer with him all right. Big, fat woman – Carla something. Rather good. Genuinely funny woman. Made me laugh.'

'That's all? No small, sexy-looking woman in a red suit?' Amy had been bloody lying about it all the time. Unless this was a subtle Gilbert cover-up. But it didn't sound as if it was.

'What's this all about?'

'Was there a driver or someone?' Norman probed on.

'No, they came on the train. I sent the pool car to pick them up. Joseph went down, if you really want to know.' Hey ho, thought Norman, in for a penny, in for a pound. 'Did you entertain anyone at the Randolph afterwards?'

'The Randolph? What, in Oxford? Bloody hell, who do you think I am? I had work to do. The photo session took for ever anyway. We were poncing about for about four bloody hours. Mary crawling in and out of various outfits. And I had to take her to Sainsbury's afterwards, too. Norman, what is this all about? Come on, tell me.'

'I don't know.'

'Who was here? In the car?'

'Someone else. I think.' The kettle boiled. He made two mugs of coffee. Black for Gilbert. No sugar.

Norman felt shell-shocked. He sat down. He couldn't concentrate. His mind was a whirl of questions and theories and conundrums. Gilbert had either decided that he was a hopeless case or that his paranoia was of no consequence. Norman's younger brother decided to take the bull by the horns and address what he saw as the more important question of the operation and staffing of various Chandos House institutions. It was, after all, their livelihood. He pulled out of his pocket a number of memos addressed to the managers of Cowsdown House and Aubrey Manor and the managers of a number of other centres, instructing them to commence the process of securing additional staff. They were dated throughout the year, the earliest having been issued in February.

Yes, Gilbert explained, they had been lacking in some areas and staff had been overstretched and had definitely felt exploited. This had mostly been over the winter. Since June, the situation had changed dramatically. There had been some cash-flow problems that, with the help of the bank, Gilbert had now virtually solved. The process of rebuilding staff levels was progressing well. The position would never be quite as good as it had been during the end of the eighties but it would be perfectly satisfactory. All this information had been covered in board papers and discussed at meetings that Norman had attended.

Norman was hardly listening. He acknowledged what his brother was trying to tell him but his brain was overwhelmed by the knowledge that Amy had lied and lied and lied and lied and lied. She had apparently lied about her liaison with Gilbert and her researches at Aubrey Manor. She had lied about where she had been and what she had been doing. She had lied about everything.

It struck Norman that Amy had been trying to make problems between him and his brother – trying to drive a wedge between them. Norman had never got on all that well with Gilbert following his time in the States, but they had always had a degree of mutual respect. Nothing like as close as in those days when Norman's house had been a bolthole for old man Magnus's youngest son. In those days Gilbert used to call around week after week for Sunday lunch with Norman, Grace and baby Joan. The young teenager would then spend the whole of his Sunday afternoon, when by rights he should have been studying, with his head tucked deep into the sofa, his bum in the air, listening to the delights of the oft-lamented Light Programme. After lunch on Sundays had meant a run of all the popular comedy repeats of the week – *Take It From Here, Educating Archie, Paul Temple, The Billy Cotton Band Show* and *The Navy Lark*. In those days they used to have proper entertainment for all the family – not like the various ghettos for the different generations that television and radio had erected nowadays. No wonder the institution of the family had broken down.

Gilbert had obviously run through his defence case in his mind before driving over to Coombe. So he made a damned fine job of it. But Norman couldn't listen properly. He nodded his assent and allowed himself to agree that all was probably hunky-dory at Chandos House. Finally Gilbert put the undrunk mugs of pallid coffee into the sink and after some prevaricatory small talk about the fourth Test match and the drought, took himself off. Gilbert did not try very hard to hide from Norman that he thought that his older brother might be getting a touch on the senile side.

Norman sat in the kitchen for a long time after Gilbert left, trying to figure out what all this new information meant. This meant he entirely missed the knock on his door and knew that Lesley-Anne was looking for him only when she placed a hand and her head against the kitchen window, from outside, trying to see where he might have got to. He got up slowly and walked around to let her in. She apologised for troubling him. He absentmindedly poured her a sherry.

'She was round here, the girl? Amy?' said Lesley-Anne abruptly.

'Yes, she was. She drove me back from the film site.' He added defensively. 'I've loaned them my Bullnose Morris until Wednesday. Silly of me, I expect. "Dressing", they call it apparently. It just stands around in the background.' He was finding it very difficult to find the energy to chat like this. 'It was very pretty over at Wormell.'

Lesley-Anne waded on with what she had to say. 'I've no right to interfere.' She sipped at her glass and seemed to be thinking how best to phrase what she felt she needed to say. 'There's something I didn't get to finish telling you about yesterday, you know, when we talked about that crazy stuff, you know, about what I'd heard was called, um, "harloting".'

'Yes,' he said irritatedly. He didn't want to hear any more of this. Everything he was hearing today was bad news.

'It's just that this man – well his business, or whatever it is – isn't just involved in trying to get people removed from office. They do worse than that. Much worse.'

'How, worse?'

'It may be impossible to believe this but it's said they undertake killings.' She was in fantasy land.

'How so?' This was so much nonsense.

'I'm sorry, it does sound impossible. It's just what I was told. It probably means nothing. But I thought I'd say.'

'What?'

'It's foolproof, they claim, undetectable.'

'What is?' he said vaguely, not really thinking, being patronising.

'I think it goes like this. All you have to do is pay a massive fee and sit back. Rajindra told Terry that these girls, they're well trained and, well, they have been known to discomfort some of their victims so badly that some of them, the men, actually go mad. Sort of. And, well, it's said, some of them kill themselves. And that's the idea. That's what they want to happen. That's how they do it. That's how it's done. I couldn't really believe it.'

Norman couldn't believe it, either. It sounded more and more like the ravings of an excitable, bored, imprisoned Pakistani than anything else. But, nevertheless, the name of Boyd-Orr swam into his mind. Was that anything to do with this? But Norman could never be in the frame. A judge might just be. But who would want to kill Norman? No one. People liked him. No one, thank God, would ever guess, apart from Amy, what a sick mind he had. To the world, he had always been seen as a kindly, avuncular old fellow. Friend to everyone. Why, it was even why Amy herself liked him. She had said so. Her words had shored up his life. 'You're such a nice, nice man,' she had said. On more than one occasion.

Lesley-Anne seemed to know that, as she said these things out loud, they sounded less and less likely. 'He said it's a foolproof, untraceable way of murdering old enemies,' she went on, 'finishing their lives. And it works, apparently. Because the victim does it himself. No one could ever be found guilty. You see? That's, um, what this Rajindra said,' she finished limply.

Norman stood up and looked out of the window, at the certainty of the sun on Bargate Hill, at the cloud of birds buzzing in and out of his willow trees. This was all so much hot air, of course. But the funny thing was that, in the last few days, possibly for the first time in the whole of a fairly fraught life, he had felt momentary suicidal impulses. It had been nothing serious and nothing meaningful. Even when, moments ago, he had been wrestling absurdly with Gilbert on the stairs, the thought had come to him that, were Gilbert to discover his guilty secret, he might not be answerable for his actions. The impulses meant nothing, of course, but it *was* odd. And Amy had, indeed, messed very substantially with his head. But that was what girls sometimes did to men. And men to girls, he supposed. But it struck him that she definitely had lied to him in ways that were far beyond teasing and kinky games.

He had never felt so all at sea, so depressed. He didn't want to be thinking any of this. What to do? What to do?

He turned to his housekeeper again. He felt grim and old. 'I'm glad you've come in here, anyway, Lesley-Anne, I have been thinking. I really do need a couple to help me run this place. That was my initial idea, as you know. The garden needs so much attention. It's getting out of hand. It's got so dry and there are weeds everywhere. In another two weeks we'll have lost it and then it will need a great deal of work to get it all back together again.'

'I'd be happy to tackle the garden as well. I'd enjoy it. I could find the time. Gladly.'

'No, no, a couple, a couple,' he said, almost to himself.

'What does that mean?' She knew. Her voice was clipped and hard.

He hated this. 'I think I will have to give you notice. I always expected to have a couple here, you see. There's so much work. One person couldn't possibly do it all alone. However willing.'

'Please let me stay.' She had wet eyes. And she was so pretty in her big floppy T-shirt. What was he doing this for? He was unhinged. Maybe her Mr Rajindra's theory was right and Amy *had* made him mad.

'No,' he said more to himself than to her. 'You did disappear on me you know. You might do it again.' He knew it was a useless and pathetic thing to say. But he wanted her out. He didn't want to hear all this nonsense about Amy seeping into his brain. 'A week,' he said. He had to give her some notice. A week wasn't truly enough.

'One week?'

'I think so. I think that's best.' He was such a bastard. She got up, angry. 'I thought I was doing all right for you here, Mr Ranburn,' she said, not allowing herself to whine. 'I'm sorry, I thought I was looking out for you here. I'm sorry if I've spoken out of turn. I was only saying. I thought you should, at least, know.'

'It's not that. Of course it's not that. Nothing to do with that.' He reached for the nearest lie: 'Only, when you left, I arranged to replace you, you see. With another couple.'

'You didn't say.'

'I was concerned for you. And they hadn't confirmed. But now they have. So I'm committed. I'm very sorry. I'll give you two weeks' notice. Put them off a week. I think it's probably the best I can do.'

'I'll go tonight. I'm not hanging around where I'm not wanted.'

'No. Don't be silly. That's not necessary. Really.'

'Yes, Mr Ranburn, tonight. Don't worry about me. I'll go. I'll be all right. We've got a sister in Ilford.'

He didn't see her go. The taxi must have taken her off at about six that evening. Norman was busy hammering six-inch nails into the architrave of his viewing room door. He wouldn't be able to get into it ever again. It was solidly nailed up. Perhaps it would be found in some generation to come. And puzzled over – like a priest's hole. And, hopefully, blamed upon his father, who would always be more flamboyantly remembered than Norman himself in the word-of-mouth history of the locality. He even tacked the bottom of the Kayseri carpet into place. He would start a new and better life.

He felt awful. And lonely now Lesley-Anne had gone. He must be mad to have let her go. She was a nice woman. On his side. A very-very-nice-woman.

Oh yes, he was quite definitely off his head.

CHAPTER EIGHT

For the lips of a strange woman drop
as an honeycomb, and her mouth is
smoother than oil: but her end is bitter as
wormwood, sharp as a two-edged sword.

PROVERBS 5:4

TUESDAY 8 AUGUST

Norman had called the Chandos House meeting for two.
He drove sombrely around the top of Oxford on the A40
in the lunchtime traffic. He had slept badly. And then he
had found it almost impossible to rise in the morning.
All night long he had worked through countless scenarios
that might explain Amy's behaviour. His limp final conclusion was that she was a pathological liar who could
not help herself. And even this didn't totally convince
him.

He felt ill. He was also bothered about the meeting that
he had called so high-handedly. From what Gilbert had told
him the previous day there was very little point to it, and the
other directors were going to be mightily peeved at having

been dragged away from their other responsibilities all the
way to Witney for so little reason.

He also missed Lesley-Anne being around. He was such a
fool.

All told, he was in a pickle. He pulled off the road at the
turning to Woodstock and sat there for a long time considering his options. None of them were all that propitious. The
best thing he could do was go away for a spell. He needed
a break from this hothouse weather and from the hothouse
psychological circumstances of the last three weeks.

He made two decisions. He would dump the meeting. He
would ring Gilbert and explain he was ill, apologise profusely
and ask Gilbert to explain their chairman's erstwhile concerns
to the board and their probable lack of foundation. He would
go home, ring Gordon Driscoll, who was now at Blair Athol,
and join him up there in Scotland in good time for the twelfth,
which was, after all, only four days away. He could take
in a bit of shooting and then return home in a week or so
with his head back on straight. By that time Amy and her
accompanying shenanigans would have evaporated and he
could get on with a quiet, sober, sensible, dull retirement.
The thought of it was like glimpses of paradise.

He found a pay-phone in a service station, rang the office
and spoke to Mrs Pettit and then to Gilbert. His brother
sounded concerned about his illness. Norman tried to adopt
a marginally throaty voice and explained his absence from
the meeting. He was aware that it was the vagaries in his
head that made him seem genuinely poorly.

'Joan rang,' Gilbert said.

'Oh yes? Why was that?'

'She was in a state. Asked after you. Had I seen you? Were
you all right and all that? She seemed bothered. I don't know
what brought that on. I told her to ring you. I told her I
thought you were under the weather. You are, aren't you?
You were a bit all over the shop yesterday.'

'Yes, probably. Sorry. I'm thinking, when I feel a little
stronger,' he added quickly, 'that I might take myself off
to Scotland to join the Driscolls. Spot of shooting.'

'I don't know what's got into Joan. Said she thought she might pop down to see you.' Norman wondered why she might want to do that. He saw her so rarely. Then he surmised that she might be making one last bid for Francesca's recording-studio capitalisation.

'I'll ring and tell her I'm not going to be there.' And they left it at that. Gilbert seemed relieved that he wasn't going to be at the meeting. And so was Norman. He felt feeble and cowardly about letting them all down, but he had got himself into a very feeble and cowardly frame of mind. He would have to begin to rebuild himself. He would certainly have to start eating properly. And taking exercise. And stop thinking about a person called Amy Shakespeare.

When he drove into the stable yard at the Aviary, Amy's car was parked by the barn.

Norman walked cautiously round the corner into the gardens and approached the house. Amy was nowhere to be seen. There were pigeons on the long yellow grass of the lower lawn and the whole garden seemed listless and unkempt. He had locked the house when he had left in the morning so he guessed that she couldn't be in there. The garden was apparently deserted. Could she be in the barn or in the stables? He had an image of her lurking in the barn, hanging from one of the main beams, ready to jump down on him, shrieking like a banshee, whatever they were. Could she be in the little summerhouse? It was very odd. He didn't know where to go and look first. Should he bother to go and look at all? Perhaps the wisest strategy would be to get back in the car and drive away. But then that was stupid. This was where he lived, for God's sake. But this young woman did make him confused. He was better off without her.

He was standing in the heat of the day, on the lower lawn, under the chocolate-coloured boughs of the copper beech when to his great surprise the door of Onan Cottage opened. A fit young man wearing just a pair of shorts came out, walked quickly around to where Amy's car was parked and returned with some pieces of paper in his hand. She must have got into the cottage somehow. The boy was her new friend, the exchange dealer Jamie. What the hell were they doing in there? He could imagine only too well.

Norman stood in the shadows of the tree and considered what to do. He could hammer on the cottage door and order them out. He could drive off and leave them to it. Or he could run surreptitiously to his house, unnail the viewing room and see what they were up to.

Norman knew only too well which of these options had the most votes in his mind. He thought wryly how absurd it was that only yesterday he had been at such desperate pains to nail up the dread door. How fervently he had promised himself never to enter that sordid little room ever again. He was living a completely asinine life. How had Amy put it? Out of his box?

To release the door he would need to fetch the claw-hammer from the barn, which, in turn would mean that he had to walk right past the cottage windows, risking being seen by Amy and the boy. He couldn't really see himself hiding – crawling on his stomach beneath the window-sills of the place. Even he wasn't that ridiculous.

Then he had the thought that Amy might like to think of his being there, behind the mirror. That would figure. So it might be all right for her to know that he had arrived back.

He walked stealthily down to the barn, collected a pair of ancient pliers and his trusty claw-hammer and walked them back to his house. He stolidly looked neither right nor left as he passed the windows of the cottage, but he got the feeling from a suspicion of activity that the occupants may indeed have spotted him. They seemed, from what few clues he could gather, to be in the bedroom. Well, of course they were.

Once he got inside his house, he locked the door and sped to the study. Sick idiot or not, this was what he had wanted most of all in his life, or so he had always thought. He would be mad not to have a peek, at least.

He discovered that he had nailed up the door with some resolution the night before. It took him a long time, effing and blinding, to remove the recalcitrant nails. Finally he had it done, but not without a bleeding finger. He entered the viewing room again, put down his hammer, and switched on the sound. God, he thought he had given all this up. He was crazy.

The bed was unoccupied. They had drawn the bedroom curtains and placed both bedside lamps on the floor so that the room had an eerie, almost theatrical quality – convoluted shadows everywhere. She was unforgivably presumptuous, helping herself to his property. But then he knew that already, didn't he?

In the middle of the room stood a grotesque seven-foot-high piece of equipment. It looked like a cross between a piece of sado-masochistic sculpture and a Gothic guillotine. It was all black and steel and was covered with mean leather straps, and buckles and chromium bats' wings. It was not what you would call an obviously tasteful piece.

The first voice he heard was Amy's, saying: 'So. Let's start. Go from the top. The little bit we've done so far. Then we'll work on.' Her soft flute music, the music with the Mau Mau beat, sobbed into the room. She had a big cassette machine on the floor, plugged into an electric socket. As Norman's eyes became accustomed to the gloom, he saw that the boy was hidden behind the centrepiece with his back to Norman, his arms suspended sideways, draped on the savage branches of the sculpture, as on a crucifix. At the front of it, Amy was hanging upside down from the top by one straight leg, her ankle caught in a leather loop, her other leg and arms spread out like thin, taut muscular wings, her short hair hanging down nine inches from the ground. One could clearly see her veins standing out through her skin.

To say they were meagerly clothed would have been the grossest understatement. Their minimalist costumes made Amy's cut-off denim shorts of yesterday look about as modest as a nun's habit. They both wore the skimpy leather-strapped outfits that she had shown Norman in Vauxhall, the leather thongs of them yanked up into their bums. As well as these, they each wore a black-and-chrome half-face mask with a sharp crow-like nose and diabolical silver-tipped horns.

Every muscle of their bodies gleamed with oil and glitter. The whole thing looked like devil-worship to Norman. It looked like a black mass with virginal sacrifices thrown in. Well, perhaps not virginal.

They were rehearsing *Hard-Up And Flummoxed.*

The beat of the music eddied on and the two bodies, on cue, began to move gently to the pulse of it. It was erotic, self-regarding movement with their hands stroking their limbs, fluttering between their legs and smoothing their exposed backsides. They looked both macabre and dangerous and wildly attractive. The boy had a fine, hard body. The choreography allowed Amy to descend from the machine and lock with the boy.

Finally Amy broke away, crouched down on her haunches and hit a button on the cassette machine. She pushed her mask up on to her forehead. So did the boy. They were both already shining with sweat. 'Yeah,' she said. 'That's cool. Right, going on, going on, going on. We do the cards. You collect the cards from the structure and pose – beefcake stuff – yeah, that's right. Yep, you can camp it up as much as you like. It's not serious. I troll around the audience sitting on a few laps, letting them have a feel. I then bring the guy up – usually it's the stag-night guy or whoever the party is for. I take the cards from you, this way round. Thank you. You go behind the structure again. You can concentrate on beginning to get yourself up – no, with your back to the audience like before. Yep. Triff. The guy selects the card, I do up his lips with lipstick. They love that. Much ado, much ado, much ado. Finally he kisses the card to mark it. So.' Amy kissed the playing card herself. 'There. One big red smacker. I fold the card, put it in my mouth and snog him. Snog, snog, snog, snog. Uproar. Then I clean up what's left of him and park him in the chair, stage left – there.' She moved the spare chair into place. 'A bit further off. Music, music, music. I go into my galactic bloody back-bend and you, dud-DAH, you reappear.' Amy lifted her arms back over her head and in profile dropped herself backwards into a crab-like, stick-insect back-bend, her masked head hanging down inches from the floor, as she presented her pelvis to the ceiling. She walked her hands slowly across the floor towards her ankles, contracting her body into a yet more articulated arch.

'Yep, ugh, OK. Come in upstage of me. The music starts again – Courtney Pine – I can't do that at the moment,' she grunted. The boy appeared behind her. Norman couldn't be sure but it looked as if he was partially erect inside his tiny leather jockstrap. 'That's it,' she continued. 'You sort of fold your body around mine, lay your cheek on my tits, knees underneath, crouching, ballet. Make it beautiful, beautiful, beautiful. Yes. Well, sort of. Slower, slower. Poetry, Jamie, poetry. When you're sorted, you tongue your way down from my tits to the little leather toggle at the waist there. Long tongue, long tongue. Take your time. Not so quickly, not so quickly. Give it time. We're not running for a bus here. I can't see, you see. Now. Pull the fucker with your teeth. The toggle. Got it? The toggle?' The boy clumsily followed what she was telling him. He gave the toggle a pull. Nothing happened. 'Oh smeg. Come on. Again. I'm dying here,' she said to the floor. This time the toggle came away and in one magical movement the whole of the leather strappings of her costume fell away to the floor and she was naked – still in her excruciating back-bend.

'Great, marvellous, wonderful. Now round to the business end. Quick, quick. But don't make it look hurried. Beautiful, beautiful, beautiful, all the time. Kneel between my knees. Oh shit, I'm out of practice. It's quite quick normally. Hold each thigh gently with each hand. Gently. Finger and thumb, finger and thumb. Quite delicate. Ballet, ballet, ballet. *Swan Lake*, dying swan, all that. Yeah, that's it. Then as if it's a new idea and you've only just thought of it, like it's a cheeky joke – whip off the mask and throw it aside. As if you really want to get to business with this. It's a good laugh if you do it OK. Like you're improvising all of a sudden. Really – you've never thought of it before. New idea. That's it. Then go for it. Nuzzle in. Make a bit of a show of it. I don't mind.' She giggled. 'I really – don't mind at all. Yeah, go on, go on. I shriek a bit when we're doing the show.' She gave Jamie a perfunctory shriek or two. 'Something like that. Only better. And more of it. And panting. If I remember. Then pull the folded card out of my pussy with your teeth. Go on. Go on. Try again. It's there. Don't worry about me. Yes. Oh yeah, that's it. Groovy, even. Pull it out. Pull it out. Galactic. Stand. Oh, Christ. Ouch. I've got to get to the gym. Get myself back together. Yowee, I'm dead. I creep round and fasten myself to your back, behind you, one arm over your shoulder, one leg curled over your hip. Yes, that sort of thing. Almost. I can't do this. Fuck. God, you're slippery. Now you show the guy in the chair the playing-card. And it's the lipsticked job, yeah? He's mighty pleased. Well, he's marginally pleased. But he's been concentrating on looking up my fanny. But I'm mighty pleased. You're mighty pleased. The audience is mighty pleased. A big applause. Yeah, and applause for our gallant helper too, please, as he goes back to his place. Music ends. Wow. Phew. Well done.'

Norman realised he was sitting motionless, hardly breathing.

Amy puffed her cheeks out and blew almost as if she had been running in a race. She sat down on the floor, back against the sculpture, exhausted, her legs straight out. Her sole apparel was her pair of high-heeled strappy shoes. 'Rest.' Amy rubbed her nose with a skinny knuckle.

'There's so much to remember,' Jamie said as he went and sat on the bed, looking eager and bright-eyed but concerned.

'The important thing is to enjoy it. Doesn't matter if we get some of it wrong then. As long as it looks as if we're having a good time, they lap it up.'

'I hope it's all right. I mean it's great. But it's just I'm a bit fazed at the idea of doing it in front of a room full of people.'

'You get used to it. You get to like it even. I really get off on it now. Well, most of the time. Exhibitionist freak, me. Sometimes they're a bit gross. If I don't feel great, I just think of the dosh.'

'Yeah, it's all right for you. It terrifies me.'

'You'll be kicking. The performers are in charge here. The punters have no idea what we're going to do. They get scared, however canned they are. We've got the power. I love it. Stick with me, babe. I'll see you're all right. OK, on we go. Next,' she announced. 'You'll like this bit. Start where we left off. Me on your back.'

She remounted him. 'The guy has just gone back to his place. I peel off, back to the audience. Like so. Lots of bum, lots of bum. You wheel the guillotine around ninety degrees so they can see what it does. Music.' She dashed off back to the cassette machine and found the track she wanted. More slow saxophone. 'It goes like this.' She showed him. The structure had a traditionally diagonal guillotine-blade which was pulled aloft with a length of rope which went through a pulley at the top. Amy hauled it aloft and then sent it crashing back down to the bottom. It sliced its way straight past a hole where a tiny Louis XIV's head could just about be inserted, at waist height. This little round space turned out to be exactly big enough to push a fat cucumber through. Amy also demonstrated the blade's effectiveness with a robust-looking carrot. In time to the music, Amy, obscured by the machine itself, pulled the blade aloft and let it thunder to the bottom, each time neatly dissecting the vegetables. A knob of carrot and the end of the cucumber fell, sliced, to the floor. Norman began, he thought, to guess at what might be in the offing.

'Right. OK? You come around here. Oh, music again,' she said. She clattered about with her various tapes. Then the music commenced once more. It was now softly insistent, but dreamy. 'You're in profile. We're both in profile. Something like this.' Amy knelt down in front of Jamie, put her hand up to the little leather toggle at his crotch and his costume fell away in much the same way as hers had earlier. They were both now naked. The boy was already creeping upwards towards being properly erect. It wasn't going to take him long. He held himself briefly and then put both hands behind his head as instructed, pushing out his neat pelvis with a clenched bum. 'Yes,' she said looking up. 'As I say, I hope this begins to make it all worth while.' Amy held the boy's thigh with one hand and after quietly stroking his balls, held his penis delicately with the fingers and thumb of her other hand. The music sighed and caressed the air as she licked her lips in theatrical anticipation. Then she slowly lowered her fiercely concentrated face like some kind of a gentle beneficence on to his now solid erection. Her tongue flashed out and licked its way around the glans of the thing. She kissed it with pursed lips. Then she sank her head over his sharply angled flesh. Forward and back went her head, the cock disappearing far into her mouth and then appearing again. Jamie had his head thrown back a little and his eyes shut.

Amy came off him, gasped for air and, looking up, said: 'You *are* allowed to groan, you know. Like as if it's almost pleasant.'

Would they really do this in public? In front of a gang of beery men? Norman couldn't believe it.

The music changed. Amy moved to fetch the structure. She wheeled it to the boy and fitted the hole in it, just as Norman had anticipated, neatly over Jamie's preening erection. It now stood at an angle, right across the path of the descending knife. Norman found he was pinching his thigh in the tension of the moment. Supposing she didn't do it right? To the accompanying threat of the mounting music, she slowly, ominously hauled the guillotine blade aloft, fastened it ready, made a joky magic pass or two with her fingers over the man's penis, stooped and kissed the condemned thing goodbye. And then released the blade.

It screamed down and clunked to a stop, right past the object that was in its way. But Jamie's manhood remained intact and proud. And in place. Amy pulled away the machinery, took Jamie by the hand and they both bowed.

'Brilliant,' she said. 'Then we put on the wraps.' There were two cotton gowns with skulls all over them that they scrambled into. 'Fuckin' brill, you. In my view. Sometimes Quentin used to come at the end when the knife has dropped. But, then, he could come at will. Come and go at will actually, the smegging bastard. But, then, Quentin is a control freak. It's not necessary but it makes for a well smart finale.'

'I don't expect I could do that.' They stood against each other, without holding on, her pelvis pressing against his thighs, her head back, looking up at him. It seemed very intimate. 'I expect you could,' she murmured.

'I'll see what I can do.'

'Galactic, you are.' And she reached up her hand and affectionately tweaked his nose with her knuckles.

'Thanks.' Was he blushing? He turned sharply away from her to go to the bathroom.

Amy watched him go. Then she turned to the mirror for the fleetest second. 'Yeah?' she said, and grinned wickedly, blowing the glass a minute kiss. She had the oldest, greyest eyes in the world. For a moment she stared deadpan at the mirror and then she inclined her head and dropped one eyelid in a graphic wink. She, too, then exited to the Onan Cottage bathroom.

Norman felt absolutely exhausted from what he had watched. Those young people and their boundless energy and puppy-dog liveliness made him feel so old. And sad. In fact, when he came to think about it, he felt worse than old – he felt rotten. He had a headache, blood on his hand, depression in his heart. He sat and watched the closed bathroom door disconsolately for a long time. Nothing happened. He couldn't even hear anything.

He supposed he had been feeling a bit off-colour, on and off, ever since he had met Amy. How long had it all been going on? How long had it been since that dread, wondrous night she had rolled him some of her marijuana and walked the beam? Three weeks was it? Nothing. It was actually eighteen days – not even three weeks. Yet it already seemed like for ever. He had been totally consumed by her. It was ridiculous in a grown-up like himself. But she had filled up this total vacuum. He had been unable to shake her off. She had got her hooks into his psyche – much as Lesley-Anne had suggested. And he felt so changed because of it. It was as if he was doped a lot of the time. Did those drugs of hers have a longer response time than he imagined? He felt as if he was suffering from some sort of misty vertigo, with Amy always further along the precipitous ledge, just out of his reach, above the dinky-toy traffic in the street thousands of feet below. An ancient Harold Lloyd film with sex appeal.

It was going to be difficult to get himself out of his chair. Watching their rehearsal, he had been hard the best part of forty-five minutes. It had virtually disappeared now, but he didn't feel very much better for it. What to do? What to do?

Have tea. That was the usual Ranburn response – stupid, prosaic, but time and time again it was what he turned to in order to get a hold on reality once more. Tea might do the trick.

So with the redoubtable Earl Grey in the forefront of his mind, Norman dragged himself out of the chair. He had a dreadful headache. It was probably the stifling heat of the viewing room. And the lack of air. He had never thought a lot about ventilation when he had built it. He staggered a little and, using his hands for support, hauled himself out of the tiny space. He adjusted his dress and generally sorted himself out. He would be all right.

He assumed that Amy would bring her new friend around to say hello once they got out of the bathroom. She would like doing that. She would – what? – 'dig' that. It would be her sort of thing. She was seriously deranged, that young woman. But he might enjoy it a little bit as well. Because he was seriously deranged as well. He and Amy would be in a situation in which only they knew the full scenario of what had been going on during their performance. The two of them knowing and the young Jamie being in the dark. He would enjoy feeling that. He could understand it in her, too. He would be in the same game-plan as Amy once again, on the same side. He put together a tea on a tray – a tea for three, including an ancient Swiss roll that Lesley-Anne had left for him in his kitchen.

He was about to take the whole thing out on to the terrace and summon the troops, when he heard the noise of Amy's car erupting in the stable yard. He just got out of the house in time to to see the open-topped Mazda, with two heads in it, leave the end of his drive and set off for the open road.

When he went into the cottage, he discovered they had cleared up. The only sign that they had been there was a residue of cooling condensation on the bathroom tiles. Nothing else.

It was about as sticky and as hot as any night they had had that summer. And Norman had slept badly for the best part of three weeks now. He tossed about fruitlessly, readjusting his pillows and trying to sleep covered by just a single sheet, which made him feel oddly vulnerable. But it wasn't primarily the heat that kept him awake – it was his swarming mind. He couldn't switch off his brain. On a couple of nights in the last week or so he had taken to walking round the garden, in the dark, in his dressing gown with the bone-dry grass underfoot, until he was dog-tired. That, together with the odd hot toddy, sometimes worked. Tonight, though, his mind was so hijacked by teeming thoughts that he might need something even more taxing. He decided to get up, dress and walk down into the village.

He had no fresh shirts left. The laundry situation seemed to have gone completely to pot. He pulled on a thin sweater and his trousers and slipped out of the house. Coombe at the best of times was always a quiet little village, but at night it was entirely bereft of humanity. The whole place was naught but hyper-neat cottages, model weedless gardens, closed curtains and a tangle of television aerials. It was strange to think of Mrs Robinson of Coombe cottage, Mr and Mrs Mackenzie and their three cats and all the other inhabitants whose names he would never know lying tomb-like in their various beds. How many of them were tossing about, unable to sleep? The sky was clear and the stars were obscured by the brilliance of a full moon.

He walked all the way to the Blenheim Arms on the green, past Mrs Thomas's shop, over the bridge to the other end of the houses. Having got that far, he slowly turned around to go back home again. He stood still in the middle of the lane

295

and contemplated the quietness. He thought about Susan Davidson, Mrs Thomas's Saturday girl. He would have been better off secretly lusting after that kid than actually getting involved with bloody Shakespeare. The air felt heavy with a dull night-time heat. There wasn't even the odd fox about – trotting purposefully around. The moon gave him a large and clearly visible shadow, which walked up ahead of him on the road. He got on the move again. He trudged slowly past the end of the churchyard. He had no reason to hurry. He didn't want to be back in his bedroom too soon. Even though he now felt boss-eyed with weariness.

He thought he might go into the churchyard as far as the church porch. It would be interesting to see if they had remembered to lock the church for the night. They sometimes forgot. He walked through the lych-gate. Beyond the two large yews were some of the newer graves. His father's was third from the left by the wall. 'Magnus Ranburn', it said – if one had been able to read it in the shadows – and gave his dates. No epitaph. There were no words adequate enough to encapsulate his father's brilliant, busy, trying, friendless life. Like father, like son – apart from the brilliance. And there was no clear rationale, in the final analysis, why they should have been so friendless. Both Magnus and Norman had been bright, well-provided-for and even humorous men. Men with considerable skills and capabilities and not bad-looking either. Why had they had no skill in making good friends? In Norman's case, that was, until Amy had come along.

Norman perched on a low stone catafalque nearby. Dad, he thought, almost out loud. What was he to believe about Amy? What was the truth? Had she ever been his friend? Probably not. The truth was that she was an immoral, disorientating, foul-mouthed, beautiful woman. But maybe that was what young women in the nineties were like. They were different creatures from the generations before. Everyone said so. It was this women's liberation thing that had done it. And he'd never disapproved of that. More power to their collective elbow.

Certainly, if one was going to select someone to 'mess

with men's heads' – probably, more truthfully, 'fuck with men's brains' – one would surely look to choose just such a one. Amy Shakespeare, or whoever she was, was the ideal executrix – wicked, teasing, revengeful, amoral. Kinky. With a riveting sex-appeal that reached into the sexual psyche of every man whose brain she addressed. She was, without doubt, about the most thrillingly attractive young woman he had ever come across. In all his whole life. If destruction *was* the name of the game she would be the perfect instrument to choose. No question.

What other pieces of information could he gather about it all? What else did he actually know? For sure? Well. She lied. She lied pretty well all the time. Congenitally. Consistently. Inconsistently. About her parentage, her work, her relationship with Gilbert, her sex life everything, anything.

What was the other thing? Oh yes, she liked him. Yes, of course it could just be part of an act. And there was no question that she was a consummate actress. But every so often, when he caught her off guard, during one of their conversations – as he had when she was crying in the church, or calling to him the cricket result that evening at Paddington Station – he had a real sense that for all their age difference, for all their different backgrounds and experience, she had a genuine fondness for him. Yes, of course, he could be wrong. But what little sixth sense he had told him that he wasn't.

What else? She was rich. Anyway, reasonably well-off – for someone who was twenty-four. Where did her bloody money come from?

And, in spite of her immediate, confrontational sex-appeal, people didn't necessarily like her. Was she too much of a challenge? To his surprise, Norman had discovered that a number of the men on the unit didn't like her at all. Fancied her right enough, but didn't care for her all that much. She was seen to be trouble – odd, mystifying, dangerous. So he wasn't alone in that. It was only on the last day when the unit was at the Aviary that he had learned that the crew's nickname for her was 'Witch'. Not exactly a kindly sobriquet.

Yes, and what else? Boyd-Orr had given her emeralds and then killed himself. She had known him, he had clearly been enthralled by her, and now he was dead.

But no one wanted Norman dead, did they? Everyone either liked him or thought nothing of him. Had anyone sufficient grudge to want to wreak some kind of vengeance on nice, retired, harmless Norman Ranburn MBE?

No one.

What about Peter Peacock?

Peter Peacock. Peter Peacock. Peter Peacock.

Until now, Norman had not thought of that as an idea. That particular young man had dropped out of his mind. Peter bloody Peacock. Yes. Norman had always assumed that Austin's son hated him with a devotion that verged on the unhinged. How had Norman forgotten about him? Had he blocked him out of his mind? How selective could one's memory get?

The last time Norman had met up with Peter, the young man had been remarkably pleasant. That may have been why he had stopped featuring in Norman's personal chamber of horrors. At Lord's, it had been – with Amy dressed as Dick. Peter had seemed, in their short conversation, to have decided to let history take care of itself – bygones were apparently to be allowed to have gone by.

But here was a thought – if one was to be party to the kind of scenario Lesley-Anne had tittle-tattled about, one might well decide to disguise one's loathing. Perhaps. Or maybe for Peter it *was* now all just water under the bridge. His father, after all, had been guilty. What had happened could hardly have been said to be Norman's fault. It was all very sad but one could not escape the fact that Austin had committed a crime. Everybody knew that.

And yet . . .

Norman closed his eyes and rocked himself quietly backwards and forwards and thought of his father's bones in their rotting box, two or three yards away. He always thought of the earth pressing around the faces of the dead. He didn't want to die.

So it was very silly to sit in a graveyard at two-thirty in the morning under a full moon, wasn't it? The ghosts' high noon. He was so tired now. He would take himself back. Open all the bedroom windows to encourage what little breeze there was. Then tomorrow he would go and fetch Bertram – the filming had finished at Wormell Water. Then he would pack and depart for Scotland. He had to leave all this behind him. Never see her again. That's all there was to it.

'Thanks, Dad,' he muttered shortly as he got up and walked away. It struck him that he probably sounded like Amy.

Norman was still not sleeping when the birds began their racket at dawn. Then he slept without waking all the way through until four-thirty in the afternoon. The television had the early-evening news on by the time he had had a bath. He must be poorly, sleeping that long. He had virtually lost a day.

The filming would have finished today. He needed to get Bertram back. It was all so late in the day.

Norman had just called a taxi to take him over to the lake to pick up the car, when to his astonishment, a cab arrived. For a moment he thought it was the result of dealing with a radio-controlled taxi service, when he saw that this one was delivering his daughter Joan.

She had a face like thunder.

'Joannie,' he managed, 'what brings you here? I was off to Scotland today. But I've got very behind – I'll have to go tomorrow now.' Joan said not a word. She paid the taxi and then pushed straight past Norman into the house. She had no luggage, just a handbag. He watched, in shock, as she marched straight up the stairs and into his office.

Oh God. She knew. She knew. She knew. She knew.

Somehow she knew.

He followed her, almost staggering, almost against his will, aghast, appalled, dying, miserable, summoning up desperate lies to explain, wondering if there was any way in which he could disclaim all knowledge of it. Why, in God's heaven's only name, had he never thought up some kind of ready alibi, some kind of bland explanation to account for his madness? Maybe because there wasn't one.

She went straight behind his desk, threw her handbag on to it and clawed aside the hanging carpet.

'Daddy, what is this?' she rapped. 'Come on, what is it?' The old panelled door, dark brown, stood there revealed, blankly accusing him. It was scarred with nails, one or two were still fastened to it, bent and battered, banged in. There were hammer marks. He didn't know he had done as much damage as that.

'I tried to nail it up,' he gasped and he sank half to his knees and half on to the chaise. His head was pounding. There were no depths to his shame. He was depraved, appalling, pathetic, ashamed, ashamed, ashamed. He *loathed* himself. He was crying. That his daughter should know the depths to which he had sunk – the little girl who had worshipped him as a baby, with whom he had built sandcastles at Birchington-on-Sea, whom he had so proudly given away in marriage one golden September day in Studham, whose beautiful daughter, Fran, he loved more than anything in the whole wide world.

'Open it,' she said.

'No. I can't.'

'Daddy, open it.'

'It's locked. I can't. I can't. It's never been open.'

What had he been doing all summer? He had been totally, disgracefully disgusting. A Peeping Tom, a dirty mac, a wanking pervert, a vomit of a person. Seeing himself, suddenly, through his daughter's eyes made him realise with dreadful clarity what mean, seedy, shocking things he had allowed himself to do – had allowed himself to revel in. What would Fran think, when she knew? Because she would get to know, wouldn't she? He groaned.

'You've got a key, Daddy.'

'No.'

'You've got a key, Daddy. Open it.'

'I can't. I can't.'

'Show me. I want to see what you've done.'

'No.'

'Open it.'

'I can't show you. Oh God. Oh God. I'm so – I can't, Joan.'

Amy must have told her. There could be no one else. No one else knew. She must have telephoned her. She wanted to kill him. He was dead. He could never look anyone in the eye ever again. He was a sneak, a pervert, a cancer, a scab, an ulcer, a warped, debased human thing. He *loathed* himself. He imagined his granddaughter's face looking bewildered, despising him.

He covered his face with two big hands. Joan stood there, looking at the back of the door, the heavy carpet still in her hands.

'It's a peep-hole, isn't it?'

'Oh God, it's worse than that.'

'Why, Daddy, why?'

'I don't know,' he started. 'I don't know. I don't know at all. I don't know what got into me. I just wanted to do it. It was a sort of madness. God knows why. God knows why. I couldn't begin to tell you.' He couldn't speak. It was all too too painful. He wanted to say that he had had so little to do. That he had been so lonely. That he felt that he might have missed out on life. But he could never talk to Joan about sex, for example, about his needs, about his sickness, about having no one, about the accursed repression that had been with him every minute, every hour, every day, every year of his life.

'Why, Daddy?' She said it calmly. Comfortingly almost.

'Too much time on my hands, I think,' he said. Joan snorted derisively. There was a long silence. He felt finished, blank, sad. 'I'm so very sorry. I'm so very sorry you had to discover this. I'm so sorry. That's all I can say. Oh, Joanie, your father's a – your father's a pervert. I'm so very, very sorry. I'm so sorry. I'm so ashamed. I am so very, very ashamed.'

'Stop it, Daddy,' Joan said quietly. She dropped the carpet back into place – the door disappeared again. She came around the desk and he felt the weight of her sit down next to him.

'Daddy,' she said, hard voiced. She was in navy blue – a navy-blue suit.

'Don't,' he mumbled bitterly. 'I hate myself. There's no excuse. I'm sick. Worthless.'

'Show it to me, Daddy,' she said very quietly.

'I don't think I could. It's too shameful. You know anyway.'

'Yes.'

'She told you?'

'Yes. The girl. That friend of Francesca's.'

'Amy.' He was calmer now.

'How did she know?'

'I told her. I showed her.'

'Why?'

'It was a sort of showing off. She bewitched me, I think.' Tears were coursing down his cheeks.

There was a knock at the front door. Joan went down and told the new taxi man who had arrived that he wasn't going to be needed after all. Norman found he couldn't move, or think, or feel angry, or betrayed, or indeed anything at all. He barely felt alive. He deserved to be buried, the earth pressing against his face.

Joan came back. She sat back down next to him again. She was calmer. She held her small round hands, palms together, in silence. She was thinking. The salt from the tears stung his eyes. He cried, not so quietly any more – snuffling – soliciting pity. Joan sighed gently. She quietly put an arm around his big shoulders. A distant daughter doing her duty by him – just. She stroked his back with small comforting strokes of the flat of her palm. He didn't deserve comforting.

'Why did she do that, Daddy?'

'What?'

'Why did she ring me and tell me?'

'Amy?'

'Of course Amy. Why did she tell me?'

'What did she say?'

'I don't know. I couldn't take it in. I couldn't understand what she was on about. Then I couldn't believe it. It sounded so bizarre. You – this – everything she said. It was yesterday morning. She said she thought I ought to know. To protect others or something. To protect you perhaps? Help you? I wasn't sure. I didn't believe any of it to start with. It didn't seem possible. And she's got a reputation, I'd heard, as a bit of a tearaway, a bit of a bolshie – you know – not one of us. Then I began to think that perhaps it was true. The detail was so convincing. You wouldn't make up a story like that. She sounded terribly upset.'

'She's a very good actress.'

'Yes. Possibly. It sounded real though – her distress. A real state, she was in. Then I couldn't sleep of course. So I got the train down.' He was crying again – agonised tears. 'Daddy, Daddy,' she said again, with more feeble patting. She was being so much more friendly than he deserved. It moved him all the more. 'She's destroyed me,' he managed. 'Have you told anyone?'

'No, of course not.'

'But they know you've come down.'

'Fran does.' Everyone would know eventually. Fran, Fran, Fran. Joan went on softly, kind but shocked: 'I think, well, I don't know, but I think – you might need some help.'

'How do you mean, help?' He sniffed.

'Therapy.' So, he *was* mad. Mad. Perverted. A shit-brain. Dangerous. He would never hold his head up again. Everyone would hear about it. Everyone would get to know – finally. One couldn't keep that sort of thing in. So this is what you felt like, Austin? Poor old Austin Peacock. This is the kind of despair you felt. Norman would never be able to smile at any of his family, any of his friends, ever again knowing that in their heart of hearts they truly believed him a good, honourable and kind man. He must so disgust his daughter. And Fran would never be able to face him. He would certainly never be able to face her, knowing that. He would have to say goodbye to his granddaughter.

If Amy had told Joan, she could have told the world. She wanted him dead. He was dead. It was all over for him. She had to be stopped. He would get her first.

They sat together in silence. There was so little that was worth saying. Her being there and not accusing him of his dirty mind was support enough. After about half an hour, Norman felt he was cried out. One couldn't cry for ever. He mopped himself up with his sleeve until Joan went into his bedroom and fetched him a handkerchief. Then she offered to make him a cup of tea. Well, of course. No, she was being kind really.

He couldn't make himself join her in the kitchen. She had to come and find him in the corridor with the two mugs. He was so uncertain as to what to do, what to say, how best to react. Eventually they sat either side of the kitchen table. Dusk was gathering outside.

'So she's been a – a friend? Amy?' she asked finally.

'I suppose so.'

'What sort of friend, Daddy? Have you had an affair?'

'Good God, no. She's just been around. A chum, you know. I'm old enough to be her grandfather. Mostly it was to do with them filming here.'

'And you decided to show her the peep-hole? Did you ask her to keep it a secret?'

'Well, of course. Well, I thought – yes, it was just a secret. Between us. So stupid. So awful. I'd nailed it up too. Before. I was terribly ashamed of it. I'd gone a little bit crazy, Joanie, during the summer. I didn't mean to do anybody any harm. It was quite innocent really. It just looks horrible, that's all.'

'Why did she betray your secret then, Daddy? Had you made her angry? Was she after money and you'd refused?'

'Nothing like that.'

'What then?'

'Nothing. I don't know.' He would have to eliminate her. Amy would see to it that Francesca got to know. Fran would never ever understand. Fran would loathe him as much as he did himself. 'I suppose I have a kind of notion why she told you.'

'Why?'

'I think she hated me, wanted me to be humiliated.'

'Why on earth?'

'I don't know. It's just an idea.' He got up.

'What are you going to do, Daddy?' She was being so kind. He was moved to tears by it. Family first – that's what Gilbert had always said. It seemed he was right.

'I'm going to have to fetch Bertram. The filming finished yesterday,' he said bleakly. 'I have to. Stay here. I'll be back in half an hour. A bit of fresh air. Then we'll talk. I'll tell you more then. Believe you me, I'm really truly disgusted by myself. I'm so very, very sorry, Joan.'

'I'll get you something to eat.'

'There's no need,' he said. 'I don't think I could eat.'

'Go carefully, Daddy.'

'Of course I will.'

'Shall I come with you?'

'No. I'll see you when I get back.'

They stood looking at each other across the kitchen. Then she stepped forward and gave him a brief hug. It was about as kind and as nice and as unwarranted as anything she had ever done. He felt he was going to cry again. He did.

He left the house. And then, as he reached the car, he had two thoughts. His brain was beginning to work once more. He went back in and returned to his miserable study. He pulled out his business reserve account cheque-book and wrote a cheque. He walked through to the bathroom and tipped the Boyd-Orr ring out of the tooth-mug into the palm of his hand. He wasn't sure why, but he put the ring into his trouser pocket. Evidence, he supposed.

He felt sick. And blank. Exhausted mostly.

Joan was standing in the living room, looking sightlessly out at the burned lawns and Bargate Hill with the evening light on it.

'I thought that was you,' she said.

'Here,' he said without emotion. He gave her the cheque. 'I should have done this before. It's for Frannie. And all that rock-and-roll stuff of hers. The studio. Synchromesh Sound. I'm sure it'll be a goer.'

'Daddy. You are such a darling.' Joan smiled ruefully at him. She had been crying too, a little.

'No,' he said seriously. 'I've made it payable to you. But it's the full capitalisation for the scheme. Eke it out. Tell her to keep a very close eye on the contractors. Read the small print. All that sort of thing. She's in the big cruel world now. And there's no more where that came from. She won't be able to go mad. Everything costs more than one thinks. Tell her I love her.' He wasn't trying to buy affection or forgiveness. It just seemed the right thing to do.

'You can tell her yourself, silly.'

'Yes, of course. Back soon.' He headed for the front door. 'Oh, get it in an account quickly, there's a love. She'll need the interest.'

'Thank you, Daddy,' Joan said. He wanted her to walk over and hug him again. Just one quick squeeze would have done the trick. She couldn't do it any more. Or, at any rate, she didn't. She just stood there with the cheque in her hand, looking strained. Yes, of course, he was trying to buy forgiveness.

He didn't notice a single detail of the drive over to Wormell Water. All he knew was that the car got there extremely quickly. And he arrived in one piece. He wasn't really sure what he was trying to do. Fetch Bertram? He would need someone to drive his own car back for him afterwards. But was this all about Bertram?

He parked the Daimler in the gathering dusk and walked slowly over the dam, trying to see where everybody was. Bertram was parked where he had been asked to leave the car three days ago, but closer to the crest of the dam, facing the depths of the valley. The drop seemed only inches away from its front wheels. He would have to reverse it with great care. They had covered Bertram with a bright-yellow, plastic cover.

Nearly all the film-unit vehicles had disappeared. There was a small team of scaffolders demounting the structure that had supported the manor-house scenery. The place looked a mess. Someone had a radio full on and tortured migraine music – guitars and painful saxophones – filled the air. That and the noisy chiming of the scaffolding poles as they dropped on to the lorry. It was getting dark. There was no sign of Amy's car.

Norman wasn't quite sure what he was expecting to do. He walked over to the men working, trying to see if he could recognise any of the faces. Most of them were the building contractor's people and had not been around for the filming. He saw one face he thought he recognised. There was a small fat man in baggy shorts, speaking on a mobile phone, whom Norman felt sure he had seen at the Aviary as well. The man looked up as Norman trudged up the dusty path towards him. The music was very loud and felt totally at odds with the setting. Norman hated their modern pop music. Aural toothache, it was.

'Hello,' he said against the noise. 'Is, um, Amy Shakespeare around still?'

The man clicked his phone shut and considered this. 'No, they've all gone. Des's around. You could ask him.'

'Right.'

'Amy?' the man said, remembering: '"Witch", you mean?'

'If you like.'

'Oh, I know about her. She's gone to LA. Her feller Quentin picked her up dinner-time. She's gone. Gone for good, I think. Job in Los Angeles. All the luck.'

'Really?' Norman was suddenly swamped with tiredness again. He had slept all day long but was still completely exhausted. And lost as to what to do. The man walked away from him, back up to where they were working. Norman felt so dead and dull that he was finding it almost impossible to breathe. The air was thick with heat and damp. He had too many clothes on. He had to sit down. He found one of the big red plastic bread trays they used for carrying cables in and perched it on its side to use as a kind of a seat. Looking away from the mess towards the lake with the pale, virtually full moon in a white evening sky should have been very beautiful. But nothing would ever be beautiful in his life again. There were seagulls wheeling about over the water. And the black silhouette of a duck paddling placidly on its surface. Birds. They were so bloody carefree.

The headlights of a car carefully picked their way over the road across the dam. It moved up the slope and parked close to where he was sitting. Des Wright got out. 'All right, squire?' he said when he saw who it was. He began to walk away from Norman towards the air-curdling music.

'I hear Amy's gone,' Norman called hopelessly. 'To the States or something.' She had got her job done, *coup de grâce* and all that, and then buggered off with her winnings. God, he hated her. He only hated himself more.

'No,' said Des coming back towards him a little. 'She was being picked up. But I got a call from her fella Quentin. He'd got involved in this shunt on the M25. So he's had to hire another motor. I shouldn't think he'd be here yet. Amy must be around. Unless she said she'd meet up with him in Oxford. I saw her here before I left, down by the lake. What – half an hour ago? She might still be around.' Des looked at him, 'You OK?'

'Yes,' said Norman. 'I've come to relieve you of the car. Meant to be here this morning,' he prattled on. 'Got delayed. Thanks for the cheque. That was quick.'

'Wow. Unusually so, I'd say,' said Des. 'Cheers,' he said. But then he would, wouldn't he? The location manager left it at that. He walked away from Norman up the hill and disappeared behind the two scaffolding trucks. The episodic noise of the sliding scaffolding was almost unbearable.

So Amy might still be around. Where?

She could be lurking around anywhere in the forestry. But she would have to show herself when the man turned up.

Norman walked down towards the lake away from the music. Where was she? Where?

Gone?

Norman went back up to Bertram, scanning the darkening lakeside all the time for any sign of movement. He removed the cover and battled automatically to fold it up.

Then he found himself looking at the boathouse. It was about fifty yards away, in the shadows, by the side of the black lapping waters of the lake. It would be as good a hiding place as any.

He left the tarpaulin half-folded in the back of the open-topped vehicle and walked circumspectly down to the building. It was small and wooden. The door creaked open. It was pitch-dark inside. Two punts side by side. Dark water moving stealthily. No one.

His eyes got used to the darkness. She was there, curled up, lying in the bottom of one of the punts. Lying as still as she could.

'Amy?' He spoke very quietly. No sound. There was a small walkway stretching along the side wall of the building, beside the punts. He edged carefully along it, feeling the wall with his hand. He would be close enough to touch her in a moment. He had the sudden thought that she might be dead.

'I'm sorry,' she whispered, her throat sodden with tears. She wasn't dead.

'Why did you tell her? Why? It was a secret. It's killed me.' She didn't reply. 'Amy,' he said again.

'I didn't want to hurt you,' she gasped. 'I didn't mean to say anything. It just popped out. It started as a joke. Fran had rung me and I rang her back. I got her mother. I didn't mean it. I wouldn't hurt you. Not ever. Oh Christ, oh Christ, oh Jesus H. Christ.' And she was crying again. Everyone was crying today.

'You betrayed me.' He was choked up too.

'I didn't want to. I didn't mean to. I wouldn't do that.'

'I thought we were a team – you and I.'

'We were.'

'But you set out to do all this, didn't you, you rotten bitch. This was all a plan. This is your job!' he seethed at her. 'Like poor old Boyd-Orr. He was one, wasn't he?' He reached into his pocket and dragged out the ring. He was close enough now to touch her. She scrabbled away from him, rocking the punt, but he grabbed her hand and pressed the sharp emeralds hard into her palm, hurting her. For a second he found he'd put a foot in the water, his shoe filling up. She was moaning and crying and he could see the wet of her tears shining on her face. She had an arm raised in defence, half across her forehead, cowering under it as if

309

he might strike her. Well, he might. He might do worse than that.

Her words were almost obscured by her crying: 'He was my godfather, William was.' Her godfather? Had he got all this wrong? He could make neither head nor tale of it. Was it not a plot?

'What hurts so much – what hurts so much, is . . .' he found difficulty in finding the words. 'Is that – is that every single expression of – of – of affection, every sneaky temptation – every twisted bloody challenge, every part of this – and, oh yes,' he said bitterly, 'I use the word with the greatest possible cynicism – this "relationship" was just you fishing for dark secrets so you could exploit them. And turn me over. I thought . . .' he was out of breath, he could hardly say the words. 'I thought you – you liked me.'

She was sobbing bitterly, her face awash, moaning, keening. 'I did, I did, don't you see?' she moaned. 'I was there for you. I did it for you, Dad.' Her words became indistinct with her crying. He could just make out what she was trying to say. 'You needed to get out – before you were history. I was *for* you, Dad – *for* you. I loved you.'

He snorted derisively. 'Rubbish, girl, rubbish. You just wanted to bugger up an old man, dish the dirt, watch him die of humiliation.'

'No, no, no, no, no, no, no, no.' She was weeping and weeping.

He wasn't going to hear any more. She'd say anything. He flung the emerald ring into the water, slammed out of the tiny boathouse and ran, stumbling, up the slope towards the dam, his leather soles slipping on the dry grass. Bertram. He'd better get Bertram out of here. Bertram was something certain. Bertram was a friend. You could trust a great old classic car like that. You could never trust a woman. Not ever. Never, ever.

It was almost pitch-dark now. The music crashed on, echoing about the valley in the night. They had working lights around the scaffolding towers which bounced jagged reflections on the surface of the water.

He reached the vehicle. He was on automatic pilot. More by feel than anything else, he opened the bonnet of his most prized possession, the only thing that had never let him down. He flicked on the petrol and adjusted the magneto. Try not to flood, he begged the car, silently. He took hold of the starting handle and, miracles of miracles, Bertram coughed dutifully into life the first time. They started so easily, Bullnoses. Thank you, Bertram, he thought, my only, only, only, only friend. He wouldn't bother to light the lamps.

'DAD!' A desperate scream reached him in spite of the noise of the motor. She was running breathlessly, stumbling, gasping, up towards him. She was in a morsel of a dress – a dark patterned shift hardly covering her bum. In the moonlight, she seemed to be all charging pale white legs, shoulders and arms. By the time he had turned to look, she had thumped into him, her arms hard up around his neck, her pelvis glued to his. 'Don't you understand? I love you Dad!' He threw her bodily away from him. She staggered and then gained her balance. Norman walloped her as hard as he could across the side of her face with a big flat hand. She fell to the ground.

He was instantly appalled. She seemed stunned. And then she was up and she came at him again. She clung to him sobbing and desperate. Now, all he could feel was her hard flesh locked to his. It was as if she was trying to get inside his body by brute force alone. She was damp and tense and the thin material she was wearing hardly seemed to exist. He stood in the billows of blue exhaust smoke as she clung to him, her legs half caught around his thighs, howling. He couldn't push her away from him but he did try to walk aside, dragging her with him. 'Love you, love you, love you, love you, Dad. Don't you understand?' she croaked at him, the bitch, her fingers fighting to seek out his face, scratching him.

He couldn't stop his arms enfolding her tight, tiny being. She was gasping and sobbing and clawing at him. She seemed almost to crawl up his body, her mouth wetly seeking out his. He would not kiss her. He would not kiss her. He would not kiss her. She was his nemesis. He hated her. He would not respond. He would get away from her. He would not kiss her.

But her body felt so urgent and warm and intimate and close. And his.

He began to taste the damp smell of her, the sunburned scent of her and the moist desire of her sweat and tears. His hands took hold of the taut roundness of her buttocks. He lifted her up and their tongues locked. She was everything that was gorgeous. And he hated her more than anything he had ever hated in all his life.

She was whispering, urging him on – desperate, cloying, pleading, seeking words. 'Oh yes, oh yes, oh yes – I want it, I want it, I want it, you want it, you want it. God, how you want it, Dad, Dad, Dad, Dad, Dad, yes, yes, yes, yes, get it, get it, get it, get it. Get it now. Now. Now. Now.' And when she wasn't feveredly whispering into his mouth, filling it with her panting, she was stopping it with her tongue, with her kissing. They were dovetailed together in an eternal embrace engulfed by petrol smoke, next to his throbbing motor car.

And she knew how quickly he had responded.

She broke away, holding him with one hand. Her other hand slid under her dress. 'God, you want this,' she whispered. 'How you want this. Have it, darling, have it. Just have it, my darling man.' She was stepping out of her knickers. They were on the ground – a scrap of black. He pulled away. 'I'm going,' he managed to gasp. He pulled himself along the side of the car with his hands and, finding the driver's door, wrenched it open and stepped up into the car. It slammed shut behind him. He would drive away. Don't stall, please, Bertram. He would drive away. Or, what would he do?

Something else. He had a thought.

'In the car,' she shrieked. 'Let the car do it. Fucking, stonking razor. Yes. Yes. Yes. Oh Dad, I want it. You want it. You know you do. God, how you've wanted this. Oh, Dad, yes.' She clambered up on to the running board and stepped over him, over the door and slid on to his lap between him and the big steering wheel. Even in the gloom he was aware

of the dark hair at her crotch under her dress as her long legs
straddled his lap. She clamped bare arms around his neck and
the wetness of her tongue and lips was on his face. She was
crazy. Breaking away from him, looking down between them,
her fingers were at his fly, feverishly seeking him out.

'God you've wanted this, haven't you, Big Daddy. Big
Daddy. Oh *Big Daddy*.' Her breath was hot on his face, her
eyes, point-blank, tearing into his soul. 'You want it. I want it.
We all want it. Want, want, want, want, want – oh gorgeous.'
She had got him right out. 'You are so gorgeous,' and this
time it was a shout. Levering herself up with bent elbows, her
hands on the top of the windscreen and on the side of the car,
she raised her pelvis high above his cock and thrust herself
down on to him. 'In we go, in we go, in we go. Yes, yes, yes.
There!' she groaned. 'Cool as fuck, cool as fuck, cool as fuck.
Oh, that's better, isn't it?' she cooed wetly in his ear. 'Yes, yes,
yes, yes.' He threw his head back. He could feel the tightly
enclosing moisture of the whole of that wondrous tunnel of
hers. He could feel her pubic hair pushing hard at his. She
was shrieking and shrieking. She would wake the dead. He
was right up her. He had her. She had him. Her mouth was
in his ear. 'Good? Good? Goody-good-good-good?' she kept
asking. It was, bugger, bugger, bugger it, it was.

Brilliant, awful, disgusting paradise, it was. He moved up
at her. Her head, with her damp hair hard up against his
own, shook in denial. 'No, no. Make it smegging last, Daddio,
let the car do the work. Swanky-doodle, swanky-doodle, it's
brilliant. Isn't it brilliant?' And then she was just moaning.
Rocking on him and moaning. Arms locked around his head,
mouth applied to his. Moaning on him and rocking.

She had sounded almost too triumphant. Too much of a
celebration. He would have to take her out. This was it. This
was what she deserved. This was what he deserved. She sat
there clamped to him, Bertram driving them on, shuddering
them together. He was going to come. This was it. This was it.
He would take her with him. He was going to come. Yes.

'God, you love it.' She began to sound like a ship's
siren approaching rocks. 'God, I love it. Fuck, fuck, fuck,

fuck, fuck.' She was in time with the revolutions of the motorcar.

'I'm going to take you over, Amy,' he grunted, warning her. And he *would* do it.

'Oh very *Thelma and Louise*,' she almost chortled, her voice obscured by his mouth. 'Yeah, go for it. Let's see you do it. Do it, do it. Come, come, come. I want to feel you come inside of me, Daddio.' She sounded almost cheerful again. His mouth was full of her sweet-smelling hair. He chewed her hair in fury and his hand found the hand brake. The ratchet clicked down. The car rolled forward slightly, but only he knew that. She wasn't thinking – she was too busy hollering. The edge of the dam was only three metres away and millions of feet above the valley. He was going to come. He was going to come. She was screeching – she was coming too. His right foot hit the accelerator with every fibre of all his might. The car wheels ripped into the turf.

He had once heard that the most truly devastating orgasm could feel strangely akin to dying.